Also by Paige Tyler

X-Ops

Her Perfect Mate
Her Lone Wolf
Her Secret Agent (novella)
Her Wild Hero
Her Fierce Warrior
Her Rogue Alpha
Her True Match
Her Dark Half
X-Ops Exposed

SWAT: Special Wolf Alpha Team

Hungry Like the Wolf
Wolf Trouble
In the Company of Wolves
To Love a Wolf
Wolf Unleashed
Wolf Hunt
Wolf Hunger

X-OPS EXPOSED

PAIGE TYLER

sourcebooks
casablanca

Published by Sourcebooks Casablanca, an imprint of Sourcebooks, Inc.
P.O. Box 4410, Naperville, Illinois 60567-4410
(630) 961-3900
Fax: (630) 961-2168
sourcebooks.com

Printed and bound in Canada.
MBP 10 9 8 7 6 5 4 3 2 1

*With special thanks to my extremely patient and under-
standing husband. Without your help and support,
I couldn't have pursued my dream job of becoming
a writer. You're my sounding board, my idea man,
my critique partner, and the absolute best research
assistant any girl could ask for.*

Love you!

Prologue

Kunduz Province, Northern Afghanistan, June 2013

Sergeant Tanner Howland quickly ducked behind the mud-brick wall along with the other members of his rifle squad as a barrage of automatic weapon fire slammed into the other side, showering him and everyone else with shards of stone and dirt. The Taliban fighters had set up a strong defensive position inside the walls of the sprawling school compound, that was for sure. Tanner and his fellow Army Rangers had been trying to get close enough to take out the truck-mounted machine guns located on either side of the compound's main entrance for the past fifteen minutes, but so far, it wasn't working. The bad guys had dug in like ticks and were shooting the shit out of Tanner's platoon.

He looked around, making sure all his troops—including the Afghanis fighting with them—were okay. Everyone was alive, but just barely. Every one of them was wounded, but Corporal Chad Hunter, the light machine gun operator, was dealing with the worst injury by far. He was visibly limping from a serious shrapnel wound across his right thigh, but even though it had to hurt like a son of a bitch, the man wasn't complaining. He refused to fall back and get help from the medics in the rear, either.

"You holding up okay, Chad?" Tanner asked, throwing him a quick look as more rounds smacked against the backside of the wall.

"I'm good, Sarge." Chad checked the extra belts of ammo for the M249 machine gun he'd slung over across his shoulder earlier. "Vas and Danny already patched me up."

Tanner glanced down at the well-placed field dressing wrapped tightly around the wound on the blond man's leg. Privates Marcos Vasquez and Danny Copeland, the other two members of Tanner's fire team, had gotten to Chad within seconds of him getting hit. By sealing the wound with a liquid bandage, they'd probably saved his life. Rangers did whatever it took to get their buddies home.

Despite the bandage, Tanner would have preferred Chad fall back to the medics, but they needed the firepower too badly. Along with Vas and Danny, Tanner had five Afghanis assigned to his fire team, but none of them were as good with the automatic weapon as the corporal. He hated doing it, but he needed the man too much to let him go yet.

Tanner cursed as a hand grenade exploded nearby. "I thought we weren't supposed to be involved in direct combat operations on this deployment."

On the other side of him, his best friend and fellow fire team leader, Sergeant Ryan Westbrook, popped up and fired a few rounds from his M4 carbine in the general direction of the incoming gunfire.

"We're not engaged in direct combat." Ryan smirked. "We're over here to advise and assist the Afghan National Security Forces as they finish mopping up the last few dredges of the struggling, demoralized, and discouraged Taliban forces."

Tanner chuckled. There weren't many people who could laugh at a time like this, but after so many years of getting shot at, not to mention witnessing friends and enemies dying, the insanity going on around him now seemed like background noise. But as funny as Ryan could be sometimes, in this case, he wasn't making crap up to get a laugh out of Tanner. His friend had merely been repeating the speech their commander had given them right before the 2nd Battalion, 75th Ranger Regiment had boarded their planes for the start of a seven-month deployment to Northern Afghanistan.

"Maybe someone should give the lieutenant colonel a dictionary, because I don't think this particular group of Taliban is struggling too much," Tanner said drily. "And we're sure as hell doing a lot more than advising and assisting."

Ryan probably would have said something sarcastic in return, but just then, a rocket-propelled grenade exploded against the wall several yards away, tearing open a hole large enough to ride a bicycle through and lighting up the night as bright as day. If that RPG had impacted only a few feet closer, it would have wiped out half their squad.

"We can't keep wandering around out here like a bunch of pop-up targets on a rifle range." Ryan looked at him, his dark eyes intent. "If my team does something crazy to get their attention, do you think you can slip your team over the wall and inside the compound? We have to deal with those machine gun nests by the entrance, or we're never going to get in there."

Tanner nodded. He'd known it would come down to this at some point. He looked around at his three guys and the handful of Afghan Nationals they were supposed to be *assisting*. None of them—especially the Afghanis—seemed thrilled about taking the lead on this assault, not when they were so obviously outgunned for this kind of operation.

This mission had been billed as a simple bag-and-grab of a regional Taliban warlord propped up by little more than a handful of poorly equipped rebels. But within minutes of assaulting the man's compound, it had become apparent that the Afghan intel had been wrong. If Tanner had to guess, he'd say there were easily more than two hundred Taliban fighters in there, armed with AK rifles, light and heavy machine guns, RPGs, and what seemed to be an unlimited amount of ammo. They sure as hell weren't demoralized or discouraged.

With two very skittish platoons of Afghan Nationals and a single platoon of Rangers short on some key personnel—like their squad leader—they simply didn't have the numbers for a fight like this. Worse, now that the United States had turned over most of the responsibilities for conducting military ops like this to the Afghanis, the coordination for this mission had been one huge clusterfuck. They had no dedicated air or artillery support, communications with the battalion were spotty at best, and scariest of all, they had limited medevac assets available in the event things went bad.

And they were definitely going bad.

Tanner hadn't exactly been able to take time for a head count, but he was fairly sure his platoon had already lost more men tonight than they had in their last two deployments. It was going to get worse before it got better. But falling back wasn't an option. The Taliban fighters would be on them like rabid dogs if they tried that. No, the only thing they could do was press the attack and try to end this quickly.

"We can get in," Tanner told Ryan. "But you'd better be there to cover our asses ASAP. If you aren't, my team won't last five minutes inside those walls on our own."

"We'll get through to you, I swear," Ryan said.

Tanner didn't doubt that. He and Ryan had grown up in the Seattle area, and even though they'd never met before going through Ranger Assessment together, that hometown connection had led to an immediate bond. When they'd both been assigned to the 2nd Ranger Battalion at Lewis-McChord, it seemed like fate had taken a hand. Through three tours in Iraq and now their second stint in Afghanistan, he and Ryan had watched each other's backs through more shit than he cared to think about. They'd each taken a bullet meant for the other and seen more death and destruction than any human should ever have to face. They'd helped each other survive impossible odds and kept the other Rangers in their rifle squad alive at the same time.

Tanner couldn't help feeling all that was about to change. He was tempted to chalk up such dismal thoughts to this insane mission. They were out here in combat when everyone back home thought the fighting was over. But he knew it was more than that. It was tough putting into words the reason he was so sure, but something told him their luck had finally run out.

Judging from the expressions on the faces of his fellow soldiers, they all sensed it, too.

"Watch yourself out there," he warned them softly. "This could get ugly."

These men were closer to Tanner than his own family. The thought of any of them getting killed filled him with dread. But Chad, Vas, Danny, and the others simply nodded, resigned to what they were about to do.

Ryan clasped Tanner's shoulder, his face earnest. "We've had a good run, brother. Better than we had any right to. It's not like we can keep tweaking the devil's nose forever. Sooner or later, we all have to pay the price."

Tanner's mouth edged up. "If it's a matter of sooner or later, I vote for later."

Before Ryan could say anything else, Tanner was up and motioning for his men to follow as he led them toward the other side of the compound. One of the Afghanis with them called out their position softly into his radio, trying to let the rest of their forces know what the hell they were up to so they wouldn't get whacked by friendly fire. But as poorly as their communications system was working lately, Tanner had no idea if anyone out there even heard the man.

They moved fast, only shooting when absolutely necessary so they wouldn't draw attention to themselves. Ryan and his team had already started laying down heavy fire on the Taliban at the front gate, giving them the distraction they needed. Less than a minute later, Tanner and his team were at the rear of the compound, hiding out in the shadows.

"They're going to be on us the moment we go over this wall," he whispered. "We can't stop, and we can't slow down, no matter how bad it gets. We have to make it to the gate and take out those two heavy-duty machine guns. If we don't, the rest of our guys are going to get wiped out when they charge the gate. Understood?"

Everyone nodded. They all knew how bad this was going to be, but they were going to do it anyway. Tanner felt his chest swell at that moment. Damn, these were some good men.

Tanner felt more than heard the uptick in weapon fire intensify at the front of the compound. Ryan and the other Rangers were moving toward the gate, giving Tanner and his guys a chance of making it over the wall alive.

"Let's go," he ordered.

Slinging his M4 over his back, Tanner leaped up to grab the top of the wall, pulling himself up. Around him, the others scrambled over the eight-foot-high obstacle. Chad's leg was wrapped so tightly, he could barely bend it, so getting him over was a pain in the ass, but the machine gunner clenched his teeth and dealt with the pain.

They started taking sporadic gunfire the moment they dropped to the ground inside the compound. Tanner and his guys ignored it as best they could, spreading out to make it harder to hit them, then picking up the pace as they ran through the buildings and narrow alleys of the school property. It wasn't time to shoot back yet. It was time to move fast—and get as close as they could to the gate before too many people realized they were in there.

They were within sight of the gate, and the two big 14.5mm truck-mounted machine guns positioned on either side of it, when the Taliban fighters finally figured out there was another threat coming at them from inside the walls. That was when the battle really started.

Bullets kicked up dirt around them as Tanner shouted orders to his men, moving them toward the left side of the gate. They'd focus all their attention on the machine gun positioned to that side and do everything they could to take it out. If they survived, then they'd worry about the one on the right. It was better to keep his small force together as long as possible and knock out one of the heavy weapons than split their forces and accomplish nothing.

Unfortunately, the fighters surrounding the machine gun on the left quickly figured out what the plan was and immediately skewed the big weapon around in their direction. The night sky suddenly lit up with muzzle flash and tracer glow. Around Tanner, members of his team went down, and he knew they weren't going to get back up.

"Keep moving!" he shouted, forcing himself not to think about the price his friends were going to pay for taking out the weapons. "Put everything you have on that gun!"

It was an easy order to give but hard to do. There was nothing as bone-numbingly insane as charging up to the barrel of a heavy-duty machine gun when bullets the size of a person's thumb were coming at you at a rate of one hundred and fifty rounds per second. There were thousands of people in the world who would never consider doing something so stupid. As for those who were brave enough to try it, most of them would give up after seeing the guy beside him get ripped in half by the vicious weapon.

But Tanner's men continued to advance, laying down their own machine gun fire and launching 40mm grenades toward the truck. Tanner glanced over and saw Chad was barely keeping up with his bum leg. That's when he realized Danny, as well as a couple of the

Afghanis, were nowhere to be seen. His heart tightened in his chest, suddenly making it hard to breathe. If Danny could have moved at all, he would have been at their side…crawling if he had to.

Tanner pushed that thought away and kept moving, knowing the rest of the team would keep going only as long as he did.

They were less than forty feet away when Vas finally put a 40mm grenade directly in the back of the truck, silencing the thunder of the big weapon. Tanner kept them moving in that direction, emptying the remainder of his M4 magazine into the back of the vehicle until some of the spare ammo back there blew up. The truck bucked under the explosion, erupting into a fireball as the gas tank caught on fire. Flaming chunks of metal rained down on them, and out of the corner of his eye, Tanner saw another Afghani go down hard as a blur of flashing debris hit him in the chest.

Tanner refused to look around anymore, not wanting to know just how bad it really was. But he instinctively knew he'd lost a lot of his guys already.

"The other gun!" he shouted to anyone who was left, reloading his weapon as he ran in that direction.

His remaining men fell into step beside him. They had taken it in the ass so far, but they weren't giving up.

The Taliban couldn't swing the second machine gun around to shoot at them, not with Ryan and the other Rangers charging hard at the gate from outside the walls. But even without that threat, the heat coming at Tanner and his team still intensified as the Taliban fighters realized they had to keep them from taking out that machine gun. If Tanner and his team succeeded, the Taliban would be overrun by the good guys within seconds.

Not that what happened to the Taliban fighters mattered to Tanner at the moment. He and his remaining men were focused only on surviving the next few minutes and getting to that machine gun.

They'd advanced another fifteen feet against the onslaught of ball and tracer rounds coming their way, far enough to start laying accurate fire on the operator of that 14.5mm gun, when Tanner heard Chad's M249 suddenly go silent. He twisted around in time to see the man who'd been on his team from day one tumble to the ground beside Vas, who must have gone down a split second earlier. Neither man moved.

As much as Tanner wanted to drop to his knees and yank his friends to his chest and make this all stop, he knew he couldn't. He had to keep going or Ryan and the rest of his platoon would end up just like Danny, Vas, Chad, and the Afghanis who'd been brave enough to follow them into this fight.

Tanner swung his M4 over his back, then reached down for the lightweight machine gun in Chad's hands. He instinctively checked the plastic ammo box mounted on the side of the gun, absently noting there was maybe half a pack of 5.56mm rounds left in it. A hundred rounds wasn't a lot, but it was enough for what he needed to do.

He turned and ran toward the machine gun, ignoring the bullets kicking up the dirt around him. To his left, the other members of his platoon were pinned down outside the gate, unable to move any closer while the weapon was still functional.

Tanner paid no attention to the individual Taliban

fighters, instead focusing on the gunner in the back of the pickup truck, firing short three- and four-round bursts from Chad's M249. It was only a matter of time before he got hit by one of the bullets flying around him. He just had to take out the machine gunner before that happened.

Off to the side, a Taliban fighter aimed an RPG in his direction. Tanner could have swung his weapon around and engaged the shooter, made him duck even if he didn't hit the man straight up. But if he did, there was a good chance he'd run out of ammo before disabling the machine gun in the truck, and he couldn't risk it.

Ignoring the man about to kill him, Tanner locked on the machine gunner and squeezed the trigger of his weapon, popping off a long string of rounds right into the back end of the pickup truck. Unfortunately, he didn't get a chance to see if they had any effect because just then, the world exploded around him.

Tanner flew through the air for what seemed like forever before slamming into the ground like a bag of bricks. He bounced and rolled a few times before tumbling down into a deep crater carved out by a previous explosion. He came to rest in the bottom of the pit, debris raining down on him as he lay there in a twisted heap, the stock of the M249 digging painfully into ribs that had to be broken as dirt landed on his face and chest, choking him and making it nearly impossible to breathe.

He had no idea how badly he was hurt, but as the world started to go dark, he realized it was pretty damn bad. He wasn't going to make it. And he was completely cool with that. The 14.5mm machine gun had fallen silent, replaced by the *pop* of smaller weapons and the sounds of running footsteps. His team had done its job. The gate was clear, and the platoon was moving quickly into the compound.

Tanner realized he must have passed out, because the next thing he knew, the shooting had stopped and someone was leaning over him, brushing dirt off his face. He forced his eyes open, wondering briefly if he was going to find a Taliban fighter standing there, an AK-47 pointed at his chest, ready to finally end this.

But it wasn't a Taliban soldier. It was Ryan. His friend was down on one knee, regarding him with eyes that were completely devoid of emotion.

"I thought you were dead," Ryan said.

"I probably should be," Tanner told him.

"Probably."

Tanner considered pushing himself up into a sitting position but then changed his mind. *Shit*. He ached all over. "Chad and Vas didn't make it. I'm pretty sure Danny's gone, too."

Ryan nodded. "Yeah. I saw their bodies a ways back while I was looking for you. My guys didn't make it either. They all bought it during the last charge through the gate. It's just you and me. We're all that's left of our squad."

All twenty members of their combined fire teams dead. Tanner closed his eyes, letting the pain wash over him. Not the physical pain that came from broken bones and torn flesh, but the deeper ache in his chest that came from knowing he was alive while all his brothers were gone. The anguish grew deeper and darker with every breath he took, overwhelming him and leaving him to wonder how he could possibly survive another five seconds, much less make it through the rest of the night and beyond.

When he opened his eyes again, he assumed he'd see his pain mirrored in his friend's gaze. But Ryan's face was calm, almost detached, like he was sitting on the beach, watching the waves roll in and out. Tanner shouldn't have been surprised. Ryan had always been able to compartmentalize shit like this better than he ever could.

Gritting his teeth against the pain, Tanner pushed himself into a sitting position and looked around at the damage inside the compound formerly controlled by the Taliban. Bodies were everywhere. His platoon and the Afghanis fighting with them had done what they'd set out to do. But they had paid a price. Tanner wondered if the people responsible for doing the math would decide it had been worth it.

"What now?" he asked, not sure what else to say.

Ryan stared off into the distance. "We keep going."

Tanner tried to imagine doing that but simply couldn't see how it was going to be possible after what had happened.

Chapter 1

Wenatchee National Forest, Northwest of Chelan, Washington, Present Day

"OKAY, MAYBE THIS WASN'T THE BEST IDEA I'VE EVER HAD."

Zarina Sokolov cursed as she stumbled over yet another tree root and tumbled to her knees in the rich, leafy soil along the dirt trail. At least she hoped she was still on the trail. It was darker out here than she'd ever dreamed possible, and the flashlight the man at the sporting goods store had sold her was a piece of crap.

She shone the dim beam around as she stood up, hoping to see something to convince her she was still following the 25 Mile Creek Trail. But after a few moments, she realized one patch of pine needle–covered dirt looked much the same as the next. She turned and took a few steps back the way she'd come but then stopped when she didn't see anything that looked remotely like a beaten path in that direction, either.

Perhaps it was time to accept she'd wandered off the trail. She flipped her wrist over and looked at her watch, stunned to see it had only been an hour since the sun had gone down. She could have sworn she'd been out here half the night. She'd been hiking since midmorning, but it already felt like days.

Blowing out a breath, Zarina tucked some long, blond hair that had escaped from her ponytail behind her ear and began backtracking along the route she'd followed to get here. Her navigational skills being what they were, it was entirely possible she'd end up farther off the trail and deeper in trouble, but she wasn't going to stop searching until she found Tanner. While the idea of wandering around the woods in the middle of the night scared the hell out of her, she was committed to finding him no matter what she had to do. She wasn't going to give up simply because she was a little nervous about being alone in the woods at night.

Zarina moved her flashlight around as she walked, relaxing a little when she recognized some obvious landmarks after a few steps. She definitely remembered that waist-high outcropping of rocks ahead of her, as well as the big tree leaning over part of it. And that thick root sticking up out of the ground like a clutching hand? Yeah, she'd almost fallen over that thing.

Within minutes, however, the route started to look unfamiliar, and Zarina second-guessed her decision to keep going. Frowning, she stopped walking and turned in a slow circle, wondering if maybe she'd missed a turn or something. Nothing looked familiar now. Not the ground, or the rocks, or the trees.

She was lost.

She probably shouldn't have been surprised. She was a scientist who specialized in genetic engineering. A normal day for her involved spending hours in a lab looking through microscopes and manipulating DNA strands, not hiking while carrying a backpack's worth of outdoor gear on her back, looking for one man in the middle of a huge wilderness.

Zarina considered pulling out the satellite phone buried

in her backpack but decided against it. She was lucky the new people in charge of the Department of Covert Operations in DC had agreed to let her come on this hopeless mission in the first place. If she called for help after looking for less than a day, they'd probably be on the next flight out to rescue her and her search would be over.

Taking a deep breath, she reached into the pocket of her jacket for the trail map she'd been following. Well, the one she was supposed to be following, anyway. As she focused her flashlight on the bewildering collection of squiggly solid and dotted lines crisscrossing the carefully folded map, she realized she could see her breath in the crisp October air.

Crap. She hoped it didn't get too much colder tonight. She might have lived most of her adult life in Moscow, but that didn't mean she enjoyed turning blue. It probably didn't help that her jacket wasn't meant for these kinds of temperatures. But in her defense, it had been much warmer in town. Plus, she hadn't planned on being out here this long.

When she'd showed the man at the sporting goods store a photo of Tanner, he'd told her he had heard rumors of a huge guy with a crazy mane of dark-blond hair camping near Grouse Mountain, just north of the trail she'd been following. The man had sworn it would be easy to find Tanner if she stayed on the path. All she needed to do was look for a big pile of rocks near the spot where the trail and 25 Mile Creek nearly crossed each other. From there, a small, unnamed side path would take her to the general location where Tanner was camping. It had sounded so simple.

But Zarina had been following the main trail since

ten o'clock that morning, and she'd never seen anything even close to the landmarks the store clerk had
described. Then again, this was the same man who'd
sworn the flashlight he'd sold her for fifty dollars would
light the forest up like it was broad daylight. That had
turned out to be a lie, so maybe he'd been lying about
knowing where Tanner was, too.

She pushed that thought aside and stared harder at
the map, trying to figure out where she'd veered off the
path. While the store clerk might have lied about the
quality of the flashlight he'd sold her, she knew in her
heart the man he'd described was Tanner. Not only was
the former Army Ranger one of the largest men she'd
ever seen, he was also graced with the most amazing
head of hair any man had ever possessed. It was the kind
of hair that made women want to run their hands through
it just to feel its softness against their skin. Well, at least
that's what she wanted to do every time she saw him.
But maybe that was just her.

Of course, Tanner's size and wild mane of dark-
blond hair were a result of the horrible serum that evil
scientists wanting to play God had injected him with
nearly a year and a half ago in an old, abandoned ski
lodge a dozen miles or so from the place she now stood.
But still, no one would ever confuse Tanner with any
other man. He was singularly unique in every way.

Zarina vividly remembered the first time she'd seen
Tanner. He'd been stripped to the waist and strapped
down to a hospital gurney in the bowels of the ski lodge
while those two psychotic doctors pumped him full of
drugs in an attempt to create the world's first viable
man-made shifter.

But while she'd been in the room, she'd been far from a willing participant in the whole thing. The man heading the horrible operation—Keegan Stutmeir— had kidnapped her four months earlier from her home outside Moscow, believing her knowledge of gene manipulation could help him achieve his goal of turning a normal human being into a shifter.

At the time, Zarina was sure Stutmeir and his scientists were insane. Back then, the idea of shifters, humans who had naturally occurring animal DNA, seemed absurd. According to Stutmeir, shifters could turn this normally dormant genetic material on and off at will, using it to make themselves stronger, faster, and more dangerous. They even had claws and fangs. It had sounded crazy to her, but she'd soon learned Stutmeir would do anything to create these shifters, no matter how many people got hurt.

Zarina thought she'd understood the depth of cruelty one human would go to in an effort to hurt another, but she realized how naive she'd been the first time she'd seen the results of their experiments. They had rounded up dozens of homeless people in the surrounding areas, administering their horrible drugs to one man after another, then letting them die and throwing their bodies away like they were nothing but garbage. And since no one besides Thomas Thorn, the late former senator who had hired Stutmeir, knew what they doing, there was no one to put an end to it.

Except her.

When her attempts to stop Stutmeir had failed, Zarina focused on helping as many test subjects escape as she could. Unfortunately, that was difficult when none of them survived very long. She'd seen so many other people die in horrible pain after being given the DNA-altering drugs that she'd been terrified the same would happen to Tanner. Her hands shook now just thinking about that awful day. His body had twisted and spasmed so hard, she'd heard muscles tear and bones crack.

Yet somehow, Tanner had survived. He hadn't come out of the process as the shifter Stutmeir had been hoping for, though. Instead, he'd become stuck somewhere in between human and shifter. He was a blend of both…a hybrid.

Whereas shifters had flawless control over their abilities, hybrids like Tanner possessed almost none. In many ways, they reacted like mistreated animals, their fangs and claws coming out as they flew into violent rages at the least provocation. Around her, however, Tanner was never violent. That was the main reason she'd been able to get close enough to him to help him escape.

By then, the damage had already been done. Tanner had been as much uncontrollable beast as man, and the rages that sometimes turned him into a killing machine had made his life a living hell ever since.

Zarina had tried to help Tanner learn to control the anger inside while she worked on an antiserum that would put his DNA back the way it had been before. A lot of good people at the Department of Covert Operations in Washington, DC, friends who cared about Tanner nearly as much as she did, had helped any way they could. But in the end, those friends were the reason he'd run away.

Two months ago, the DCO training complex outside Quantico had been hit by a large group of highly functional hybrids led by Thorne. Tanner had had no choice but to fight alongside everyone else and had ended up completely losing control. He'd killed a lot of bad guys, but he'd also come close to killing some of his friends, too.

Tanner had run away that same night, fleeing back to the forest where all his nightmares had started. Zarina knew he was looking for the isolation he thought would keep him from ever hurting anyone he cared about again.

She understood why he'd left. He was the type of man who always worried more about the safety of others than himself. But she cared about him, and she wasn't going to let him live out here by himself. Not when there was something she could do to help him.

Blinking back tears, Zarina folded the map and slipped it back into her pack. She had a fairly good idea where she'd gotten off the main trail. More importantly, she knew how to get back on it. If she headed left—west, she guessed—she should stumble across the 25 Mile Creek Trail again within a mile or two. If she was lucky, she'd find Tanner's campsite by midnight.

Cutting cross-country in the direction she thought the main trail might be had seemed like a simple solution, but it turned out to be a lot more difficult than the map suggested. If she wasn't heading up a steep slope of rock and pine needles, she was heading down the far side. But it wasn't like she had a lot of options. She didn't trust her navigational skills enough to do anything other than head in a straight line. She was going to have to deal with the rough terrain until she reached the trail.

To take her mind off the hike, she thought about the

conversation she'd had with Tanner a few days before the hybrid attack on the DCO complex, when he'd not only come damn close to admitting he loved her, but also confessed he'd rather isolate himself in this forest than risk hurting her. Hearing him say he'd willingly live in total seclusion because he was terrified he'd harm her had torn at her heart.

That was the moment Zarina had realized she was in love. It was true. A man she'd never even kissed completely owned her heart. How crazy was that?

She was still pondering that when she heard a strange noise to her right. She froze and slowly turned that way, her pulse kicking up a notch. It sounded like heavy panting, as if someone was having difficulty breathing.

The doctor in her urged her to see if someone needed help, but she stopped. She wasn't sitting in a restaurant in DC. She was hiking through the forests of Washington State, one of the few true wilderness areas left in this country. Whatever was out there making that noise didn't need her assistance.

Heart still beating a little fast, Zarina turned and headed in the direction she'd been going before. As much as she wanted to run, she resisted the impulse. Her time with shifters and hybrids had taught her running away was a very bad thing to do around any animal. She definitely moved with purpose, though.

Zarina thought her plan had worked and whatever was behind her would leave her alone, but the panting grew louder, like the animal was following her. She gripped the flashlight tighter, refusing to give in to the urge to look over her shoulder. She didn't really want to know what was back there.

She crested a hill and started down the other side, picking up her pace even as she told herself to slow down.

"Don't look like prey," she whispered, remembering something her father had told her a long time ago back in Russia. "Rabbits get eaten."

But the reminder did no good. Her feet decided they knew better and began propelling her faster down the slope. The flashlight in her hand swung wildly as she moved, casting crazy shadows and making her wonder how long she could keep going before she tripped over something…and got up just in time to find the animal stalking her ready to pounce.

That terrifying image fueled her fear, and by the time she reached the bottom of the slope, she was practically running. That's when the panting behind her stopped and the long, drawn-out grunting started. Halfway between a loud moan and a low roar, Zarina had never heard a sound like it. But it was loud and menacing, and she couldn't imagine anything cute and cuddly making it. Whatever was back there, it was big and it didn't like her in its territory.

At the thud of heavy paws hitting the ground, Zarina abandoned caution and ran as fast as her legs would carry her. Playing it cool and calm hadn't worked. Maybe giving in to panic might.

She didn't even attempt to head up the next slope, instead running along the flat valley she was in. But the creature behind her was fast, and she barely made it fifty feet before it caught up to her. It was so close, she swore she could feel its overheated breath stirring her hair.

Knowing she wasn't going to get away, Zarina slid to

a stop and spun around, ready to shout at the beast that wanted to kill her. She'd seen Tanner let out a roar that could paralyze almost anything crazy enough to attack him, so perhaps she could do the same thing.

But her cry of defiance died in her throat as she came face-to-face with a gigantic grizzly bear. The beast reared up on its hind legs, towering over her for one heart-stopping moment before dropping to all fours and roaring at her so loud, her bones felt like they'd turned to jelly.

She vaguely remembered the store clerk in town trying to sell her a can of bear repellent. If she wasn't so terrified, she'd laugh at the idea. What the heck would a can of pepper spray do to something this big?

The bear took a step in her direction with another roar, showing off fangs large enough to bite right through her.

For a split second, Zarina considered running again, but it would be pointless. She'd never outrun a bear.

Rabbits get eaten.

So instead, she screamed as long and loud as she could.

The grizzly looked shocked for a moment, but instead of scaring the animal off like she'd hoped, all it did was seem to make him mad. Head low, the bear started toward her.

She was going to die.

But suddenly, the bear stopped, a look of what could only be confusion on its face as it focused on something behind her. A second later, a roar ripped through the night that shook the ground. She jerked her head around, almost collapsing in relief when she saw Tanner standing there in the dark, dressed in jeans and a T-shirt, his eyes glowing vivid red, fangs bared as he let out a roar that sounded exactly like that of a lion. Which made sense, because those were the DNA strands blended with his own.

Zarina stood transfixed. Tanner's fangs were longer and looked more terrifying than the bear's.

The rage and anger on his face must have been enough to scare the grizzly, because the huge animal gave one more half-hearted chuff in Tanner's direction, then turned and scurried back into the pitch-dark forest.

To her right, she caught movement. *Crap!* Tanner was going after the bear. Not because he wanted to hurt the animal, but because by running, the grizzly had become the prey, and Tanner's lion half simply couldn't stop itself from hunting the animal down now that the rage had taken over.

"Tanner," she said softly. "Let the bear go."

He stopped like he'd hit a brick wall, then stood there, unmoving, for what felt like forever, facing away from her and staring off into the darkness in the direction the bear had run. Not that it was probably all that dark for Tanner. With his animal-enhanced eyesight, he could probably see the grizzly's big, fuzzy rump bouncing off into the woods. And if his eyes lost the creature, then his keen sense of smell would fill in the details. Which was a good thing, since she'd have probably been a bear treat if it hadn't been for that nose of his.

After what seemed like an eternity, Tanner turned and looked at her. His fangs and glowing red eyes were gone now, replaced by a mesmerizing blue gaze and a ruggedly handsome face that had made her heart almost stop beating the first time she'd seen it. He had a bit more dark-blond scruff along his jaw and chin now.

Actually, a lot more. Maybe it was because she'd grown up in a cold-weather environment where the opposite sex went all caveman in an attempt to stay warm, but she wasn't usually a fan of facial hair. On Tanner, though, it looked incredibly scrumptious.

His T-shirt clung tightly to his chest and shoulders, showing off all the muscles he had upstairs, while his jeans fought to contain thighs that looked poised to tear their way out at any moment. Had he actually gotten more muscular since he'd been out there?

Zarina almost ran to him right then so she could throw her arms around him and hold him tight for the rest of the night. But she didn't, because she knew he wouldn't be ready for that. Not after she'd showed up in the forest out of the blue and almost gotten eaten by a bear.

But damn, it was hard.

Tanner looked better now than when he'd been living in the dorms at the DCO complex. He had been put up there since the agency's covert agents had found him out here all that time ago. Even the stress lines that had been etched into his features had completely faded. It almost made her sorry she'd come out here to disturb the serenity he seemed to have found. But she couldn't stay away, not with the way she felt about him. And especially not when she could finally help him.

"What are you doing here, Zarina?" he asked bluntly.

So much for him sweeping her into his arms and saying he was happy to see her. Clearly, he wasn't. She tried not to let that hurt too much.

"I'm here to help you," she said, equally blunt.

She'd learned a long time ago that dancing around a subject wasn't the way Tanner did things. It wasn't the way she did, either, so that was okay. She didn't bother mentioning that his disappearance had caused her more sleepless nights than she could count and had nearly driven her insane with worry. That would have been emotional blackmail, and she wasn't going to do that to him.

His jaw flexed. "I don't need any help. I'm doing a good job of controlling my hybrid impulses all on my own."

She looked pointedly in the direction the grizzly had run. "It doesn't seem like it to me."

Tanner flinched, and she immediately regretted her choice of words. Dammit, she was out here to help him, not push him further away.

"I haven't lost control in the two months I've been out here," he said through clenched teeth. "Not until you decided to do something stupid like wander through the middle of a grizzly's territory by yourself."

Zarina wanted to point out that she hadn't planned to be out here this late and that there was no way she could have known she was in a bear's territory. But she bit her tongue and focused on trying to defuse the situation.

"I'm sorry I made you lose control again," she said. "But I'm here to make sure it doesn't happen again...ever."

She waited, expecting Tanner to ask her what she meant by that, but he didn't. Instead, he stood there regarding her and looking way better than any man should considering he'd been camping in the woods for two months. She had met plenty of guys who couldn't pull off his level of masculine perfection after primping in front of a mirror for an hour. That was one of the other things she'd learned about Tanner. He didn't have to work hard at being so amazing. It came naturally to him.

After another minute of silence, Zarina accepted that if they were going to talk, she was the one who would have to get the conversation started. "I finished the hybrid drug antiserum that will return your DNA back to what it was before Stutmeir's doctors experimented on you. You can be a normal human again."

She waited for some reaction—relief, doubt, elation. Something. But Tanner looked as interested as if she'd told him it might rain tomorrow.

"I'll never be normal again," he finally said quietly.

"Yes, you will." She stepped closer, anguish coursing through her when he immediately took a step back. "I worked on the antidote every minute since you left. It will work. It will keep the beast from ever slipping out again."

"I don't want it, dammit!" he shouted, making her jump. He cursed and ran his hand through his hair. "I'm sorry," he said, his voice softer. "For yelling at you. And for making you come all the way out here and hiking halfway across the Wenatchee Forest to find me. But I don't want the antidote. Just go home, okay? Leave me out here where I can't hurt anyone."

Zarina's heart tore in two at the pain in his eyes. She had no idea why he was turning down her offer, but she wasn't leaving without him.

"I'm not going home," she said, standing her ground and leveling her gaze at him.

Having this conversation would have been a lot easier without holding a flashlight. Then she could have folded her arms to emphasize her point.

"Then you'd better have a lot of books on that e-reader of yours, because you're going to get bored damn fast waiting for me at whatever hotel you're staying in."

"I'm not going to a hotel," she told him. "I'm staying
out here."

Red flared in his eyes but faded just as quickly. "Like
hell you are."

"I'm not leaving," she said firmly. "You can run off
into the woods—we both know I can't keep up with
you—but I still won't leave. I'll keep walking all over
the forest looking for you."

His eyes flickered red again, and he muttered something under his breath she couldn't catch. "You irritate
me like no one else on the planet, do you know that?"

"Yes," she replied, even though it was probably a
rhetorical question. "So, which way to your camp?"

Tanner was so mad, he could have punched a hole
through a tree trunk. Getting a grip on his temper, he
took a deep breath and forced himself to walk slower. If
he moved too fast, Zarina wouldn't be able to keep up,
and while he might be pissed as hell, he wasn't going
to leave her alone out here in the dark. They could have
made better time if she'd let him carry her pack, but
even though it was obviously too damn heavy for her,
she adamantly refused.

He bit back a growl. For a brilliant scientist, Zarina
did some frigging stupid stuff. Like hiking out here in
the middle of the night looking for him. She could have
gotten herself killed, and probably would have if he
hadn't jerked awake from the middle of a deep sleep,
one hundred percent sure he was picking up a trace scent
that was impossible for his nose to miss—or ignore.
He'd almost convinced himself he'd been dreaming.

God knew he'd been thinking enough about her over the past two months for that to be possible. His hybrid sense of smell had been jerking him around a lot lately.

It kind of sucked when you couldn't even trust the stuff your head was telling you was right there in front of you. Then again, that was why he was alone in the forest in the first place. He couldn't trust himself anymore. Not his hybrid side or his human side.

Even so, he'd dragged himself out of his tent just to be sure. It was a good thing he had, because he'd picked up the grizzly's scent at the exact same moment he'd figured out Zarina's scent wasn't an illusion. He had no idea what she was doing in the woods, but he had no doubt it was her. No one on the planet had a scent quite like hers.

He'd slowed only long enough to pull on his boots and T-shirt, then sprinted across the mountainous terrain like his life depended on it. He'd smelled that bear a few times over the past several weeks. The grizzly had been getting bold when it came to following campers around looking for food. The animal probably had no desire to hurt Zarina, but a grizzly could do strange things if it thought its territory was being poached. Tanner thanked God he'd found her in time.

Now he was taking her back to his campsite. But just for the night. First thing in the morning, he was dragging her cute ass back to town and sitting it down in the first bus or cab heading for the airport.

As angry as he was with her for coming after him, he'd be lying if he said it wasn't good seeing her. He hated his traitorous heart for going there, but the beautiful Russian doctor had stirred something inside him from the moment he'd opened his eyes and seen her leaning over his bed in that damn place where those assholes had turned him into a monster. She'd saved his life in that hellhole—and saved his soul several times since then. But as beautiful and mesmerizing as she might be, she was also the most stubborn woman he'd ever met. That damn grizzly would have killed her if he hadn't found her in time, and she barely seemed to care. He'd told her she needed to go home, and she'd firmly refused. When he'd threatened to leave her out there on her own, she'd called his bluff.

Damn, she could be irritating as hell when she wanted to be. That made it damn hard to protect her from the most dangerous thing in all these woods—him.

Tanner did his best to ignore Zarina as they headed northwest along the top of the ridgeline that led to his campsite. Of course, that was useless. It wasn't like he had to even look over at her stomping through the darkness beside him to know exactly what she looked like. Her perfect skin; plump, kissable pink lips; and long, wavy blond hair were permanently etched into his mind. He'd never forget a single part of her as long as he lived.

"I can't believe John Loughlin let you come out here on your own," he grumbled, needing something to distract him from thoughts of how insanely gorgeous she was and how much he'd missed seeing her since sending himself into exile, even if it was for the best. "Didn't he have anyone available to send with you? Declan, or Landon, maybe?"

There were plenty of other operatives and shifters at the Department of Covert Operations, people who could have tracked him down easily enough. But Declan

MacBride was the big natural-born bear shifter who had found him when he'd been wandering these woods after being turned into a hybrid, and Landon Donovan, a former Army Special Forces A-Team Commander, was the best operative in the DCO. Sending either of those guys with Zarina would have made perfect sense. Sending her out here alone had been crazy. What the hell had John been thinking?

"Well, Landon couldn't come because he's busy running the DCO now," Zarina said, waving her flashlight from side to side in an effort to keep from falling over the rocks along their route. "And Declan is spending most of his time close to home. Those twins of his are a handful. Neither he nor Kendra are getting a lot of sleep."

Tanner completely got the part about Declan needing to stay near his wife and kids, but the stuff about Landon having a new job caught him off guard.

"What do you mean, Landon is running the DCO now?" He frowned. "What happened to John? He's okay, right?"

Two months ago, he and everyone else at the DCO had thought John had been killed by a bomb. Thankfully, the director of the DCO—former director now, Tanner guessed—had a guardian angel out there in the form of a shifter named Adam who'd gotten him out of the building just in time. Tanner had been relieved to see John alive and would hate to think something had happened to the guy after he'd left.

"Yeah, he's fine," Zarina said. "But all the stuff he and his family went through convinced him he needed to reprioritize his life. He took a sabbatical from the DCO and made Landon deputy director. No one really knows if he's coming back or not. Heck, I'm not sure if anyone even knows where he is right now."

Tanner shook his head. Apparently, a lot had changed at the DCO since he'd been gone. "If Landon is deputy director, who's the new director?"

"Some political mover and shaker named William Hamilton."

Zarina reached out to grab his arm for balance as she stumbled over a rock. The feel of her hand on his skin immediately sent tingles racing through him. Tanner cursed silently, hating how his body reacted to her touch.

"I don't know anything about the man, but he seems capable," she continued, squeezing his biceps as she made her way over the uneven ground.

Tanner stifled a groan. She was doing that on purpose, wasn't she? Considering she was smarter than he'd ever be in his life, she had to know the effect she had on him. He hated to think she'd manipulate him like that, but he wouldn't put it past her. She knew he didn't want her here, and she was going to fight him every step of the way when he made her leave. But he had to do it. It was too dangerous for her, and it had nothing to do with him or the grizzly. There were things going on in these woods he didn't want her getting mixed up in.

He was still pondering that when she slid her hand to the top of his shoulder before moving it away, all the while acting like she was unaware of what she did to him.

He moved to the right a little, putting some space between them and focusing on what she'd said.

Landon Donovan as deputy director. Tanner hadn't seen that coming. The guy was a dirty boots soldier through and through, built from the ground up to spend his life fighting the fight and leading his troops. Trying to imagine him behind a desk running a covert organization didn't seem to fit.

"So Landon's the one who let you come wandering around out here on your own, huh?" he asked Zarina.

From the corner of his eye, Tanner saw her throw him a withering glare. "It wasn't up to him whether I came or not," she said sharply, reminding him yet again that she was a woman who did whatever she felt was right regardless of what anyone told her. Which had a lot to do with him being alive at the moment, he supposed, so maybe that wasn't such a bad thing.

"When I told him I was coming to find you, he wanted to send someone with me, but I pointed out you'd only run again if he did," she explained. "I convinced him I could find you on my own and talk you into coming back."

More likely Zarina had browbeaten the new deputy director until he relented and let her do what she was going to do anyway. Landon had a strong-willed woman for a wife in Ivy Halliwell. The man knew enough to conserve ammo when he was in a fight he couldn't win.

"How did you know where to look?" Tanner asked, leading her down the ridge toward his camp. "Don't tell me those analysts at the DCO have been watching me on one of their spy satellites."

Zarina laughed. "No. It wasn't an analyst figuring out where you were. It was me. Remember the conversation we had when we were sitting on the bench overlooking the obstacle course at the DCO complex? You told me that you were thinking about coming back here."

"Oh." He remembered the conversation all too

vividly. Mostly because he'd nearly slipped up and told Zarina how he felt about her. Thank God, he hadn't made that mistake. If she was stubborn now, what would she be like if she knew he loved her? "That explains how you knew I was in Wenatchee. How did you know where to find me once you got here?"

"You're an easy man to remember." Her lips curved in the darkness. "I simply walked into every camping and outdoor store I could find in the surrounding towns and asked if they'd seen a man fitting your description. I had a general idea where you were within hours."

Tanner did a double take. "A general idea? You came up here and wandered around the woods because you had a general idea of where I was? Do you have even an inkling of how stupid that is?"

She glanced at him. "It worked, didn't it?"

He didn't bother pointing out that her wonderful plan had almost gotten her eaten. She'd probably have something snarky to say about that, too.

"I'm serious, Zarina," he said softly. "There are things up here that can hurt you, and I'm not just talking about the bears. Several locals have gone missing in the past few weeks, and no one has a clue what happened to them. It's not the kind of place you should be wandering around on your own."

She was silent, as if considering that, then shrugged. "It was a risk I was willing to take. I thought you'd know that about me by now. I'm not a foolhardy person, but for you, I'll take any risk."

Tanner cursed silently. He knew that all right. He simply didn't understand why the hell she'd do something so selfless for someone like him.

He knew she meant well by coming after him. She thought she could make everything better with her magic antidote, that all his problems would simply go away if he wasn't a hybrid anymore. He didn't have the heart—or the words—to tell her it wasn't that simple.

When they reached his camp, Zarina moved her flashlight around, taking in the clearing, the small tent, and the even tinier fire pit encircled with rocks. It wasn't much, but that was because he didn't need much. The fire was out now—he never left the camp with it still burning—and he wordlessly walked over to get the flames started again, then put on a bit more wood to build up some extra heat and provide a little more light.

Switching off her flashlight, Zarina stowed it in her pack, then knelt down on the far side of the fire pit opposite him. She held out her hands toward the flames. "Is this where you've been staying this whole time?"

He shook his head, trying hard to keep from looking at her too closely in the light coming off the fire. She looked way too damn sexy in the flickering orange and reddish glow. He didn't need anything making this situation harder than it already was. He was going to have a tough enough time convincing her to leave tomorrow, and it would only be worse if he let himself think too much about spending time with her.

"No," he said, realizing he hadn't answered her question yet. "This is about the tenth or eleventh place I've made camp since coming here. The rangers from the forest service aren't too keen about people living out here full time, so I move every few days to make it harder for them to find me."

She looked around. "It's hard to believe someone

could stumble across this place by accident. It's so well hidden, I didn't even know it was here until we walked into the clearing."

"That's one of the biggest factors when it comes to the places I set up camp," he admitted. "It has to be well off the beaten path and difficult to find. I don't like taking risks, though, so I move a lot."

She frowned, as if considering that. "It must be difficult having to move your stuff and set up somewhere new all the time."

He shrugged. "Not really. Everything I have can fit in my pack. I can grab my gear and move everything I own in less than ten minutes. That's the way I like it."

Her expression softened, and he knew she was about to say something meant to be comforting. He stood up quickly, cutting her off. "You need to get some sleep. We'll have to leave early in the morning if I'm going to get you back into town at a reasonable time."

He expected her to protest, to stubbornly tell him once again that she wasn't going anywhere, but instead, Zarina simply nodded. Tanner wasn't fooled into thinking that meant she was going to comply with his wishes. She was simply putting off the argument until morning. He was okay with that. He had no desire to get into it with her right now, either. Not after the evening they'd both already had.

"There's some more wood over in that pile," he said, gesturing to the branches he'd broken into manageable-sized pieces and stacked off to the side of the camp. "If you toss a few logs on the fire right before you go to sleep, that should keep you warm enough through the night."

Once again, Zarina didn't complain but merely nodded

and began taking stuff out of her pack. First came a light-weight sleeping bag, then a self-inflating sleeping pad. That was followed by a blanket and a frigging pillow, of all things. Damn, no wonder that pack had been so heavy. She'd brought her whole damn apartment with her.

"If you have to…you know, use the facilities, I've dug a slit trench in the ground over there behind those trees," he added. "There's a stream about twenty-five feet or so downhill from my tent, but I don't recommend going that far outside the circle of the firelight. That grizzly probably won't come back, but he may have friends."

Tanner felt like crap for scaring Zarina. Hell, he could hear her heart thumping harder already. But he didn't want her getting comfy out here. He wanted her going home tomorrow, and that wouldn't happen if he went easy on her. That's why he was making her sleep outside rather than in the tent.

He hesitated a moment before turning away, his heart begging him to say something meaningful to her before walking away. But what the hell could he say that would help?

Thanks for coming. I appreciate the thought. Now go home.

"Good night," he finally murmured, then quickly yanked down the zipper of his tent and ducked inside.

Zarina told him to have a good night in return, and her soft, mesmerizing voice was almost enough to make him turn around and go back outside. The urge to yank her to her feet and kiss her was so strong, his inner hybrid was practically panting in anticipation. Ignoring the beast, he zipped the tent flap closed with a muttered curse.

He yanked off his boots and T-shirt, leaving his jeans

on like he always did just in case he had to run out and chase off a stray animal, then lay back on his sleeping bag. He wiggled around a bit, getting comfortable on the balled-up sweatshirt he used as a pillow and waited to fall asleep. Instead, he stared up at the inside of his tent, inhaling Zarina's intoxicating scent. Damn, how could any woman smell that good? She was like a slice of heaven with a Russian accent.

He tried to block it out, but it was useless. Short of not breathing, there was no way to keep her scent from invading his nose and reminding him exactly how spectacular she was. The fact that it was giving him a boner sure the hell didn't help.

Tanner closed his eyes only to open them again when his ears picked up an odd tapping sound. It sounded a little like a woodpecker, but they didn't usually come out at night. He pushed himself up on his elbows and listened again.

Crap. It was Zarina. Her teeth were chattering. Dammit to hell, he knew that sleeping bag wasn't heavy enough for her.

Biting back a growl, Tanner yanked open the zipper on the tent and crawled out. If he wasn't so worried about her, he would have laughed at the sight of her snuggled up dangerously close to the fire pit, completely cocooned in her sleeping bag with nothing but her nose and eyes showing, the blanket wrapped around her shoulders like a shawl.

Zarina blinked at him. "What's—?"

Her words trailed off as he dropped down to one knee and slipped his arms under her, then scooped her up, sleeping bag, blanket, and all.

"What are you doing?" she asked.

"Keeping you from freezing to death," he muttered. "I'm tempted to carry your blue butt into town and put you in a hotel room right now." He knelt down to slip her through the open door flap of his tent. "Put your bag inside mine and zip them both up. That should keep you warm enough."

"What about you?" Zarina asked.

"What about me?"

She unzipped her sleeping bag from the inside. "Aren't you going to sleep in here, too?"

Tanner thought his jaw might have dropped, but he wasn't sure. Before going to bed, Zarina had taken off her coat, along with her shirt, jeans, and boots, and was now wearing pajamas with cute cartoon moose printed on them. Holy hell, she'd brought pj's with her? Apparently, the lightest, snuggest pair she could find. And holy hell part two, she wasn't wearing a bra, either. She definitely hadn't been faking how cold she was. Damn. It was all he could do not to cup her perfect breasts in his hands and kiss her until neither of them could breathe.

"That would be a no," he said, working overtime to keep the growl out of his voice and the hard-on from showing through his jeans.

She frowned. "Take my blanket at least. It's cold out there."

Even though he didn't need it, he snatched the blanket from her outstretched hand, then quickly ducked out of the tent before he could change his mind and climb in the damn sleeping bag with her.

Stomping over to the fire, he tossed another few

pieces of wood on it, then stretched out on the blanket and tried to get comfortable. Fat chance of that with the tree branch throbbing between his legs. Well, he sure as hell wasn't going to be cold tonight, that was for damn sure.

"Tanner?" Zarina called softly from inside the tent.

He tensed. If she suggested she needed him to come wrap his arms around her because she was still cold, he was seriously going to lose it.

"I left my pillow out there by the fire," she said. "Could you bring it to me?"

He didn't bother muffling his growl this time. Grabbing the pillow, he got up and walked over to the tent. The moment he unzipped it, Zarina's scent hit him like a two-by-four. Hurriedly tossing the pillow to her, he headed back to his makeshift bed by the fire before he did something he'd regret.

Chapter 2

"I can't believe Landon split up your team," Trevor Maxwell said.

Tate Evers grunted. He'd joined the dark-haired coyote shifter and his partner/girlfriend, Alina Bosch, on one of the benches along the edge of the training area on the DCO complex a little while ago to watch his former teammates navigate the obstacle course with their new partners. Tate had worked with Brent Wilkins and Gavin Barlow, along with bear shifter Declan MacBride, for nearly a decade, but the DCO was currently going through a lot of changes, and that meant a lot of changes for his team, too.

"Landon needed veteran agents to pair up with the shifters they recently recruited," Tate said. "Brent and Gavin are two of the most experienced field agents he has, so it makes sense to pair them up with the newbies."

Some of Alina's strawberry-blond hair had come loose from its bun, and the fall breeze toyed with it. She reached up to tuck it behind her ear. "That all sounds very professional, but aren't you pissed you're losing your guys?"

Tate opened his mouth to say he wasn't, but then stopped. Why bother? He might have recently met Alina, but he and Trevor had been working together since he'd first come to the DCO. The coyote shifter knew him as well as anyone. Besides, Trevor had always been clever. He'd see right through the lie.

"Yeah, it does kind of suck," Tate admitted, scratching his scruff-covered jaw. "I've always worked with a partner, even back when I was in the marshals. When the DCO started bringing in new recruits, I saw the writing on the wall and figured I was going to lose Brent or Gavin, if not both of them. But Declan, too? That's tough."

Trevor did a double take. "Wait, what? Declan has a new partner?"

"No," Tate said. "Landon has him training the new recruits instead of going on missions so he can stay close to Kendra and the kids."

Understanding lit Alina's face. "Can't blame him for that. I've heard the twins are a little wild. What are they, two months old?"

Tate couldn't help grinning. "Yeah. They're growing like weeds. I think they're going to take after their dad."

The mountainous bear shifter was like a brother to him, so while Tate was genuinely happy Declan was able to spend time with his growing family, he was also bummed not to be working with him anymore. Without his team, Tate felt damn useless at the moment. The DCO seemed like it was moving at a hundred miles an hour these days, and he was stuck in neutral.

"So is Landon going to team you up with someone new soon?" Trevor asked.

"Yeah, just not sure when. Kendra's been working overtime with that fancy compatibility computer program of hers trying to find someone for me, but no luck so far."

Trevor's hazel eyes glinted with amusement. "Are you saying you're a hard man to work with? Say it isn't so."

Tate snorted. "Yeah, I'm not too sure how to take that, either."

If this were any other organization, Tate would probably go on missions solo, but that wasn't the way the DCO did things. The whole purpose of the DCO partner program was to pair shifters and humans together. The shifters had the ability to handle themselves in the field. The human part of the equation was to make sure their secret never got out. If people knew the government had shifters working for them, there was no telling what would happen. In Tate's experience, most people didn't like anyone who was different than they were. And saying shifters were different was an understatement.

As he watched the new teams move from one part of the obstacle course to the next, Tate had to admit that Brent's and Gavin's partners matched up with them well. His buddies were moving through the ridiculously difficult terrain faster than they ever had with him and Declan. He guessed Kendra really did know what she was doing with that compatibility program of hers.

"Speaking of changes," Alina murmured, motioning off to the left with her chin. "If someone would have asked me to lay odds on Hamilton ever letting that happen, I would have said slim to none."

Tate followed her gaze to see Sage Andrews and Derek Mickens strolling along the perimeter of the training area, their shoulders bumping occasionally as they walked, their mouths moving in soft conversation. There wasn't an armed guard in sight.

It wasn't the fact that the feline hybrid and the Army Special Forces soldier were having a quiet conversation together that was so unusual to see. The couple had been attached at the hip since Landon had gotten the army to allow Derek to spend a couple of months here on temporary duty. No, the fact that the DCO had let Sage out of her room at all was the big shocker. The hybrid had been held prisoner at the DCO for months, locked in a secure dorm room supposedly for her own protection.

"I'm starting to think that we grossly underestimated Hamilton and Rebecca," Trevor said. "So far, they're doing a damn good job of running this place."

Tate couldn't argue with that. Everyone at the DCO had been stunned, not to mention more than a little worried, when John, their former boss, had told them he was walking away. Tate could understand why he'd done it—his wife and kid had almost died. There was also the whole issue of his ten-year-old daughter going through her first shifter change years before she was supposed to thanks to the fear and stress of seeing her mother get shot. If anyone deserved some time away, it was John. Rumor had it he'd moved his family to the Seychelles Islands…or maybe Fiji. Then again, they could be living in Iceland. Who knew?

"I agree they're doing a good job—they've definitely brought in more shifters than I ever would have thought possible—but that doesn't mean I'm ready to trust them," Tate said. "Especially since we know for a fact that Rebecca Brannon was involved with hybrid research up in Maine." He pinned Trevor with a look. "It's almost a certainty she was funding Mahsood's program at that mental institution where you went undercover, even if there isn't any proof."

Alina shuddered. "I'm less concerned about the

possibility that a congresswoman was funding the research than I am that she knew Mahsood was using her daughter as a guinea pig. It scares me to think how cold-blooded a woman would have to be to allow that."

Trevor grunted "Oh, I never said Rebecca was a saint. She's definitely up to something, which means we still need to keep an eye on her, as well as that Hamilton guy she handpicked to serve as director. I'm just saying she's doing a good job rebuilding the DCO. Landon and Ivy are only bringing in all these new recruits because Rebecca has given them the go-ahead. As for Hamilton getting rid of the bars and locked doors on Sage's dorm room, that's okay with me, even if it turns out later he's an evil bastard."

"Okay, I'll buy that," Tate said. "But have you noticed how much time Ivy and Landon are spending out on the road? I know they're busy recruiting new agents, but a suspicious person might think Rebecca and Hamilton are purposely keeping them, as well as most of the other teams, out of the way for some reason."

Shit. Another reminder Tate didn't have a damn thing to do to keep himself occupied while everyone else was going balls to the wall. Effing great.

Maybe he could go out to Washington State and check on Zarina. It'd been a while since anyone at the DCO had heard from the Russian doctor. She might have gotten herself into some trouble. And since she was probably keeping the satellite phone she was carrying turned off to conserve the battery, they couldn't even get a fix on her location.

He was just wondering if she'd found Tanner when Alina's phone rang. She pulled it out of her back pocket and held it to her ear, then listened attentively for a few moments before throwing Trevor a look.

"We're on the way," she said, then hung up.

Trevor stood. "We'd love to stay and chat some more about no one liking you enough to be your partner, but duty calls. That was the operations center. They have us booked on a plane for London. Some crisis involving thieves with claws and fangs."

Tate wasn't surprised Trevor was the one to fill him in on the conversation instead of Alina. Of course, the coyote shifter had picked up every word that had been said over the phone. Shifters had exceptional hearing to go along with their other skills.

"Lucky you," Tate muttered. "Bring back a souvenir for me."

"Sure thing." Alina smiled as she got to her feet. "One tourist T-shirt coming up."

She and Trevor were a match made in heaven. Tate wondered if they spent their free time trying to one-up each other in the sarcasm department. He scowled as he watched them walk away, acutely aware his professional life—and his social one for that matter—sucked.

Chapter 3

ZARINA WOKE TO THE SOUND OF VOICES OUTSIDE THE TENT. She frowned and pushed herself up on an elbow, trying to hear what Tanner and the other man were saying, but they were speaking too quietly for her to make anything out. Sighing, she flopped back down on the sleeping bags. Considering she'd never spent the night in a tent in the middle of the forest, she was surprised by how well she'd slept.

Of course, she probably wouldn't be nearly this well rested if she'd been huddled outside by the fire trying to stay warm and freaking out about every little sound she heard. Instead, she'd snuggled down in Tanner's sleeping bag, surrounded by his scent and secure in the knowledge that absolutely nothing was going to get past him in the darkness, not even a big, pissed-off grizzly bear.

She started to smile at that, but then froze as she remembered what Tanner had said the night before about park rangers not liking people staying in the forest for extended periods of time.

She bolted up, reaching for the zipper on the door flap only to realize she was still cocooned in the double sleeping bags she'd slept in the night before. The arrangement had been cozy when she'd been freezing her butt off, but now it was claustrophobic.

She scrambled around inside the bag until she found the first zipper and got that one down, then searched for the second one. As she moved her fingers furiously around the quilted material, she strained her ears, listening for the sounds of an argument. Or worse, growling. Tanner would never hurt her, but if another person irritated him—or implied some threat to her—all bets were off. Tanner had already demonstrated on numerous occasions that he could be extremely dangerous if he thought someone he cared about was in jeopardy.

Zarina yanked down the second zipper and shoved her way out of the sleeping bags. Goose bumps spread over her skin as the cold air hit her. That's when she realized she wasn't wearing anything but the flannel pajamas she'd bought in town before hitting the trails. The things had looked absolutely adorable on the store shelf, and the salesman had insisted they'd help keep her warm. That had been another lie, like the one about the flashlight.

The pajamas were also a bit snugger than she'd realized. She didn't mind Tanner seeing her in the curve-hugging clothes, but she wasn't as crazy about a complete stranger ogling her. Unfortunately, the rest of her stuff was out by the fire, so all she was left with was one of Tanner's sweatshirts that he'd rolled up and tucked to one side of the small tent. She quickly pulled it over her head, reveling in his masculine scent for a moment before shoving aside the door flap and crawling out of the tent.

Zarina wished there was a more dignified way to scramble out of it other than on her hands and knees, but she didn't know one. She got out as fast as she could and stood up, then pushed her long hair back from her face, fearing the worst.

But Tanner merely stood there talking to their visitor, no claws or fangs in sight. The newcomer had dark hair and a thick beard and was dressed in jeans and boots similar to Tanner's, as well as a heavy jacket. Tanner, on the other hand, was standing there bare-chested. The sight of him made her both hot and cold at the same time.

Tanner gave her an apologetic look. "Sorry we woke you." He glanced at the man. "This is Burt."

She waited for Tanner to elaborate on who Burt was, but instead, he introduced her with the same amount of eloquence.

"Burt, Zarina."

The man gave her a nod, clearly not impressed by her moose-print pajama pants in the least, then turned his attention back to Tanner.

"They hit the south end of the camp this morning," he told Tanner. "There were at least half a dozen of them, and they were armed with automatic weapons this time. I'm assuming you heard the gunfire?"

Tanner nodded. "Yeah, I heard." He jerked his chin in Zarina's direction. "I wasn't able to come help. Sorry."

Zarina had no idea what they were talking about, but she definitely hadn't heard any gunfire. Then again, with Tanner's hearing, the shooting could have come from very far away. But that would suggest Burt knew about Tanner's enhanced hearing.

"Just as well you didn't," Burt said. "They raided us with military efficiency and were in and out in less than five minutes. As fast as you are, you still wouldn't have gotten there in time."

Zarina frowned. That answered the question about whether Burt knew of Tanner's abilities.

Tanner didn't comment on that assumption one way or the other. "Was anyone hurt?"

Pain flickered across Burt's face. "Three people, including Lorraine. She got shot in the leg. She'll make it, but I doubt she's going to be able to walk again for a long time, if ever."

Zarina stepped closer to Tanner, hugging herself with her arms in an effort to ward off the morning chill. "What did the doctor say?"

She was surprised the woman was already out of surgery with injuries that bad.

"No one in our camp goes to doctors." Burt's mouth tightened. "We don't trust them."

Zarina gaped at him. "Why not?"

Beside her, Tanner sighed. "It's a long story."

Zarina fought the urge to throw her hands in the air. "Then you can tell me on the way to Burt's camp. I'm going to check on Lorraine and the other people who are injured."

Zarina ignored Tanner's scowl as she crouched down beside her pack. No doubt he'd been planning to take her into town this morning and get her on the first plane out of Seattle. She wouldn't have gone anyway, but now she had even more reason to stay. This woman Lorraine needed medical attention, and she might be the only one who could give it.

As she rummaged through the pack for fresh clothes, Zarina tried to make sense of Tanner's behavior the previous night. He'd been angry with her, but she'd expected that. He was a stubborn man who'd decided to run off and live like a hermit in the wilderness rather than risk hurting the people he cared about. She'd never expected him to be happy about her tracking him down.

But something told her there was more to it than that. When she'd explained about the antidote that would repair the damage the hybrid serum had done to his DNA, she'd expected him to jump at the chance to be human. Instead, he'd started talking about never being normal again. That made no sense.

Even more confusing—if that were possible—was the way Tanner had reacted after he'd carried her into his tent. She could tell from the bulge in his jeans he'd been aroused, but instead of taking her up on the offer to share the sleeping bags, he'd bolted. It was like he couldn't stand the sight of her, and that rejection had hurt more than she could ever have imagined.

"Did they grab anyone this time?" Tanner asked Burt.

Zarina stilled, hand on a long-sleeved T-shirt. The thought that whoever attacked Burt's camp had kidnapped people hadn't even entered her mind. Who were these lunatics? She glanced over her shoulder to see Burt's eyes fill with sadness.

"Josh is missing." Burt shook his head. "He was right beside me during the fight, but then next time I looked, he was nowhere to be found. We're still looking, but…"

Tanner growled. "What the hell was Josh doing fighting? He's frigging seventeen years old!"

Burt met Tanner's gaze. "He's old enough to carry a weapon, so he's old enough to protect the camp."

Tanner cursed and turned away from her and Burt to gaze into the forest. Zarina wondered if it was because his eyes had turned hybrid red. She tightened her grip on the shirt in her hand, fighting the urge to comfort him. Something told her he wouldn't appreciate a gesture like that at the moment.

"Chad thinks it would be a good idea if you stayed with us until we figure out how to stop these people," Burt said. "He doesn't think you should be out here on your own."

Tanner grunted but didn't turn around. Zarina didn't have to see his face to know he was still angry. "Chad wants me in his camp to help protect the place."

Burt shrugged. "Maybe. I know I'd feel better if you were there."

Tanner made no comment.

"Look, I have no doubt you'll be fine on your own, but are you ready to risk Zarina?" Burt demanded. "Are you sure you can keep her safe from these psychos?"

That must have struck a nerve, because Tanner swung around, his face dark. He went crazy at the mere notion she might so much as stub her toe. The idea that she might be in danger would make him go ballistic. She appreciated that he wanted to keep her safe, but she hated that he thought he could do it without asking her opinion on the matter.

"It's not really an issue," Tanner stated flatly. "She's leaving after she checks on Lorraine."

Straightening up, she glared at him. "No, I'm not."

Burt must have found that amusing, because his mouth twitched under his mustache. "Do what's best for you and Zarina, Tanner, but if you want to stay with us, you're welcome to. Like I said, we could use your help." He gave Zarina a nod. "I'll tell Lorraine you'll be stopping by."

Zarina waited until Burt had disappeared into the trees before looking Tanner's way. "Okay, what the heck was all that about? Who are Burt and his friends?

Why don't they trust doctors? And who are these crazies that keep attacking their camp?"

"They're preppers," Tanner said casually, as if that explained everything. "They have a place north of here, just on the edge of the federal property above Lake Chelan. They don't know who keeps attacking their camp, but a few nearby prepper communities have been hit recently, too."

Zarina waited for him to say more, but he didn't. Instead, he crouched down and started folding the blanket he'd slept on last night. She couldn't believe he'd been comfortable using nothing but a thin piece of fabric to keep him warm, but that came with being a hybrid.

She forced her attention away from the display of rippling muscles as he moved and focused on what he'd said. "Okay, maybe I'm losing something in translation, but what's a prepper? And why would anyone want to attack them? Are they wealthy or something?"

Tanner chuckled softly. "No, they're definitely not wealthy. Preppers are people who think there's going to be a big disaster in the world at some point, so they stockpile food, water, and other supplies. As for why they don't trust doctors, they just prefer to depend on themselves instead of outsiders."

Zarina folded her arms. "So they're paranoid kooks waiting for the zombie apocalypse?"

Tanner finished folding the blanket and stood, his eyes twinkling with amusement. "They're not kooks. I'll admit, some of them are a little more paranoid than others, especially when it comes to the authorities, but most of them are normal, everyday people who live off the grid."

"Who keep a year's supply of food in their pantry," she said.

"Who keep a year's supply of food in their pantry," he agreed. "A lot of them—like Burt and his friends—have community farms, too."

Zarina nodded. That she could understand. Farms were a way of life back home in Russia. She even got the part about not trusting the authorities. That was a way of life in Russia, too. But living off the grid and keeping that much food on hand sounded a little odd to her.

"So why are these people attacking the preppers if they're not wealthy?" she asked. "Is it to take their food and supplies?"

"The attackers weren't after food or supplies, that's for sure."

Tanner dropped to one knee beside her pack, then took everything out. He hesitated a moment when he ran into the stack of panties that must have been all the way in the bottom, maybe overwhelmed by the sheer number of them. But there weren't any washing machines out here, and the idea of wearing panties more than once made her feel gross. She reached out and snagged a pair from his hand so she could change into them later.

Tanner didn't look at her as he stuffed them back in the pack. "If they grabbed Josh, that makes him the fifth person who's been abducted in the past few weeks. That's not counting the people missing from the homeless camps located in other parts of the forest. I'd assumed it was the locals trying to chase them off, but now I'm not so sure. My gut tells me there's something else going on, though I don't have a clue what it might be."

"What are the police saying about the abductions?"

she asked as Tanner finished with her pack. "Do they have any leads?"

"I doubt the police even realize anything is going on," he said, walking over to his tent.

Zarina watched as Tanner leaned in and pulled out the sleeping bag, then rolled it up. If he was packing up, that must mean they'd be staying at the prepper camp. She wasn't surprised. The moment Burt had suggested she might be in danger, she'd known Tanner would agree to move to their camp. That also meant he was smart enough to know he wasn't getting rid of her.

He quickly finished shoving his stuff in his pack before starting in on the tent. Zarina would have volunteered to help, but he was moving so fast, she'd only get in the way.

"Like I said, preppers don't trust outsiders, especially the police. I'm pretty sure they didn't even report it," Tanner told her.

She blinked. "So the preppers are going to try to find their friends on their own?"

Tanner shrugged. "Probably."

She didn't see them having much success. "Okay, so they don't like the police, but what's the deal with doctors and hospitals? They're willing to let Lorraine lose the ability to walk simply because they have trust issues?"

Tanner was silent as he finished strapping the tent on top of his pack. "Hospitals mean paperwork, lots of questions, and ultimately, cops. None of them want that."

Zarina shook her head. Picking up her backpack, she dragged it on over her shoulders. "How long will it take to get to this prepper camp?"

It could already be too late for Lorraine. A person

could go into life-threatening shock within an hour of a major injury. Burt didn't say whether the woman had been hurt sometime last night or early this morning, but either way, that was a long time to go without proper medical attention.

As Tanner shrugged his pack on his broad shoulders, Zarina looked around and realized he'd been right. There was nothing left to show anyone had made camp except for the cold fire pit. Tanner really did carry everything he owned on his back.

"The trip would take me a solid hour at a steady walk." Reaching out, he snagged her pack off her back and hung it casually off one of his shoulders. "It would take you a lot longer, especially weighed down with all this stuff. I'll carry your pack so we can get there faster."

In any other situation, Zarina would have complained, but Tanner was right. This wasn't about her or her pride. There were people hurt who needed her help.

"Okay," she said. "But don't think this means I'm going to let you carry my pack all the time."

Tanner snorted and turned in the same direction the prepper had gone a few minutes ago. "I wouldn't dream of it." He glanced over his shoulder. "You coming or what?"

Zarina started after him, jogging to catch up. Five minutes later, they were heading up a steep slope, and she was already gasping for breath. Maybe if she asked nicely, Tanner would carry her and her pack?

Zarina stepped onto the front porch of the small cabin, closing the door quietly behind her. She'd expected to find the camp's residents waiting expectantly for her, but no one was around. That wasn't surprising. Lorraine's surgery had taken a long time. Reaching around, she pressed the heels of her hands to the small of her back and stretched, letting out a groan. From the position of the sun, it must be midday, which meant she'd been working for at least three hours straight. The backache was worth it, though. Lorraine wasn't going to lose her life—or her leg—even though it felt like Zarina had just performed surgery in the middle of the Stone Age.

She and Tanner had practically run all the way to the prepper camp. Okay, maybe she was exaggerating. Tanner had walked at a brisk pace. She'd mostly stumbled over rocks and tree roots every five feet, trying to keep up.

She looked around at the collection of cabins and tents, searching for Tanner. She and Tanner had been moving too fast when they'd first gotten here to give the place more than a quick glance, but now that she had a minute to take it in, she had to admit it reminded her of something you'd see on *The Walking Dead*—without the zombies.

Zarina found Tanner standing off to one side of the porch, his back against the cabin wall, his face heavy with exhaustion. He'd been at her side while she'd treated Lorraine for almost the entire morning, helping out any way he could. Even though he didn't say as much, it was obvious it hurt him to see the old woman in so much pain. But there was nothing Zarina could do to relieve the woman's agony. The camp's supply of heavy-duty drugs had been used up in the previous attack or given to the other prepper camps that had also been hit.

"Is she okay?" he asked softly.

He'd left a few minutes earlier, after one of Lorraine's more vocal moments. It had been difficult for Zarina to take, but she knew it'd been worse for him. His hybrid half had immediately responded to the primal sounds of pain, his eyes flaring red, his fangs and claws extending. Zarina didn't blame him for walking out. She would have left if she could.

"She's better," Zarina said, moving off the porch and walking over to him. "Lorraine will be in pain for a while, but it should start to taper off within the next twelve hours or so."

Sighing, Tanner closed his eyes and leaned his head back against the wall of the cabin again. Zarina didn't say anything else, not wanting to interrupt him if he was silently saying a prayer of thanks. She frowned a little, realizing she didn't know whether he was religious or not. Then again, there was a lot about Tanner she didn't know. He kept a lot of stuff to himself. She wished he didn't do that. Maybe she could make his life better if she knew more about him. Which, strangely enough, was part of the reason she was so attracted to him. That stoic, stubborn nature of his was alluring—when it wasn't driving her crazy.

Tanner's eyes abruptly snapped open, and he pushed away from the wall, completely alert. A moment later, Zarina heard the sound of footsteps approaching the cabin. She turned to see Burt, along with another man and a dark-haired teenage girl who was about eighteen or nineteen. The man was probably the same age as Burt, but his face was more lined and his eyes more weary.

It wasn't until the trio stopped in front of them that

Zarina caught sight of the half-healed scar along one side of the girl's neck. Four parallel wounds, the two in the middle deeper than the ones on either side. It took Zarina only half a second to recognize those scars had come from a shifter—or a hybrid.

Zarina shot a quick look Tanner's way, telling herself it wasn't possible. She searched his face for some indication he was the one who'd hurt the girl, but he merely returned her gaze.

"Zarina, you know Burt already," Tanner said. "This is Chad and his daughter, Lillie."

Burt gave Zarina a nod while Chad and Lillie took turns shaking her hand. Zarina should have realized the girl was the man's daughter as soon as she saw them together. They had the same gray eyes, aquiline nose, and arching brows.

"I can't tell you how much I appreciate you getting here so fast, Tanner," Chad said. "And for bringing your friend." He looked at Zarina. "I don't know what we would have done without her, except maybe lose Lorraine. How is she?"

Zarina opened her mouth to point out that there would have been a lot less drama if they'd simply taken the woman to a hospital like normal people, but the sight of three huge, fierce-looking men coming toward them made her forget what she'd been about to say.

It wasn't just the blatant anger on the men's faces that stunned her speechless. It was the fact that she recognized them. But even as she stood there with her mouth hanging open, she told herself she had to be wrong. There was no way they could possibly be the men she thought they were, because the last time she'd seen them, Stutmeir's goons had been dragging their dead bodies out of an abandoned ski lodge not more than fifteen miles from here.

"What the hell is she doing here?" one of the men snarled, showing off inch-long fangs to go along with his suddenly flaming red eyes. Dark-haired with a broad nose and full lips, he was nearly as tall as Tanner. "She's one of those damn doctors who tortured us. I'd know her fucking scent anywhere."

Zarina was still trying to wrap her mind around the fact that the hybrids were alive when the one who'd spoken strode toward her, his clawed hands itching to do damage. She barely had enough time to get out of the way before Tanner stepped in front of her and stiff-armed the guy in the chest.

"Back off, Spencer," Tanner growled, his tone more menacing than Zarina had ever heard it. He pinned the other two hybrids with a glare. One had blond hair and a stocky build while the other was a tall, muscular, dark-skinned man. "Peter and Malcolm, that goes for you too."

That warning only got them more riled up. Zarina watched in alarm as Peter and Malcolm snarled and bared their fangs. Clearly, they were ready to go through him to get to her.

Tanner didn't give them a chance. He dropped his hands to his sides, his claws extending to their full length so fast that blood splattered on the wooden planks of the porch. Then he bared his fangs at the men and roared so loud, people five miles away probably heard it.

Zarina reached out to grab his arm, desperate to stop the fight before it started, but Tanner slipped left and caught the blond-haired Peter in midjump. Latching onto the man's shoulders, Tanner spun him around and sent him crashing into one of the pillars supporting the porch. Peter slammed into it with an audible crunch. Something told Zarina the sound wasn't entirely from the wood breaking.

Peter hadn't even tumbled to the ground before Tanner was moving again. He intercepted Malcolm just as the man lashed out at Zarina's face with his claws. Their sharp points missed her by mere inches, and she gasped as Tanner ran headlong into her attacker, shoving him away from her.

Tanner and Malcolm went down in a pile, quickly becoming a rolling ball of muscles, snarls, growls, and flashing claws. A split second later, Spencer joined the fray.

Crap. This was going to get so much worse.

Heart pounding, Zarina hurried forward to intervene, but an arm wrapped around her waist, jerking her to a stop before she'd gone more than a few feet. She glanced over her shoulder to see Burt holding onto her. A few feet away, Chad was doing the same to his daughter. All around the camp, people poked their heads out of doors and windows, a few of them venturing out of their cabins to see what the commotion was about.

"You can't get between them, not while they're like this," Burt insisted. "You do, and you're the one who's going to get hurt."

Zarina knew Burt was right, but that didn't keep her from fighting against his grip anyway. Tanner was in danger. That was all she cared about.

But Burt refused to let her go, so she was forced to watch as Peter joined Spencer and Malcolm. The three hybrids looked barely human now, their eyes completely lost in a glow of red and fangs flashing.

Tanner might be bigger than all three of them and a former Army Ranger to boot, but there was no way he could fight that many out-of-control hybrids all at once. He was so focused on Spencer and Malcolm that he never saw Peter coming at his back. Malcolm gripped Tanner's shoulder, digging his claws in deep and flipping Tanner over. Peter immediately lunged forward and sank his fangs into Tanner's free arm, pinning it to the ground and holding him tight. That's when Spencer leaned in close and lifted his hand, his claws aimed at Tanner's exposed neck.

Zarina's heart seized in her chest. *Oh God*. Spencer was going to kill him.

Just then, Lillie broke loose of her father's grip and threw herself into Spencer's arms, ignoring his claws as if they weren't there. Her father shouted for her to get away from the hybrid, but Lillie didn't pay any attention. Instead, she placed her small hands firmly in the middle of Spencer's chest and pushed, resolutely facing down the snarling hybrid like she wasn't scared of him at all.

That interruption was all Tanner needed.

He broke loose from the two hybrids holding him, blood flying as he roared so loud, Zarina swore she felt the ground tremble beneath her. He slashed Peter across the chest as he got to his feet, knocking the air out of the hybrid and putting him on his back. The wound wasn't deep enough to kill, but it was bad enough to jerk Peter out of his shift. The red faded from the man's eyes, and he rolled over, groaning in pain.

Tanner quickly moved over to put himself between Malcolm and Zarina, as if he still thought she might be in danger. From where she stood, she had a three-quarter view of Tanner's face, and the rage she saw there shocked her. She'd seen his hybrid side many times, but she'd never seen him like this.

He roared again, louder than even before. That, along with the display of three-inch-long fangs, which were much larger and more terrifying than any other hybrid's, was enough to make Malcolm take a step back, the red glow fading from his eyes.

That should have ended the fight, but Tanner was too far gone for that. He stalked toward Malcolm, his clawed hands ready to strike.

Zarina froze. He was going to kill Malcolm because the hybrid had tried to hurt her.

She yanked away from Burt before he could stop her and lunged for Tanner. This time, she wasn't worried about protecting him from physical harm but from something much worse. If he killed the other hybrid in cold blood like this, it would crush his soul. For him, that would be more than he could take.

Zarina ran around in front of Tanner, putting herself between him and Malcolm. But the sight of her wasn't enough to halt him in his tracks like it usually was. His eyes were as ruby red and feral as the three other hybrids' eyes had been mere moments ago. He was so far gone, she wasn't sure if she could get him back from the edge.

"Tanner, it's me…Zarina," she said in the calmest, softest voice she could manage. "It's okay now. You can relax. The danger is past. Breathe, Tanner, just breathe."

He hesitated, and she stepped closer to him, saying the words over and over again, first in English, then in Russian, before repeating them in English. She knew he couldn't understand her when she spoke in her native language, but when he was this far gone, she doubted he could understand what she was saying in English, either. But the words she used never mattered. It was her tone and the soft sound of her voice calming the beast that fought to completely take control of him.

Little by little, the red glow in his eyes began to fade, and she knew she was getting through to him despite the fact that his claws and fangs were still fully extended.

"I'm safe, Tanner," she murmured as she moved closer. "You can relax."

Stopping in front of him, she put her hands on his chest and leaned in, letting her scent envelop him until the red glow finally disappeared from his eyes and his fangs and claws retracted.

Zarina nudged him back, wanting to put a little more distance between him and the other three hybrids.

Out of the corner of her eye, she saw Lillie doing the same thing to Spencer. Even more shocking, the big hybrid let her do it, though the girl was literally half his size and his eyes were still blazing a deep, angry red. That answered Zarina's earlier question about how Lillie had gotten those scars on her neck. She'd put herself in front of an angry hybrid, something Zarina had done more times than she could count.

Now that the hybrid testosterone had finally receded, Chad got his hands on Peter while Burt urged Malcolm back, putting a little more space between everyone.

"Move away from Spencer, Lillie," Chad ordered.

She didn't answer but simply met his gaze and stayed where she was.

Chad gave his daughter an angry look but didn't argue. Muttering something under his breath, he checked the slash on Peter's chest.

While Tanner had calmed down, Zarina could feel his body shaking as he fought to keep control of his inner hybrid. He stood there with his hands at his sides, breathing deeply, blood running down his arm from the wound on his shoulder. The lion was gone, and in its place was a man who looked exhausted and crushed to his core. She longed to check his wounds, especially the bite, but that could wait. A hybrid wouldn't bleed to death from a wound like that, and right now, getting him completely relaxed was the most important thing.

It took a lot longer for the other three hybrids to get it together. But even after Spencer's fangs and claws had retracted, he and his friends stared at her with hate in their eyes.

"What the hell are you doing with her, Tanner?" Spencer finally demanded, his voice rough with emotion. "She was there. She helped turn us into monsters."

Zarina opened her mouth to tell her side of the story, but Tanner spoke before she could.

"She was there, yes, but she was as much of a prisoner as we were," he said firmly.

"What does that mean?" Peter asked.

"Stutmeir kidnapped her and forced her to work for him. If she didn't, he would have killed her," Tanner explained. "She had nothing to do with what happened to us. In fact, she did everything she could to stop it. I know it doesn't mean anything to you, but Zarina risked her life to get me out when it looked like the other doctors were going to keep pumping me full of drugs until I died for real. She saved my life, so if you have a problem with her, you have a problem with me."

Tanner didn't so much as let out a growl, but his message came through loud and clear anyway. All three of the hybrids backed off. Spencer even let Lillie nudge him another few feet away. While none of the men looked happy, at least they weren't eyeing Zarina like they still wanted to attack her.

Zarina was eager to use the pause in hostilities to ask how the three men had gotten there. Or more precisely, how it was possible they were still alive. She'd personally checked their pulses after Stutmeir's doctors had injected them with the hybrid serum, and they'd been dead. Of that, she was certain.

Before she could get her first question out, Tanner asked one of his own.

"Where's Bryce?"

The three hybrids visibly tensed. Zarina stiffened, too, afraid there was going to be another fight. But Spencer merely shook his head.

"He disappeared right after the attack. We were hoping he was out tracking Josh, but he still hasn't come back. We're starting to worry maybe those assholes grabbed him, too."

"We tried to follow his trail, but we lost the scent pretty quickly," Malcolm said. "Maybe you can try. Your nose is way better than any of ours."

Tanner didn't answer but instead threw a quick look at Zarina. "Stay here. I'll be back soon."

He was gone before she could say anything, leaving her standing on the porch with a group of preppers she didn't know and three hybrids who still didn't act like they thought very much of her.

Chad and Burt headed into the cabin to check on Lorraine while Lillie and Spencer moved several feet away to talk softly to each other. The young woman turned and looked Zarina's way a few times, like they were talking about her. Zarina couldn't help but wonder what they were saying.

The other two hybrids stood off to the side, Malcolm tending to the wound on Peter's chest. Zarina would have offered to help, but she was pretty sure her gesture wouldn't be appreciated. So she simply walked back onto the porch and took a seat in the Adirondack-style chair there and waited. Even the preppers who'd come out of their cabins before had disappeared inside.

Tanner jogged back into the camp five minutes after he'd left, a concerned expression on his face. Zarina could tell he'd been running fast, because there was a sheen of sweat covering his skin, but he wasn't breathing hard at all. He stepped onto the porch just as Chad came out of the cabin. Spencer, Lillie, Peter, and Malcolm moved closer to listen in.

"Well?" Chad asked.

"Bryce's trail converges with Josh's and the men who attacked your camp not more than a half mile into the woods," Tanner said, his face grim. "There was a gunfight, and Bryce was hit. I found brass from an M16 or M4, as well as Bryce's blood. The amount of blood didn't suggest the injury was severe, but it must have been bad enough to knock him out. I found marks along the ground indicating they'd dragged both Bryce and Josh several hundred feet to the dirt road that runs along the south side of the farm. From there, they put them in a big vehicle, a van or SUV judging by the tire tracks."

No one said a word. The preppers and hybrids simply looked around at one another like they were hoping Bryce and Josh would appear and announce Tanner had been wrong, that they'd merely been lost in the woods.

"We need to call the police," Zarina finally said when no one spoke.

Chad shook his head, his mouth tight. "No cops."

Not that again.

"Your community was attacked by someone with weapons, and two of your friends were captured—or worse," Zarina pointed out.

"Don't you think I know that?" Chad shot her an angry look. "There are people we know and trust in the other camps near here. We'll get some trackers out there. We'll find them."

Zarina stared at Chad in disbelief. Was he insane? Not even Tanner could track Bryce and Josh if the men were in a vehicle.

"That hasn't worked so far, and now there's what, half a dozen people missing?" Zarina folded her arms. "You don't even know who captured them or where they took them. You need trained professionals if you ever hope to find them."

Chad stood silently, his jaw clenched tight.

Zarina was tempted to walk over and slap the man. His damn pride and his stubbornness were going to get his friends killed. If they weren't already. But then she had a better idea. She pointed at where her backpack leaned against the side of the cabin alongside Tanner's.

"I have a satellite phone in my pack," she said. "Tanner and I can call some friends of ours in DC. They're very good at dealing with this kind of situation."

The man's eyes sharpened. "DC?" he said warily. "What kind of friends? You mean feds?"

Zarina started to answer, but Tanner got the words out first. "Yeah, they're feds. But they're good people I'd vouch for any day of the week."

If Zarina thought Chad seemed suspicious before, it was nothing compared to the expression on his face now. "No. No feds of any kind."

"Dad," Lillie said softly. "They're trying to help."

"We don't need that kind of help," her father insisted. "Chad and Bryce are my responsibility. I won't risk their lives calling in the feds. We'll do it our way, just like we always have."

Zarina cursed silently. She'd never dealt with anyone so infuriating in her life, and that included Tanner.

"What do you expect, that Tanner and I are going to stand around here and do nothing?" she demanded.

Chad shook his head. "I don't expect you and Tanner to do anything. This is our problem, and we'll handle it. You've done more than enough for us already." His expression softened. "If you really want to help, then maybe you could go into town and pick up some supplies? We've been sticking close to camp for the past couple of weeks, and we're out of just about everything, especially medical supplies. Since you're a doctor, you might have an easier time replacing the antibiotics and pain meds we're out of."

Zarina frowned. Yes, she was a doctor, but she wasn't licensed to practice in Washington—or the United States for that matter. Even if she was, she couldn't simply walk into a pharmacy and load up a cart full of prescription drugs, then walk out the door with a wave and a smile. It didn't work that way.

"I'll do the best I can with the meds," she said. "But I'm not too sure how successful I'll be. It's not like I have any connections out here."

He nodded. "That's all I can ask. I can give you the names of the doctors who have helped us out in the past. Maybe with you doing the asking, they'll help us again."

Chad stayed long enough to tell them where they could get the supplies they needed and give them a key for a vehicle.

"I want your promise you won't call your friends back in DC," he said as he handed it over.

Tanner's jaw tightened, but he nodded. "You have my word."

Chad walked off after that, disappearing into a big building on the other side of camp. The hybrids followed suit. Lillie stood where she was for a moment, gazing at Tanner and Zarina like she wanted to say something but couldn't, before she left as well.

Zarina watched her go. She didn't understand these people at all. Sighing, she turned to Tanner.

"Are we really going to go along with Chad's demands and do absolutely nothing while his trackers run around in the woods on the off chance they stumble across Josh and Bryce?" she asked.

When Tanner didn't say anything, Zarina was afraid he was going to go along with Chad. But then he bit back a growl, and she knew he was as frustrated as she was.

"I promised I wouldn't call the feds, and I won't. I owe Chad that much," he said. "But that doesn't mean we can't call someone else."

"Who?"

"My brother."

Chapter 4

TANNER PULLED THE BIG PICKUP TRUCK THEY'D BORROWED from Chad into a space in front of Darryl's Diner in Wenatchee a little after two that afternoon. But instead of climbing out, he sat there with both hands on the wheel and the motor running, aware of Zarina sitting quietly beside him. He hadn't said much to her since they'd left the camp and even less after talking to his brother on the satellite phone, and he braced himself, expecting her to demand answers now that they were about to meet with Cam. But she didn't.

How the hell had he gotten to this place? Everything around him was spiraling out of control, and there was nothing he could do to stop any of it.

When the first few preppers and homeless people had disappeared, he'd convinced himself it wasn't his problem and the best thing he could do for the world was stay as far away from other people as possible. That was the only way to make sure he didn't lose control at the wrong time and kill someone.

But where had that decision led? To over half a dozen innocent people going missing, including some he'd come to think of as friends. His desire to not kill anyone had almost certainly led to those disappearances regardless. The only difference was now he felt like a coward for not doing a damn thing to stop it.

Then there was Zarina. He'd intended to get her off

the mountain at first light this morning, even if he had to tie her up in her sleeping bag and carry her all the way to the departure gate at Sea-Tac. But those plans had been shot down the moment Burt had walked into their camp and told them about the attack. Now that she knew about the missing preppers, there was no way he was getting her to leave, cinched up in a sleeping bag or not.

Everything he'd done over the past two months had been in the name of keeping the people he cared about safe, especially Zarina. Now the woman he loved was in more danger than she'd ever been, not only because of those assholes who were attacking the prepper camps, but because he was a monster who should never be allowed around anyone.

He bit back a growl as he replayed the fight with Spencer and the other hybrids at the prepper camp. *Shit.* That had been bad. He hadn't lost control like that in a really long time. He could have easily killed all three of those hybrids, not to mention Chad, Burt, and Lillie. And yes, probably Zarina, too.

He'd convinced himself that coming out here and staying away from people and situations that might set him off would help him get a better grip on the animal inside. He'd obviously been wrong about that. The truth was he was worse off now than he'd ever been at the DCO compound. As much as he hated to admit it, being away from Zarina had caused him to lose even the small amount of control he'd fought to gain over the past year. He felt as on edge as he had when the DCO had first dragged him out of the woods a wild, feral monster.

He guessed he'd made a lot of bad decisions lately. He'd made them for the best possible reasons, of course, but they were still terrible decisions regardless. Now he was heading into a diner to meet a brother he hadn't seen in years in the crazy hope that somehow it'd make things better. The only problem was that he couldn't imagine how this family reunion could possibly end well.

To say he hadn't been planning to see his brother or any other members of his family while he was out here was an understatement. He'd been living in the Wenatchee Forest within two hours of the home he'd grown up in and had never even considered calling them. The fact that he was meeting with Cam now only because he needed help made him feel kind of dirty.

"How's your shoulder?" Zarina asked softly from the passenger seat.

Tanner glanced at her. It was obvious from the concern on her beautiful face that she was worried about the damage he'd sustained in the fight, even though she knew he'd survived far worse. In addition to bandaging the wounds at the camp before they'd left, she'd checked his injuries twice on the way down the mountain. He flexed his shoulder, feeling the fresh scar tissue tighten and pull across his deltoids and biceps. It hurt, but the gouges and bite wounds were healing. Within a day, he wouldn't even notice them.

"Shoulder's fine," he said.

Zarina nodded, turning back to gaze out the windshield at the brick diner with its metal roof and photographs of happy people enjoying burgers, fries, and Cokes pictured in each of the windows. "You never told me your brother was a cop."

She hadn't mentioned his brother once on the drive down or while they'd picked up supplies and equipment for the camp. Not even after he'd talked to him on the satellite phone. But now that they were about to meet Cam, he supposed her curiosity had finally gotten the best of her.

Tanner didn't blame her. He'd never talked about himself much, even though Zarina had tried to engage him on the subject hundreds of times. The obvious tension in his voice during the short phone call with his brother probably hadn't done anything to lessen that curiosity.

"Cam was only fifteen years old when I left to join the army," Tanner told her, smiling a little as his mind filled with images of his little brother. "I tried to get home as much as I could, but my Ranger battalion deployed all the time, so I didn't get a chance to see him or the rest of my family nearly as much as I wanted to. Time just sort of gets away from you, and you tell yourself there'll be time to make it up to them later." He sobered at that thought. "When I finally got out of the army, I expected to come back and see the same little brother I'd always had, only to discover he'd gone out and grown up on me when I wasn't looking. He'd already joined the Seattle Police Department and was close to finishing the academy before I got a chance to talk to him. I didn't even know he wanted to be a cop."

Sighing, Tanner glanced at the Seattle Police cruiser parked beside them. It was crazy to think the brother he'd tossed the football around with in the backyard between army basic training and reporting to Fort Lewis after Ranger School was a cop.

"Was that the last time you saw him?" Zarina asked, turning her head to look at him. "When you got out of the army, I mean."

Part of Tanner wanted to tell her what happened the last time he'd seen Cam, about all the horrible things he'd done and how those few short days had changed his whole life. But it would be stupid to unload his problems on Zarina when there was nothing she could do to change any of it. More than that, though, it would be unfair. His burdens were his alone to carry, no matter how much she might wish otherwise.

He reached out to switch off the engine. "It was a long time ago."

Beside him, Zarina got that same determined look in her eye she got whenever she wanted something, and it was all Tanner could do not to chuckle. He'd come to be wary of that part of her personality at the same time as he'd grown to adore it. When Zarina felt she was doing the right thing, there was little that would stop her from continuing down the path she was on.

"I think it's time we head inside," he said, opening his door. "This meeting won't get any easier by putting it off."

Tanner stepped out of the truck before Zarina could try to stop him—or ask him what he'd meant by that comment. He busied himself for a few moments tightening the tarp over the load of supplies they'd already picked up before going around to help Zarina out.

Tanner resolutely led her to the door of the diner. He forced himself to ignore his racing heart, the quiver in his stomach, and the nearly overwhelming urge to run back to the truck and get the hell out of there. Instead, he focused on putting one foot in front of the other, moving closer to the entrance and a meeting he dreaded with every step. He might have slowed a bit, maybe even stopped once or twice. He wasn't sure, since Zarina didn't call him on it or ask him what was up.

Cam was still his little brother, all grown up or not. He could do this.

He picked up Cam's scent the moment he stepped inside the diner. Which was kind of crazy, considering he hadn't seen his brother since he'd been turned into a hybrid. But in some strange way that only made sense to the animal living just beneath the surface of his awareness, Tanner knew his brother's scent even though the diner was packed with people.

Tanner ignored the awards filling the walls proclaiming Darryl's one of the best restaurants in Wenatchee and instead followed his nose, taking Zarina's hand and winding through a maze of red laminate-topped tables until he found his brother seated near the very back, around a corner that shielded the booth somewhat and provided at least some measure of quiet in the otherwise bustling restaurant. His brother was seated facing the door, dressed in the dark blue uniform of the Seattle PD. It suited him.

His brother glanced up from his menu at their approach, as if sensing Tanner. They locked gazes for a moment, Cam's blue eyes widening slightly. Tanner had always been taller and more muscular than Cam, but now that he was a hybrid, the differences were even more pronounced.

Cam recovered quickly, taking in Tanner's long hair, old jeans, worn hiking boots, and the scruff on his jaw. When he was done with him, Cam turned his attention to Zarina, no doubt wondering who she was and what the hell she was doing with someone like Tanner.

"You look different," Cam said, glancing his way as he put his menu back in the rack near the wall.

Tanner didn't blame him for not shaking hands or giving him a man hug. Could this get any more uncomfortable?

"You've changed, too," he said.

He wasn't lying. Cam had changed a hell of a lot since the last time Tanner had seen him nearly three years ago.

For one thing, his brother's dark-blond hair was shorter than he remembered. His shoulders and chest were also quite a bit bigger. He even had biceps to fill out the sleeves of his uniform shirt. Joining the police force had clearly done him good.

Tanner and Cam regarded each other in silence for what must have been at least a minute before Zarina sighed and moved around Tanner to slide into the booth across from his brother.

"I don't know about the two of you, but I'm starving," she declared, taking a menu from the rack. "What's good here? By the way, I'm Zarina. You must be Cam, though that's completely a guess on my part, since Tanner has told me next to nothing about you."

That seemed to break the ice. Cam chuckled as Tanner took a seat beside Zarina on the wooden bench seat.

"Nice to meet you, Zarina." Cam gave her a warm smile and extended his hand. "I've never eaten here, but I was going to order the chili cheeseburger. The menu says they mix chili cheese corn chips into the burger before they cook it."

Zarina raised a brow. "I have no idea what that would even taste like, but it sounds delicious. Though to be truthful, I've been living on beef jerky and granola bars for days. Anything with grease sounds good at this point."

Cam chuckled again, then fixed Tanner with a glare. "So, where were you for the past three years? Mom has worried herself sick, and Dad thinks you're dead."

Shit. This was why he hadn't wanted to see Cam. Because his brother was going to ask him questions he couldn't answer.

"It's complicated," he said.

"I'm sure it is," Cam snapped. "But I still expect an answer. Unless you want me to just get up and walk the hell out of here."

Tanner glanced over at Zarina, hoping for some guidance, but all she did was shrug, as if to say there wasn't an easy way out of this.

"Dammit, Tanner," Cam swore. "Talk to me! You can't call me out of the blue after being gone for three years and expect me to act like nothing ever happened."

Tanner ground his jaw. His brother was right. But how the hell could he explain all the crap that had happened to him without sounding like he'd escaped from a mental institution? He couldn't.

Across from him, Cam started sliding out of the booth.

Shit.

"After what happened with Dad, I lived in a homeless shelter in Seattle for a couple of weeks," Tanner said quietly. "But I couldn't handle the noise and the crowds, so I moved out here to live in the forest."

Across from him, Cam stopped moving and gaped at him. Zarina looked equally stunned.

"I ran into some other guys who'd gotten out of the

military recently." Now that he'd started talking, Tanner couldn't seem to stop. "We helped each other out as much as we could, but I couldn't stay around them for long either. I wasn't fit to be around people back then."

Tanner didn't say why, and he prayed neither Zarina nor Cam asked. Because then he'd have to admit he'd almost killed his own father.

"I'm not sure how long I lived out here on my own," he continued. "Days of the week stopped having any real meaning. But I remember camping out through summer, then winter, and well into spring before some people showed up. Bad people."

Tears filled Zarina's eyes. She knew where he was going with this and didn't want to relive it any more than he did.

"Bad people?" Cam asked. "What are you talking about? What kind of bad people?"

How much could he divulge without telling his brother the classified stuff? "People who were looking for test subjects to use in a series of medical experiments. They decided people like me wouldn't be missed. They grabbed me and some other guys and they…did things to us."

Cam leaned forward, eyes narrowing. "What kind of things?"

"Things I'd rather not get into." Tanner swallowed hard. "Not because I don't think you can handle it, but because I'm not sure if you'd believe me."

Cam's gaze went from him to Zarina, then back again. "Does this have anything to do with the fact that you're half a foot taller and forty pounds heavier than you were the last time I saw you?"

Damn. How the hell had Cam made the connection? Then again, his brother was a cop. He was paid to be observant.

"Yeah," Tanner admitted. "But like I said, I'd rather not get into any more details than that. Suffice it to say, people died—a lot of people. I would have died, too, but Zarina was there, and she got me out. She risked her life for me when I was ready to give up and die."

Cam regarded Zarina thoughtfully. "I get the feeling there's an epic story behind all this, but I'll take it on faith that you can't tell me any more than Tanner can. So I'll just say thank you. My big brother might be a pain in the ass, but he's the only brother I have, and I love him. Thanks for risking your life to save him."

Zarina nodded, reaching up to wipe a tear from the corner of her eye before it could run down her cheek.

Cam sat back in the booth, his gaze on Tanner. "All that stuff would have been what, two years ago at most? Where have you been since then?"

Okay, he was going to have to be careful around his brother. Cam was piecing together little details fast as hell. If Tanner wasn't careful, Cam was going to be neck-deep in more secrets than he'd know what to do with.

"After Zarina got me out of that place, I was messed up. Even more messed up than I'd been before, if that's possible."

Zarina opened her mouth to protest, but Tanner cut her off with a look. She'd defend him to the death, but this was one time when the truth couldn't be denied.

"Long story short, I've been living on a federal compound in DC trying to get my head back together," Tanner explained. "Unfortunately, I still have some issues, so it's not good for me to be around other people. Especially people I care about. That's why I never called."

His brother frowned. "What are you doing back here then?"

Tanner shrugged and stared down at his hands loosely clasped together on the table in front of him. "Some things happened a little while ago that made me think it would be better if I came back out here to Wenatchee to see if living on my own might help."

"A decision I didn't get a chance to be a part of and was adamantly against," Zarina put in. "Tanner was doing well back in DC, but he's stubborn, and when he thinks he's a danger to those close to him, he tends to go with the most extreme option available."

Cam's mouth twitched in amusement. "Well, at least one thing hasn't changed about my brother. He never did anything halfway."

Tanner opened his mouth to protest, but just then, a young guy with dark hair appeared at the table with three glasses of water and an order pad shoved in the pocket of his apron. "Sorry you've been waiting so long. No one told me you were back here. Do you have any questions about the menu?"

The poor guy looked like he was about to have a nervous breakdown, and Tanner couldn't help but take pity on him. "Don't worry about it. We're not in any rush."

The three of them decided to go with chili cheeseburgers, fries, and Cokes. After their server left, they turned to relatively safe topics while they waited for their food. Like where Zarina was from and why Cam became a cop. Cam quickly figured out Tanner and Zarina were in some kind of relationship—following him all the way across the country was pretty much a dead giveaway—but he didn't make a big deal out of it.

Once the safe topics were covered, the elephant in the diner couldn't be ignored any longer, and Tanner forced himself to ask the question that had been on his mind since he'd called his brother.

"How are Mom and Dad and the girls?"

His brother pinned him with a look. "You want the BS answer that will make you feel better, or do you want the truth?"

Tanner didn't have to ask to know his family would take his absence hard. They'd always been close. Right up until the point when he'd walked out on them.

"The truth can't be any worse than my imagination has made it out to be," he said.

Cam sighed. "Like I said before, Mom worries about you a lot. She lights a candle for you at church all the time. And while I don't have any proof, I'm pretty sure she hired a private investigator to track you down. She refuses to let Dad change anything in your old room and keeps it the same way it was when you were in the army, on the off chance you come back and need a place to stay."

Tanner groaned. Maybe this was worse than he'd imagined. He'd known his mom would be upset when he left, but he told himself she would recognize he was doing it for their own good. Apparently, she hadn't.

"Dad blames himself for you leaving." Cam sipped his drink. "He insists everything that happened that morning was his fault. He spent about the first year driving around town looking for you like you were a lost puppy before he finally stopped. He doesn't join Mom when she goes to church to light those candles for you. In fact, he doesn't go to church at all now."

"Shit," Tanner muttered, wishing Cam would stop. He would have been better off not knowing any of this.

"Kellie had some problems for a while," Cam continued. "She missed you like crazy, but she's doing okay now. She's a lot more serious than she used to be. Same pixie-style haircut with all the crazy colors, but she got rid of her piercings. She's a senior in high school now. Plans to join the army as soon as she graduates, which is freaking Mom out."

Tanner would have crawled under the table at that moment if he would have fit. Kellie was his youngest sister and also the most bubbly, idealistic, and outgoing member of the family. At least she used to be. Getting a chance to see her had been one of the highlights of his visits when he used to come home on leave. She would sit for hours and listen to his stories. It sounded like he'd barely recognize her now.

"But on the bright side, Raquel hasn't changed a bit." Cam's mouth tightened. "She's pissed you left, but only because it hurt Mom, Dad, and Kellie. She never says your name, never talks about you, even changes the subject anytime your name comes up. She finally got married to that accountant boyfriend of hers, Darrin."

Raquel was two years younger than Tanner, so there'd always been a lot of sibling rivalry between them. She'd started dating Darrin when he'd done her taxes, and Tanner had teased her about it, saying she only went out with him for the free tax advice. His sister had never said he was wrong.

"You know, with the exception of Raquel, they'd all

love to see you," Cam said cautiously. "I could arrange something casual if you want to work your way back into things slowly."

Tanner's heart suddenly started racing, and he cursed silently as he felt his fangs trying to force their way out. He quickly dropped his hands under the edge of the table, terrified his claws would spring out and give him away. Without a word, Zarina reached over and placed a warm hand on his forearm, silently letting him know she was there. He closed his eyes, focusing on that touch as he tried to get his breathing back under control.

This was what he'd worried about most when he'd agreed to meet with Cam, that his brother would say something that would make him mad and the animal inside would make an appearance at the worst possible time.

Tanner took a breath, calming his racing pulse and envisioning the hybrid part of himself as a physical animal that he had to shove back into a cage and lock away. He'd been working on this technique for the better part of a year, and normally, it worked. But now that he was in a crowded diner with his brother sitting across from him, it wasn't doing a damn thing.

He breathed deep and tried again, mentally shoving his inner lion into its prison and slamming the door shut. When he finally got himself together, he dreaded opening his eyes, afraid to see the look on Cam's face. But Tanner couldn't sit there like that forever.

As it turned out, his brother was sitting there calmly sipping his soda. Tanner waited for Cam to ask what the hell that was all about, but thankfully, the waiter chose that moment to bring their meals.

Tanner immediately picked up his cheeseburger and

bit into it, mostly to avoid having to say anything. He almost groaned in appreciation at the combination of the spicy chips and scrumptious beef. It had been a long time since he'd eaten anything like that. Damn, he'd missed it.

"Okay, so as much as I'd like to think you called me just because I'm your brother and you wanted an update on your family, my gut tells me that you didn't," Cam said in between bites. "I'm guessing you needed a cop and didn't feel like you could call one out here in Wenatchee. So, what's up?"

Tanner took another bite of burger, using it as an excuse to delay answering for a moment. Once again, Cam had surprised him. First, by moving beyond the near hybrid shift he'd almost certainly seen, and second, by the way he'd pegged the situation with the preppers perfectly. On the downside, Cam's blunt words made Tanner feel shittier about using him than he already did.

"Over the past couple of weeks, at least half a dozen people have gone missing in the Wenatchee Forest," Tanner said.

Cam frowned as he dunked his waffle fries in ketchup. "I haven't heard anything about that. I mean, we don't hear about everything back in Seattle, but something as big as half a dozen missing people moves the needle. I would have thought it would be all over the news."

"The people who have gone missing are either homeless or preppers," Zarina explained softly, almost like she hated admitting that was a valid justification for the media to ignore it.

"Ah, I see," Cam said. "So these missing people aren't even being reported, are they?"

"No," Tanner told him. "Which is probably why

they're being targeted. Whoever is capturing them has to know there's little chance anyone will call the cops. These kidnappers are smart, well armed, efficient, and know exactly what they're doing."

Cam looked at him sharply. "Well armed? Okay, this is sounding like more than just some homeless people disappearing. What's the rest of the story?"

Tanner and Zarina told him everything they knew about the first few people who'd gone missing, the attack on the preppers' camp last night, the use of automatic weapons, and how he'd figured out both men from the encampment had been thrown into a waiting van or SUV.

Cam looked at Tanner a little oddly when he mentioned tracking Josh and Bryce through the woods, but he didn't ask for details.

"This is way too big for me, Tanner," his brother said after hearing the whole story. "We need to get the state police involved. Maybe even the feds."

Tanner shook his head. "These preppers don't trust anyone in authority, especially the feds. I promised I wouldn't call them."

"That was stupid," his brother said dryly.

"Probably, but I was hoping you could do a little digging on your own and see what you can find out. And before you tell me that you don't have any contacts in Wenatchee, I'm pretty sure this isn't a local thing. I can't explain why I think that, but my gut is telling me there's something weird going on with these kidnappings."

Cam regarded him curiously again but didn't question his suspicions. "Okay, I'll dig around and see what I can find. What are you and Zarina going to be doing in the meantime?"

Tanner shrugged. "We have a few more supplies to pick up before we head back up the mountain, but after that, the plan is to stay close to the prepper camp and hopefully keep anyone else from getting kidnapped."

Cam's brow furrowed. "That sounds dangerous. And stupid."

"Probably," Tanner agreed. "But I don't have a choice."

They spent a little while longer going over everything Tanner knew about the abductions, including when they'd happened, what the victims' names were, what they looked like, and what kinds of weapons the kidnappers used, anything Cam thought might help him get a lead on either the missing people or the assholes who'd taken them. After that, the conversation slipped back into casual things, mostly Cam and his personal life... or lack thereof.

As they talked, Tanner realized he was eating more slowly now. He didn't want this meal to end. It seemed like a lifetime since he'd talked to his brother. It felt good.

But at some point, the food was gone, and the conversation came to an end. When they slipped out of the booth, Tanner expected his brother to walk off, but instead, Cam gave him a hug. They missed each other more than either would want to admit, and Tanner hugged him back with the same fierceness.

At least neither of them started crying. That would have been awkward.

"You know," Cam said as he stepped back, "I was serious about you seeing the rest of the family. I can see you're not ready for that yet, but when you are, I'll help make it happen."

Tanner was still thinking about that as Cam gave Zarina a hug, too, telling her he was glad he'd had a chance to meet her and thanking her once again for helping Tanner.

"Something tells me I owe you for making this lunch happen," he added with a smile. "Thank you for that, too."

Without another word, his brother turned and walked out of the diner, leaving Tanner and Zarina standing there.

"Your brother's an amazing person," Zarina said.

Tanner chuckled. "Yeah, I guess he is. Other than the fact that he just stuck me with the tab for lunch."

———

"It's not London, but at least it's a mission," Tate muttered as he pulled into the parking lot of the funeral home.

Killing the engine, Tate got out of the rental car and walked past the sheriff's patrol car, heading for the tree-shrouded building. Even though it was only a little after six p.m., it was getting dark. A lone streetlamp illuminated the entrance, casting the doorway in deep shadows and making the place seem even creepier. Not that funeral homes were inviting to begin with.

Landon had called him that morning, telling him to get his butt up to Oxford County, Maine, ASAP. The police had found a body that looked like it had been attacked by a wild animal, which wouldn't have been odd except for the fact that the body had been found in a log cabin with the door closed.

Based on the last update he'd gotten from the DCO on the flight up, the locals seemed to be working hard to make the animal attack angle work. Probably because they had no other way to explain what the hell had happened to their victim. Maybe they assumed the animal that had attacked the victim was simply polite and had closed the door to the cabin after it was done because that's what nice, polite animals did after they attacked a person.

Admittedly, the whole funeral-home thing was a new wrinkle for Tate. Every other time he wanted to see the victim of a crime, he stopped by the local coroner or medical examiner's office. But in this case, the coroner had already finished with the autopsy and turned the body over to the funeral home outside Hiram for embalming. Apparently, the locals were completely comfortable with the animal attack explanation and were moving fast to close this case. If Landon hadn't pulled some strings, the body might be in the ground already.

He didn't doubt that the locals knew how to do their jobs, but because he was an agent with the DCO, he had access to more information on how the world really worked. Since this attack occurred less than three hours away from the mental institution in Old Town where Mahsood had been conducting his hybrid research a few months ago, Landon and Ivy had wanted someone up here to sniff around on the off chance the doctor was at it again.

Tate wouldn't be surprised if he was. From everything Trevor and Alina had told him, Mahsood had been close to creating a fully in-control hybrid that could blend into the everyday population. If that was true, it was doubtful the psycho would stop his research now. Hard to believe he'd set up shop so close to the mental institution, though.

Of course, Landon and Ivy had suggested another

rationale for the victim's death—the possibility that Ashley Brannon had murdered the guy.

There had been a few sightings of the woman slipping back across the border from Canada, where she'd apparently been hiding out since July. It wasn't that much of a leap to think she might have come this far south looking for revenge on the people who'd been holding her prisoner. Or maybe she'd simply gone rogue and enjoyed killing people now.

Either way, Landon had asked Tate to come up here and see what was going on. Even though they were already familiar with the place, Landon couldn't send Trevor and Alina for obvious reasons. For one thing, they were still in London. For another, if either Ashley or Mahsood were involved in this, they'd recognize Trevor and immediately bolt. Landon wanted Ashley and Mahsood in custody, not on the run again.

Besides, Landon didn't want Brannon and Hamilton knowing what they were up to. That meant sending someone who wasn't currently on their radar. Since Tate didn't have a teammate, he was perfect for the job. As far as Brannon and Hamilton knew, Tate had decided to take a little time off while the organization tried to find him a partner.

Tate opened the door and walked in, expecting to find the sheriff waiting for him. Instead, he was met by a tall, skinny man in a dark-gray suit who had to be the funeral home director. Either that or the Crypt Keeper. No joke. With the lank, thinning hair, lifeless eyes, and sallow complexion, the guy could easily be mistaken for the lead character in *Tales from the Crypt*. Tate had seen enough episodes on Netflix to know.

Tate pulled his badge from his pocket and flashed it at the man. "Tate Evers, Homeland Security."

"We've been expecting you." The man extended his hand. "I'm Silas Arnold, director of this facility."

Tate wasn't sure if it was the man's choice of words or his flat, emotionless baritone that made the hair stand up on the back of his neck. Damn, this guy took creepy to a whole new level. As Tate shook Arnold's hand, he had to resist checking for a pulse just to make sure the man was among the living.

"I'm supposed to meet the sheriff here and see the victim's body?" he prompted when the man continued to gaze at him in a way that suggested he wasn't used to dealing with people in the vertical position.

Arnold nodded stiffly. "Follow me."

Turning, he led the way down a long, dark hallway. A little voice in the back of Tate's head shouted that he shouldn't follow Arnold. This was exactly how your average B-grade horror flick started. But he ignored his inner movie fan and started after the man.

At the end of the hallway, Arnold turned into a room on the right. Tate squinted as the bright fluorescent lights assaulted him, and it took a second for his eyes to adjust. The space looked a lot like something you'd find in a morgue, right down to the two porcelain pedestal tables in the center of the room. Counters lined two walls with cabinets above and below. A big sink took up a good portion of a third wall.

Tate ignored the decor and focused on the two police officers standing near one of the tables. It wasn't until they turned his way that Tate got a glimpse of the body laid out there. A sheet covered the man from the waist down, but one look at the slashes crisscrossing his torso told Tate this was the victim.

The older of the two men stepped forward and held out his hand. Judging by all the brass on his collar and the number of service stripes on the arm of his long-sleeve khaki uniform shirt, he had to be the sheriff. "Agent Evers, I take it?"

Tate nodded. Like Arnold, the sheriff had a thick Maine accent. "Sheriff Bowers, sorry for making you wait. It took me a bit longer to get here from the airport than I thought it would. I appreciate you arranging for me to see the body tonight."

The sheriff nodded before gesturing at the officer with him. "This is Deputy Chase York. He was the responding officer who discovered the body."

York was about Tate's height with green eyes and short blond hair. Tate couldn't put his finger on it, but something about the deputy screamed former military.

"Thanks for coming, Deputy York," Tate said, shaking his hand. "I read your initial report on the flight, but I wouldn't mind hearing your account firsthand."

Tate didn't necessarily need to hear the deputy's thoughts, since York probably couldn't tell him anything that hadn't been put in the written report, but he'd always found it was a good idea to treat the locals with as much respect and deference as possible. It went a long way to smoothing over ruffled feathers.

"I don't mind you talking to my deputy." Bowers regarded him thoughtfully. "But I'd appreciate a little clarification on exactly how this case involves Homeland. Things so slow in DC that your bosses have you out investigating animal attacks now?"

Tate knew this question would be coming, so he'd prepared an answer before he got here. Well, kind of. "So, you've confirmed it was an animal attack?"

The sheriff motioned at the dead man on the table. "I think that's obvious, isn't it?"

Tate didn't reply, instead moving closer to the table to examine the corpse. He ignored the big Y-shaped incision left behind by the coroner's autopsy, focusing instead on the scratch marks. No way was this a normal animal attack. The guy had definitely been clawed to shreds by something, but if you knew what to look for—and Tate did—it was clear he hadn't been savaged by a wild animal. There were a few swipes thrown in here and there to make it look good, but there wasn't a single bite wound. Moreover, the claw marks were almost surgical in nature. Clean, precise, and controlled, the killer had sliced deep into nonvital areas that would produce the most amount of pain with the least amount of life-threatening damage.

Tate had seen these kinds of wounds before. One of the primary jobs he and his former team had done for the DCO was tracking down shifters who'd gone rogue and started killing people. It was a rare occurrence, but it did happen. Based on those experiences, Tate was left with no doubt now. This guy had been tortured by a shifter or a hybrid.

While the majority of the damage was to the torso, there were some slash marks on the victim's shoulders and arms. Taking a pair of gloves from the cardboard box on the shelf under the table, Tate slipped them on, then nudged the body onto its side. There weren't any marks on the man's back.

Tate frowned. The bruising on the man's arms

indicated he'd been strapped down during the attack. Not with ropes or anything else that would leave obvious ligature marks, but something had definitely been wrapped around the arms.

He leaned in closer to look at the bone-deep slice along the inside of the man's left thigh. That had been the killing strike, delivered after the shifter or hybrid had gotten whatever information he or she was after. Or had simply tired of torturing the victim.

"Did the coroner identify the animal?" Tate asked, glancing at the sheriff.

"The coroner's report listed the animal as a bobcat or Canadian lynx," Deputy York said, holding up the folder in his hand. "I'm leaning toward bobcat. Lynx are pretty rare in these parts, and I've never heard of one large enough to do this. But bobcats up here can easily get up to forty or fifty pounds."

Tate nodded, wondering how the coroner had explained the bruising on the victim's arms and the deep slash on the inner thigh. What, did he think the bobcat was carrying a switchblade? Not even a fifty-pound bobcat could slice open a person's leg like that.

But Tate had seen feline shifters and hybrids do things exactly like this. Of course, that sort of screwed up the likelihood Ashley was the attacker. According to Trevor, she was a coyote shifter like he was. While they were still sharp as hell, the claws on canine-based shifters like coyotes and wolves tended to be thicker. He couldn't see one of them making a slash this clean and surgical. Then again, he'd never met a female coyote shifter. Maybe Ashley's claws were more delicate than Trevor's. That could make the difference.

Regardless, he couldn't take her off the table as a suspect yet. Based on everything Trevor had told him about Ashley, the woman was certainly unbalanced enough to do something like this.

Tate continued to study the dead man's body, hoping there'd be something that would tell him why the guy had been killed. But other than what he'd already seen, the body had nothing left to tell him.

He turned his attention to the two cops. "What do we know about this guy?"

York glanced over at the sheriff. Bowers's jaw tightened, but he gave the deputy a nod.

"His name's McKinley Bell. He was a doctor at the medical center in Scarborough, which is just south of here," York said. "He was well respected by all accounts and part of several prestigious research and education programs involving genetic testing. He lived alone and had no family I could locate."

Well, damn. A doctor with a background in genetic research? It wasn't anything conclusive, but it definitely increased the possibility this guy had been working with Mahsood on a new hybrid program. Wasn't much of a hop, skip, and a jump from there to the notion that Bell had been tortured by one of his own creations to get back at him for turning him or her into a monster.

Tate glanced at the body again. Would a hybrid be patient enough to spend hours slowly slicing a man to ribbons? The hybrids he'd dealt with in the past were a lot of things, but patient wasn't one of them. Even the ones who worked for the DCO would best be described as mercurial. They could go from fully in control to wild animal in a matter of seconds.

That left Ashley. He could see her torturing Bell if she thought there was a connection between him and Mahsood.

"So, Agent Evers," Sheriff Bowers grumbled. "You ever plan on answering my question about why the Department of Homeland Security spent so much money to send an agent all the way up here to personally look at a man killed by a bobcat?"

Tate cursed silently. If he didn't deal with this now, he wouldn't get any more assistance the rest of the time he was here. He glanced at Arnold standing over by the doorway, then at the two cops.

"Nothing I'm about to tell you can leave this room," he said softly. "It's extremely confidential information provided by protected sources outside the U.S. Is that completely understood?"

That definitely caught everyone's attention, and all three men practically leaned forward as they nodded in unison.

"Homeland, as well as the FBI and NSA, have been tracking a terrorist known as Kyfus through Europe, across the Atlantic, and into Canada. We don't have confirmation yet, but there's a good chance he's already crossed the border into the U.S. en route to his next target."

"Kyfus?" The sheriff frowned. "Never heard of him."

Tate shook his head. "Not many people have. That's because he never takes credit for his attacks. He kills, then moves before the dust has even settled. No one knows why he does what he does, and as far as why he's in the States, we don't know that, either. We have no clue what his target might be. Worse, we're not even sure what he looks like."

Tate paused, partially to let his words sink in, but mostly to give himself time to fabricate the rest of the story. He'd come up with the name Kyfus on the drive from the airport, piecing together parts of two different street signs. The whole thing was complete BS, but he had to admit the name sounded pretty damn cool.

"The only thing we know for sure is that Kyfus frequently travels with a big cat like a mountain lion or jaguar that he's been known to let loose on those who irritate him. He apparently takes great pleasure in watching his cat kill people."

Sheriff Bowers eyed Bell's body for a moment before turning back to Tate. "And you think this terrorist is here in Oxford County? That he killed this man?"

"It would be premature to even consider saying something like that," Tate said quickly. He didn't want the sheriff declaring martial law or something. That wouldn't help anything. "I think you'd agree the chances of an international terrorist being in Hiram, Maine, are pretty low. Bell's death is most likely nothing more than a tragic run-in with one of your local critters. But Homeland doesn't want to leave any stone unturned, so they sent me here to poke around a bit, that's all. I don't expect anything to come of it, and I'm not trying to step on your jurisdictional toes."

The sheriff nodded. "I understand, but I'm going to need you to be very discreet. I can't have anyone getting wind of any of this, or they'll lose their minds."

"No one will get anything from me," Tate assured him. "You have my word."

"That's good to hear," Bowers agreed. "And I have no doubt you and Deputy York will have this situation taken care of quickly. I have a feeling you two will work well together."

Tate had thought everything was going well up until that moment. The last thing he needed was a local deputy sticking his nose into something that very well might involve shifters, hybrids, illegal human research, corrupt doctors, and a crooked congressional representative from the state of Maine. None of those things were something he wanted York learning about.

"I understand your concern, Sheriff Bowers," he said, giving the man a smile. "But I'll be out of your jurisdiction much faster if I work on my own. I appreciate your offer of assistance, though."

Bowers pinned him with a look. "It wasn't an offer of assistance. I don't trust you DC people as far as I can throw you. I'm putting Deputy York with you to ensure someone is watching out for the best interests of Oxford County instead of a bunch of folks inside Homeland headquarters. If you don't like that idea, I'll drop everything else my entire department is doing and put every officer I have on following you around for the duration of your investigation. Your call."

Bowers must have known which way Tate was going to go, since he gave him a nod, then walked out of the room. Arnold left with him, acting like he hadn't heard a thing.

"I guess we'll be working together, Agent Evers," York said.

Tate regarded the man he was apparently going to be stuck with for the next few days. Unless he could come up with a way to ditch him, of course. "I guess so, Deputy York."

"I can take you out to the cabin where I found the body now if you want. But it's at least forty minutes north of here by back roads, and the place doesn't have any power, so it'll be dark as hell."

Tate glanced at his watch, wondering whether he'd get anything useful out of rummaging around a dark cabin with a flashlight. Probably not. He could make better use of his time sitting on a phone with one of the DCO intel analysts digging into Dr. McKinley Bell's background. He was damn interested in knowing if Bell and Mahsood had ever crossed paths.

"It would be better to head out to the cabin in the morning," he told York. "Any idea about where I can find a room for a couple of nights?"

"There's a Marriott up in North Conway, across the state line," York said. "But if you'd rather stay someplace local, the Middleton Inn is your best bet. It's a simple place, but there's free Wi-Fi, the rooms are clean, and the price is right."

Tate nodded. "You had me at free Wi-Fi. Meet you at the sheriff's office at eight in the morning?"

York shook his head. "Too far out of your way and mine. It takes over an hour to drive to Parish from here, and then we'd only have to head back this way. How about I meet you at the Dunkin' Donuts off Highway 25. That'll be easier for both of us."

Damn, he might have just figured out how to ditch Deputy Chase York already. "Sounds good. See you then."

Chapter 5

TANNER STARED OUT THE WINDSHIELD AT THE POSTERS ON the store's big front windows advertising discount camping gear and cheap tickets for local kayaking adventures and scenic cruises on Lake Chelan. "You bought your camping supplies here?"

In the passenger seat, Zarina looked at him, then at the store before swinging her gaze his way again. "Is there something wrong with it?"

Tanner almost laughed but stopped himself. Zarina was a scientist. She wasn't used to shopping for outdoor gear. He gestured to the signs plastered all over the place. "Would you buy your lab equipment from a store that advertised their stuff as cheap and discounted?"

"No, of course not. But what does that have to do with camping supplies?" No sooner were the words out of her mouth than understanding dawned on her face. "Oh, now I see. I shouldn't buy camping gear from a place I wouldn't buy lab equipment from."

"Something like that," he muttered. "If nothing else, we can return the crappy flashlight they sold you. The sleeping bag, too. It's a summer-weight model they never should have given to someone heading up the mountain at this time of year."

Zarina looked at him sharply. "Is this another trick? Are you trying to get me to give up my sleeping bag as a way to get me to leave?"

He sighed and shook his head. "No. You'll have to
use mine as long as you're here anyway, unless you
want to freeze to death. I'm merely trying to get your
money back."

She relaxed but still looked hesitant. "When I bought
my stuff, the clerk was quite specific about the store's
return policy. No refunds or exchanges. He was adamant
about that."

Tanner clenched his jaw. "I bet he was."

Getting out of the truck, Tanner grabbed her pack
from the back where he'd tossed it on the off chance
he could convince her to leave after they met with his
brother. That hadn't worked out so well.

They'd spent the past two hours working through
the rest of the supplies on the shopping list Chad had
given them. It wouldn't have taken nearly as long if
he and Zarina hadn't spent most of the time arguing.
When he hadn't been harassing her about going back to
DC, she'd been badgering him with endless questions
about what had happened to put such a rift between
him and his family and why he refused to consider
taking her antiserum.

Neither conversation had gone very far, and in the
end, they'd agreed to disagree. He didn't intend to take
her new wonder drug or run home to see his family anytime soon, and she wasn't going to get on a plane back
to DC in the foreseeable future.

He felt like crap for nagging at her about leaving,
especially when being with her felt so damn right, but
she wasn't cut out for life up here. Or any life with him,
for that matter. The sooner she figured that out, the
better. But she was so damn stubborn, it was like talking

to a brick wall. If he was lucky, maybe Lillie would tell Zarina the story about how Spencer had nearly killed her a while back, and Zarina would finally figure out what kind of price she might have to pay being around a hybrid like him. It was only a matter of time before he lost it and did the same thing to Zarina—or worse.

He was just as terrified that something equally bad was going to happen with the assholes who were attacking the preppers. But what the hell could he do? He might threaten to drag Zarina down to Seattle and stuff her on a plane, but she knew he would never actually do it. He only hoped he didn't end up regretting his decision to let her stay.

Mouth tight, he pulled her sleeping bag and the cheap-ass flashlight out of the pack, then walked around to open Zarina's door.

He could practically smell the second-rate quality of the merchandise the moment he stepped inside the store. He usually had a let-the-buyer-beware outlook on business and didn't mind someone making a profit selling cheap crap to tourists who were simply going on a short hike along the trails. But the clerk had seen Zarina coming and ripped her off, knowing he was sending her into the wilderness with shit for gear. That pissed Tanner off. His inner hybrid wasn't too happy about it, either.

Or maybe they were both still mad at Zarina and looking for someone to take it out on. That would work, too.

Zarina led him past racks of jerky, fishing poles, and brightly colored rain ponchos to the checkout counter, a big monstrosity of a thing made from local fir trees. A skeevy-looking middle-aged man stood behind the counter, flipping through a catalog and ignoring the half dozen customers wandering around the store looking at gear they clearly didn't know the first thing about. He glanced up at their approach, eyeing Zarina with obvious interest before turning his attention to Tanner. The man straightened to his full height, which still made him a foot shorter than Tanner.

"I guess you found who you were looking for," he said to Zarina.

"She did," Tanner answered, tossing her sleeping bag and flashlight on the big wood counter.

The clerk frowned. "What's that?"

"The camping equipment you sold me," Zarina said politely. "I won't need either of these and would like to return them."

The man jerked a thumb at the poster on the wall behind him that said No Returns! No Exchanges! in big red letters along with paragraphs of fine print only a lawyer could love. "Like I told you yesterday, we have a strict no returns or exchanges policy, ma'am. No exceptions."

Tanner bit back a snarl. They didn't have time for this crap. They still hadn't gotten any of the drugs and medical supplies, and he wanted to be back at the camp before dark in case those assholes with the automatic weapons decided to come back and hit the place again.

"Time for your first exception," he told the clerk in a voice that was little more than a growl. "You sold cheap camping gear to a woman you knew had no experience in the mountains," he said through gritted teeth. At least his fangs weren't out—yet. "That sleeping bag you foisted off on her for ten times what it's worth is so thin that if she'd been forced to depend on it last night, she probably would have died from hypothermia by morning."

The clerk's eyes narrowed. "Now, just a damn minute. I can't be held responsible…"

Tanner stopped him with a glare. "Well, I am holding you responsible."

When the man continued to glower right back, Tanner's hybrid half itched to grab the man by the throat and jerk him out from behind the counter. Tanner might have done it, too, if Zarina hadn't placed a hand on his arm while sliding the receipt across the counter.

"I've circled the items I'm returning." She smiled at the clerk. "But I'm definitely keeping the pajamas. They're very comfortable."

The clerk seemed happy to hear that. Or maybe he was simply thrilled Tanner had stopped tearing gouges out of his countertop. Either way, he worked fast to apply a credit to Zarina's card. A few minutes later, Tanner and Zarina walked out of the store with most of her money back. It was probably too much to hope she'd use it on that plane ticket he wanted her to buy.

"If I'd known you were so good at negotiating store returns, I would have taken you with me to the Galleria after the spring sales," Zarina said. "I spent hours arguing about their store policies."

Tanner snorted. "Yeah, I don't see my technique working out nearly as well at the Galleria."

"I see your point." Zarina stopped and glanced back at the store they'd just left. "I wonder if I should have exchanged the sleeping bag and flashlight for more of those pajamas. They're so comfortable. I could wear them around my apartment in DC in the winter."

He stifled a groan as an image of Zarina and her pj's flashed through his head. He immediately wished he hadn't let his head go there, since it was damn tough walking with a boner. *Shit*. What the hell was it about her that got him hard at the drop of a hat?

Tanner was so focused on thinking about anything other than Zarina romping around a campfire in her pajamas that he nearly missed someone calling his name. When the man's voice finally broke through, he was surprised to realize he recognized it. But he had to be wrong. He hadn't heard that voice in years.

Sure he must be imagining things, Tanner stopped and turned around to see his old army buddy standing ten feet away from him on the sidewalk. His friend looked just as shocked as Tanner.

"Tanner, is that you?"

Tanner nodded. "Ryan?"

His friend still looked the same as he had when Tanner had last seen him the day he'd gotten out of the Rangers and walked away from his old life. Ryan's blond hair was even cropped close enough to still pass army regulations. Only Ryan wasn't in the military anymore. He'd been in the process of bailing at the same time as Tanner had.

But while Ryan might look the same on the outside, there was a scar on his jaw and lines around his eyes that hadn't been there before. His nose looked like it had been broken a few times, then poorly set as well.

Tanner wasn't sure which one of them moved first—or maybe they both moved forward at the same time—but the next thing he knew, they were pulling each other in for a man hug that made him wonder why he hadn't worked harder to stay in touch with his friend.

"Damn, you look good," Ryan said as he pulled away. "Are you bigger than you used to be? It looks like you're four or five inches taller than you were the last I saw you."

Since he'd never run into anyone who'd known him before those scientists had turned him into a hybrid, Tanner never had to explain how he'd added the extra inches and more than fifty pounds of muscle. Now he'd had to do it twice in one day. He laughed it off.

"I guess I was still growing when you knew me, so I might be a little bigger than you remember," he said casually.

Ryan frowned and opened his mouth, no doubt to call BS on that. Time to change the subject.

"You look good, too, man," Tanner said, interrupting whatever Ryan had been about to say. "It looks like you could do a fifteen-mile ruck march with no problem. Makes it even harder to believe you got out."

"Yeah, I intended to do my twenty years and retire with full benefits," his friend admitted. "That all changed after our last deployment to Afghanistan."

Tanner couldn't do anything but nod. Ryan was right. Being in the Rangers wasn't the same after all those guys in their platoon had died. The battalion had arranged a solemn ceremony and handed out a lot of posthumous awards, then expected everyone to move on. But Tanner hadn't been able to do that. So instead of reenlisting like he'd planned, he'd gotten out a few months after getting back from Afghanistan.

He'd honestly thought Ryan would stay in, though. While Ryan hadn't been unaffected by their fellow soldiers' deaths, he hadn't seemed as traumatized as Tanner. But maybe Tanner had been wrong about that.

Beside Tanner, Zarina softly cleared her throat, reminding him of her presence. He cringed and gave her an apologetic look before making introductions.

"Ryan Westbrook, Zarina Sokolov," he said, then stopped as he realized he had no idea how to introduce her. He obviously couldn't say she was the Russian geneticist who'd attempted to keep a psychopath from turning him into a hybrid. But he also couldn't say she was his girlfriend, because he had no idea if she'd ever want to be described that way. Camping buddy didn't hit the right note either, though.

Finally, he punted the ball and finished with the most truthful answer he could come up with. "She's a very important person in my life."

Ryan's gaze went from Tanner to Zarina and back again, as if he was envisioning them together in the biblical sense. Ryan had never been good at biting his tongue, but at least this once, his friend didn't say anything stupid.

"Very important person, huh?" he murmured as he shook Zarina's hand. "Something tells me there's an interesting story there, but I'll keep my curiosity to myself for now. Regardless, it's nice to meet you."

Zarina hit Ryan with the kind of smile that never failed to make Tanner weak in the knees. He was relieved to see it didn't have the same effect on Ryan.

"Nice meeting you, too," she said. "From the conversation the two of you just had, something tells me you and Tanner were in the army together."

Ryan nodded. "Nearly seven years, all in the same Ranger squad. Which is rather remarkable, since the army likes to move people around just for the fun of it. Tanner and I did three tours in Iraq and another two in Afghanistan. Saw a lot of shit, pardon my French."

Zarina laughed. "Your French is fine. I'm Russian. We use that kind of French all the time."

"Russian, huh? I thought I detected an accent." Ryan threw Tanner a sideways glance. "So, what's the deal? Is there some kind of James Bond angle going on here, or did she just buy you on Craigslist?"

"Curiosity killed the cat," Tanner deadpanned.

Ryan chuckled. "Okay, okay. I get your point. At least throw me a bone. What have you been up to? You back in Seattle working security for Boeing or something?"

How the hell did he answer that? Especially since he hadn't held a real job since getting out of the army. He'd never been good at lying. But it wasn't like he could tell the truth either.

I've been working part time at a covert organization in Washington, DC, you've never heard of.

"Nah, nothing like that," he finally said. "Actually, I've been between jobs for a while now. I get a little bit of money each month from the VA on account of all the times I got blown up. Head trauma and stuff, you know? I don't have many bills, but what I get from the government takes care of them."

Zarina's eyes widened at the mention of head trauma and disability pay from the Veterans Administration, but Tanner pretended not to notice. He hadn't told her about any of that, and he didn't want to get into it now, especially with Ryan standing there.

"How about you? What are you doing for a living these days?" Tanner asked, mostly so his friend wouldn't be tempted to dig any deeper.

Ryan regarded him thoughtfully for a moment, as if knowing Tanner was trying to change the topic. But he didn't call Tanner on it.

"I own a club called The Cage outside of Redmond on Highway 203," he said. "It's a nice gig, and the money is way better than I ever could have imagined when I first started it."

Tanner fought hard not to gape as Ryan told them about buying an old logging mill on the outskirts of town and repurposing it as a nightclub. He tried his best to picture his friend doing that kind of work and failed. When they were in the army, Ryan had spent a good portion of his free time in a hundred different clubs and bars scattered around the world. Hell, they both had. Tanner simply couldn't wrap his head around Ryan owning a club and doing all the work that went with it now.

"Actually, that's why I'm in Wenatchee today," Ryan added. "I'm looking for a few new acquisitions for the place to entertain the customers."

Tanner couldn't help frowning at the odd word choice. "Like a band, you mean?"

"Not exactly," Ryan said.

"Well, Redmond is a two-and-a-half-hour drive from here," Tanner said. "Whoever you're looking to hire must be damn good."

Ryan's mouth quirked. "My customers are always looking for something new and interesting. I've been lucky enough to find some of that out here, so I keep coming back. Never know when I'll hit the jackpot." He studied them thoughtfully. "You and Zarina should stop by sometime."

Tanner cringed inwardly. He'd come out here to get away from people. Going to a crowded nightclub probably wasn't the best idea. He couldn't exactly explain that to Ryan, though. So he lied. Again.

"We might do that." Tanner glanced at Zarina, then turned back to Ryan. "We'd better get moving if we're going to get back up the mountain before dark."

Ryan nodded. "Where are you two planning to set up?"

Tanner opened his mouth to tell Ryan about the prepper camp but then closed it again. Chad and his group had never hidden where they were, but for reasons Tanner couldn't explain, he didn't feel like advertising it to the world—or an old buddy. "We're planning to set up around Crow Hill or Graham Mountain. Maybe even a little farther north of there."

Ryan frowned. "You might not want to do that. A lot of crazy preppers have been hanging out near Graham Mountain, causing trouble."

It was Tanner's turn to frown. "Is that so? I didn't know that. Thanks for the tip. I'll keep that in mind."

"Good," Ryan said. "There are a lot of good campsites over to the southwest side of the forest. You should check out some of those."

"We will," Tanner said noncommittally.

He was glad now that he hadn't mentioned staying with Chad and his group. He didn't know where Ryan's crap about the preppers was coming from. Maybe those events over in Afghanistan had changed his buddy more than he'd thought.

Ryan glanced at his watch. "I have to get out of here,
too. It was good seeing you again, man. If you two come
to the club, let me know so I can make sure I'm there.
We can catch up on old times."

"Will do," Tanner said.

Ryan gave Zarina a nod. "Nice meeting you."

"You, too." She waited until Ryan was out of earshot,
then turned to Tanner with a frown. "Okay, what was all
that stuff about the preppers about?"

"I don't know," Tanner admitted, watching his friend
walk down the street. "But something tells me Ryan and
I won't be getting back together to talk about the good
old days anytime soon."

—◦◦◦—

Tate rubbed the back of his neck as he walked out of
his motel room. He'd seen a coffeemaker on the counter
beside the front desk when he'd checked in last night
and prayed he'd still be able to get a cup. That crap they
put in those little single serving pots in the rooms should
be outlawed. Who the hell did they expect would drink
the stuff?

As he headed toward the front of the building, he tried
to work out the kink in his back from the too-soft mattress
he'd slept on last night. The cold morning air didn't help.
Anytime it was below forty degrees, his lower spine got
stiff. Getting shot in the back could do that to anybody.
Though to be fair, he couldn't entirely blame his nearly
sleepless night on the poor mattress. That mostly had to
do with the fact that he had spent much of his evening
digging through databases and newspaper articles looking
for anything and everything he could on McKinley Bell.

Unfortunately, the effort had been a waste. He'd found nothing of interest on the recently deceased doctor. If the man had ever been involved in anything remotely resembling hybrid research, it didn't show up in his background history. By all appearances, Bell had been an honest, conscientious doctor from a well-off family in Boston. He'd been a leader in his field of genetic birth defects and had donated huge amounts of his time and money in the search for genetic therapy and cures for a list of childhood conditions that sounded pretty frigging horrible to Tate. The man had won a ton of prestigious awards from various research institutes around the country but had no apparent social life of any kind. From what Kendra could find out, the man had never dated, gone on a vacation, or had personal communications with anyone.

It was damn hard to imagine the guy being involved in hybrid research. But Tate had been fooled before, so he rarely took anyone or anything at face value. Besides, Bell had definitely been tortured by a shifter or hybrid, which meant he was involved in something. Hopefully, getting a look at the cabin where the man had been murdered would give him an idea what that something might be.

He rounded the corner leading to the motel lobby, already tasting coffee he hoped would be fresh, only to stop dead in his tracks when he saw Deputy Chase York leaning casually against the side of his patrol car in the parking lot, two large cups of coffee in his hands, a familiar-looking Dunkin' Donuts box on the hood, and a knowing smile on his face.

Tate frowned and double-checked his watch. "I

thought I was supposed to meet you at the coffee shop at eight? Did I get the time wrong?"

Chase's smile broadened. "I thought I should show up here in case you forgot you were supposed to meet me before heading out to the cabin."

"What makes you think I'd forget?" Tate asked, walking over to him.

Dodging the deputy had actually been his plan. It bruised his ego to know Chase had seen through him so easily. Maybe he'd gotten slow after all those years working on a team with people he trusted.

"Let's just say I know how busy you federal types are." Chase pushed away from the car and held one of the cups out to him. "I wouldn't want you feeling bad if you ended up driving all the way to that cabin only to realize you'd forgotten to meet up with your temporary partner. That would be damn inconvenient."

"I'm sure," Tate said dryly, reaching out to snag the coffee. "Well, since you're here, lead the way. I'll follow."

Chase's mouth twitched. "Why don't we go in my car? Just so there's less chance of us getting separated. Some of the back roads on the way up to the cabin are twisty and confusing. It'd be easy to get turned around out there and lose each other."

"I bet," Tate muttered, impressed despite himself.

He sipped his coffee. Damn, it was good. Maybe teaming up with York might not be so bad after all.

"I figured you took it black with no sugar or cream," Chase said as he motioned toward the passenger seat. "I've been a coffee addict long enough to know the signs."

Tate scooped up the box of donuts as he walked

around the front of the car. "Okay, you get extra points for knowing I like my coffee black, but if there are any chocolate-glazed cake donuts in here, then I'll be seriously impressed."

Chase chuckled as he opened the driver's side door. "Please. What kind of cop do you take me for? Half the box is chocolate-glazed."

Tate lifted a brow at that. Damn. Maybe he should get Landon to recruit this guy. For his knowledge of coffee and donuts if nothing else.

Shit, Chase drove fast. The fact that they made the forty-minute trip to the cabin in less than thirty was a sure sign of that. Tate had never been one to necessarily obey every traffic sign out there, but he assumed a few of them, like the one warning unsuspecting drivers that the road ahead was about to do a ninety-degree dogleg, could occasionally be useful.

"Where'd you learn to drive, Beirut?" Tate asked, gripping the handle on the passenger door as the deputy maneuvered the patrol car onto a gravel road at a silly rate of speed. Hopefully, the gravel meant they were almost at the cabin, because he wasn't enjoying this tour of backwoods Maine as much as he would have thought.

"Close," Chase said. "Baghdad and Mosul actually."

That explained a lot. He glanced at the deputy. "Marines?"

Chase nodded. "Five years, three deployments. Never been able to drive within the speed limit since. How about you? You strike me as the kind of man who's seen his fair share of firefights and car chases."

Tate considered how to answer that, thinking about all
the scraps he'd been in with his old team, then decided
honesty probably wasn't the best policy here. It was too
much to get into with somebody he was going to have
to majorly lie to at some point. Easier to fib a little now.

"Me?" He chuckled. "Nah, nothing like that. I spent
a while in the U.S. Marshals chasing a few averagely
mean bad guys, then moved over to Homeland, where
I've pretty much hugged a desk ever since."

The deputy glanced at him as he stopped at the end
of the gravel road, his expression doubtful. "Sure, whatever you say."

Tate stared out the windshield, stunned. After hearing where Bell had been found, he'd been expecting
some kind of broken-down hovel with vines covering half of it. Instead, he got a neat, well-maintained,
split-level log cabin with a wraparound deck and
large windows overlooking a sloping yard and the
picture-perfect pond just beyond it. The place looked
like something on a postcard, for crying out loud. In
fact, Tate could see himself burning up a few weeks of
excess leave renting the place and catching up on all
the reading he'd been putting off. Well, if a man hadn't
been murdered there.

"Not the kind of place you expected?" Chase asked
as he opened his door and stepped out.

"Not really."

As Tate headed for the front door of the cabin alongside the deputy, he glanced over his shoulder at the highway, confirming that somebody passing by would never
even know the place was here.

"How did anybody realize there was something going

on out here?" he asked. "There doesn't seem to be a person close enough to hear anything."

"The owners are an older couple who spend their winters down in Florida, so they pay a handyman to come out here every week and keep the place up," Chase said. "When the guy came by the other day, he saw a couple of black bears pawing at the door and figured there was something in there attracting their attention. He chased them off, took one look inside, then called me."

Tate did a double take. "He called you, not 911?"

Chase shrugged as he stepped onto the porch. "The Oxford County Sheriff's Office doesn't have a lot of deputies, so the people on our beats know each of us by name. The handyman has called me before when there's been trouble, so it made sense for him to reach out to me when he peeked in the window and saw the body."

Tate shook his head. He had a hard time imagining working in a place so small that people not only knew the deputies by name but had them on speed dial. Heck, he had a hard time remembering the names of half the people he worked with at the DCO. He probably only had phone numbers for a dozen of them.

Chase used a pocketknife to cut the crime scene tape on the door, then pushed it open. "We were planning to turn the house over to the cleaning crew this morning, but when Homeland contacted us, we put them on hold. Nothing has been touched since the coroner took the body out."

Tate had barely stepped foot in the cabin when the acrid metallic scent of blood slapped him in the face. Thank God the weather was cool. He didn't want to think about how bad the odor would be if it had been the middle of summer.

Breathing through his mouth so he wouldn't yak, he moved through the small entryway, then across the living room with its wood-burning fireplace and leather couches, following the bloody footprints into the kitchen. One look at the knocked-over chairs, broken table, and big puddle of sticky, nearly dried blood was enough to tell him that this was definitely where all the action had occurred.

Besides the blood on the linoleum floor, there were some spatters decorating the far wall. Arterial spray from Bell's slashed femoral, he guessed. At least a half dozen different shoe impressions had traipsed through the reddish-brown mess on the floor. Probably from the first responders who'd come in hoping there was a chance Bell was still alive. Some of the tracks likely belonged to the coroner's team, too. Since Bell's death had been declared an animal attack from the start, no one had seen the need to preserve the scene. It would have been nice to know if one of the shoe imprints belonged to the killer, but it was too late to do anything about it. Besides, his gut told him the person who did this was too good to leave behind any obvious evidence.

While there were undeniably a lot of footprints around the crime scene, the one thing he didn't see were animal tracks. How the hell had the local cops explained that little detail?

Tate wandered around the room, carefully avoiding the blood that was still wet as he looked for anything that might give him an idea of how McKinley Bell had ended up in the middle of nowhere getting sliced up by a shifter or hybrid. But other than one of the kitchen chairs having some scuffs on the arms from the restraints used to hold Bell down, there was nothing.

He wished Declan was there. Having the bear shifter's sensitive nose would have told him a lot, namely whether he was dealing with a shifter or hybrid, if the attacker had been working alone, maybe even if Bell had been drugged. Without Declan, Tate was swimming blind, hoping to stumble over a clue the police had missed. It made him wonder how he'd ever gotten anything done before having a shifter partner.

He crossed the room to check the dead bolt on the back door that led out of the kitchen and onto a walkway toward the pond. The bolt and doorframe were intact with no sign they'd been kicked in or even tampered with. When they'd first come in, Tate had glanced at the front door and noted that was in good shape, too.

"What's the theory on how this all went down?" Tate asked, turning back to the deputy.

Chase was casually looking in the cabinets, like he was searching for a snack, which was crazy, considering how many donuts the guy had eaten. At Tate's question, the deputy glanced his way, his face serious. "You want the narrative that's in the final report?"

Tate frowned. Did Chase know the whole animal attack angle was BS regardless of what he'd said about the bobcat in front of his boss? "Yeah, the official party line would be good. Unless there's another one you'd like to tell me about?"

Chase shrugged and closed the door of the cabinet. "Bell's car was found out on the main highway about a half mile from here with the left front tire blown out.

The official police report says he must have pulled over due to the flat and started walking along the road looking for help. Time of death was around two a.m., so there weren't many people out there to see him. At some point, Bell realized he was being followed by an animal, and when he saw the cabin, he headed this way, either looking for a phone or just a place to get away from the thing behind him."

The deputy paused, maybe to gauge whether Tate was buying any of this shit. Tate didn't bother to point out that you couldn't see the house from the road in the daylight. How Bell had supposedly seen it in the dark was beyond him.

"Any idea why the man would have been driving around here so late at night?" he asked. "He lived in Scarborough near the medical center, right?"

Chase shook his head. "No idea why he was up here. We've checked with the people at the hospital and his service. It wasn't like he was making a house call or anything." He wandered over to the next cabinet and opened it. "The handyman swears he always locks the door behind him, but since Bell got in without breaking any windows or locks, the assumption is that the handyman made a mistake and left the front door unlocked. Unfortunately, the bobcat, or whatever it was, followed him in before he could close the door. The animal chased Bell into the kitchen and attacked him, and the wind blew the door closed at some point after the animal left."

Tate didn't say anything, instead waiting to see if Chase was going to add anything else to the fantasy, but apparently, the man was done. With everything except digging through the cabinets.

"What the hell are you looking for in there?" Tate finally asked, unable to contain his curiosity any longer.

Chase held open a cabinet door and pointed inside. "There's food in at least half of these cabinets, yet the animal never bothered trying to get into them. I mean, there's not even a scratch on them. A hungry bobcat might chase a person into a house and attack them, but if it did, it would sure as hell take a few nibbles. If it didn't, it would at least dig around the house looking for something else to eat. This one didn't. There are also no animal prints anywhere in the house. I saw Bell's body after the attack. No way any animal tears into a man like that without leaving a single fucking paw print."

Tate crossed his arms over his chest. "What are you trying to say? If an animal didn't kill Bell, what do you think happened to him?"

Chase rested his hands on his gear belt and met his gaze. "I was hoping you'd tell me. And don't bother trying to sell me that lame-ass pet mountain lion story, because we both know that was a load of shit."

"You sure of that?" Tate asked.

"I don't know what the hell to think or what I'm sure of. But I know there's some strange crap going on with this case, and you know way more than you're saying."

Tate regarded the deputy for a moment. Chase was obviously sharp as hell. The kind of cop who saw things most officers made sure they didn't and asked the questions other officers wouldn't. Right now, he had that glint in his eyes that a man gets when he knows he's involved with something big and wants to know exactly what it is.

Tate recognized that look and the insane urge that

came with it. The one where you wanted to throw yourself into the far end of the pool just to see how deep the water really was. He'd felt that urge himself nearly a decade ago when he'd stumbled onto the existence of shifters and made a decision that changed his life. He'd never looked back, but every once in a while, he couldn't help but wonder how his life would have been different if he hadn't opened the door all those years ago. Or if someone had pushed it closed before he saw too much. Would he still be in the marshals? Would he be married with two-point-three kids, a house with a white picket fence, and a dog? He supposed he'd never know.

But this moment wasn't about him. It was about a small-town cop from Oxford County, Maine, and whether Tate was going to open the door for him or push it closed.

"Maybe I'm not saying anything because you're not ready to hear what I have to say," he murmured.

"Why don't you let me decide what I'm ready to hear?" Chase asked. "I think I can handle anything you throw at me."

Tate almost laughed. Damn, this guy was so much like him when he was younger. So sure he had all the answers and could deal with anything.

He turned and looked around the kitchen again, doubting there was anything else to see here. Yeah, he could search the rest of the house, maybe even check out the yard. It would be nice to find some footprints or tire tracks that might tell him something about the person who'd killed McKinley Bell. But his gut told him he was wasting his time.

So instead, he focused on where to dig next for clues

and how to deal with Deputy York. The first part was easy. The second, not so much. He knew for sure he wasn't ready to tell Chase how Bell had died or that shifters existed. The guy wasn't ready for that.

"You want to know what's going on. I get that," he told Chase. "But what we're dealing with here is complicated and kind of tough to deal with all at once."

Chase opened his mouth to say something, but Tate stopped him. "The one thing I can tell you is that Bell wasn't chased in here by an animal. He was brought to this place to be tortured. I have no idea if he talked, but when the person who tortured him was done, he or she sliced open the man's femoral artery and let him bleed out."

"Why?" York asked.

Tate shook his head. "I don't know yet. Which is why I'm going to dig a little deeper into the doctor's background, his life, and the people who knew him. I could use your help with that, but you're going to have to accept that until I'm ready to tell you the rest of the story, you'll just have to trust me. Think you can handle that?"

Chase's expression was half pissed, half amused. "Do I have a choice?"

"Sure," Tate said. "You could drop me off at the motel, then go back to your office in Paris and tell the sheriff I've left already. Then you can go back to your normal everyday routine."

Chase snorted. "Like that's going to happen."

Chapter 6

ZARINA GAZED AT TANNER FROM WHERE SHE SAT IN BED, HER heart aching at how incredibly beautiful and peaceful he looked sleeping atop the cot on the far side of the small cabin. Early morning sunlight was just creeping through one of the small windows, enveloping Tanner in an almost heavenly glow. Which was fitting, since he was already an angel in her mind.

It took all her willpower to keep from climbing out of bed and walking over to caress his scruff-covered jaw simply so she could feel the warmth of his skin beneath her fingers without him pulling away from her.

But she didn't move, afraid she'd wake him up and ruin the moment. Tanner needed his sleep. He'd pushed himself hard last night, spending almost two hours after they'd come back from town putting supplies away. Then he'd stayed out half the night with Spencer and the other hybrids, patrolling the woods around the prepper camp and making sure no additional trouble came their way.

Even though he'd been quiet, Tanner had woken her when he finally slipped into the cabin a few hours ago. She'd thought he might want to talk, but instead, he'd tumbled onto his cot in an exhausted slumber. She hated seeing him that way. It was like he was carrying the weight of the entire camp's safety on his shoulders.

She sighed. At least he'd slept in the cabin with her.

When Chad had told them Bryce's house was the only place he had for the two of them to sleep, Tanner had resisted. Okay, that was an understatement. What he'd said was he preferred to sleep outside on the ground than share the small space with her. She'd known he wasn't trying to be hurtful with his words, but they'd cut deep nonetheless.

She'd solved the problem by announcing that if Tanner was going to sleep outside, then she would, too. It might have been juvenile, but if Tanner could be stupid, then so could she. Besides, it had worked. He'd agreed to stay in the cabin with her, even if he'd slid his cot as far away from the bed as he could. He was in the same room with her. That was a big improvement as far as she was concerned.

Zarina swung her legs over the side of the bed and tiptoed over to Tanner, needing to be closer to him. She loved him so much, it made her heart ache. How could they ever be together if he kept working so hard to keep them apart? As much as she'd wanted to come here and make everything better for him, she didn't know how that could ever be possible. She wasn't sure where that left her. If he kept shoving her away, how much longer could she hang around and pretend she could make this work all on her own?

Tears stung her eyes, and she stifled a sob. If she didn't get out of there, she was going to start crying and wake him up.

Grabbing her coat from where she'd tossed it on the chest at the foot of the bed, she slipped it on, glad she'd decided to sleep in her shirt and jeans last night instead of pajamas. Picking up her boots, she carefully opened the door of the cabin and left, closing it quietly behind her.

She was a little surprised she hadn't woken Tanner up. Perhaps he was even more exhausted than she'd thought. Or maybe he was faking sleep so he wouldn't have to face her.

Pushing that horrible thought from her mind, she put on her boots and stepped off the tiny porch, trying to remember where the main building was. In addition to serving as the camp's meeting hall of sorts, it was also their communal kitchen and dining area. Hopefully, she'd be able to find something to eat there. She was famished. It was why she was awake at this ungodly hour in the first place.

"You're up early," a voice said behind her, and Zarina turned to find Lillie standing there with a basket in her hands. "I thought you and Tanner would sleep in this morning since you were out so late last night."

Zarina didn't mention she and Tanner weren't actually sleeping together. It was too complicated to get into.

She smiled. "Tanner was up late last night, so I let him rest while I went looking for breakfast."

Lillie's mouth curved. "I know what you mean. I like getting up early to grab something to eat before everyone else is up and about. In fact, I was just about to make some breakfast. Want to join me?"

"I'd love to." Zarina glanced at Lillie as they made their way across the camp. "Any word on Bryce and Josh?"

The girl's face fell. "Uh-uh. Dad was out all last night talking to people in the other nearby settlements. He's hoping someone will turn up something soon."

Zarina hoped for the best, too, but limiting the search like Chad was doing seemed myopic to her.

The building Lillie led her into was bigger than she expected. Based on the number of benches and tables set up along one side of the interior, it looked like it could easily seat thirty or forty people.

Lillie set the basket on the counter in the kitchen, then stirred up the embers in the four wood-burning stoves at the back of the room and added some fresh wood to each. Zarina moved closer to the heat they gave off, groaning in appreciation as the big space immediately began to warm up. It seemed like she'd been cold since she'd gotten to Washington State. The aroma of fresh coffee brewing on the stove didn't hurt, either.

"You're not used to spending so much time outdoors, are you?" Lillie asked with a laugh as she flipped open the basket she'd been carrying, revealing a large pile of eggs.

Zarina blinked. They had chickens there? She hadn't heard a peep from them since she'd arrived. The idea of eating eggs for breakfast made her mouth water. She'd love to help Lillie cook, but it had been a long time since she'd made anything over an old-fashioned wood-burning stove.

"Is it that obvious?" Zarina asked.

Lillie smiled over her shoulder as she walked over to the counter. "Just a little."

"Believe it or not, I actually grew up on a farm. It was nothing like this, though," Zarina admitted. "How about you? Have you lived here long?"

Lillie cracked half a dozen eggs into a glass bowl and beat them vigorously with a whisk. "About five years. Since I was fourteen. When my mom passed away, my dad decided to sell everything we had and move out here from Montana to start up the camp. I've been here ever since."

"I'm sorry about your mom," Zarina said.

Lillie's eyes filled with sadness. "Thanks."

"Moving here must have been quite a change," Zarina said.

The girl shrugged as she sliced mushrooms and added them to the eggs. "I didn't want to come here at first, that's true. But looking back on it now, I realize why Dad did it." She picked up a block of cheese and deftly grated a small amount. "I didn't handle my mom's death very well and was heading down a destructive path. My dad had already been a prepper back in Montana, so trading in our farm there for this camp wasn't really that much of a change. Besides the fact that we don't have TV or internet." Her lips curved slightly. "But I don't mind missing those things, because if we hadn't come here, I would never have met Spencer."

If Zarina had any doubt the girl was in love with the hybrid, she didn't now. It was obvious from the look in Lillie's eyes when she said the man's name.

"What does your father think of you and Spencer?" Zarina asked.

Lillie placed two thick slices of bread on a cooking sheet and slipped it into the side compartment of the closest stove, then poured the eggs into the cast-iron skillet already sitting on top.

"He absolutely hates it," she said. "He thinks Spencer is bad for me, that he's dangerous, and that I could do so much better."

Zarina took two plates from the open cabinets above the counter. "Silverware?" she asked.

"Top drawer on your right," Lillie said.

Zarina took out two sets of forks and knives, then set the table nearest to them. "Is he right? Is Spencer bad for you? More importantly, is he dangerous?"

Lillie frowned as she lifted the heavy pan and brought it over to the table. She spooned the scrambled eggs onto the plates in silence, then placed the pan on the counter. With practiced ease, she pulled the toast out and brought that over to the table, too.

Pouring two mugs of coffee from the pot on the stove, she placed one in front of Zarina, then sat down across from her. Flipping her hair over her shoulder, she pointed at the scar on her neck. "This was totally my fault. Spencer and I have had a special connection since the day we met, and I've always felt safe around him even when his control is at its worst. But then I made the mistake of slipping into his cabin and trying to wake him up from a nightmare. It was a stupid thing to do. I knew better. But I couldn't stand to hear him shouting in fear. It tore me apart."

Zarina spread butter on the toast. She'd heard Tanner do the same more times than she could count. Lillie was right. It was hard to listen to. "What happened?"

Lillie ate a forkful of eggs before answering. "Exactly what you'd expect from startling anyone armed with claws out of a night terror. Spencer lashed out without even knowing I was there. The minute I cried out in pain, it immediately pulled him out of the dream. Or maybe it was just the scent of my blood. Either way, he snapped out of his rage. He almost lost his mind when he realized he'd hurt me. I swear, for a second, I was worried he was going to kill himself when he saw how bad it was. But instead, he picked me up and carried me to Lorraine's cabin. She fixed me up just fine."

Looking at the scars, Zarina reminded herself to never let Lorraine sew a tear in her clothes. The woman had obviously focused on the practical aspects of keeping Lillie alive, not the cosmetic ones.

Lillie shrugged and stared down at her plate. "We don't have a lot of mirrors around here, so I barely think about them, but I know they bother Spencer. To him, they're a constant reminder of how dangerous he is and why we shouldn't be together. Which is silly. To me, these scars are a sign of how much our love can endure. Not that I expect Spencer to understand that of course, since he's a guy."

Zarina couldn't help but smile. "Lillie, you might not know it, but you are wise beyond your years. Can I assume your father doesn't share your view on the matter?"

She let out a snort. "Dad went ballistic. He wanted to toss Spencer and his friends out on their butts. I told Dad that if he did, I'd leave with Spencer. My dad knew I'd do it, too, so he backed off."

Zarina was stunned by how brave and strong Lillie was. She wasn't sure she could have stood up to her father over something like this at the girl's age.

"You must love Spencer very much," she said softly.

Lillie nodded, her mouth curving again. "I know it's crazy to fall for a guy with Spencer's issues. He'd be the first one to tell you that between his PTSD from the years he spent in the army and what those crazy doctors did to him, he's dealing with a lot of crap. But love doesn't care about a person's past or what issues they have. When you meet the person you're meant to be with, nothing else matters."

Zarina silently agreed. She wished Tanner would take a page out of Spencer's book and stop pushing her away. Or maybe she was the one who needed to be more like Lillie. Zarina had just met her and could already tell the girl was a force of nature.

She sipped her coffee, studying Lillie over the rim. "So, how did Spencer and the other hybrids end up in your camp?"

Lillie eyed her in confusion, quickly finishing the bite of toast she'd just taken. "Hybrids? What's that?"

Of course. Stutmeir's doctors hadn't started using that term until after Tanner had survived the first dose of the serum. That was after Spencer and the others had already supposedly died.

"It's a term the doctors who experimented on Spencer and Tanner came up with," Zarina explained. "They used it to describe a person who's half human, half animal."

Lillie blinked. "So you really were there in that ski lodge with those lunatics who wanted to turn humans into monsters?"

"Unfortunately, yes." Zarina pushed her scrambled eggs around on the plate with her fork. "But like Tanner said, I wasn't there because I wanted to be. The man who employed the doctors kidnapped me from my apartment in Moscow a few months before and forced me to help them come up with a drug to create hybrids." Even now, she shuddered at the memory. "I tried everything I could to slow down and sabotage their work, but it didn't help.

I was able to get Tanner out, but I couldn't do the same for Spencer and the others. I was sure they'd died."

Lillie nibbled on her toast. "The guys don't talk much about what happened in the lodge, but from what little they have told me, the doctors must have thought they were dead, too. They took their bodies into the woods and left them in shallow graves, probably thinking some wild animals would make everything disappear. But Spencer woke up and dragged his friends to a cave about a mile from where they'd been dumped." She picked up her coffee mug and wrapped both hands around it. "That's where Burt found them last January. It was in the middle of a blizzard, and they were freezing and starving to death. They'd been surviving on whatever food they could forage, too scared to go down into any of the nearby towns for food and shelter because they were worried they'd lose control and hurt someone. When Burt brought them back here, a lot of people in the camp were scared of them at first, but that changed as soon as Spencer and the other guys proved they could be trusted. My falling in love with Spencer probably helped a little with that, I guess."

Zarina smiled. "Probably so."

She and Lillie continued to talk while they ate, with Zarina telling her about hybrids, shifters, and Tanner, while Lillie told her how Spencer and the others helped out around the camp and worked to control their aggressive behaviors. Maybe it was simply because they'd both fallen in love with hybrids, but Zarina found it incredibly easy to talk to the girl despite the fact that they came from completely different backgrounds.

"Are you and Tanner getting married?" Lillie asked, setting her fork and knife on her empty plate and pushing it aside. "You can tell me to back off if it's none of my business, but after seeing how he defended you yesterday, not to mention the look you get on your face every time you say his name, I'm figuring the two of you have been together for a while." She shrugged. "I can't help thinking if the two of you can make it work, then Spencer and I might, too."

Zarina hesitated, hating to dash the girl's hopes. But she couldn't lie.

"No, we're not getting married." Tears stung her eyes as she suddenly realized marrying Tanner had been a dream buried deep in her heart all along. She swallowed hard and blinked them back. "Tanner and I care about each other, but in our case, it's not enough to overcome the obstacles life throws in front of you."

Lillie set her mug down on the table with a frown. "Sure it is."

Zarina gave her a sad smile. "I wish it could be. But like Spencer, Tanner is constantly worried about hurting me or someone else who's important to him. That's why he's been living out here on his own for the past two months. He thinks that's the only way to keep other people safe."

Lillie let out a sound of frustration. "What is it with guys? Spencer has said the exact same thing to me a dozen times. He thinks it'd be better for everyone if he goes up to Alaska and lives alone in the wilderness. Are all men born with that macho crap in their DNA?"

Zarina laughed. "Probably. The worst part is that it doesn't have to be that way. I came out here with an antiserum that will make him human again, but Tanner won't even consider taking it. He's so damn stubborn, it drives me insane."

Lillie's eyes widened. "You have a cure for this hybrid thing? Would it work on Spencer?"

Zarina considered that. She hadn't thought about it until now, but there was no reason it wouldn't. "Almost certainly. I developed the antiserum specifically for Tanner's type of hybrid DNA. Since Spencer and the others were created using the same hybrid serum, it should work on them, too."

Excitement danced in Lillie's eyes. "Taking the drug wouldn't be dangerous, would it? There wouldn't be any side effects, right?"

Zarina sighed. Unfortunately, it wasn't that simple. "It won't kill him or cause any significant damage. If there was any chance of that, I'd never consider giving it to Tanner. But Lillie, this drug is designed to make drastic changes to a hybrid's DNA to reset their body back to what it once was. There's a price to pay for that."

"What kind of price?" Lillie whispered hesitantly, like she was afraid to hear the answer.

"There could be slight physical and personality changes," Zarina said. "He'd probably look a little different, maybe shorter and less muscular. His voice and eye color could change. Maybe his hair color, too."

She nodded. "That's not so bad."

No, but there were other possible side effects that might be. Ones she didn't want to so much as consider in Tanner's case. But she'd deal with them if it meant helping him.

"Lillie, there's a small chance Spencer might not

remember certain things, maybe not even you. You'd have to start your relationship all over."

The girl swallowed hard but then took a breath. "Is that all of it?"

"I wish it were," Zarina said sadly. "I'm not sure if Spencer can father children now that he's a hybrid, but after taking the antiserum, there's a very good chance he won't be able to. I didn't test the antiserum for that possibility, but everything I know about medicine makes me think the back and forth changes to his DNA are probably going to be too extreme to ever let that happen."

Lillie's eyes filled with tears. "I could deal with losing the parts of what make him the Spencer I know, but not the part about him being unable to have kids. He comes from a big family and talks about having a family of his own all the time. I couldn't let him give that up. I'd rather he stay like he is."

"Do you think he'd feel the same?" Zarina asked gently.

The door opened, and a group of preppers walked in before Lillie could answer. The girl quickly wiped the tears away and gave them a wave as they headed over to the stoves to make breakfast. Then she turned her attention back to Zarina.

"I don't know. Spencer would take any risk if he thought it might change him back to what he used to be, especially if he thought it would keep me safe." She reached across the table to take Zarina's hand. "Please don't mention the antiserum to him. Let me tell him."

"I will," Zarina assured her. "I promise."

That seemed to satisfy Lillie. The girl released her

hand and sat back with a sigh. "Is that why Tanner won't take it? Because he knows about the side effects?"

Zarina shook her head. "No. I never got the chance to get into that level of detail with him. He said he wouldn't take it the moment I brought it up. I'm sure he has his reasons, but he won't tell me what they are. In fact, he doesn't tell me much of anything. Instead, he keeps saying he needs to stay as far away from me as he can, and it's infuriating as hell."

Lillie rolled her eyes. "Tell me about it. Please tell me he doesn't pull the same crap Spencer does and use that line when you tell him you love him."

"Actually, I haven't told him," Zarina admitted.

"But you love him, right?"

"More than anything. But I've always thought a conversation like that should wait until we're...I don't know...closer, I guess you'd say. Why tell someone you love him if he isn't ready to hear it?"

"Because Tanner is a guy," Lillie said as if that explained everything. "Besides, sometimes you might have to both lead the horse to the water and make him drink."

Zarina had absolutely no idea what that meant. Maybe it was an American thing. "I don't understand."

Lillie sighed, and for a moment, it seemed the nineteen-year-old girl was years beyond Zarina in both age and wisdom.

"I mean that if you want to be in Tanner's life, you might need to put yourself in it regardless of what he says."

"So, how did you stumble across these preppers in the first place?" Zarina asked as she pulled the vial of antiserum out of her backpack to check on it. "Did you smell Spencer and the other hybrids?"

Tanner momentarily turned his attention away from the ax in his hand and the wood he was chopping, glancing suspiciously at the vial in her hand. They were on the edge of the camp, and while they weren't exactly alone considering there was a whole group of people nearby, she wasn't worried about anyone overhearing them. Well, maybe except for Spencer and the other hybrids, but they were off patrolling the woods.

"Yeah," Tanner said. "I picked up their scent within the first couple of days of getting here. At first, I thought I was having some kind of olfactory flashback, but I figured it out soon enough it was real. It wasn't difficult to track them down after that."

From where she sat on a nearby tree stump, Zarina watched Tanner position a big log on its end a few feet in front of him, turning it this way and that like he was a diamond cutter looking for that one perfect place to strike. She waited for him to tell her the rest of the story she'd been curious about hearing since seeing the hybrids yesterday, but he seemed to be done.

"Weren't you stunned when you realized the men who'd gone through the hybrid experiments with you were still alive?" she prompted.

He didn't say anything for a moment, but then he shrugged. "I guess so. I'd figured I was the only one who'd made it out of those labs. Finding out I was wrong was a relief in a way."

She was about to ask him what he meant by that, but

he gestured to the vial in her hand. "You planning on injecting that stuff into a bear or something?"

Zarina sighed, giving up on the idea of digging deeper. It was obvious this particular conversation was finished. She flipped the vial's protective case over in her hands, looking for signs of damage.

"No, I'm not injecting it into any bears," she told him after she was satisfied it was completely intact. "It was designed around the specific serum used on you and tailored for your particular hybrid variant. It would have no effect on a bear at all. Or any other animal for that matter."

Tanner grunted "That's good, I guess." He turned his attention back to the ax in his hand and the big log standing on its end in front of him. "Not that it matters, since I'm not taking it."

"I know," she said. "You've already mentioned that to me several times."

Tanner's jaw twitched a little, like he wanted to say something, but he didn't. Instead, he bounced the ax in his hands a few times, then swung it violently over his head, slamming it into the log in front of him and splitting it neatly in two. He then moved over to the next log he'd already set up and whacked that one in half, too, before turning his attention to the next, and the next, and the next. After he split all of them, he patiently collected up the pieces, brought them back to the center of the flat piece of ground he'd been working on, and set them up to do it all over again. He'd been doing this same thing for over an hour like he was some kind of machine.

Zarina didn't say anything, either. Mostly because she was too busy eyeing Tanner's bare chest and enjoying the way his sweat-covered muscles flexed and strained in the cool mountain air as he worked. She'd seen him without his shirt plenty of times before, but she still found herself transfixed at the sight of his broad shoulders, thick pecs, bulging biceps, and rippling abs. Even that little trail of dark-gold hair that led from his belly button down into his jeans was mesmerizing.

When she'd come out here with him to the far end of the camp where the firewood supply was stacked up as tall as she was, it had been with the idea of getting Tanner alone for a serious conversation. Regardless of whether anyone could overhear or not, she still would have preferred it to be somewhere more private, but Tanner was worried about getting too far from the camp in case those jerks with the guns came back.

It wasn't a perfect place, but it would do.

She'd come here intending to follow Lillie's advice and ask him why he wouldn't consider taking the anti-serum. If that conversation went well, maybe they could talk openly about how they felt about one another, too. But instead of talking, Zarina had spent more time gazing at him like she was now. She tried to tell herself it was to make sure the injuries he'd gotten yesterday in the fight with the hybrids had healed properly, but in truth, she was ogling him because he was so damn hot. It was almost embarrassing to be so discombobulated at the sight of his bare chest that she couldn't think straight, but she was powerless. It was like his body had been designed specifically to enthrall her.

Some of her reticence also had to do with the fact that Tanner wasn't simply against the idea of taking the antiserum. He seemed to completely hate the idea that it was even out here in the woods with him. When she had pulled out the case, he'd looked at her like he thought she was going to yank it out and jab the syringe in his neck when he wasn't looking.

Although, if she was being honest, the biggest reason she hadn't brought up the subject of the antiserum—or the fact that she loved him—was because she was a big chicken and not nearly as bold as Lillie apparently was.

Sighing, she popped open the plastic protective case around the vial and studied the auto-injector nestled inside. She sagged with relief. The case for the serum was rugged and well built, but her pack had been jostled around a lot over the past couple of days, so she'd been a little worried. The antiserum had taken her a year and a half to create. To say it was valuable was an understatement.

Thankfully, the auto-injector was fine. She'd been worried it might have been accidentally triggered or started to leak. Not that either of those things was likely, but then again, she hadn't exactly planned to carry the thing around with her for so long. She thought she'd administer it to Tanner the moment she found him. She had multiple degrees in everything from genetics to medicine, and she still didn't understand the male half of the species.

"Shouldn't that thing be kept in a refrigerator?" Tanner asked as he wedged the ax head out of a gnarled log that didn't seem to want to let the blade go.

He asked the question so casually, she'd almost think he didn't care about the answer one way or the other, but the look in his eyes made her think he was more concerned about the drug than he let on.

"No, because it's not a live vaccine," she explained patiently. "It isn't protein based at all, for that matter. I constructed it using catalytic RNA molecules so it would be stable for longer periods of time at ambient temperatures. It's less likely to break down in your body as well."

"I don't really know what any of that means," he murmured. "But it doesn't matter. I'm still not taking it."

She bit her tongue to keep from saying something she'd regret and put the case back in her pack. She wanted to ask Tanner what the hell his problem was, but that would only play into his hand. If the conversation became combative, she'd lose the battle before it got started.

So instead, she took a deep breath and attempted to see this situation from his perspective, trying to understand why he was turning his back on something like this. She thought yesterday's fight with the other hybrids had demonstrated better than anything why he couldn't keep acting like he could hide from the animal inside.

Some of his reluctance probably had to do with the fact that he didn't want to get his hopes up only to have them dashed if the antidote didn't work. She could understand that. She'd be the first to admit she'd been working on this cure for a long time without success. But if that was the reason, why couldn't he simply tell her that? Then she could discuss all the medical possibilities and probabilities. She might not understand men, but science? That she got.

"Have you tested it on anyone else?" Tanner asked suddenly. "Any other hybrid, I mean? Like Minka or Diaz?"

Zarina was so surprised by the question that all she
could do was stare at him. A minute ago, he'd told her
he wasn't interested in the antidote. Now, he wanted
to know if she'd tested it on the feline hybrid, Minka
Pajari, and the Special Forces soldier, Carlos Diaz.

"No. I haven't tested the antiserum on anyone else,"
she said after a moment. "I designed it specifically for
the first-generation hybrids Stutmeir made, like you.
It wouldn't work on Minka, because she's a third-
generation hybrid made from Ivy's DNA, and it wouldn't
work on Diaz, because he's a natural-born shifter."

Tanner did a double take. "Diaz is a shifter? I thought
he turned into a hybrid because he'd been bitten by one."

Zarina frowned. Had Tanner forgotten the last time
he'd seen Diaz? It had been the night the hybrids had
attacked the DCO complex. Tanner had completely lost
control and nearly killed the Special Forces soldier. Diaz
had survived, but only because he was a shifter. Tanner
had almost certainly smelled Diaz and recognized him
for what he was.

Then again, maybe his hybrid episodes were like an
alcoholic having a blackout when almost all the memories were lost. Zarina wasn't sure which would be worse,
knowing you'd lost control and having no memory of it,
or losing control and remembering every horrible detail.

She opened her mouth to ask what he remembered
of that night but then thought better of it. He'd obviously remembered enough to force him to go on the run.
There was no reason to make him relive events he'd
likely prefer to forget.

"I told Diaz a dozen times it wasn't possible for a
person to become a hybrid from a bite, so I have no idea

why he insisted he was one," she said instead. "He's a coyote shifter. A late bloomer, but still a full shifter."

"A late bloomer?" Tanner grunted. "I know he's a small guy, but I had no idea he was still waiting to go through puberty."

"Very funny." She made a face. "That's not the kind of late bloomer I'm talking about. It's something I've learned since you left. It turns out that being a shifter is a bit more complex than we originally thought. There are a lot more people in the world with shifter DNA in their system than we ever imagined, maybe as much as one percent of the population. For most people, that DNA stays in a dormant state for their entire lives, but for a very small number, the chemicals released into the body during puberty activate the dormant gene and turn them into shifters. In Diaz's case, for some reason, the change occurred really, really late in his male growth cycle instead of early on in the process."

"Huh." Tanner shook his head. "Diaz must be disappointed. He was all in on the theory that the bite was what changed him."

"You have no idea," she muttered. "As much as he wants to blame the hybrid bite for changing him, in reality, it was pure coincidence that his body decided to go through the change at that point."

Tanner muttered something under his breath she didn't quite catch. "I don't know what he's complaining about. Better to have shifter DNA in your blood than hybrid. God knows I'd rather be a shifter."

Zarina chewed on her lip. "Actually, in a way, you are."

He slammed the blade of the ax into the top of the

next log and turned to look at her, his eyes narrowing. "What do you mean by that?"

"That's something else I learned after you left," she told him. "It also explains why some people made it through the various hybrid experiments while others didn't. It turns out having dormant shifter DNA in your blood is essential to surviving the hybrid serum."

"You mean…" His voice trailed off.

She nodded. "Yes, you have shifter DNA. So do Minka and Sage. Not enough to start the change on its own, but enough that you all survived the hybrid serum when the drug killed so many others."

That suddenly made Zarina wonder about Spencer and the other hybrids at the prepper camp. None of them had possessed a discernible pulse when they'd been dragged out of the lodge. But the more she thought about it, the less surprised she was that their bodies had somehow revived themselves. If certain people were already genetically predisposed to surviving the hybrid process, was it that crazy to believe they'd be able to put themselves into some kind of coma-like stasis to help them live through the worst of the changes? It was an interesting hypothesis for sure, and one she'd love to study.

Zarina's big reveal seemed to have put Tanner into a thoughtful mood, because he went back to splitting logs, his expression showing he was struggling with something. She let him think for a while but then stood up and moved closer. He stopped what he was doing, lowering the ax to let it hang down at his side.

"Sage is thinking about taking the antiserum," she said softly.

Maybe if he knew another hybrid—a friend—would take it, he might be willing to do the same.

Tanner looked at her in surprise. "I thought you said it would only work on me?"

Zarina shook her head. "I said it would only work on first-generation hybrids like you. Technically, Sage is third generation like Minka, but the serum that created her was developed a few months after you were turned. It might have shifter DNA in it instead of an animal's, but it's very similar to what they used on you. In some ways, she has more in common with you than Minka. I'll still have to tweak the formulation a bit, but it shouldn't take me too long."

Tanner didn't say anything for a long time, his eyes filling with pain. "The relaxation and visualization techniques I taught Sage were finally starting to help. I never thought about her having a setback after I left."

"Actually, she's doing okay," Zarina said. "Landon was able to get Derek Mickens transferred to the DCO from Special Forces temporarily."

Derek had been the one who'd rescued Sage from the hellhole where she'd been captive all those months ago, and they'd developed a connection. He was the only one who could seem to calm her inner hybrid when she lost control.

Tanner looked confused. "If she's doing well, why take the antiserum?"

"Because Sage doesn't want to live her entire life in a locked room on the DCO complex. She's come to the realization that she might be able to have the life she used to have before all this happened. If she takes the drug I'm offering."

That seemed to take him aback. "When is she going to do it?"

"Not right away," Zarina said. "She still wants to see if she can learn to control her feline side on her own. I'll also need time to modify the structure of the drug to perfectly match her hybrid breed and DNA."

Tanner stared out into the surrounding forest, his expression thoughtful.

Zarina moved around in front of him, trying to catch his eye. "Look, I'm not saying you should take the antidote because Sage might." Actually, that's exactly what she'd been trying to do. "It's just that I've learned a lot about shifters and hybrids since you left. Rebecca Brannon is extremely interested in supporting my research and has given me a nearly unlimited budget. Between the money and the countless hours I spent in my lab for the past two months, I've pushed the science of shifter and hybrid DNA miles beyond where it was. All so I could come up with an antidote for you. And I've done it. The drug I developed is designed to counteract the effects of the hybrid serum used on you. I swear it will work, Tanner. With everything in me, I swear it will work."

She knew now was the time to mention the less-than-thrilling side effects of the antiserum, but she couldn't bring herself to do it. Those details could wait until later, when Tanner let the idea of taking it seep in a little.

He turned to gaze at her intently, and for a moment, she thought he might actually agree, but then he shook his head. "I appreciate everything you've done for me, Zarina, I really do. But I'm not going to take the drug."

It was all Zarina could do not to scream in frustration.

What the hell was wrong with him? She'd never wanted to smack someone so much in her life. But it wasn't in her to hurt anyone, especially Tanner. So instead, she yanked the ax out of the log with both hands and swung it at the piece of wood in an awkward attempt that took a lot more effort than she would have thought. It didn't land with nearly enough force to split the log and ended up getting stuck. It took her a few seconds to get it out, which only frustrated her more. But once she had the blade out, she attacked the wood again, swinging even harder this time. It still didn't split, but it did get a crack in it. That was a start.

It took her five minutes to finally get the log split, and by the time she did, her arms were numb with fatigue. *Crap*. Tanner had made it look so easy. But even as tough as it was, it felt good to do something physical and take her pent-up frustrations out on an inanimate object.

She'd just shifted her focus to the next log in the line when she realized Tanner was standing there, his muscular arms crossed over his chest, an amused expression on his face.

"What?" she demanded. If he made a crack about her swinging the heavy ax like a girl, she was going to throw it at him.

Tanner shrugged. "Nothing. It's just while I've always thought of you as a city girl, it never struck me until now how completely out of your element you are here in the wilderness. This outdoor living thing really isn't for you, is it?"

She knew Tanner was likely trying to distract her from the previous topic of conversation. While it was irritating as crap, there wasn't much she could do about it. But just because he wasn't ready to deal with the subject didn't mean she had to give up. One way or the other, she was going to figure out what was going on in Tanner's head.

"Ha! Shows what you know," she said as she got lined up to aim the ax at the second log. "I grew up on a farm. It's been a long time since I've done anything like this. It takes a little while to get back into the swing of things."

As if to emphasize her point, she swung the ax, trying her best to bring it straight down into the center of the wood. The result was a very pleasing-sounding thud as the blade bit in deep and the log split cleanly in half. She was so excited, she almost started dancing.

"See?" She gave him a smile. "Like that."

Tanner stared at her, a dumbfounded look on his face. "Wait. What? You grew up on a farm?"

She winced as she realized she'd never told him about that part of her life. "So, I guess I never mentioned that?"

"No, you didn't. In fact, in all the time we've known each other, I don't think you've ever mentioned your family. I got the feeling it was a touchy subject, so I stayed away from it."

"I'm kind of private when it comes to my family." She shook her head. "It's complicated."

He shrugged. "Family usually is."

She silently agreed as she lined up another log. But instead of taking a swing at it, she stared down at the big piece of wood thoughtfully.

"I grew up in a rural area about three hundred kilometers south of Moscow near the Ukrainian border," she said quietly. "During the day, my dad worked in a factory building trucks and tractors, then in the evening, he helped my mom and me on our five-acre farm. We grew mostly potatoes, along with some other vegetables when the season was right. I helped with all the planting and harvesting when I was younger, but that trailed off when I started secondary school, which is when I began to get serious about my science classes." She rested the ax against the log and walked over to Tanner, shoving her hands in the pockets of her coat. "My parents didn't understand most of the stuff I was learning and used to joke that maybe I'd been switched at birth, since neither of them had ever been good at academics. But they recognized that a career in science would be a way for me to get out of the hard life they'd grown up living, so they made sure I dedicated my time to studying instead of helping out on the farm. I felt bad about that, but it was what they wanted. They didn't even complain when I went off to the university in Moscow right after I finished school."

"Huh," Tanner said. "You seriously grew up on a potato farm? I did not see that coming. I had visions of you sitting around with your parents at breakfast discussing the periodic table and the theory of relativity. I can't believe you never mentioned the farm thing to me."

She gave him a sheepish look. "This is going to sound horrible, but I spent a lot of years feeling embarrassed about where I came from. Most of the other students I studied with at the Lomonosov University in Moscow were more sophisticated than I was. I grew up a potato farmer with parents who never made it beyond the ninth grade. I guess I got used to not talking about my family even after I got away from that world."

"Hey," he said softly, reaching out to brush some hair that had come loose from its ponytail back from her face. "It's nothing to beat yourself up about. You wouldn't be the first person to hide your parents' background from your friends. The important thing is you love them, and they know it. Do you get to see them very often?"

She smiled. Sometimes, Tanner could say stuff so perfect, it was hard to believe that other times, he could be such a pain in the butt. "I used to see them all the time, but not as much over the past few years. My work back in Moscow consumed all my time in the months before Stutmeir's goons grabbed me. I was so bad about calling my parents that they never even realized I'd been kidnapped. And when I did call after coming to the DCO, they simply assumed I'd moved to the United States to further my genetic research. I send them money all the time, trying to make things easier on them, but I know they'd rather I come home for a visit."

Tanner nodded. "You should. The DCO could help you get a flight home. In fact, you could probably leave straight from here."

Zarina fought the urge to roll her eyes. She didn't know who he thought he was fooling. He was suggesting she visit her parents because he wanted to get rid of her. She'd be lying if she said it didn't hurt a little, but she knew he wasn't trying to be mean. Knowing him, he thought he was keeping her safe.

Well, she wasn't going to let him push her away, and she definitely wasn't leaving him out here by himself, even if that was what he wanted. If that meant living through the winter with him in this prepper camp, badgering him about taking her hybrid antiserum, she was prepared to do it. She'd freeze to death, but she'd do it.

"I'm sure you're right," she said with a smile. "But because it's been so long since I've seen Mom and Dad, I'm sure another couple of months won't matter. I think I'll just stay here with you for now."

Tanner's jaw clenched, but other than that, he gave little sign her words had bothered him. Instead, he walked over and started lining up more logs to split, as if he planned to spend the entire day doing it. Knowing him, he probably did.

"What about your family?" she asked when the silence began to stretch out to the point of discomfort. "Cam said your mother hasn't changed your room since you joined the army, which means they must still live in Seattle, right?"

"Olympic Hills, actually." Tanner turned his attention from the logs he still needed to split to stacking the wood he already had, aligning the pieces almost like a jigsaw puzzle so the wall of firewood was straight and stable. "It's the northernmost part of Seattle."

From the conversation with Cam yesterday, it was obvious Tanner hadn't been in contact with his family since he'd left three years ago. And he'd burned all his bridges behind him when he walked out. Something told her whatever had driven him away from them was still playing a major role in his life now.

"When we were at the diner with Cam, you mentioned something happened with your dad. I'm guessing that would have been right around the time you got out of the army," she said, suddenly desperate to keep him talking. "Did he have a problem with you getting out? Is that why you left and came to live out here?"

Zarina held her breath, waiting for Tanner to turn and walk away because she'd trespassed into forbidden territory. But he simply shook his head, his expression introspective. "No. Dad was fine with me getting out. And Mom was frigging thrilled."

"But?" she prompted when he didn't say more.

He shrugged, almost looking at a loss as to what he wanted to say. That was hard for her to see. Regardless of the whole hybrid thing, Tanner was a smart, confident man. Seeing him unsure of himself was something new for her.

"But things didn't work out the way anyone planned, and I realized being around my family was a really bad idea," he finally said. "That's why I left."

Zarina cursed silently. Tanner was like a broken record, using the same excuse to turn his back on his family as he did with her and his friends at the DCO, that he was going to make a mistake and hurt them. But this stuff with his family had been long before he'd been turned into a hybrid. So what had him running so scared back then?

She wasn't sure how to even get into it with him, until something Tanner had said to Ryan popped into her head. Something that scared the crap out of her far more than his hybrid-induced rages.

"When did all this start?" she asked softly. "This need to get away from people?" When he didn't answer, she followed her instincts and the horrible suspicion that had started creeping into her mind. "Did it have to do with why you got out of the army and why you're on VA disability?"

Tanner stood there, staring at nothing, his blue eyes

looking so lost and confused, it nearly tore her heart out to see it.

She knew she should probably back off and wait until he was ready to talk, but she couldn't do that. She couldn't stand there and act like she didn't see the pain etched clearly on his face.

She wanted more than anything to yank him into her arms and squeeze him until everything was better. But she knew that wasn't how it worked.

So instead, she lifted her fingers to his strong jaw and gently turned his face to hers. "Tanner, why won't you talk to me about this? I want so much to be able to help you, but I can't do that if you won't even talk to me."

"This isn't something I can talk about." He gazed down at her with eyes filled with so much sorrow that it took her breath away. "Sometimes, there just aren't words to explain what's happening."

Zarina felt the tears she'd been holding back slide down her cheeks, and she opened her mouth, ready to beg if she had to. Anything, as long as he would let her help him. He stopped her with a single tormented glance.

"I can't talk about this stuff, but maybe I can show you," he said, his voice so low, she had to strain to hear it. "Maybe then you'll understand."

Turning, he walked over to the stack of firewood and grabbed his T-shirt from where he'd left it earlier, pulling it on as he walked away. Zarina grabbed her pack and joined him, ready to follow him anywhere. She thought for a moment that they were heading back to their cabin, that maybe he was going to show her a picture or memento to explain all this. But instead, he headed into the forest.

"Where are we going?" she asked, hurrying to catch up with him. "I thought you said we needed to stay close to camp."

He shrugged his broad shoulders, his long strides covering more ground than she could ever hope to. "We won't be gone very long. The camp will be safe enough until we get back."

"Back from where?" she said, running to keep up. "Tanner, where are we going?"

"To the place where I died."

Chapter 7

"I STILL CAN'T BELIEVE HE'S GONE," ABBY WARNER SAID over her shoulder to Tate as she unlocked the door of Bell's office and pushed it open. "He was absolutely the nicest person I've ever worked with. I swear I'm not just saying that. I don't think I ever heard the man complain, not even once. And he was beyond brilliant. One of our very best doctors and an even better genetic researcher."

Tate exchanged looks with Chase as he followed the chief administrator into the office. He and the deputy had talked to several other doctors and nurses at the Scarborough Medical Center before checking in with Abby Warner, and the story had been consistent so far. McKinley Bell had been hardworking and friendly, passionate about his patients and his research, and more than willing to pull extra shifts if they needed him to. Even though he'd won a lot of awards and recognition for the work he'd done in the field of genetics, they couldn't find anyone who'd admit having a beef with him. Tate wasn't surprised. He didn't think anyone there had anything to do with Bell's death. Not unless they were using the large hospital as a cover for hybrid research, of course, which wasn't very likely.

Still, there was always a chance he might stumble over someone who knew what Bell might have been involved in and point him in the right direction.

"Ma'am, can you think of anyone who might have wanted Dr. Bell dead?" Chase asked.

The woman frowned. "That's an odd question. Wasn't McKinley killed by a wild animal?"

Tate let the deputy dig himself out of the hole he'd just dug. Abby Warner had already expressed a goodly amount of suspicion, wondering why there was a deputy from a neighboring county and an agent from Homeland investigating an animal attack. Asking if the man had any enemies had definitely put her antennas up.

While Chase smoothed over the woman's concerns by explaining that since he was assisting in a federal case, he was forced to follow the standard checklists, Tate wandered around Bell's office. It wasn't a big space, but it was neat and orderly and as spotlessly clean as an operating room. There were framed pictures mounted on the walls, everything from landscapes and wilderness photos to smiling people dressed up in fancy clothes. Oddly enough, there weren't any framed degrees on the wall. Every doctor he'd ever encountered proudly displayed them.

Tate looked around again, thinking he must have missed them. Nope, there wasn't a single degree in the entire place. Bell's decision to leave his sheepskins in the closet made Tate's mouth edge up. That said something about the guy. Something good.

He wandered over to the big oak desk by the window. While most people would have positioned their desk to face the door, Bell had turned his around so he could look out over the carefully landscaped lawn. The foliage on the trees was an explosion of orange and yellow with a bit of green thrown in here and there from the firs. Tate had never thought of himself as a nature lover, but even he had to admit this scene was breathtaking.

Yet another thing to like about the man.

Tate forced his gaze away from the brilliant display of colors outside the window and studied the desk. It was just as neat and orderly as the rest of the space, the handwriting on the desk calendar so legible, it almost looked like it had been printed. In addition to the computer, there was also one of those fancy pen sets mounted on a polished hardwood base. Kendra had already remotely accessed the computer, copied everything last night, and found absolutely nothing of interest, so there was no point in wasting time doing it again. Bell didn't even have any suspicious-looking emails worth reading. From the looks of it, the man hadn't used his work computer for anything personal.

Tate started to open one of the desk drawers but stopped as the engraving on one of Bell's fancy pens caught his eye. Tate picked it up, turning it toward the window and the late afternoon light.

The engraving read *Hearts Lost but then Found*.

Tate was a guy, and even he recognized romantic crap when he saw it. Obviously, Dr. Bell had a girlfriend out there. The fact that the pen set was positioned strategically front and center on the desk so the man could see the inscription every time he looked up told Tate this secret someone must have been a pretty big deal to him.

"Was Dr. Bell in a relationship with anyone that you know of?" he asked Abby, putting the pen back in its holder.

The fact that nothing about a relationship had shown up in the DCO's background scrub had Tate curious.

The only way that happened was if Bell had gone out of his way to hide it.

Abby looked at Tate. "I don't think so. If he was, he never mentioned it to me. You could talk to his clinical research assistant, Joanne Harvey. They worked together for years and were good friends. If anyone would know if he was seeing anyone, it'd be her."

Tate glanced at Chase, but he shook his head. Apparently, the deputy didn't know anything about Joanne Harvey either. "I wasn't aware that the doctor had an assistant."

Abby waved her hand. "That's because, technically, she wasn't McKinley's assistant. On all the HR paperwork, she's a general researcher, but that's just a formality. She's worked exclusively for him for the past five years."

Another quick look in Chase's direction told him the deputy was thinking the same thing he was. If anyone knew what the doctor had gotten himself into, it would probably be Joanne Harvey. Hell, she might even be the finder of lost hearts mentioned in the engraving.

"Is Ms. Harvey here now?" Chase asked Abby. "We'd like to talk to her."

The woman shook her head sadly. "Joanne didn't come in today. In fact, she's been out since we learned of McKinley's death."

Huh. Okay, the chances of Joanne Harvey being in a relationship with Bell just increased. "We'll need to get her home address from you," Tate said.

Abby nodded. "Of course. Follow me."

Tate was halfway to the door when the photo in one of the frames caught his attention, bringing him to a standstill so fast, Chase almost ran him over. He ignored the deputy and moved closer to the photo. Damn. He wasn't seeing things. It was Mahsood in the picture with Bell. The two men were standing with several other people, and all of them except Mahsood were proudly holding some kind of award plaque.

"Excuse me, Ms. Warner," he said, keenly aware that Chase had taken an interest in what had caught his attention. "Do you know when this picture was taken?"

The woman slipped her reading glasses on and leaned closer. "Ah, yes. That was the award banquet last December in Portland. McKinley and his team had just won the Allan Lasker Genetic Research Award. It was the highlight of the entire evening."

Tate pointed at Mahsood. "Was this man part of the team?"

"Dr. Mahsood? Technically, he wasn't, and his name didn't officially appear on the award, but he'd mentored all the doctors on the team at one time or another over the years, so they insisted he join them for the photo." Abby's lips curved. "He's very respected in this part of the country for his innovative work in the field of genetic engineering. As I remember it, he'd been out of the country for some time just prior to the banquet, and McKinley was thrilled he'd made it back in time."

Tate stifled a snort. Mahsood had been out of the country prior to that because he'd been in Costa Rica creating a group of insane hybrids. Tate couldn't believe Mahsood had been ballsy enough to go straight from that bloodbath to a formal award ceremony, like everything that had gone on down there had been nothing more than a day at the office. Heck, maybe for Mahsood, creating monsters *was* just another day at the office.

Regardless, it was now a certainty that Mahsood and Bell knew each other, and the chances were getting better and better that the link was the thing that had gotten the man tortured and killed.

Tate was still considering the ramifications of that as Abby led them out of the office and toward the administrative section. Even if he went with the assumption that Bell and Mahsood had been working together on a new hybrid program, that didn't explain how Bell ended up in a cabin in the middle of nowhere sliced and diced. The theory that they were creating a new hybrid out for revenge didn't feel right. And he seriously doubted Mahsood had killed Bell.

He was still wondering where that left him when they walked past a brass plaque mounted on the wall with the name *Brannon Memorial Wing* emblazoned on it. Tate stopped to take a closer look, noticing Chase must have been catching onto how he worked, because the deputy swerved before he mowed him over.

"Ms. Warner, is this Brannon as in Rebecca Brannon?" Tate asked.

He seriously doubted it could be anyone else. How many Brannons could there be in this part of the world?

Abby beamed. "Yes. Do you know her? She's an amazing woman, isn't she? This whole wing of the facility was built with funding from her charitable organization."

"Really?" Tate said. "A whole wing?"

He'd be a lot more impressed if he didn't know the woman so well.

Abby nodded, her head bobbing like one of those toys. "She's very generous, but that's to be expected. The Brannons have lived in the area for generations and have always been very supportive of the local community. They've funded the construction of hospitals, libraries, children's centers, as well as domestic violence and homeless shelters for decades. Everyone adores them."

Tate wondered if people would revere the Brannons as much if they knew how many people had died at the hands of Rebecca's hybrid research projects or that she'd abandoned her own daughter in a mental institute for most of her life, almost certainly because she didn't want the girl getting in the way of her political career.

He reached into his jacket pocket and took out his notebook, then flipped through it until he found the picture of Ashley he'd taped in it that morning before leaving his hotel room. It was a crappy photo, taken from a cheap convenience store camera a few hours after the shifter had escaped the mental institution. It was a grainy, black-and-white image, but it was the best shot they had of her.

"Have you seen this woman around by any chance, possibly with Dr. Bell?" he asked Abby.

This was Rebecca Brannon's hometown. Maybe Ashley had come back here looking for Mommy Dearest instead of Mahsood, and Bell had simply been collateral damage.

Abby frowned at the picture and shook her head. "I'm sorry. She looks familiar, but I don't think I've ever seen her. Who is she?"

Tate slipped his notebook back into his pocket. "Just a person of interest on another case."

The woman nodded and continued leading the way down the hall, but one look in Chase's direction suggested the cop wasn't so gullible. While Tate doubted the deputy recognized Ashley as a relative of Rebecca's, he was smart enough to know Tate wouldn't flash her picture if she wasn't important.

"So, you going to tell me yet what the hell all that was about in there?" Chase asked when they left the research center a little while later. "Who the hell is this Mahsood guy, and what's his involvement in all this? Don't try to tell me he's not involved, because your face lit up like a Christmas tree when you saw him and Bell in that picture. And how do Congresswoman Brannon and that woman in the surveillance photo fit into this?"

Tate came to a halt beside the passenger side of the police car, trying to figure out how much of the story to get into. He didn't want Chase walking into a situation totally blind, because confusion at the wrong moment could get the guy—and possibly him—killed. But full disclosure wasn't an option, either.

Ultimately, he decided to tell Chase enough to give him a clue what kind of crap he was wading into without revealing details that would completely freak him out.

"Mahsood has been involved in some extremely unconventional medical research both here in the United States and abroad," he said after they'd both climbed in the police cruiser. "Research that has led to a lot of people ending up dead—or worse."

Chase regarded him thoughtfully. "Does this research Mahsood is doing have anything to do with the way Bell was killed?"

Damn, this guy was dangerously good when it came to his gut.

"Yes," Tate said, not elaborating further.

Chase didn't push for more on the subject. "Okay. What about the woman in the photo?"

"The picture came from the security camera of a convenience store a few hours from here. She stumbled in there a little while after escaping from one of Mahsood's research facilities."

"Escaping? She was held there against her will?"

Tate inclined his head.

Chase sighed. "And Brannon? How is she involved in this?"

"You sure you want to know?" Tate asked. "And before you answer, stop and seriously think about this. Brannon is a powerful woman. You get on the wrong side of this, and kissing your career goodbye will be the least of your concerns."

"I'm sure," Chase answered without hesitation. "If I only wanted to walk down the safe paths, I never would have joined the marines, become a cop, or gotten involved in this case. I said I'd trust you. Now, it's time for you to start trusting me."

Tate took a deep breath, knowing he was taking one hell of a big leap of faith. But his gut was telling him it was the right thing to do. "Rebecca Brannon has been funding Mahsood's research. The woman in the picture from the security camera is her daughter. Mahsood was experimenting on her, almost certainly with Brannon's full knowledge and support."

If Chase tried to hide his surprise, he wasn't able to pull it off. "You have any proof of this? Proof solid enough to go after a woman this powerful?"

Tate shook his head. "No. And to be truthful, I doubt

I'm going to be finding any up here. Which is fine, because that's not why I was sent here."

"Then why are you here?"

"To figure out what killed Bell and make sure it doesn't kill anyone else," Tate said. "Let's get over to see this research assistant and see if she can help with that."

Chase started the car and put it in gear but then hesitated. "You mean *who* killed Bell, right?"

It took Tate a moment to realize exactly what he'd said, and by then, it was too late to worry about it. He turned to gaze out the passenger window. "Yeah, sure. That's what I meant."

—◦◦◦—

"What is this place?" Zarina asked as she set down her pack and knelt beside him on the ground.

Tanner didn't answer her question. They were a dozen feet from a deep, slow-moving stretch of the Entiat River, less than an hour's hike from the camp. Tanner could hear the crunch of tires on gravel as a heavy vehicle moved along the forest access road a couple hundred yards away. He remembered that rough, narrow road well, even if he'd only been semiconscious the last time he'd traveled over it.

He closed his eyes, vividly remembering the smell of the humid summer air the night Stutmeir's men had brought him here. He could almost feel the hard bed of the pickup truck digging into his spine as the vehicle bounced and jounced along the unpaved route that was little more than a firebreak through this section of the forest. It had been a night he'd never forget.

The weight and scent of the four dead bodies that had been piled on top of him in the back of the vehicle guaranteed that.

As much as he'd never wanted to come back here, there was a part of him that always knew he would. In the privacy of his own mind, he could admit that the place terrified him. But at the same time, it called to him. He had a history with this stretch of riverbank.

Opening his eyes, he reached out and scooped away some of the pine needles that had collected in the shallow depression in front of him, making it easier to see the outline. There were even a few telltale sections of dirt as evidence that the soil had been broken up and pushed to the side.

"This is the place Stutmeir's men brought the bodies after the hybrid experiments," he said softly. "This spot right here was my grave. As things go, it wasn't bad, I guess. It had a nice view of the river."

Zarina stared at him, understanding and horror crossing her face in equal measures. "Oh God. You were...?"

"Buried?" Tanner finished, because he knew she wouldn't be able to. Her beautiful, amazing mind simply couldn't envision something that terrible. "Yeah, I was buried here, along with Spencer, Bryce, and all the other homeless people and hikers Stutmeir's doctors experimented on."

Zarina's head whipped around as she took in the dozen or so other shallow depressions scattered around the clearing. "Are the bodies still here?" she asked hesitantly, her voice low as if she was worried about disturbing them.

"No. At least I don't think so. The DCO cleaned the

place up after taking down Stutmeir so no one would stumble over the remains and draw attention to the area."

Even though the bodies weren't there, the thought of them was enough to make him remember Stutmeir's men dragging him out of the back of the pickup truck along with the others and tossing him into the holes they'd dug. Then they'd started dumping dirt on him. They'd buried him alive, and there hadn't been a damn thing he could do to stop them.

He remembered everything so clearly because the drug Zarina had injected him with to trick the doctors into thinking he was dead had made his heart rate drop and trapped his fully functioning mind inside a nearly comatose body. He'd been completely aware the whole time the men had buried him, and the sensation of the dirt hitting his face and covering his helpless body had taken him back to the very worst day of his life and almost crushed his soul.

Kneeling there now, reliving the memories, was enough to send his pulse racing and make his fangs extend. He didn't realize how close he was to completely losing it until Zarina reached out and rested her hand on his forearm.

Tears filled her eyes, spilling over and running down her face. "I'm right here, Tanner. You're not alone."

His pulse slowed at the sound of her voice, his fangs retracting. For about the millionth time, he wondered what it was about Zarina that gave her the ability to pull him back from the edge with nothing more than a touch or even a whispered word or two. He'd never fully understood how she did it, but it had been like that from the very first moment she'd spoken to him mere hours after Stutmeir's doctors had given him the first dose of hybrid serum.

He wanted to reach up and wipe her tears away, but his hands were too dirty. Literally and figuratively. Sometimes he didn't think he'd ever be clean enough to touch her.

"I'm sorry," she whispered. "I never knew what they were planning. I thought they were going to dump you in the woods. If I'd known they were going to bury you, I would have never given you that drug. I should have tried to stop them from taking you."

"If you hadn't given me the drug, they would have kept giving me dose after dose of that serum until my body ripped itself apart," he said hoarsely. "And if you tried to stop them from taking me, you probably would have found yourself in one of these graves without the possibility of ever crawling out. So don't be sorry. You saved me. That's all that matters."

Zarina shook her head, her mouth opening but no words coming out.

Before he could stop himself, he reached out and grabbed the hand she had resting on his forearm, giving it a firm squeeze. "When those men grabbed me that day in the forest, I was sure I was dead. When they gave me those two doses of hybrid serum, turning me into a monster, I prayed I would die. And when things were at their darkest, you came and risked everything for me. I can't put into words how much that means to me, because you did more than save my life that day. You gave me a reason to keep going."

She wiped the wetness from her cheeks with her free hand, blinking at him in confusion. "Keep going? What are you saying? That you'd given up on living? Why?"

He shook his head, opening his mouth to tell her that

wasn't it. But the truth was, at that point in his life nearly eighteen months ago, he had been close to giving up. He'd pulled so far away from the rest of the world, there wasn't much left other than ending it all.

Zarina's hand tightened around his. "Tanner, talk to me. Please."

He regarded her silently for a moment. Maybe it was time he got everything out in the open. Maybe then she'd understand why he couldn't take her antiserum and why she was wasting her life staying out here trying to help him.

"This isn't the first time I ended up flat on my back in a shallow depression, getting dirt dumped in my face," he said quietly. "The other time it happened, I was pretty sure I was going to die, too."

He ran his free hand over the grave he'd clawed his way out of after Zarina's drug had worn off. As the loose, earthy soil shifted between his fingers, he vividly remembered the sensation of the rich dirt getting sucked up his nose and into his lungs as he'd fought to get out of the hole. It had seemed to take forever, and he'd almost given up. But it was the memory of the beautiful Russian doctor with the voice of an angel that had kept him clawing for the surface. At the time, he remembered thinking that he had to make it out so he could find a way to help her.

Zarina didn't say anything, didn't prompt him. Instead, she knelt there in the dirt beside him, holding his hand and waiting for him to get the courage to say the things that needed to be said.

"Ryan and I were in northern Afghanistan on our last deployment with the 2nd Ranger Battalion," he said, the pain of thinking back to the last battle he'd fought with his friend making it hard to get the words out. "It was in a little place called the Kunduz Province that I doubt ninety-nine percent of the world could find on a map, even with the help of Google. The mission was supposed to be easy. All we had to do was babysit a bunch of Afghanis as they picked up a local warlord. But everything fell apart, and we ended up in a meat grinder. All three members of my fire team died right in front of me. Ryan's guys bought it, too. In the span of ten minutes, our entire squad was wiped out."

Thinking about Chad, Vas, and Danny dying was enough to push him to the edge of his control again. His fingers tingled and his gums ached. He breathed through it, focusing on Zarina's warm scent and her gentle touch until the urge to run—or tear something apart—passed.

"I was almost taken out by a Taliban fighter with a rocket-propelled grenade and ended up getting flipped through the air," he continued. "I came down in an artillery crater and immediately got pelted with falling dirt and rocks. It felt like I was being buried alive."

Zarina looked down at the depression in the ground in front of them, her face going pale as she recognized the similarities to what had happened here.

Tanner swallowed hard as he remembered what it had been like lying in that hole over in Afghanistan, every part of his body hurting while he wondered if he was going to die. Wondering if anyone would ever find him in that damn crater. They were exactly the same feelings and emotions he'd experienced here.

"Going through something like that once was bad enough, but having the same thing happen to me again here?" He shook his head. "I…I didn't handle it well."

Zarina took his other hand in hers, and he used the strength she gave him to keep talking, to get the rest of the story out.

"I thought I'd get over everything that happened over there, all my guys dying, you know?" He shrugged. "I'd seen other men in the battalion die in combat before, and it hadn't shaken me up too bad. I mean, I'd be upset about it for a couple of weeks but then get right back into the job. That's what soldiers are supposed to do. It's what I'd done for years. But for some reason, that time was different. I couldn't shake the memories. The images of my guys dying were there every time I closed my eyes. I stopped sleeping at night and couldn't concentrate on anything. Everything became a haze, and I barely remember coming home from Afghanistan after the deployment. The only clear memory of that time I have is what happened to my guys, and I had the crystal-clear knowledge that I couldn't be a Ranger anymore. When it came time to reenlist, I couldn't do it. So I walked away."

"Did you talk to Ryan at all during this time?" Zarina asked. "He'd gone through the same thing. Was he having problems dealing with it, too?"

"Yeah, but most people probably didn't notice it. I knew him well enough to recognize he was hurting, too, just in a different way."

She frowned. "What do you mean?"

"Before what happened in Kunduz, Ryan and I were like brothers. But after that, we both changed. It was like there was this big pink elephant in the room, but both of us acted like we didn't see it. I pulled away from everyone, Ryan included." Tanner sighed. "As for Ryan, he bought a big motorcycle and started street racing and staying out in the clubs around Seattle until the early morning hours, stumbling in hungover just in time for morning physical fitness training. It wasn't long after that we stopped talking to each other altogether. It was like we woke up one morning and realized we didn't know each other anymore. I didn't even tell him when I made the decision to walk away from the Rangers."

"Didn't anyone in your unit notice what was happening?" Zarina asked, frustration clear in her voice.

He shrugged. "Sure they noticed. The army really tries, but as a general rule, soldiers tend to stay out of one another's heads. If you show up to work on time and do your job, the thoughts rolling around in your bean are your own business. But I had to talk to a few docs in order to get out-processed, and they figured out I'd had my brain bucket rattled a few times. That's where the VA disability came from. I didn't want to take it, but it's pretty standard in the military now. Get blown up a time or two, get a few bucks from the Veterans Administration. I'm not even sure if there's a way within the VA bureaucracy to give it back."

Zarina scowled. "That's crazy! Why the hell wouldn't you want to take the money? Traumatic head injury is serious, and it's a common side effect of concussive blasts."

Tanner couldn't refute that. Zarina was a doctor, so she was probably right. But for him, getting money simply because you'd been knocked unconscious a few times didn't feel right. Not when there were soldiers out there coming home with body parts missing. His problems were nothing compared with that.

"Regardless," he said. "After I filled out a few forms and watched a couple of videos about dealing with stress, I was done with the army, and they were done with me."

That answer didn't seem to make Zarina very happy if the look on her face was any indication, but she let it go. "Okay, so you got out of the army and went back to see your family?"

"Yeah. I thought spending time with them would fix everything." He winced at how incredibly stupid and naive that sounded. "My family had always been close, so I assumed being with them was what I needed to get me out of the fog I was in after getting out of the army."

"But it wasn't?"

He shook his head. "It was like I didn't know how to fit into their world anymore. They wanted to hear stories about what I'd seen and done, but I wanted to forget it all. They tried to help, but they couldn't understand the mood swings, the anxiety, the strange sleep patterns, the hypervigilance, the hours I spent staring up at the ceiling. Hell, I didn't understand it, either, but it was tougher on them. I was someone wearing the face of the man they knew as their son, their brother, their friend, but I wasn't the person they'd known all their lives. It scared the hell out of them."

Zarina was quiet for a moment. "Did you try to get professional help?"

"Sure. I wasn't stupid. I knew there was something wrong with me. I tried to get an appointment to talk to someone at the VA in Seattle, but the waiting list was insane. There are way too many vets needing help and way too few people helping them." He shrugged. "I made the appointment even though part of me knew I'd never show up. I felt like I was a car flying down the interstate at a hundred miles an hour with one lug holding each tire on. I knew it was only a matter of time until a wheel fell off and I crashed and burned. I was right."

"What happened?" Zarina asked in a hesitant voice, as if she really didn't want to know.

Tanner took a deep breath, shame and embarrassment nearly overwhelming him. "Dad came downstairs one morning and found me sitting at the kitchen table where I'd been the night before when he and Mom went to bed. I was staring out the window at the sun coming up. He said good morning, then started to make coffee like he always did. When I just kept sitting there without saying anything, he figured out pretty damn quick something wasn't right with me."

Tanner raked his hand through his long hair, wishing he didn't have to tell Zarina about what happened next, but he needed to.

"He wanted to know what the hell was wrong. I know Dad meant well, but I couldn't explain the things I was feeling. I don't know what happened. One second, we were shouting at each other, and the next, my hands were around his throat, and I had him pinned against the wall."

Tanner didn't look at Zarina, afraid to see the horror in her eyes. But when he risked a glance in her direction, he saw that she didn't seem horrified at all. Maybe because she'd seen him lose it so many times that nothing he did shocked her anymore.

"That wasn't even the worst of it," he continued. "When Cam jumped out of bed and ran downstairs, I thought it was gunfire. I went into total combat mode and tossed my dad across the kitchen right as my mom and brother hurried in. I'll never forget the look on her face. It was like she'd seen a monster. That's when I realized what the hell I'd done." Tears blurred his vision, and he forced them back. "That's when I left. I knew if I didn't, I'd end up hurting someone at some point, so I bailed."

"Was that when you went to the homeless shelter?"

He nodded. "Yeah, but that didn't work out any better than being at home. Too many people and too much noise. That's actually where I met Spencer. He's the one who suggested coming out here, that the solitude of the forest might help. I didn't realize he'd taken his own advice until Stutmeir captured me and I saw Spencer in the cell next to mine."

Zarina's lips curved into a small smile. "You must have been thrilled when you came back out here and discovered he was okay."

"Yeah, it was good seeing him," Tanner agreed. He'd been freaked out when he'd first caught the hybrid scent on the breeze and followed it all the way to the prepper camp. He'd been sure he was losing his marbles. "But if we're being honest, there was some baggage that came along with finding them, too."

"What do you mean?"

"I expected that seeing Spencer and the others would bring back some bad memories from my time in the lodge, and they did. But after I'd found them, I started having flashbacks about the battle in Kunduz again."

"That's not surprising." Zarina rubbed her right thumb back and forth over his hand. "I'm not an expert in psychology, but I've read enough to know that when it comes to PTSD, flashbacks can be triggered by anything that pulls you back into those horrible moments when the trauma first happened. Hearing Spencer and the other guys talk about crawling out of the same kind of shallow grave you were in put you right back in that crater in Afghanistan. All these horrible events are interconnected in your mind, and they're not going away until you find a way to deal with them."

"That's easy to say but hard to do." He knew Zarina was right, but he wasn't sure how to deal with them. "At some level, I blame myself for the death of the guys on my team as well as the Afghanis working with us. In my gut, I know that's crazy. There was nothing I could have done differently that would have prevented their deaths. Every one of us was living on borrowed time the moment we went on that mission. That doesn't do anything to change the feelings of guilt I have, though."

"Guilt." Understanding slowly dawned on her face. "Is that why you don't want to take the antiserum? Because you're beating yourself up about being alive when everyone else on your team in Afghanistan died?"

He dropped his gaze to their intertwined hands. "I suppose that's part of it. Part of me keeps thinking I have no right to be alive when men who depended on me to bring them home didn't make it. But it's more than that."

She frowned. "I don't understand."

He was so screwed up, he barely understood himself most of the time.

Tanner didn't say anything for a moment, using the time to figure out how to put into words what he'd kept hidden in the darkest, most private corner of his mind for a very long time.

"I've lied to myself from the day those doctors turned me into a hybrid," he finally admitted. "I allowed myself to believe the beast inside me was entirely to blame for me being an out-of-control monster. That it wasn't me doing all those things but the animal inside me."

She sagged a little, her body relaxing as if a weight had been lifted from her shoulders. "You're scared to take the antiserum because if it works and you're still out of control, you'll have to face the fact that it was never the beast inside you. You'll have to accept that it's your PTSD and a past you've never wanted to deal with."

There it was. Out there for the world to see. Or Zarina at least. As far as he was concerned, she was the whole world.

"Stupid, huh? Especially since I had violent episodes way before I ever became a hybrid." He snorted. "I guess I'd rather hide away and lie to myself by blaming the corrupt part of my DNA than face the fact that I'm broken."

Zarina's eyes flashed. Tightening her grip on his hands, she stood and tugged him to his feet. "You are not broken! You're a man who went through one horrible event after another. But you've kept going, fighting against your inner demons as hard as you fight to protect the people you care about. Instead, all you see are those moments when you've lost control. You forget that every time you lost control, you regained it before you hurt anyone important to you. If you choose not to take the antiserum, that's your decision, and I'll support it. I won't push you to take a drug you don't want to take. But I refuse to stand around for one more second and watch the man I care about wallow in this pain by himself."

Tanner opened his mouth to speak, but she cut him off.

"I won't let you push me away, and I won't let you deal with those issues alone anymore. If you don't want to talk about your PTSD with anyone else, then you'll have to talk about it with me. If you want to isolate yourself from the rest of the world, that's fine, too, but we'll do it together."

Zarina's heart was beating a hundred miles an hour. He'd never seen her get this upset before. Suddenly, a little bit of the weight he'd been carrying on his shoulders disappeared. He was still carrying an ass load of baggage, but by standing up to him and refusing to let him go it alone anymore, Zarina had somehow taken some of it herself.

He gave her a lopsided grin. "So, you care about me, huh?"

She seemed taken aback for a moment, eyeing him like she thought he was up to something. Or stupid. "Yes, but that should be obvious. I've chased you all the way across this very wide country and hiked alone through the wilderness to find you. Of course I care about you. You're the most important person in the world to me."

His inner lion let out a soft hum of contentment. "Then I guess I should admit one other reason I had for not taking the antiserum."

"What's that?"

"A part of me was worried you wouldn't be interested in me if I wasn't a hybrid anymore. That I wouldn't be the same scientific challenge I am now."

She regarded him thoughtfully for a moment. "Tanner, I'm interested in you because of who you are, not what you are. I thought that was obvious."

He shrugged. "I'm a guy. Sometimes we miss the obvious stuff. It's genetic."

"I know for a fact it isn't," Zarina said. "You're simply a stubborn man who would rather be alone than let a woman put herself at risk for you or share your pain. It's time to let me in."

Tanner suddenly realized the feelings he had for her weren't one-sided—she felt the same way about him as he felt about her. It was insane to believe. She was a beautiful, intelligent woman who could have any man in the world, while he was an unemployed, damaged veteran with a moody personality and claws that came out at the worst possible time. He didn't see the attraction on her part, but maybe it was time to accept it. That was why he stopped thinking so damn much and let instinct take over.

Cupping her face in his hand, he lowered his head and covered her mouth with his, kissing her like he'd wanted to kiss her since the day she'd swept in and risked her life to save his. Her taste nearly made him delirious, and he groaned in appreciation.

Zarina sighed and weaved her fingers into his hair, urging him to kiss her harder. He grasped her waist, tugging her close even as he pulled her ponytail holder off with his other hand and buried it in her silky tresses.

His body responded immediately, desire rippling through him as his tongue found hers, his cock hardening, his gums and fingers starting to ache. For once, he ignored the signs of a hybrid episode and simply lost himself in Zarina. This moment was exactly the way he'd dreamed it would be, even if he'd never imagined it would happen.

She glided her tongue along the tip of his, teasing it and making him chase her. Tanner pursued with a soft growl, fitting her more snugly against him. She was all womanly curves against the hard planes of his body.

He'd just about caught her tongue when she pulled away.

The move yanked Tanner out of the moment so quickly, it was painful. Breathing ragged, he gazed down at her, terrified he'd done something wrong. Pushed too fast. Nicked her tongue with his fangs.

But Zarina was regarding him with a drowsy, languid expression, a fire burning in her eyes so bright, he wondered if she possessed shifter DNA of her own.

"Maybe we should finish this back at the cabin," she suggested.

He would rather have gone to someplace that had a big, luxurious bed made with soft sheets, fluffy blankets, and mountains of pillows. But the cabin would do just fine. Unless...

"Unless you think we should wait until later," he said. "For a better time and place?"

Zarina went up on tiptoe to press a gentle kiss to his lips. "There will never be a better time or place to be with you."

Stepping back, she took his hand and gave it a tug. He reached down and scooped up her pack, falling into step beside her and praying he was doing the right thing.

Chapter 8

IT WAS ALREADY DARK WHEN THEY PULLED INTO THE DRIVE-
way of Joanne Harvey's secluded home on the north-
east edge of the Scarborough city limits, and Chase was
forced to slow down to almost a crawl on the curvy
gravel road. Tate's mouth twitched. That must have
seriously irritated the former marine.

"Is it a law that every home up here has to be hidden
in the woods at the end of a creepy driveway?" Tate
asked.

Chase grinned. "Haven't you ever read Stephen
King? The man has spent most of his adult life convinc-
ing people this state is the scariest place in the world.
We can't go ruining all that work with a bunch of well-
lit subdivisions sitting on perfectly manicured lawns.
What'd be scary about that?"

Tate nodded. "Point taken. Maybe that should be on
your license plates. *Maine, the Scary State.*"

The deputy seemed to consider that. "It could work,
but I think the tourist association might have a problem
with it."

Tate chuckled. It was funny how well Chase was handling all this cloak-and-dagger crap. He'd expected the
guy to hound him with nonstop questions all the way out
here. What kind of research was Mahsood doing? Where
was Brannon's daughter now? How did anything Tate
had told him explain the wounds that had killed Bell?

But Chase had barely said a word, other than making an occasional comment on the how they might handle the impending conversation with Joanne. Tate was relieved as hell the deputy wasn't asking questions he couldn't answer yet.

Tate was just thinking that he was going to have to answer them eventually and about what the hell he was going to say when the patrol car jerked to a halt on the gravel driveway.

"Oh shit." Chase killed the engine and turned off the headlights. "This can't be good."

Tate cursed at the sight of the two dark SUVs parked diagonally across the driveway, blocking the garage. Beside him, Chase grabbed his radio and called for immediate backup. Tate barely heard him identifying himself as an off-duty deputy from Oxford County and reporting suspicious activity at Joanne's address. He was more interested in what the hell was happening in the house.

Jumping out of the car, he pulled his DCO-issued 9mm and approached the pair of SUVs. Based on the position of the small two-door coupe half in and half out of the garage, it looked like Joanne had been in the process of leaving just as the SUVs had shown up, but she was nowhere to be seen.

The driver and passenger doors of both SUVs were wide open, and the engines were still running. That meant there were probably four bad guys on the scene, which weren't horribly terrible odds. Unless one of those four bad guys was the shifter or hybrid who'd torn Bell apart. Then they were shitty odds.

Tate took a quick look in the first SUV he passed,

confirming it was empty before moving into the garage. The door leading into the house was open, and he could make out the outline of a hallway with a dim glow of light at the end.

Chase caught up with Tate as he approached the door. The deputy nodded once as he took up a cover position. Tate returned his nod, then led the way into the house and down the hall.

They'd just entered the country-style kitchen when Tate heard a woman's scream. It was immediately followed by the sound of struggling, then a low-pitched growl.

Tate cursed. There was definitely a shifter or a hybrid in there, which meant he and Chase probably only had a few seconds to get to the woman before their scents gave them away. It also meant the cop was about to get his first introduction to the real world the hard way.

He glanced at the deputy. "You're about to see some crap you're going to have a hard time dealing with," he whispered. "But it's real, so watch yourself. These things are more dangerous than you can imagine. If you get a chance, shoot to kill."

Tate knew Chase would have liked more information, and in a different situation, he would have supplied it. But right now, there simply wasn't time. Ignoring Chase's questioning look, he hurriedly crossed the kitchen and into the living room beyond, hoping the man would follow.

The living room was as poorly lit as the kitchen had been, but there was enough light to see the two men coming down the stairs, a struggling Joanne Harvey in their arms. A third man moved slowly behind the others, his graceful movements giving him away as the shifter or hybrid. There was another person on the upstairs landing, but the angle was bad, and Tate couldn't make out enough details to even tell if the last person in the group was a man or a woman.

Tate didn't recognize any of the men, but he knew their type immediately. Big, fit-looking mercenaries, they seemed completely unfazed by Joanne's cries of pain as they dragged her down the stairs.

The shifter must have smelled them at the same time as Tate stepped forward and lifted his weapon, because his head snapped up, his eyes glowing vivid green. That answered one question. They were definitely dealing with a shifter. Probably the one who'd shredded Bell.

Well, on the bright side, they weren't dealing with a psychotic, out-of-control hybrid. Instead, they were up against a psychotic, completely in-control shifter. That was so much better.

"Police! Stop where you are, and let the woman go!" Chase ordered as he moved past Tate and farther into the living room in an attempt to cover everyone on the stairs.

Judging from the firm, authoritative tone of voice Chase used, the deputy was used to people doing exactly what he told them. Too bad it wasn't likely to work out that way this time.

Everyone did freeze, though, for all of three seconds. Then all hell broke loose.

One of the two goons on the stairs yanked Joanne against his chest like a human shield while the other leaned close for cover. In a blur, both men reached behind their backs and came out with a matching set of Micro Uzis. A split second later, the shifter launched himself off the second-floor landing, heading straight for Chase, eyes blazing, claws and fangs on full display.

Tate would have tried to shove the deputy out of the way, but before he could move, the living room exploded with the sound of two fully automatic submachine guns tearing the place apart. He barely avoided the hail of gunfire, darting into the kitchen just as the carpet in front of him was riddled with bullets.

Out of the corner of his eye, he saw the shifter hit Chase square in the chest. But instead of the graceful feline killer driving the cop down to the floor like he probably intended, the deputy rolled back with the impact, getting a foot planted in the shifter's gut at the same time and sending him flying over his head and bouncing him off the coffee table.

The shifter was up in a flash, rage twisting his features. Chase scrambled to his feet and ran full speed toward his attacker, driving him backward and straight through the big picture window in the living room. Breaking glass was accompanied by a few curses and a whole lot of growling, then both men disappeared from sight into the darkness.

Seeing their shifter buddy vanish like that must have stunned the two men on the stairs, because the shooting came to a sudden halt. Then again, maybe the men were just reloading. Micro Uzis tended to go through ammo quickly. Either way, Tate wasn't going to waste the opportunity.

He stepped into the living room and aimed at the gunman still holding Joanne up on the stairs, knowing he didn't have much of a target to work with. A couple of inches the wrong way and he'd completely miss the guy or hit Joanne instead. But he hit what the hell he was aiming at, clipping the guy in the shoulder. It wasn't a fatal shot, but it rattled the man enough to make him release Joanne and take a step back.

Joanne seized her chance. Swinging an elbow at the second man, she whacked him in the face, knocking him backward. The moment she was free, she hurried down the stairs.

Tate charged forward to meet her, popping a few more shots at the men on the steps at the same time. He ended up putting another 9mm through the leg of the guy he'd already shot in the shoulder. The man just about took a header off the stairs, but then a woman's arm suddenly reached out and yanked him back, practically picking the man up off his feet as she got him and the second guy out of the line of fire.

Even though her face was visible for barely a second, that was all the time it took for Tate to realize he'd seen her before. She was the wolf shifter Declan and Kendra had fought with back in February after the group she was with had tried to murder William Hamilton and his daughter. Tate and the rest of his team hadn't gotten there until everything was over and the female wolf shifter was long gone, but he'd seen photos of her afterward. While she might be attractive as hell, she was also a hired killer.

He aimed his weapon, ready to take a shot, but before he could fire, she and the two men disappeared from sight. He cursed. Everything in him wanted to go after them, but he still had Joanne to worry about. If the growls coming from outside were any indication, he needed to worry about Chase, too.

Tate urged Joanne into the kitchen, keeping an eye

on the landing above him in case the two men or the wolf shifter came back. But when he heard a window breaking up there, he knew the three of them had bailed. Which was kind of crazy, since they could have overwhelmed him by sheer numbers if they'd tried.

"Stay here," he told Joanne, then turned and raced across the living room, praying he wasn't too late to help Chase.

He dived out the window, tucking and rolling as his shoulders crunched through the broken glass littering the porch outside. He came up with his weapon ready just in time to see the feline shifter lean over the deputy, one of his clawed hands cocked back, ready to rip Chase's throat out.

Tate didn't have time to aim. He simply pulled the trigger, letting instinct guide him as he emptied his magazine at the shifter. He must have hit something, because the shifter staggered back a step and shot him a green-eyed look of pure rage.

For a second, it looked like the shifter was going to charge him before he could reload, but then Chase rolled over on the grassy lawn and grabbed his weapon, lying a few feet away. That was enough to convince the shifter it was time to go. With a growl of frustration, the man turned and darted for the main road. Chase tried to get a shot off at him, but the shifter was too fast. He disappeared into the darkness like a ghost. A few seconds later, there was a roar as the two SUVs tore off down the driveway and melted away into the night, one of them slowing only long enough to pick up the feline shifter. Tate reloaded in time to get a few rounds off in their direction. He didn't hit anything, but it made him feel better regardless.

Jaw tight, he shoved his gun back in the holster under his coat and walked over to Chase. "You going to live?"

The front of the deputy's uniform was shredded, but Tate didn't see any blood. That was only because the deputy had been wearing a bulletproof vest. Thank God, or he would have been screwed.

From where he still sat on the ground, Chase nodded. "Joanne Ward okay?"

"She's a little bruised and probably going to be sore as hell tomorrow, but she's alive," Tate said.

Chase nodded and reached out a hand for Tate to help him up. As he got to his feet, he glanced down at the tattered remains of his shirt and the Kevlar vest under it. Even in the darkness, it was impossible to miss the four perfectly aligned slash marks.

"Glad to hear that," Chase said as he fingered the sliced material that had barely protected his chest. "Now that we got the rescuing part out of the way, maybe it's time you tell me what the hell just happened. I've seen a lot of crap in my life, but nothing like that. The guy had frigging claws."

Sirens echoed in the distance, heading their way.

"Yeah, I guess it is time we have that talk." Tate glanced at Chase as they walked toward the house. "But before we go there, let me ask you a question. Are you more of a cat person or a dog person?"

———

It was well after dark by the time Tanner and Zarina walked into the prepper camp. He expected someone to remark on their absence, but as they moved slowly toward their cabin, no one said anything one way or the other. The

few people who were out and about nodded pleasantly in
their direction, then went back to what they were doing.

Zarina held his hand tightly in hers, and he could feel the
drumming of her pulse against his palm. Not that he needed
to feel the rapid thumping of her heartbeat to know she was
excited. The scent her body had been putting off during
their casual slow stroll through the woods told him everything he needed to know. Her arousal was so obvious, he
probably could have smelled it even if he wasn't a hybrid.

But as intoxicating as Zarina's scent was, it was the
simple, honest conversation they had as they walked that
did it for him. For the first time ever, he stopped tiptoe-
ing around the subject and admitted how much he cared
about her. And she'd done the same. While the word
love hadn't come up—neither of them seemed ready to
go there quite yet—they'd both admitted they needed
the other. That was a huge step. At least it was for him.
He'd spent a good part of the past three years pushing
everyone as far away as possible. He wasn't sure he
knew how to behave any other way around people anymore, especially someone as amazing as Zarina.

In addition to talking about their feelings, they'd also
discussed his PTSD and what they might be able to do
to get him help. He wasn't ready to go running into the
nearest VA clinic for a group therapy session, but maybe
he could handle a one-on-one setting with a psycholo-
gist if Zarina was there with him.

It was crazy, but a part of him was almost ready to
believe he could get to a point where he didn't have to
fear losing control and hurting the people he cared about
the most. He wasn't so delusional to think it would be
easy to get to that place, and he knew it would probably

take some time, but simply being able to imagine that day as a real possibility was pretty damn awesome.

Tanner was still lost in those thoughts when he realized they'd reached the cabin he and Zarina had shared the night before. Had it really been one day since they'd left the campsite behind and moved into the prepper cabin together? With all the emotional terrain they'd covered today, it felt like they'd been here weeks.

He turned and gazed down at Zarina, finding her looking up at him with excitement as well as a little hesitation.

"Hey." He reached out to tip her chin up, marveling at how her perfect, plump lips looked oh-so-kissable. "We don't have to jump into anything if you'd rather wait. We're not in any rush."

Zarina smiled and closed the distance between them until she was so close, he could feel the heat pouring off her body through the zipped-down opening of her jacket. "No more waiting. We've been putting this moment off for a year and a half. That's the textbook definition of not jumping into things."

He waited, checking for any reluctance in her voice or doubt in her eyes, but all he saw now was passion, need, and certainty. That was Zarina. When she knew what she wanted, she went after it and let nothing get in the way.

Even so, a part of him still worried he was making a mistake, that he should keep Zarina at arm's length for her own good. But he'd be lying if he said he didn't want this too, that the urge to pull her into his arms and lose himself in her body and soul was nearly overwhelming.

He reached out and tugged her forward the last few

inches until her breasts were pressed tight to his chest, then dipped his head and found her mouth with his. A growl immediately rumbled through his throat as her body melted against his and the delightful taste of her tongue scrambled his senses.

Tanner moved his lips urgently against hers, slipping his tongue in deep and playfully teasing every inch of her mouth as he glided his hands down and over her hips, finding his way to that perfect ass of hers by pure instinct. She whimpered, the sound making his cock tighten in his jeans and his fingertips tingle. He was on the edge of giving in to his hybrid and letting the animal come out to play, and it took everything in him to get a grip on the beast. He wanted Zarina so badly right then, he could barely think.

It wasn't until she started unbuttoning his flannel shirt that he realized they were damn close to having sex right there on the doorstep of the cabin.

While he wanted Zarina worse than anyone he'd ever been with, he knew they'd end up regretting it if their first time together came complete with an audience. He forced himself to pull away and take a step back.

"Maybe we'd better go inside before we draw a crowd?" he suggested hoarsely.

Zarina blinked, looking dazed. Then she gave him a sheepish smile. "I completely forgot where we were."

Tanner chuckled and reached around her, pushing the cabin door open. Inside, he moved across the small room and flipped the switch on the small lamp on the bedside table. Since it was being powered by nothing more than the small bank of batteries located behind the main hall and recharged each day by an equally small array of solar cells, the light wasn't very bright. But it would do.

Zarina had already lowered the piece of wood that barred the door of the cabin from the inside by the time he turned back to her. The sultry look she gave him made his jeans very uncomfortable all of a sudden.

She crossed the room and wrapped her arms around his neck, pressing her body teasingly against him. "Of all the places I imagined making love, a tiny cabin in the middle of the wilderness was definitely not one of them."

He couldn't help but smile. "So, you spent a lot of time imagining us making love?"

The look she gave him was hot enough to scorch his skin. "You have no idea."

He trailed his mouth along the curve of her jaw, then down the soft, perfect skin of her neck. "Actually, I have a really good idea, because I spent a lot of time thinking about it, too. What do you say we see if we can make our fantasies become reality?"

Skimming her coat off her shoulders, he tossed it aside, then undid the buttons on her shirt. As much as he wanted to tear them open, he forced himself to work slowly, revealing her creamy skin a little bit at a time. As he got his first glimpse of the mouthwatering curves of her bra-covered breasts, he had to remind himself he was in control of this, not his inner hybrid. He was going to take his time and enjoy the moment. But when her sexy belly button came into view, he had no choice but to say to hell with that.

With a groan, he dropped to his knees in front of her and buried his face in her taut tummy, kissing, licking, and nipping every square inch of exposed skin, especially that delightful belly button. He'd never realized that particular part of a woman's body did it for him, but

clearly hers did. He was so turned on, he had to fight to
keep his fangs from coming out as he traced the outline
of her navel with his tongue.

He forced himself to focus on pleasing Zarina, letting
his senses tune in to the quivering of her muscles, the rapid
beating of her heart, the surge and flow of the pheromones
her body was pumping out as he teased her. There was
no denying she was enjoying it. Her body was practically
singing with excitement. She even buried her hands in his
hair, holding him close and silently begging him to con-
tinue. Well, she wasn't all that silent. In fact, she let out a
few moans loud enough for anyone walking by outside to
hear. But if she didn't care, he sure as hell didn't. At this
moment, they were the only two people in the world.

As he dipped his tongue in her belly button, he carefully worked open her belt, then popped the top button
of her jeans. The scent that hit him then was so intoxicating, it was a battle to stay in control and not give in
to the animalistic urge to rip them off her.

He pulled back, taking a second to push his inner beast
further down into the recesses of his mind, then slowly
popped the remaining buttons of her jeans, kissing each
small section of skin that his efforts exposed. When his
mouth reached the top edge of her panties—and his
human mind was this close to taking a backseat to what
his hybrid half wanted—he stood and scooped Zarina into
his arms, carrying her over to the cabin's small bed. It
wasn't the king-sized one he would have preferred, but it
would definitely do for now. Then again, at that moment,
the cabin's floor would have worked just as well.

That image in mind, he set her gently down on the
bed. Face flushed and lips parted, she propped herself

up on her elbows and tracked the movements of his fingers as he unbuttoned his shirt. She looked so damn gorgeous lying there with her shirt hanging open and her jeans undone enough to show off her panties. This was going to be the most incredible night of his life, he could feel it.

Tossing his shirt on the chest at the foot of the bed, he slowly eased himself onto the bed with her. Zarina must have figured out he was being extra careful not to put too much of his weight on her, because she frowned.

"Don't you dare treat me like I'm made of glass," she chided. "You aren't going to hurt me, I promise."

Before he could say anything one way or the other, she grasped his shoulders, then pulled him down on top of her and kissed the hell out of him. When she spread her legs, he automatically settled between them. His erection was so hard, it hurt, but nothing had ever felt so right in his life. Even when the tips of his fangs slipped out unbidden, he knew this was where he was supposed to be.

He had just reached down between their bodies to unbuckle his belt when he heard shouting somewhere outside, accompanied by the thump of feet hitting the ground fast and hard. He ignored the sounds, telling himself it wasn't important, that being here with Zarina was the only thing that mattered.

"Tanner!" Spencer called even as he pounded on the door. "We just got a call over the radio from the camp south of Pyramid Mountain. They're under attack and need our help."

Shit.

Tanner dragged his mouth away from Zarina's and

lifted his head to find her looking up at him wide-eyed. He hesitated. If there was trouble, the last thing he wanted was to be separated from her.

"Tanner, let's go!" Spencer said, banging on the door again. "The camp up there is smaller than ours and doesn't have nearly the kind of firepower we do."

"Go," Zarina said softly. "They need you. I'll be okay here."

Even though he knew she was right, he still didn't move. The prepper camp north of them was nearly defenseless. *Shit*. He rolled off the bed and grabbed his shirt.

"Stay here and bar the door behind me when I leave," he ordered as he shrugged into it and buttoned it up.

He was at the door in two strides, ready to leave, when the beast inside forced him to turn back and look at Zarina. She was still lying where he'd left her, looking so damn beautiful, the thought of leaving her made his chest ache. But he had to go.

Cursing silently, he crossed the room and dropped to a knee beside the bed, leaning forward to kiss her hard. "I'll be as fast as I can, but I need to know you'll be smart and stay safe. Don't open the door for anyone but me."

She nodded, her eyes taking on a fierce glint. "You be careful, too. These people were able to grab one hybrid already. Don't take them lightly."

He wouldn't, but it wasn't his safety he was concerned about. He didn't care about anything except Zarina.

He kissed her again, then strode over to the door and yanked it open to find Spencer still waiting on the other side, two semiautomatic AR-15s in his hands.

The hybrid's eyes were glowing, and his fangs were extended. The guy was wound up already, and they hadn't even gotten involved in the fight yet. Tanner was going to have to keep an eye on the man, as well as any other hybrids coming with them. It wouldn't do anyone any good if the people helping lost control and hurt the people they were supposed to protect.

He and Spencer found Chad at the far end of the camp getting armed men loaded into the backs of three pickup trucks. Chad had already decided that while Malcolm could join Tanner and Spencer on the rescue team, Peter would stay there. That was smart as far as Tanner was concerned. They needed to keep at least one hybrid here for security.

Lillie was beside her father, checking the men as they climbed into the trucks, giving them words of encouragement and making sure they had enough ammo.

"How bad is it?" Tanner asked the older man.

Chad shook his head. "No way of knowing. They called the moment their perimeter guards picked up movement outside the camp. That was at least five minutes ago. You'll lead the men when you get them there?"

Tanner hated the idea of being responsible for any of these men in a fight, but he knew he couldn't avoid it. Who the hell else was going to do it if he didn't?

"I'll take care of them, but tell them it's their job to reinforce and defend the camp. Spencer, Malcolm, and I will get there first and worry about dealing with the attackers ourselves."

Chad frowned. "You aren't riding in the trucks with the others?"

"No. It's twelve miles to the Pyramid camp by truck but less than three if we go cross-country. We'll be much faster on foot," Tanner said, already envisioning the route he and the other hybrids would need to take as they crossed the four ridges that stood between them and the other encampment. "Make sure your guys know we'll be out there. I have no desire to get shot by any of them."

Giving Chad a nod, Tanner took off running, Spencer and Malcolm on his heels. He veered due north the moment they hit the wood line, heading in a nearly straight shot for the other prepper camp. Running full out up one mountainous ridge and straight down into the next valley would have been impossible if he and the others weren't hybrids. A normal human couldn't run up a nearly vertical rock outcropping or jump from a twenty-foot height to hit a steep slope. The pace bruised flesh and cracked bone on a hybrid. It would have killed anyone else.

As tree branches slapped his skin hard enough to draw blood, Tanner let his instincts guide him. With his mind free to wander, his thoughts immediately went to Zarina. The image of her lying back on the bed, hungry for his touch, immediately made him get hard all over again. Even with the stress of the moment pumping adrenaline through his body, one thought of her was all it took to excite him.

While he had no doubts about the direction he ran nor about what he'd do when he got to the other camp, when it came to the woman he loved, doubts abounded.

Was it right to leave her there? Was it right to sleep with her in the first place, knowing how dangerous it was to be around him? Was he simply setting them both up for pain and heartbreak later when things went bad and it turned out he would never be whole again? Even though Zarina made him think anything was possible, his life was scattered with dozens of moments when situations had gone bad and people he cared about paid the price.

Tanner determinedly shoved those thoughts from his mind as he got closer to the Pyramid camp. That's when he realized he'd outrun Spencer and Malcolm while he'd been lost in thoughts of Zarina. They were barely a minute behind him, so that was okay. Actually, he preferred it. This way, he could get there first and figure out what the hell was going on before the other hybrids arrived and complicated the situation.

He'd been hearing sporadic gunshots for the past few minutes, but by the time he got to the edge of the camp, near silence reigned. There was a lot of whimpering and crying coming from the people who lived there, but no sounds of fighting.

He let his nose guide him, tracking the scent of smokeless gunpowder to the far side of the camp and back into the wood line. He picked up the scents of several men within a few more feet. It was difficult to describe how he knew it was the bad guys. They had a different smell to them—commercial cleansers in their clothing combined with the persistent stench of blood.

Tanner passed three injured preppers as he tracked the intruders' scents, one woman and two men. All of them were alive, but they were in too much pain to do much more than point farther into the woods as he ran past them. He kept going, knowing Spencer and the others would find the wounded people and get them back to the camp.

He found five of the bad guys a mile later. They walked casually toward two large SUVs parked on the road, their weapons down at their sides as if they didn't

fear a counterattack. All the men wore military-grade
tactical gear and night-vision goggles. Tanner frowned.
They looked more like people the DCO would tangle
with, not a group of preppers out doing their best to live
their lives completely separate from the rest of the world.

Four of the raiders were dragging two unconscious
preppers behind them by their heels, bouncing their
limp bodies across the ground like they couldn't care
less how much it was going to hurt the guys. Tanner bit
back a growl as his fangs slipped out. He wanted to kill
these assholes in the very worst way possible.

A fifth man trailed slightly behind, like he was pulling rear security. Except it was obvious he wasn't worried about anyone coming after them. He wasn't even
paying attention to his six.

Tanner didn't slow down as he caught up to the tail-
end Charlie—the last guy in the group. Reaching around
to grab the mounting post of his NVGs, he savagely
twisted the man's head around backward. The snapping
sound was as loud as a gunshot in the relatively quiet
forest but disappeared into the shadows like a ghost
before the body had even hit the ground and the other
four men had spun around to see what the hell happened.

Tanner hoped for a few seconds of what-the-fuck
confusion. But at least one of the remaining men knew
what he was doing. He immediately ordered the others
to drop the unconscious baggage they'd been hauling,
then spread out and get to their SUVs fast.

His inner beast growling in irritation, Tanner stepped
out from behind the tree he'd been waiting behind and
started popping off shots at the retreating figures. He hit
two of them, though not mortally. Unfortunately, they

all retained discipline, the injured duo laying down a heavy suppressive fire in his direction while the healthy ones helped them keep moving.

Spencer and Malcolm showed up then, but the bad guys made it to their vehicles anyway. Tanner charged forward and put a few more rounds into one of the guys as the bastard clambered into the SUV. The instinct to chase after fleeing prey was tough to ignore—not to mention the desire to go after the shitheads and end this right now—but he wasn't there to kill people; he was there to save some. At the moment, he was more worried about the two unconscious preppers lying on the ground in the middle of the crossfire than in getting revenge.

He put enough rounds in the escaping vehicles to discourage them from stopping, then ran to the injured men along with Spencer and Malcolm. He knew there was something odd going on the moment he approached the deathly still men. Both were young and healthy, strong looking and in their late twenties. There were no obvious wounds on them, but they weren't moving. Even their heartbeats were slow. Too slow.

Spencer and Malcolm must have thought the same thing, because they looked worried as they kneeled beside the unconscious men. Tanner frowned as he realized he recognized both guys. He'd talked to them more than a few times since moving back to the forest. They were good people.

"What's wrong with them?" Malcolm whispered.

Tanner was about to say he had no idea and that they should get both men back to Zarina as fast as they could, but then he saw a flash of metal buried in one of the men's coats. Curious, he reached down and pulled a pencil-thick metal tube with a needle on the end. Even in the pitch blackness of the heavily forested area, he could see the little bead of milky white liquid dripping from the tip of the needle. He sniffed the air, not wanting to get too close to the stuff. He had no idea what it was, but it had a distinctly medicinal stench to it.

"I think they've been drugged," he said. "Tranquilized."

Tanner checked the second man and found a similar dart.

"Holy crap." Spencer growled. "They were darted like frigging animals in a zoo."

While Spencer and Malcolm picked up the unconscious men and headed back to the Pyramid camp, Tanner searched the man he'd killed, hoping he'd find an ID. Unfortunately, he didn't have any on him. In fact, he didn't have a damn thing in any of his pockets. That, along with the military buzz-cut hairstyle and the army infantry badge tattooed on the left side of the guy's chest, told Tanner everything he needed to know. The guy was former military for sure, which meant he could be a mercenary or even a fed. The gear and submachine gun were certainly top-of-the-line stuff that the government might issue.

Back at the Pyramid camp, Tanner discovered the rest of Chad's men had arrived and were loading the injured preppers into the backs of the pickup trucks. He glanced at the blond woman he'd seen out in the woods earlier. She'd been hit in the shoulder and was bleeding badly. It looked like a serious wound, and they made sure she was in the first vehicle heading back to Chad's camp. Other than the hair color, the woman didn't resemble Zarina at all, and yet she reminded Tanner of her anyway.

Swallowing hard, he turned away, watching as

people ran around the camp, helping the wounded and consoling crying children even as they packed up to move everyone to Chad's camp. Tanner wondered if they realized how lucky they'd been. They'd gone up against five heavily armed men who were much better trained and equipped than the preppers would ever be. If those men had wanted to, they could have killed every man, woman, and child in this camp.

But for some reason, all they had done was tranquilize and drag away two of the healthiest males, like they'd been culling the fittest members of the group. Or merely trying to scare the shit out of these people by showing they could walk right in here and waltz out with anyone they pleased.

Another possibility suddenly occurred to Tanner, freezing his guts. What if this had been nothing more than an elaborate distraction staged to get everyone running in the wrong direction? If so, it had worked, because at that moment, most of the men from Chad's camp were here instead of protecting their own place.

Shit.

Tanner almost went through a total shift right on the spot at the realization that he'd left Zarina nearly defenseless.

"Get everyone loaded up as fast as possible, then get them back to our camp," he called out to Spencer as he ran for the forest. "I'm going there now."

Worry filled Spencer's eyes. "Is something wrong?"

Tanner knew why the hybrid was concerned. If Zarina was in trouble, so was Lillie. He didn't answer. Instead, he ran, letting his body shift in an effort to gain every ounce of speed he could muster.

Chapter 9

"YES, SIR, I'M AWARE I WAS OUT OF MY JURISDICTION," Chase said calmly into his cell phone. "But the people shooting at me didn't seem to care about the fact that they weren't allowed to kill me while I'm outside Oxford County."

Tate bit his tongue to keep from laughing. The deputy had been on the phone with the sheriff for the past ten minutes as they sat in the patrol car in a store parking lot off Highway 101. To say the conversation had not gone well was an understatement.

Apparently, one of the cops on the scene at Joanne Harvey's residence had called Sheriff Bowers and given him a fairly good rundown of everything that happened, including the parts about the machine-gun-wielding bad guys, the shattered living room window, and the shredded bulletproof vest. Chase had tried to downplay the severity of the incident, but the sheriff had been in no mood to be pacified. He definitely didn't find any of this amusing, no matter how much sarcasm Chase dumped into his explanation.

"No, sir, I don't think this is funny," Chase said, his jaw clenching. Bowers had been grilling him hard, and it was obvious the deputy had taken about as much as he could handle. "But if I remember right, Sheriff, you're the one who told me to keep an eye on Agent Evers and his investigation. When he decided to go first to the medical center in Scarborough, then Joanne Harvey's house, I had to go with him even if it was outside our jurisdiction. I never expected to get into a shoot-out."

Anger was starting to seep into Chase's voice, but Tate knew it wasn't only the third degree he was getting from his boss that was pissing the deputy off. A lot of it probably had to do with the fact that he and Chase had spent the next hour buried in questions, giving answers no one quite believed. A little while later, Bowers had called.

"It's fortunate I did go with him," Chase added, "or it's likely Joanne Harvey and Agent Evers would be dead right now."

Tate snorted. The way he remembered it, Chase had been the one close to getting snuffed, not him.

"No, sir, there's no one else in the car with me," Chase said, shooting Tate a look that blatantly suggested he keep his opinions to himself. "Evers called it a night, so I'm heading home… No, I still have no idea exactly where this is all going. All I can say for sure is Bell was involved with some very bad people, and it got him killed."

When Chase finally hung up several minutes later, he stared silently out the windshield for a while, likely contemplating how much trouble he was going to be in when his boss figured out Chase had been lying his ass off about almost everything, including the part about him heading home now instead of out to Bell's second residence. The one nobody but his personal research assistant had known about. Yeah, lying to your boss like that could get a cop fired pretty damn quick.

After another moment, the deputy put the car in gear

and pulled out of the parking lot and back onto the highway, heading toward Lewiston.

"We'll be crossing the Androscoggin River in a few miles," Chase said. "We should see the turnoff for Bell's after that."

Tate nodded. After rescuing Joanne Harvey from her attackers, the woman had been more than willing to tell them everything she knew about Dr. Bell, including the fact that the man had two homes. The small apartment near the medical center was where he spent most of his evenings after work. It was the address he listed on all the hospital paperwork and the only place associated with his name from a property tax perspective. Joanne had been there many times and told them it was essentially nothing more than a place to sleep. However, Bell had a much bigger home outside Lewiston where he stayed when he wanted to get away from everything. The house had been owned by his parents and was currently managed by a trust set up in their names. That's why no one at the hospital knew about it. Apparently, no one else did either, since Kendra hadn't come up with anything on it. Joanne was sure Bell was in a relationship with someone but said he'd been a very private man and she respected that privacy.

"Okay, let me see if I have this right," Chase said. "There are these shifter creatures in the world that are half human, half animal. They look completely normal but have all these incredible abilities, not to mention fangs and claws. This guy who jumped on me at Joanne's house and just about ripped me apart was a shifter, right?"

The deputy was clearly handling this better than Tate thought he would. "Batting a thousand so far."

"Then there are hybrids, people who psycho doctors like Mahsood tried to turn into man-made shifters thanks to financial backing from rich, powerful people like Rebecca Brannon," Chase continued. "With Bell's background in genetics, I'm guessing you think he and Mahsood were working together on one of these hybrid projects?"

Damn, this guy was quick. Tate had touched on every one of those subjects but hadn't tied them together in the neat bundle the way Chase already had. But before Tate could tell the deputy he was impressed, the cop spoke again.

"You said hybrids can have control issues, which probably means a hybrid wasn't responsible for Bell's murder, since he was tortured, not butchered. That leaves us with the shifter who attacked me or the one on the stairs you told me about. Unless you think Rebecca's daughter did it. Is she a shifter or a hybrid? I'm guessing a hybrid since Mahsood was experimenting on her."

"Actually, Ashley's a coyote shifter," Tate corrected. "But beyond that, you nailed everything else. I gotta say, you're processing this much better than I thought you would, and I'd already pegged you for a pretty sharp cop."

Chase let out a snort. "I'm a marine. Improvising and adapting to our environment is what we're trained to do. But if Rebecca's daughter is already a shifter, why was Mahsood experimenting on her?"

"To figure out how her shifter genes work and take DNA samples from her," Tate said. "Rebecca and Mahsood have had Ashley locked up in that mental facility outside Old Town since the girl was a teenager. She's in her midtwenties now."

"Crap, that's cold." Chase frowned. "Also puts her at the top of the suspect list. I know I'd be pissed as hell if my mother locked me in a mental institution for a decade or so and had doctors experiment on me. Mahsood in particular would be first in line for an ass whooping."

"I agree," Tate said. "But unfortunately, I get the feeling Mahsood is the kind of man who makes lots of people want to whoop his ass. Ashley might have killed Bell as a way to get to Mahsood, but it could just as easily have been those people at Joanne's place, whoever the hell they were. All I can say for sure about them is they're definitely hired guns, either paid by someone wanting to kick-start their own hybrid program or slow down Rebecca's. Bottom line, we don't know enough to jump to conclusions about any of our suspects yet."

Chase nodded and fell silent. They both stayed that way as they crossed over the river and turned onto Highway 126, then headed east.

"One thing you didn't mention, and maybe you can't talk about it," Chase said, glancing at him. "This part of Homeland you work for. All you do there is hunt down shifters and hybrids and kill them?"

Tate hadn't expected that question, and it took a second to regain his balance. Some of it had to do with the barely hidden tone of disapproval in Chase's voice, but most of it had to do with the fact that hunting down rogue shifters and hybrids is what Tate and his former team had spent a good portion of their time doing. It was something that needed doing, but it wasn't always a job Tate necessarily liked.

"The people I work for don't go out of their way to hunt down shifters or hybrids and hurt them. In fact, it's the reverse," he said. "We look for these special people, because they make damn good agents. But I'll be honest with you. Sometimes these special people do bad things just like anyone else. When that happens, people like me are sent out to deal with them, because the normal police aren't equipped to handle them."

"Have you ever had to kill any of them?" Chase asked.

There was no point in lying. It seemed like an odd question for a former marine, especially one who'd seen as many deployments as Chase. "Unfortunately, yes. But only when there was no other option. You have a problem with killing?"

"Yeah." Chase looked at him, his expression carefully devoid of emotion. "Only a sociopath kills without remorse or regret."

Tate locked eyes with the other man for a few seconds before Chase turned his attention back to the dark, tree-lined highway. "And?"

"And I'm wondering if you look at these shifters and hybrids as something less than human and therefore somehow easier to kill?" Chase answered. "Because while only a sociopath enjoys killing, in my experience, the world is full of sociopaths."

It wasn't until that moment that Tate realized how much Chase reminded him of Landon Donovan, the current deputy director of the DCO and former Special Forces captain who had a habit of asking pointed questions and leading the way when it came to doing the right thing, even when it came at a steep cost.

"I have a friend who's a two-hundred-and-seventy-pound bear shifter and another who's a coyote shifter and sarcastic as hell. I have another friend who's a big hybrid, and he's totally terrifying when he loses control. I don't judge people by the shape of their fingernails. I judge them by their character," Tate told him. "Yes, I've killed shifters and hybrids, as well as regular humans. But every one of them died for a reason, and that reason always included keeping someone else safe."

More silence reigned before Chase finally looked at him again, the corners of his mouth edging up.

"I think we'll get along just fine then," he said.

Tate blew out a breath. "Thank God. Because that's what I've been worrying about the entire night. The thought that we might not get along brings tears to my eyes."

Chase chuckled and turned into a driveway.

Five minutes later, Tate was picking the lock on the back door of a big two-floor colonial. Red brick, black shutters, and nice landscaping. No wonder Bell kept this place off his official records. The taxes must be a bear.

He pulled his weapon as he led the way inside. Beside him, Chase did the same. A quick sweep of the house told them no one was there. Tate holstered his gun as he wandered back into the kitchen. The place was neat and tidy, right down to its pristine chandeliers. No shock there. Bell's office had been spotless, too.

Curious, he wandered over to the brushed nickel trash can that probably cost as much as his big-screen TV at home and pressed on the foot pedal. The doctor had been dead long enough for things to start getting ripe in a normal person's trash, but this one didn't smell at all. The can was empty except for a frozen dinner package and a plastic tray with the remains of some kind of pasta dish that looked like it had been thrown out only a couple of hours ago.

Intrigued, Tate opened the dishwasher. Water droplets clung to the plastic containers lined up neatly on the upper rack. Someone had been eating leftovers, then was nice enough to wash the dishes.

It probably hadn't been Bell, since dead people didn't eat pasta. Or wash dishes.

"Tate, you might want to come into the living room and take a look at this."

Closing the dishwasher, Tate walked into a living room that would make Martha Stewart swoon in approval to find Chase looking at a framed photo on the far wall.

He glanced at Tate over his shoulder. "I think I finally figured out who Bell was in a relationship with."

The photo was a close-up of Bell and Mahsood sitting on a small sailboat, the wind tousling their hair as one of them took the selfie. Mahsood had an arm thrown around the other doctor's shoulder, and Bell looked genuinely happy. Hell, Mahsood looked happy, too.

"This probably explains why Bell was tortured," Chase said.

"I guess so," Tate agreed. "Either Ashley or the mercenaries we ran into at Joanne's place knew about Mahsood and Bell's relationship and carved up the doctor to try to get him to talk. But if the signs of recent activity in the kitchen are any indication, they didn't get what they wanted. Mahsood is still in town."

Zarina lowered the big wood crossbar across the cabin door the moment Tanner left, then climbed in bed and prayed he'd be okay out there. The bed was still warm from his recent departure, and she pulled the blanket around her shoulders, trying to ward off the chill. The small cabin had seemed so much warmer when he'd been with her. She knew there was no scientific basis for that, but it was true nonetheless.

Shouting came from outside the cabin followed by the sound of vehicles speeding out of camp. She pictured Tanner in one of those vehicles, speeding toward danger.

Zarina cursed. If she let her mind wander too far in that direction, it would drive her insane with worry. Instead, she forced herself to think much more pleasant thoughts, specifically the things she and Tanner had been doing right there in bed.

Her lips still felt deliciously abraded from where the scruff on his jaw had rubbed against her as they kissed. She smiled. She'd never been kissed with such complete and utter abandon like that before. The memory of how his strong hands had caressed her body at the same time as he'd teased her with his mouth almost made her moan.

And when Tanner had dropped to his knees in front of her and kissed her belly button? There weren't words to describe how amazing that had been. Heat had pooled between her thighs the moment he'd pressed his lips to her navel. She'd been so turned on, it was unreal. It had only gotten better when he'd unbuckled her belt and begun kissing and licking his way downward. For a moment there, she thought she might actually orgasm with her clothes still on.

She'd been with other men, but it had never been like this with any of them. Then again, she'd never experienced a man like Tanner. He was beyond special.

Zarina had known that about him from the moment she'd slipped into his cell in the ski lodge right before those crazy doctors had shown up to give him another injection. She'd been shocked he'd survived the first dose of hybrid serum and knew the chance of him making it through a second without help from her was slim to none. So she'd rushed in with a sedative mixture that she hoped would keep his body from tearing itself apart and another drug cocktail she'd put together to drop his heart rate down low enough so they'd think he'd died. If he didn't die for real. It had been a risky plan, but it had been the only thing she'd been able to come up.

Zarina wrapped the blanket more tightly around her, remembering it like it had been yesterday. Tanner had been strapped to a gurney, his shirtless chest straining as he'd growled and fought to pull his arms loose from the heavy manacles holding him down. As she'd leaned over him, his eyes glowed vivid red and his fangs extended, but they'd both disappeared the moment she told him she was going to save him. He'd stared at her wide-eyed before telling her it was too dangerous, that she was putting herself at risk and should get out of the cell before it was too late.

That was the first indication of how amazing Tanner truly was. He'd been terrified, in horrible pain, and mere seconds away from being given a drug that would almost certainly kill him, and yet he'd been more worried about her than he'd been about himself. As she'd learned in the weeks and months following that day, that was simply the kind of man Tanner was. Courageous, fearless, gentle, and unselfish.

Zarina wasn't exactly sure when she'd fallen in love with Tanner, but there came a point when she had stopped thinking about him as someone who needed her help and instead began seeing him as someone she wanted to spend her life with. That was why she'd come out here. Not merely to deliver the antiserum, but to spend her life with him. Admittedly, it had been tough breaking through the damn wall he'd built up around himself, but now that she had, she wasn't going to let him build it back up again.

It had been difficult hearing about what had happened to him in Afghanistan, then afterward here in Washington, but she was glad he'd told her. Not only had it helped her understand what was going on with him, but it had also been good for him to get it off his chest. During the walk back to camp, Zarina noticed a lot of the tension that had been a near-constant companion for Tanner for as long as she'd known him had disappeared.

Unfortunately, hearing the other prepper camp was under attack had immediately made him tense all over again. She only hoped everything would be okay. As soon as Tanner was back in her arms, they'd see about getting those tight muscles relaxed again.

She was still thinking about all the things they could do to make that happen when an urgent knocking at the door made her jump.

"Zarina, are you in there? It's Lillie."

She threw off the blanket and was halfway to the door before she remembered her promise to Tanner that she wouldn't open the door to anyone but him. That was before Lillie, or someone else in the camp, might be in trouble.

Zarina shoved the lock bar up and pushed it aside, then yanked open the door to find Lillie standing there holding a handgun that looked way too big for her.

"Dad sent me to round everyone up and get them to the main building," Lillie said. "It's sturdier and easier to defend."

Zarina nodded. "I'll help you look for stragglers. Let me grab my coat."

Picking it up from the floor where Tanner had dropped it when he'd undressed her earlier, she slipped into it, then stopped, her gaze locking on her backpack. Tanner might not be interested in taking the antiserum anytime soon, but it was still too valuable to leave lying around. Grabbing it from the floor, she slung it over her shoulders.

"Here," Lillie said, holding out a gun to her.

It was much smaller than the one Lillie was carrying, but it was still a weapon. That kind of worried Zarina.

"I don't really know how to use a gun," she admitted.

Lillie didn't so much as bat an eye as she shoved her weapon into a holster on her hip. Zarina was relatively certain it was the automatic kind, but she was only guessing. Not that she knew what that meant. She might work for a covert organization, but she was a doctor, not a soldier. She couldn't be expected to know things like that.

"This is a basic revolver, so all you have to do is point and shoot." Lillie attached a small holster to Zarina's belt, then stepped back and pointed at a little piece of metal sticking out on the side of the gun. "This is the cylinder release. Just push it to swing the cylinder out. Like this." She nudged the cylinder out, showing Zarina the backside of the five bullets. "If you have to reload, point the weapon up and push here. The shells will fall out. Put five more back in, then close the cylinder. Once it snaps into place, you're ready to go. There's no safety, so all you have to do is point it in the direction of the bad guys and then squeeze the trigger."

Lillie pushed the cylinder back in and held it out to Zarina again. She carefully took it from the girl, then stared down at it, her fingers as far away from the trigger as she could get them without dropping the thing.

"I'm not sure I could do that," she whispered. "Shoot someone, I mean."

"It's hard to do, so I get that," Lillie said. "If you can't shoot, then run like hell. Just remember there might be a time when you can't run, and you'll have to decide what you're capable of doing to protect yourself or someone you care about."

Lillie turned and walked out of the cabin, moving quickly and deliberately across the camp. As Zarina hurried after her, she couldn't help wonder if she would ever be as confident and sure as the younger woman if she found herself in one of those situations Lillie had just described. Zarina prayed she never found herself in a position where she had to find out.

Chapter 10

TANNER'S HEART WAS POUNDING LIKE A DRUM BY THE TIME he ran into Chad's camp and raced for the cabin he and Zarina shared. It was possible his elevated pulse might have something to do with the fact that he'd run back from the other camp at breakneck speed. He'd nearly killed himself half a dozen times over by jumping off cliffs and outcroppings he never would have normally tried in an effort to get there faster.

That wasn't why his heart was beating so fast, though. It was fear that he'd be too late and get to the camp to find that those guys with the guns had attacked and Zarina was already dead.

But there was no indication the camp had been attacked. No scent of gunfire or strangers. No stench of panic. That didn't keep Tanner from sprinting for the cabin anyway, only to slide to a stop when he realized the door was wide open. He burst inside, looking around wildly, but Zarina was nowhere to be seen.

His clawed hands clenched and unclenched as his inner beast fought to take control. The animal wanted to tear apart the camp piece by piece until it found Zarina. Tanner cursed and shoved the beast back, desperate to get the thing under control. He needed his human half in charge right now, not a raging hybrid.

It took a few seconds, but he got the animal into its cage so he could think clearly. That's when he picked

up Zarina's scent—along with everyone else's—coming
from the main building. They must have barricaded
themselves in there in case trouble came this way.

Not a bad plan if it wasn't for the fact that he'd told
Zarina to stay put before he'd left. Then again, why the
hell did he think she'd do a damn thing he'd told her?
She never had before.

Tanner strode toward the big building, claws and
fangs retracting. He was still a few feet away when the
door opened and Peter stuck his head out, relief mixed
with worry on his face.

"Are you the only one back?"

"The others will be here soon," Tanner said, walking
past Peter into the meeting house/dining hall. "They're
transporting the wounded."

Chad intercepted him before he could take more
than a few steps. Tanner ignored him for the moment,
focused instead on finding Zarina. He let his nose guide
him, following her scent to the far corner of the big open
building. She and Lillie were surrounded by a bunch of
scared-looking kids. As if feeling his gaze on her, Zarina
lifted her head and looked his way. Smiling at him, she
said something to the kids, then detached herself from the
group and moved in his direction. His heart slowed drasti-
cally at the sight of her until he realized she was wearing
a gun on her hip. What the hell was she doing with a gun?
She didn't have the first clue how to even use one. Not
that she had any business using a weapon in the first place.

He started toward her, but Chad sidestepped to block
his path. "How bad was it? Was anyone badly hurt?"

Tanner resisted the urge to pick Chad up and physically move him out of the way. He knew the older man

was simply worried. The prepper communities up here were like an extended family, and like family, they looked out for each other.

"No one from here was injured," Tanner said as Zarina reached them, Lillie at her heels. "But the other camp took some serious injuries. Five people, three with gunshot wounds."

"I'll get the medical supplies set up in Lorraine's cabin," Lillie said. "It worked well as an operating room before. We can make it work again."

Zarina nodded as Lillie hurried off, then looked at Tanner. "You said five people were injured. What happened to the other two?"

"They were hit with some kind of tranquilizer darts. They were still unconscious when I left."

"Tranquilized?" Chad's eyes filled with confusion. "Why?"

"I don't know," Tanner admitted. "All I can say for sure is that whoever attacked the camp was in the process of dragging them away when I got there."

Tanner hadn't realized that the rest of the building had gone quiet until surprised chatter suddenly filled the silence. Chad frowned and turned to field questions, even though he had no answer to most of them. Tanner used the interruption to finally focus on Zarina.

"Why the hell do you have a gun?" he demanded.

She lifted her chin to look up at him. Something told him she didn't like the question. "Why do you think?"

"Dammit, Zarina. This isn't a game." He stepped closer and lowered his voice. "There are some seriously bad guys out there. They're well trained and heavily armed, and they haven't shown any hesitation when it comes to hurting

people. You're not some kind of comic book superhero.
You should have stayed in the cabin like I told you."

Her brows rose. "Like you told me? What am I, your
pet?"

"That's not what I meant, and you know it."

She folded her arms. "Then what did you mean?"

This wasn't how this conversation was supposed to
go. "Just that I want you safe."

"You mean you want me to stay all safe and tucked
away while you go out and risk yourself for others."

He ran his hand through his hair. Why was she turning this around on him? Couldn't she see how terrified
he was at the thought of something happening to her?
"Zarina, you know how much you mean to me. You
have to be careful."

"And you don't?" she demanded, her voice rising.
A few of the preppers looked their way. "We've been
together long enough for you to know me. If someone
is in trouble, I'm going to help them the same as you
would. I'd never expect anything less of you, so don't
expect anything less of me."

He was trying to come up with a reasonable response
to that when a ringing noise interrupted him. He frowned.
None of the preppers had cell phones, so where the hell
was it coming from?

When the sound came again, he realized it was from
Zarina's backpack. The satellite phone. She must have
figured it out at the same time, because she shrugged
the bag off her shoulder and quickly dug the phone out.

"This is Zarina Sokolov."

She said it so tentatively that Tanner would have
smiled if he wasn't still mad at her. He guessed she

wasn't used to answering a DCO satellite phone. But the urge to grin disappeared the moment he recognized the voice on the other end of the line.

"It's Cam," Zarina said, holding the phone out to him. "He said he needs to talk to you, that it's urgent."

Ignoring the curious looks Chad and the other preppers were giving him and Zarina, he took the phone from her and put it to his ear. "What's up, Cam?"

"I tracked down two of the missing preppers and three of the homeless people you mentioned," his brother said. "It took a while, because the descriptions you gave me were the only thing I had to work with, but once I found the first one, locating the others went faster."

"And?" Tanner prompted, even though he had a feeling he already knew the answer.

"Two of the men and a woman washed up along different stretches of the west shore of Lake Washington. The other two guys were found way over in Elliott Bay. Without any IDs on them, they all ended up getting labeled as John and Jane Does and their cases put on the back burner, but when I started poking around, the ME office noticed the connection and started digging. He says that all five victims were beaten to death."

Tanner cursed. "Were any of them drugged?"

"Yeah," Cam said. "How'd you know about that? Even if you could get TV up there, we're keeping that detail out of the news."

Tanner took a deep breath and told him about the attack that had just happened and the men he'd seen trying to kidnap the preppers. "I don't know what they're doing with the people they're grabbing, but I recognize professionals when I see them."

"Dammit, Tanner, what the hell is going on up there?" Cam demanded. "I'm trying to do what you asked and keep this low-key, but it's starting to get out of hand. My captain thinks this is gang-related and that I know more than I'm saying. I don't know how much longer I can keep the lid on this, especially if more bodies show up."

Tanner sighed. "I understand. Try to give me a little more time, but don't do anything to risk your career. Let me know if you hear anything else."

"Was that the police?" Chad asked, his jaw tight.

Tanner nodded. "Yeah. My brother. He's a cop with the Seattle PD."

Chad cursed, his fists clenching like he wanted to punch something. Probably him. "Dammit, Tanner. I trusted you! You know how we feel about cops. You promised you wouldn't get them involved."

Tanner could have pointed out he never promised not to get the cops involved, just the feds. But the distinction would likely be lost on the man. Besides, none of that mattered now.

"Yeah, well, they are involved, so you need to get the hell over it," Tanner said. In the background, his inner hybrid was pacing back and forth in its cage restlessly. It wanted out—bad. "While you're standing here worrying about the authorities rousing your people, someone is out there right now picking you off one or two at a time. This is bigger than your damn paranoia, Chad. There are some sickos out there tranquilizing and murdering your friends. The Seattle ME has five bodies in their morgue, and two of them are preppers. Someone beat them to death, then dumped their bodies."

Chad's shoulders sagged, the color draining from his face as he sank down onto the closest bench. "Why the hell is this happening? Why would someone do something like this?"

Tanner sighed. "I have no idea." He moved closer to Chad while keeping one eye on Zarina. She was staying put, but likely only until the vehicles full of injured arrived from the other camp. "Is there any chance you or anyone else pissed someone off?"

Chad shook his head. All around the building, everyone else did the same. Tanner thought as much.

Outside, the trucks started arriving from the other camp. When Zarina headed for the door, Tanner immediately followed.

"I need to talk to you," he said as he fell into step beside her.

She kept walking. "I don't have time to talk right now. There are injured people coming in, and I have to get ready for surgery."

"I know, and I'm not stopping you," he said. "I just want you to know I'm taking you back to Seattle and putting you on the first plane to DC."

Zarina stopped outside Lorraine's cabin to glare at him. "You'll only be wasting your time, because I'm not going."

With that, she spun on her heel and walked into the cabin. A moment later, Spencer ran up carrying the wounded girl from the other camp and disappeared inside as well, leaving Tanner standing there alone with the memory of Zarina's words for company.

Seeing the injured woman with hair the same color as Zarina's only firmed his resolve. He didn't care what he had to do; he was putting her on a plane tomorrow.

"So you think Mahsood somehow heard about Joanne Harvey getting attacked and decided to bail in case she gave up this address to somebody?" Chase asked, flipping the light on as they walked down the narrow stairs to the basement of Bell's home.

The basement was the only part of the house they hadn't gone through yet, and Tate hoped they'd find something useful down here. Because the rest of the house had been a bust. Beyond the two toothbrushes in the bathroom, a closet full of clothes that wouldn't have fit Bell, and several dozen banking documents with Mahsood's name on them confirming he'd indeed lived here, they hadn't discovered anything worthwhile. From the clothes hangers lying on the bedroom floor and dresser drawers half open, it looked like Mahsood had recently packed a bag and left in a hurry.

"It's as good a guess as any," Tate said. "Ultimately, it doesn't matter. While I'm fairly confident we're right about Mahsood being the real target here, nothing we've found tonight gets us any closer to him or Bell's killer. For all we know, Mahsood may have already left the country. He has a history of doing that. Plus, with Bell gone, I can't imagine where else a man like Mahsood could be hiding. He's a doctor, not a spy. He doesn't have the training to stay off the radar and survive for long."

"Any chance he's getting help from Rebecca?" Chase asked. "You said Mahsood has been on her payroll for a while."

"Maybe." Tate said. "He's being hunted for damn sure, so it would make sense that he'd turn to the woman who's been paying the bills for all these years. Hell, if it wasn't for his relationship with Bell, I would have said that's why Mahsood came back to Maine. Something doesn't feel right about this."

Tate did a double take when he reached the basement. The place wasn't some kind of dank hole in the ground used for storing Christmas decorations and old magazines nobody had the heart to get rid of. Disappointingly, it also wasn't any kind of hybrid lab either. There wasn't a holding cell, hospital gurney, or tray of evil gleaming medical equipment in sight. Instead, Bell's basement was a tidy office space. The walls were lined with metal shelving units filled with file boxes while an expensive desk and computer occupied the center of the room alongside a long table.

"What do you mean, doesn't feel right?" Chase asked, glancing around.

Tate shrugged. "I don't know. It just seems to me if Rebecca was interested in taking care of him, what the hell was he doing hiding in his boyfriend's house, living off leftovers?"

Chase seemed to consider that for a moment before nodding. "I see your point. We're missing something here."

"Obviously." Tate walked over to the shelving unit nearest the computer desk and chose a heavy cardboard box at random. "Maybe we'll get lucky and something in one of these boxes will help us figure out what we're missing."

"Wouldn't it be a better idea to check out the computer first?"

Tate set the box on the desk and took off the lid. "Probably, but I don't have the first clue how to hack a computer. How about you?"

Chase lifted a brow. "You're kidding, right? I don't even have a password on my computer at home because I can never remember it."

"That's why I always write mine down," Tate agreed, pulling out his phone. "I'll have the intel people back in DC hack into it from their end while we dig through these boxes."

The cop walked over and selected a box. "If we open up the first few of these boxes and find nothing but old tax records, I'm going home, and you can find your own way back to the hotel."

But they didn't find old tax records. Instead, they discovered a good portion of Mahsood's adult life chronicled in photos, newspaper articles, awards, personal letters, and lab journals. The stuff led them on a convoluted journey as a man with a promising medical career decided to create monsters for money for no other reason than because he could. Tate understood Bell and Mahsood had been involved, but he couldn't understand why Bell would keep crap like this in his basement. If anyone had ever seen it, somebody would be going to jail. Or losing their medical license at least.

"Damn. You have to look at this," Chase said from where he sat on the other end of the table, folders scattered everywhere. "I did not see this coming."

Tate pushed his chair back and walked over to Chase's side of the table. While he'd focused his attention on the past ten years of Mahsood's life, the deputy had been sorting through the stuff from his college days.

Chase held up a picture that stopped Tate in his tracks. At first, he thought he was looking at Ashley, but then he realized it was a very young Rebecca Brannon cuddled in the arms of an equally young Mahsood. The doctor's jet-black hair was longer than it was now, and he had his shirt unbuttoned halfway down his chest to show off several gold necklaces.

"Yup, Mahsood and Rebecca used to be a thing," Chase said with a laugh. "Pretty serious based on the number of photos in here."

Tate took the picture, looking more closely at it. Rebecca and Mahsood were leaning against the railing of an outdoor deck. The fancy house it was connected to was just visible to one side while the blue-green water of a sun-dappled lake comprised the rest of the background.

"Any idea how long they were an item?" he asked Chase.

The cop motioned at the folders on the table. "Maybe four or five years, most of it while they were in college. There are lots of pictures of them at that house, wherever that might be. It seems the relationship ended when they were both in their midtwenties."

Tate thought about that for a moment. "If I remember right, that'd be about the time Rebecca went into politics."

"Hmm. So Mahsood was good enough for a college fling but a liability when it came to a political career?"

"Probably," Tate agreed. "Twenty-five years ago, I don't think people would be so accepting of their differences."

Chase grunted and jerked his chin at the medical journals Tate had been reading. "Anything good on your side of the table?"

"Depends on your definition of good." Tate reached across and picked up the journal he'd been skimming. "On the bright side, Mahsood kept meticulous notes. Unfortunately, that means I've been reading page after page of exactly how he experimented on Ashley and everyone else he managed to get his hands on."

Chase's face twisted. "When did it start? On Ashley, I mean."

"When she was fourteen."

Tate leaned back on the table and flipped through a few pages. He couldn't believe someone would write all this depraved shit down. It was like Mahsood thought it was completely normal.

"Rebecca ran off to Europe when she got pregnant with Ashley, and Mahsood never mentioned a father in here, so I have no idea who he is," Tate said, forcing down the sour taste in his throat. "She hid Ashley with some loyal family servants, and for a while, that was the end of it. But when Ashley turned fourteen, the couple made the mistake of mentioning she was special. Rebecca took her away from the couple and had her thrown into the mental institution. Let's just say Mahsood was excited to have the opportunity to study something so completely new and different. According to this journal, he was also thrilled to be back in Rebecca's life and have her unlimited financial backing to do anything he wanted. And he definitely did anything he wanted."

Chase shook his head. "Did Rebecca have any idea what he was doing?"

Tate flipped a few more pages until he got to a photo of Mahsood and Rebecca at the institution. "If what Mahsood wrote in here is true, they had frequent meetings to discuss his progress, especially in the past few years when he was developing his hybrid serum."

"Good to see she overcame her concerns about their

ethnic differences so they could work together again," Chase said sarcastically.

Tate snorted. He wouldn't be surprised if the two of them sat on the deck of the lake house in the photo Chase had shown him sipping wine and discussing how to experiment on Ashley next.

"So, what now?" Chase asked.

Tate had been thinking about that himself. Maybe he could figure out how to get this data to Kendra and the other DCO analysts they trusted while at the same time keeping it away from Rebecca. He opened his mouth to say as much to Chase—without mentioning the DCO of course—when a creak on the stairs stopped him cold. He and Chase both pulled their weapons just as Ashley appeared on the steps, eyes glowing yellow-green and small fangs partially extended.

Tate held up his free hand in a placating gesture and holstered his weapon. Beside him, Chase lowered his gun but didn't put it away.

Tate didn't know Ashley well, but she was looking a little rough around the edges. Her long, curly dark hair fell wildly around her shoulders. The jeans and sweater she wore were scuffed and ragged in places, and her tennis shoes looked like they were about to fall apart. She seemed tired, too, like she'd been on the go for a while. It took a lot to wear out a shifter, so if she truly was exhausted, that meant she'd been pushing for a while. Maybe since escaping the mental institution.

On the bright side, she wasn't soaked in Bell's blood. She could have washed it off, he guessed. Then again, washing blood off her clothes didn't seem like something Ashley would care about.

"It's okay, Ashley," he said softly. He needed to calm the coyote shifter before things went bad. "No one is going to hurt you."

She tilted her head to the side and regarded him thoughtfully. "Where's the doctor?"

"Bell or Mahsood?" Chase asked.

Ashley turned her gaze on the deputy, eyeing him like something she scraped off her shoe before letting out a low growl. Flashing fangs in public wasn't something most shifters did very often, but apparently, she hadn't gotten the memo.

"Mahsood," she sneered. "Where is he?"

"We think he left a couple of hours ago," Tate said. "We're not sure where he is. Any chance he's running from you?"

Tate wanted to keep her talking long enough in the, hope that she'd retract her fangs. Then maybe they could think about capturing her somehow. But the moment he said they didn't know where Mahsood was, Ashley's interest in both of them flipped off like a light switch. One moment, she was standing tense and ready on the steps; the next, she was up the stairs and through the door that led to the kitchen.

Even though Tate knew there was no way in hell they could catch her, he raced after Ashley anyway, Chase at his heels.

"Holy crap," Chase said breathlessly when they both pulled up after sprinting a few hundred yards through the trees, watching as Ashley bounded off silently into the darkness like a ghost on nitrous oxide. "How fast can these damn shifters run?"

Tate leaned over with his hands on his thighs, catching

his breath. "Faster than we can, obviously. Makes me wish I still had my shifter partner. You're worthless."

Chase grunted, falling into step beside Tate as he started back toward the house. "I can definitely see how a shifter partner might come in handy. Makes me wonder what the hell you added to the team."

Tate chuckled. "Me? I was the brains of the operation."

The deputy shook his head. "I'm not doing anything with that one. It would be too easy. So, what's the plan now that our best suspect left us staring at her butt as she ran us into the dirt?"

Tate let out another laugh. He seriously needed to get Landon to recruit Chase for the DCO, because he definitely wouldn't mind working with the guy again. Considering the fact that the deputy was almost certainly going to get fired from the sheriff's department, Chase would need it.

"First, we need to get all those photos we found scanned and sent out to an intel analyst back at my office," Tate said. He considered taking pictures with his phone and emailing them, but there were way too damn many for that. "You know where there's a FedEx or UPS store around here?"

Chase looked at him like he was crazy. "At this time of night? Are you kidding me? Nothing is going to be open."

Tate scowled and climbed over a fallen tree. "I didn't ask if they were open. I asked if you know where one is."

Chase muttered something about losing his job for sure after tonight.

"Come on," Tate cajoled. "How hard can it be? You're wearing a uniform."

"Yeah, I am," Chase said. "Which will make it much easier to ID me in the lineup tomorrow."

Chapter 11

ZARINA WAS EXHAUSTED — MENTALLY AND PHYSICALLY — BY the time she finished surgery on the three preppers a few hours later, but as she slowly walked toward the cabin she and Tanner shared, she knew the night wasn't over. He would almost certainly be waiting for her, and when she walked in, the argument would start up all over again. She had only a vague idea what he'd been upset about, since he hadn't bothered to tell her before announcing he was sending her home. She didn't know whether it was the attack on the other camp, or the gun she'd been carrying, or the fact that one of the preppers who'd been injured was a woman. If she knew him, it was a combination of all three.

Fortunately, Zarina had been able to put thoughts of arguing with Tanner out of her mind long enough to deal with her patients. The two men who'd been shot would be on their feet in a matter of days, while the ones who'd been darted with tranquilizers would be up and moving by morning. The girl, on the other hand, was probably going to be flat on her back for at least a month. She'd nearly bled out from a small nick on the right thoracoacromial artery in her shoulder. If it wasn't for the fact that there were three people in camp with O negative blood, which was compatible with all other blood types, the woman would have died.

Zarina stopped outside the door of the cabin,

wondering if maybe she should sleep somewhere else for what was left of the night. While that was tempting, it was also pointless. She and Tanner needed to talk. Before he tried to bundle her up in a sleeping bag and drag her off to the airport.

Opening the door, she stepped inside, then quietly closed it behind her. Tanner was sitting on the floor on the far side of the cabin, his head back against the wall, his eyes closed. The lamp above him cast long shadows across the angular planes of his handsome face, and she wondered if he was asleep.

She was just trying to figure out whether she could climb in bed without waking him up when he opened his eyes.

"Did the girl make it?" he asked.

"Yes. It was close, but she's out of danger for the moment."

Tanner sighed. "That's good."

Zarina waited for him to say something else, but instead, he closed his eyes and rested his head again. Hoping that meant he was too tired to argue—she knew she certainly was—she crossed the small cabin and sat on the corner of the bed. She would have preferred sitting on the floor next to Tanner, but she wasn't sure that was a good idea. Being so near him made it difficult to think straight, and she needed a clear head right now.

As much as she'd rather not bring up the subject, it looked like she was going to have to be the one to do it. Taking a deep breath, she opened her mouth to tell him she wouldn't be leaving in the morning no matter how much he yelled and threatened, but Tanner spoke before she could say anything.

"I'm sorry for berating you about having a gun earlier," he said without opening his eyes. "And for suggesting you don't have the same right to fight for the people
you care about that I do. And while I'm busy apologiz-
ing, I guess I might as well say I'm sorry for being such
an ass about constantly trying to send you home to DC."

Zarina was so surprised by the sudden flurry of apologies that she nearly fell off the bed. She was reaching
down to figuratively pick her jaw up off the floor when
Tanner opened his eyes and looked at her.

"But in my defense, when I think about the woman
I love getting hurt, it makes my head go to some really
crazy places."

Zarina was still processing the fact that Tanner had
apologized when his words finally sank in. Her heart
suddenly beat out of control, and her stomach began
doing all kinds of flips and barrel rolls. She'd never
imagined a simple four-letter word could have such an
impact on her. She'd always considered herself to be
the calm, rational type, but hearing Tanner say he loved
her was beyond special. Even more so because it wasn't
what she'd expected him to say when she walked in.

Getting to his feet with all the grace of the big cat
whose DNA was mixed with his, Tanner closed the
distance between them in two strides and knelt down in
front of her. "I know I've been stupid, Zarina. Trying to
bully you into leaving…" He shook his head. "That's
not how it's supposed to work when two people love
each other. I may be terrified of you getting hurt, but I
promise I'm done with trying to send you away."

He started to say more, but Zarina reached out and
placed one finger against his lips, shushing him.

"Apologies accepted," she said softly as she pulled her finger away. "You had me at *I've been stupid*. What's with the sudden change of heart, though? I mean, I'm not complaining, but a few hours ago, you were planning to drag me to the airport first thing in the morning."

He shrugged, still kneeling in front of her, his eyes were level with hers. "Spencer and Peter came out and took over patrolling the perimeter, so I came back here to get some sleep. But I couldn't bring myself to lay down in the bed, not when your scent was all over it. It reminded me of what we'd been doing before the other camp was attacked, of how much I love you, and of how bad I've been at showing that."

Even though Zarina had already accepted a man as amazing as he was truly did love her, it was still nice hearing him say it out loud. It made her feel all gooey inside.

"Anyway, I've been sitting here since then, waiting for you to come back and thinking about how I've treated you," he continued. "It dawned on me that I'm pushing you away exactly like I did my family, and if I don't stop, I'm going to lose you the same way I lost them."

He leaned closer, his warm eyes caressing her tenderly as he gently cupped her face. "I guess what I'm trying to say is I know I've been a complete asshat, and I'm so incredibly sorry."

Zarina knew Tanner was being serious and that this was something that had obviously been weighing on him heavily. But still…*asshat*? It was such a silly word that made no sense to her at all; she couldn't help laughing. Then again, perhaps it wasn't the word that made her laugh but relief at the knowledge that somehow, beyond all possible expectations, maybe everything was going to work out after all.

Tanner stared at her, like he didn't know what to make of her laughter. But then he started chuckling, too. It was the first real, completely uninhibited expression of happiness she'd ever seen from him. It was a beautiful sound that make her heart beat even faster than before. Being this happy was the only thing in the world she cared about.

Still smiling, she leaned forward and kissed him.

Tanner groaned and slid his hand in her hair, urging her closer as his tongue slipped inside her mouth and began to tease hers. A flavor so distinctively his suffused her whole body, making her sigh and yearn for more.

But as Tanner started to give her exactly what she wanted, she found herself pulling away, needing to say something first.

Cupping his jaw, she gazed deeply into his eyes. "I love you so much that sometimes it feels like I can't get any air into my lungs because there's no room for anything but you. And I understand why you were worried I was going to get hurt, because I'm constantly worried about you, too. But we can't wait for life to send us some perfect moment in the future when all the stars line up and everything will be sane and quiet. That moment may never come. All we can do is live for right now and make this moment as perfect as we can."

Tanner didn't say anything. Instead, he stared at her with an intensity that might have scared some people. But not her. Because she knew him better than he knew himself and better than she knew anyone else in the world.

He tugged her in for another kiss, the feel of his lips on hers almost making her dizzy with all the emotions that simple touch conveyed. It wasn't until Tanner broke the kiss and reached down to unlace her boots that Zarina realized he'd nudged her to lie back on the bed. She would have wondered when that had happened if she wasn't more interested in what came next.

As one, they kicked off their boots and stripped off their socks, sending them flying across the cabin. The bed was small, and it was going to be complicated making love on it, but she wasn't going to complain as she squirmed out of her coat and tossed it aside.

She reached for the buckle on her belt when a look from Tanner stilled her hands.

"Let me do that," he whispered in a voice rough with a little growl.

A shiver ran through her at the feral sound. When she had a chance to think about it, she was going to have to figure what it was about this primal version of him that turned her on so much.

She let Tanner undo her belt and the buttons on her jeans, lifting her butt so he could slide them down and off. She shivered as his fingers teasingly traced across her hips and down her bare thighs. A jolt of warmth bloomed in her middle, coalescing between her legs and making another little sound of pleasure escape her lips. She knew without having to look that her panties were wet, and her instincts screamed at her to get the damn things off so they could hurry this up. But another glance from him stopped her cold.

"I'll take those off, too," he growled. "When I'm good and ready."

She peeked down at the sizable bulge in his jeans and gave him a smile. "I don't know. You look pretty ready to me."

He gave her a heated look, but he must have agreed with her, because he reached out and hooked his fingers into the hem of her panties, slowly tugging them over her hips and down her legs. Moisture clung to the inside of her thighs, leaving a warm reminder that she'd been waiting for this moment for a long time.

Tanner's eyes flared bright red, and another growl slipped out of his throat, a little louder this time. Zarina wasn't sure what had brought out his inner animal until he inhaled sharply, his eyes half closing in pleasure. He must be picking up the scent of her arousal.

Knowing he was fully aware of how turned on she was right then only served to nudge her excitement level a little bit higher. But she was okay with him knowing how hot she was. It meant there would be no games between them. They both knew how much the other was aching for this.

When he opened his eyes fully again, the glow had diminished a bit but not completely, something that pleased her tremendously. For the first time ever, Tanner wasn't fighting his inner beast. They were both there with her at the same time.

He held out a hand, and she gladly accepted the help as he pulled her up to a kneeling position in the center of the bed. As he slowly unbuttoned her shirt and slid it off her shoulders and down her arms, she could feel the heat of his eyes on her skin as his smoldering gaze raked over her stomach, then traveled up to her bra-covered breasts.

The bra quickly found its way to a corner of the cabin, leaving her completely naked for her fully clothed lover. She expected Tanner to immediately sweep her into his arms for another kiss or at least yank his clothes off.

But he did neither. Instead, he knelt at the side of the bed and regarded her with an expression of pure desire and total awe. There was something extremely arousing about being on display like this in front of a man who obviously found her completely captivating.

"You are so incredibly beautiful," he whispered, and Zarina wasn't sure if he even realized he'd spoken the words out loud.

She would have thanked him for the compliment, but Tanner yanked his shirt up and over his head so fast, all she saw was a blur, then his arms were around her, pulling her close so her breasts were pressed tight to his powerful chest, making her sigh as her nipples pressed into unyielding muscle. His body was so warm, it was like she was wrapped up in a hunky blanket.

Zarina tilted her head back, eager to feel his mouth on hers again, and was surprised when Tanner trailed a path of kisses along her jaw, then all the way from her right earlobe down to her collarbone. She gasped and buried her fingers in his hair, urging him to keep going. Not that Tanner seemed to need any urging from her. He appeared completely content to ravish her neck until she passed out from the sheer pleasure of it.

Zarina thought for sure she'd melt into a puddle right there on the bed. Just when she couldn't envision this getting any better, he gently nipped at the skin at the junction of her neck and shoulder with his teeth.

No, not his teeth. His *fangs*.

He didn't bite down hard enough to hurt, but she felt it in the most delicious way she could have ever imagined.

Considering Tanner usually treated her as if she were made of glass, she was a little surprised at how aggressive he was. Maybe it had something to do with him opening up to her. Perhaps he felt like he could finally be himself with her. Not that she was complaining. If he wanted to let out a husky growl and nibble on her neck, that worked for her. Actually, it more than worked for her. It drove her insane.

Zarina was so caught up in how good his fangs felt as they grazed her skin, she almost missed his hand sliding down to cup her butt. However, when he pulled her close, she couldn't miss how hard his erection was beneath his jeans. The rest of his clothes needed to go—now.

She pulled away from him, only realizing after the fact that doing so when a guy with sharp fangs was still busy nibbling on her neck might not be such a great idea. But she avoided injury and managed to get his attention. The raw lust in his gaze was enough to almost keep her from forming coherent thoughts, and she had to really focus.

"Take your jeans off," she commanded softly.

Even as she said the words, her hands slid down his bare chest and tight abs until they found his belt. She was half afraid he'd insist they do this his way, like he had before. Fortunately, Tanner was of the opinion that foreplay was over, too.

Working together, they got his jeans down, and Zarina laughed a little as he tossed them aside and climbed into bed with her. She blinked at the sight of his extremely hard cock straining at the material of his boxer briefs.

She reached for the waistband of his underwear, eager to free his hard-on from the confining cotton fabric, if for no other reason than so the material wouldn't tear apart. But on the way there, she decided to take a detour, pausing to caress the outline of his erection, easing herself as much as him.

Zarina smiled at the growl that slipped from his throat as she toyed with him. "Don't worry. I'll take these off when I'm good and ready."

He groaned at the way she tossed his own words back at him but then grinned. "You're forgetting my nose, which is telling me you're as ready for this as I am."

She didn't argue, knowing there was no way she could deny it. Still, she moved slowly as she inched up and hooked her fingers in the waistband of his briefs, dragging them down until she finally freed his shaft. Like the rest of him, it was strong, beautiful, and perfect, and it took all her efforts to keep her hands off him long enough to get his underwear the rest of the way down.

Once that was done, she eagerly wrapped one hand around him, putting the other on his chest and nudging him back onto the bed. The look he gave her suggested he was thinking about resisting, but he must have realized she already had him firmly in her grasp, and it was obvious she wasn't letting go. So he settled back and let her have her fun.

Zarina moved her hand up and down his erection, marveling at how he pulsed under her grasp. She especially liked the little bead of essence that formed at the very tip. She smiled as she ran the pad of her thumb over the silky liquid pearl, swirling it around him.

Tanner's abs and thighs tightened and flexed as she caressed him, and she had to admit she enjoyed watching his rippling muscles as much as she did touching him. But soon enough, her hunger for more made her lean forward and take him into her mouth. She felt as much as heard the low rumble that came from his chest. His sounds of pleasure only grew louder as she took him deeper and swirled her tongue around his most sensitive parts.

Zarina had every intention of continuing exactly what she was doing until Tanner exploded in her mouth, but he had other ideas. Reaching down, he gently but firmly urged her up until she was lying atop his chest with her lips inches from his. She opened her mouth to make a quip about him interrupting her, but Tanner rolled her over and pinned her to the bed with his big body and smoldering gaze. Vivid blue, his eyes were lit from within by a soft red glow.

A woman could lose herself in eyes like those.

"Were you about to say something?" he teased.

She wet her lips with her tongue. "I'm sure I was going to say something witty and insightful, but for some reason, I suddenly can't remember what it was."

Tanner grinned, his mouth a mere hairsbreadth from hers, his hard-on pressing urgently against her tummy. "Perhaps we should wait until you remember. It might have been important."

"No more waiting," she told him, pulling his head down and kissing him hard on the mouth.

He chuckled, kissing her back, then carefully nudging her legs wide and settling between her thighs. But just as the tip of his cock touched her wetness, a look of concern crossed his face, and he froze.

"What's wrong?" she asked.

Had he picked up a scent or sound that made him think danger was close? Her mind started spinning at a hundred miles an hour as she tried to imagine what it could be. *Crap*. What if the camp was about to be attacked again?

"I can't believe I'm bringing this up now, but I just realized, I didn't even think about birth control," he said. "Condoms haven't really been on my list of essentials lately."

Zarina let out a sigh of relief. No one was attacking the camp. Thank God. "That's not something we need to worry about," she told him softly. "I began taking birth control pills as soon as I knew I was coming out here so I wouldn't have to worry about dragging all that monthly female stuff around with me."

He looked at her in confusion for a second, but then understanding dawned on his face. "Oh. I hadn't thought about that."

She reached up and draped her arms around his shoulders, tugging him close again. "Now we have that out of the way, maybe we can get back to what we were doing."

He flashed her a sexy grin, then paused. "Wait. What were we doing again?"

She pressed a kiss to the corner of his mouth. "I'm pretty sure it had something to do with you sliding into me and giving me multiple orgasms."

The grin was back, along with the smolder. "Oh yeah. Now I remember."

She laughed, but the sound was cut off as Tanner slowly slid halfway in with a single thrust. Half sigh, half gasp, she threw back her head and arched off the bed as he pulled out a little, then plunged in again, going even deeper this time. Even though she was wet and ready for him, the feeling of his thick shaft buried inside her took her breath away. The shock waves of pleasure rippling through her as he began to pump made her pant, and it was all she could do to wrap her legs around his hips and hold on tight.

Zarina buried her face in his neck, lost in the sensation of him gliding in and out, feeling the telltale tremors of a strong orgasm building deep inside her. If Tanner kept moving like he was, she was going to explode soon. Even so, she wanted more, wanted him to move faster, thrust harder. She tightened her legs around him, digging her heels into his muscular ass, moving her body under his and urging him on.

But Tanner ignored her unspoken but obvious demands, instead continuing to tease her with his gentle thrusts as he carefully held his body weight off of her. That was when her instincts told her something was off. Even though what they were doing felt amazing, she couldn't shake the feeling Tanner was holding back.

When she saw his tight jaw and expression of total concentration, she knew she was right. Tanner's head was a hundred miles away, focused on maintaining complete control of his inner hybrid and not on making love to her.

She reached up and threaded her fingers in his hair, then dragged his face down until he was staring straight into her eyes. His gaze sharpened, and he slowly stopped moving. "What's wrong? Am I hurting you?"

If it wasn't for the fact that Zarina had her legs wrapped around him too tightly for him to move, he almost certainly would have pulled out. No way in hell was she letting that happen.

If she hadn't been sure before, she was now. Tanner had been aggressive and confident when it came to getting her naked, but now that they were making love, his worries about going full hybrid were making him pull away. Well, she wasn't going to stand for it.

"Don't you even think about holding back on me," she said firmly. "Not now. Not after everything we've been through together."

She expected him to deny it, and if he did, she was going to smack him. Surprisingly, he didn't even try.

"I don't want to hurt you," he whispered. "Being with you here, like this, has me close to the edge. I don't think I can stay in control if I don't focus."

She cupped his face in her hand. "Then don't be in control. You think I want our first time to be like this, with half of you not even here? I want you to be in the moment with me right now."

He shook his head. "It's not that simple. If I lose it, I could kill you."

"You're not going to lose it, and you are not going to kill me. You're going to let go of all those worries, and you're going to make love to me for hours. And it's going to be incredible."

Tanner shook his head. "I wish it could be that way, but I can't take the risk."

She knew he was seconds away from sliding out. If he did that, she couldn't imagine how this moment was ever going to happen again. The thing that had been forming between them would be gone like it had never even been there.

She couldn't accept that.

She wouldn't.

Zarina pulled him down and kissed him so hard, his slightly extended fangs nicked her tongue and drew blood. But she didn't care. The only thing that mattered was showing Tanner he didn't have to be held captive by the beast inside him, that they could be together in every way that mattered.

The kiss caught him by surprise, and in that moment of stunned confusion, she took control of the situation, shoving at his shoulder at the same time as she twisted violently beneath him. She normally would never have been able to move a guy his size, but he'd been so careful to keep his full weight off her that she was able to flip him over onto his back. She didn't waste the advantage, keeping her balance on top of him as she drove him deeper inside her than he'd been before. Then she leaned forward and looked him straight in the eye as she began to ride him exactly the way she'd wanted all along.

"Zarina," he warned, his voice a soft rasp.

She kept moving, fighting to hold in the moans that threatened to spill out of her. "I'm not going to stop. If you want me to, you're going to have to physically move me, and I don't think you're willing to manhandle me that way."

He gritted his teeth, his eyes flashing bright red as her body clenched more tightly around his shaft. She took it as a sign he was enjoying what she was doing, even if he refused to admit it.

"Why are you doing this?" he demanded.

His hands settled on her grinding hips, almost as if he was trying to control—and slow—her sensual movements. She ignored them and moved faster, her breath coming now in little gasps as she felt the tremors building up inside her again.

"Because I trust you," she panted, tingles spreading

from her center outward until they covered her whole body. "More than you trust yourself. You, and your hybrid half, would never hurt me. I know that in my soul."

Tanner might have argued, but Zarina didn't give him a chance. Switching into high gear, she bounced up and down on him even faster as she felt her orgasm beginning to crest.

That was the breaking point for him. His eyes went completely scarlet, and his upper fangs extended far enough to protrude over his lower lip. His big hands tightened on her hips, not to slow her movements this time, but to yank her down on his cock even harder so he was touching her in places she'd never known existed.

Zarina came not in a cresting wave but in an avalanche of sensations that felt like a fireball exploding inside her. Tanner drew her climax out as far as it would go, making her scream so loud, she was sure it echoed through the camp.

She was wondering if it was possible to pass out from so much pleasure when Tanner suddenly flipped her over onto her back, thrusting into her hard and fast. That was when she realized he hadn't come with her. From the growls he was letting out, she knew that was about to change.

That was when she saw the most beautiful thing she could have ever imagined. Tanner had fully shifted, his fangs completely extended as he gazed down at her with nothing but lust, love, and adoration. There wasn't a trace of anger or rage to be seen in his glowing red eyes.

She'd been right about him all along.

Then Tanner's whole body stiffened as he shoved deep inside her and held himself there. The feeling as he poured his essence inside her was enough to make her orgasm again, but this time, she kept her eyes open. She didn't want to miss a single moment of his pleasure.

Tanner bucked half a dozen times, drawing his climax out—and hers, too—before he collapsed against her, his face nestled comfortably in the curve of her neck.

Zarina wrapped her arms and legs around him, holding him close. They lay like that for a long time, their heartbeats slowly returning to normal and syncing up with each other's.

"That was incredible," she whispered, gliding her hands up and down his powerful back, tracing her fingers over the muscles. "And without making it sound like I told you so, I told you so."

He chuckled, his fangs teasing her skin. "Yeah, I guess you did."

She threaded her hand in his hair, urging him up so that she could see his face. He started to look away, like he was ashamed to let her see his hybrid features. She tightened her fingers in his hair, holding him still. She saw nothing to be embarrassed or ashamed of. Instead, she saw an amazing man she was insanely in love with.

That was when Zarina realized Tanner was never going to need the antiserum she'd created. While he was going to need a lot of work to help his PTSD, after making love with him—and his inner beast—she was sure that at some point, he'd gain complete control of his animal half. It would take time, but it would happen. Which meant she'd never have to have that conversation with him, the one where she described the drug's possible unpleasant side effects.

Putting those thoughts out of her mind, she pulled

Tanner down and kissed him, unconcerned by the presence of his fangs. Neither he nor his hybrid half would ever hurt her.

He hesitated for a moment but then gave in and kissed her. It was like he was finally letting it all go. The doubt, the worry, the fear. He kissed her like a man kissed the woman he loved.

"So, what now?" she whispered when they finally pulled away.

He grinned, displaying his fangs. "Now we make love for hours. And it's going to be incredible."

She returned his smile. "Yes, it will."

Chapter 12

TATE CROUCHED DOWN BESIDE CHASE IN THE WOODS A quarter mile away from a gorgeous house on the west shore of Sebago Lake. The sun was just coming up over the calm body of water, burning off the morning haze. Except for the occasional bird sounds, the place was quiet.

"See anything?" Chase asked softly, like he was worried someone would hear them out here, even though it looked like there wasn't another living soul within five miles of the place.

Tate looked through his binoculars, scanning first the forest and lakefront surrounding the house before focusing on the home itself. But there was nothing to be seen and hadn't been since they'd gotten there ten minutes ago.

"Nothing." Tate lowered the binoculars. "If Mahsood is in there, he's playing possum."

"If I had as many people after me as Mahsood does, I'd be playing some serious possum, too."

It had taken the better part of two hours to collect all the photos and critical data from Bell's basement, drive into Lewiston and break into a full-service UPS store, then scan and transmit the stuff to Kendra at her house. After that, they'd had to sit in Chase's patrol car outside the store for another hour while Kendra dug through the data and got them the address and directions for this place. It had been owned by the Brannon family for close to seventy-five years, and Rebecca used it as a private retreat when she wanted to get away from Washington politics. Or maybe hide an old boyfriend.

The crazy thing was, the house was ten miles from Hiram and the cabin Bell had been found dead in. It made Tate wonder if the man had been heading here to check the place out and make sure it was safe for Mahsood when he'd been grabbed by the people who'd killed him. Kind of ironic if that was the case.

"We going to go take a look around?" Chase asked. "At least see if Mahsood has been here?"

Tate glanced at the deputy. "You seem to be getting awfully comfortable with this breaking-and-entering thing. First Bell's house, then a UPS store, and now the house of a sitting member of Congress. If your sheriff hears about this, you're toast for sure."

"I'll just claim you told me you had federal warrants. Nobody up here trusts the feds. So they'll have no problem believing me over you."

Tate couldn't find fault with that logic.

They moved slowly through the woods, using the trees for cover and coming at the house from a direction they hoped provided cover if Mahsood happened to be in there looking out a window. It took a few extra minutes, but they were able to slip all the way up to the back of the house and onto the deck overlooking the lake without raising an alarm. Tate considered that a fair trade.

"You're damn good at picking locks," Chase pointed out softly as Tate opened the French doors leading into the fancy house. "Homeland teach you that?"

"They wish," Tate whispered before moving into the huge living room that looked out over the deck. "But I owe it all to my misspent youth. Maybe I'll tell you about it someday."

Chase didn't say anything as they spread out to search the house. The place was eerily quiet, making Tate think there was no one else there. Once again, he wished he had Declan with him. The bear shifter's nose would have told them in a flash if they were wasting their time.

While Chase headed toward the kitchen, Tate moved down a long hallway to a room that was supposed to be a library, then a large office. He thought "supposed to" because the floor plans Kendra had gotten for the place had been a decade old. A lot could have changed since then.

He peeked his head into the first doorway on the left, relaxing a little when he saw that it was indeed a library. Well, their intel was right. Unfortunately, the room was empty, and there was no sign anyone had been there recently.

He kept one ear cocked for sounds of trouble from the other side of the house as he made his way down the hall. Not that he was too concerned about Mahsood getting the drop on Chase. He didn't see that happening.

The office was an interior room, which made it darker than the library. But he saw enough to know there wasn't much reason to check it out. Mahsood wasn't in there unless he was hiding under the desk. But then a glow on the surface of the desktop caught his attention.

He flipped on the overhead light and moved around the desk to check it out. The glow he'd seen was from the computer monitor sitting there. Specifically from the six black-and-white camera images displayed there in two even rows. Even as he watched, the images changed, showing him different views of the outside of the house, including the lake and the woods surrounding the home. One of those places was where he and Chase had been standing as they surveyed the property.

Mahsood had been here and seen them coming. Since they hadn't seen or heard a vehicle speed away, that meant their doctor was trying to get away on foot.

"Shit."

Tate ran out of the room and down the hall. Chase was just coming out of the kitchen as Tate reached it. He motioned toward the front door.

"Mahsood picked us up on security cameras before we even got close," he shouted. "He's probably hauling ass through the woods right now!"

Tate expected the deputy to immediately head for the door, but instead, Chase shook his head and slowly walked across the living room, lifting his hands at the same time.

"I don't think so," Chase said. "In fact, I'm pretty sure he's still in the house."

Mahsood stepped out of the kitchen behind Chase. He was dressed in jeans, loafers, and a cardigan, a small automatic pistol in his hand, pointed at the cop's back.

Tate stopped to stare at Chase incredulously. "Are you shitting me? You let a guy in slip-on loafers sneak up on you? That was the marines you were in, right, not your high school marching band?"

"Stop right there, or I'll shoot!" Mahsood warned, shaking his weapon in Tate's general direction, while still attempting to keep it aimed at Chase, too.

"Hey, if you haven't noticed, loafers can be really

quiet," Chase said angrily as he moved, putting more space between him and the doctor. "And if you think I'm going to let you badmouth the marines, buddy, you are so fucking wrong."

Mahsood was trying to interrupt the argument when Tate darted past Chase and knocked the doctor's right arm—and the gun—to the side. Then he flipped the older man over his hip, ripping the weapon out of his hand at the same time. Mahsood crashed to the floor and lay there groaning as Tate unloaded and cleared the .380 auto. At least the man had remembered to take the safety off before threatening them with it.

"Why the hell are you pointing a gun at us?" Tate demanded before tossing the empty weapon on one couch and the full clip on another. "We're not the ones you've been hiding from. I'm with the DCO."

Chase gave him a confused look at that, but Tate shook his head. Explanations would have to wait until later.

"How was I to know that?" Mahsood winced as he sat up. "When I saw the two of you sneaking up on the house, I naturally assumed you were with the people who've been hunting me for weeks."

"People," Chase echoed. "Ashley Brannon isn't the one after you?"

Mahsood seemed a little surprised—and worried—to hear the name. "Ashley is here, too? I didn't know that."

"Yeah, we ran into her a few hours ago," Tate said. "She implied she'd love to get together with you and talk about old times, but something tells me you're not nearly as eager for a reunion."

Mahsood slowly got to his feet and moved over to the couch, careful not to get too close to the empty weapon Tate had tossed there as he sat down. "Ashley is an unstable woman who believes I'm responsible for separating her from her adoptive parents and keeping her away from her mother as well. She doesn't like me, and I do not think meeting with her would be very beneficial to me."

Chase chuckled. "I agree it probably wouldn't be beneficial, but it would be entertaining as hell. Considering you held her prisoner in a mental institution for years while conducting all kinds of painful experiments on her, I imagine she has hundreds of wonderful things planned for you."

The doctor gave the deputy a dismissive glance. "The woman fails to understand the significant role she has played in the advancement of genetic science."

After hearing something like that, Tate found himself wondering how difficult it would be to let Ashley know where they were. Maybe they could give her a few minutes alone with Mahsood.

Unfortunately, that wasn't something they could do, even if they had a way of reaching Ashley. Landon would want Mahsood brought back to the DCO so they could question him about Rebecca and her role in his hybrid research. But before Tate could think about getting the man back to DC, there was one other issue they had to deal with first.

"Tell me about these people hunting you," Tate said. "Who are they?"

Mahsood shrugged. "I have no idea who they are. I'd been safely off the grid for weeks in Quebec City, but then four men and two shifters appeared out of nowhere and tried to grab me. I was fortunate enough to escape and make my way back here, but they found me again, killing someone very important to me in the process."

"McKinley Bell," Chase said softly.

Mahsood nodded, his dark eyes filling with sadness. Tate had to admit the man seemed genuinely devastated. He supposed even demented psychopaths could have a place in their hearts for someone. It didn't mean Mahsood was any less of a monster. It simply reinforced the old saying about there being someone out there for everyone, including psychopaths.

"Yes," the doctor murmured. "I'd been staying at his place, but I was worried the people who were after me would come there at some point. I knew I had to find another place to hide and decided on this house. I'd been here many times in the past and knew it would be empty at this time of the year. But McKinley was concerned for my safety, so he insisted he come out here first and look around. He even promised to drive a circuitous route so he'd know if he was being followed. Unfortunately, he never came back. I understand they tortured him as a way to get to me."

Tate had a stupid urge to say something consoling, like McKinley's death had been painless. Before he had a chance to lie, a soft chime from somewhere in the house caught his attention.

Mahsood's head snapped up sharply, his wide-eyed gaze locked on the hallway behind Tate. "That's a security alarm in the office. It means one of the sensors on the property has been activated."

Leaving Chase to deal with Mahsood, Tate turned and ran for the office. Several more of the chimes had gone off by the time he got there. That couldn't be a good thing.

He slid to a stop behind the desk, cursing when he saw the intruders moving quickly through the woods behind the house, tripping multiple alarms as they went. The two shifters were in the lead, while four heavily armed men spread out behind them. No doubt, the shifters knew they were setting off the alarms and didn't care. They knew no one Mahsood called would be able to get here in time to help.

Tate cursed as the team of well-trained operatives converged on the house. His gut told him they'd followed him and Chase since the fight at Joanne Harvey's house. They'd led the hired guns right to the man they were after.

"What's the word?" Chase walked into the office with Mahsood. "Do we fight or make a run for it?"

"That depends," Tate told him. "Do you consider six against two bad odds?"

"I can help fight," Mahsood said. "Let me have my gun back."

Chase snorted and shook his head. "We run."

Tanner knew he'd made a lot of stupid decisions in his life. In fact, it wasn't a stretch to say his life—at least recently—was nothing more than a collection of one terrible decision followed by another. But deciding to stop being a moron and tell Zarina how he felt about her wasn't one of them. It might just be the smartest thing he'd ever done.

Zarina was sleeping contently on his chest, her perfect naked body lightly coated with a sheen of sweat. They'd made love for hours, and it had been incredible. He'd never been with anyone like her. He was so in love, it hurt to even think about being apart from her for more than a few minutes.

Folding his arm under his head, Tanner glanced at the cabin's lone window with its makeshift curtain. The sun would be coming up soon, and he and Zarina would be facing another day. But for the first time in forever, he was looking forward to the day and what it might bring.

While they'd made love, he'd shifted as far as he'd ever gone, and Zarina hadn't flinched once. But as far gone as he'd been, he'd never felt the urge to do anything other than love the hell out of her. He and the beast had both been consumed with a single goal—making Zarina feel more pleasure than she'd ever experienced. Coming to accept that his hybrid half would never be a danger to the woman he loved was a life-altering moment.

Zarina murmured something in her sleep, cuddling closer to him. Tanner was about to snag one of the blankets they'd pushed around on the bed, sure she was cold, but then her eyes fluttered open, and the look she gave him took his breath away. Her blue eyes were so captivating, it felt like they could take possession of his soul with a single glance. He was more than okay with that.

"Ready for round two?" she asked, pressing her lips to his chest and making him shiver. She'd been doing a lot of that over the past few hours, but he was sure he'd never get tired of it.

He grinned. "Technically, it would be at least round four. Or five if you count that thing you did with your mouth."

Zarina smiled, pushing herself up on her elbow and putting her beautiful breasts on display. His cock immediately went hard at the sight of all those curves.

"Only if we count by the number of orgasms we've had, which I don't," she said. "I prefer to go with how many times I pass out from pleasure, which has only happened once. So, in my mind, we've just gotten started."

He chuckled. "You're amazing, you know that, right?"

She slipped a warm thigh across his hips, gracefully climbing on top of him. "Yes, but feel free to keep telling me. I promise I won't get tired of hearing it."

Tanner shook his head as he grabbed her hips, getting her settled carefully on his shaft. "I'm never going to stop letting you know how amazing you are or how much I love you. I can promise you that."

Zarina leaned forward, pressing her breasts against his chest as she kissed him. "It's a promise, then. We never stop saying I love you, no matter how crazy things get in the future."

He slid his hands down and cupped her ass. "Deal."

Tanner had just leaned in to nuzzle Zarina's neck when a pair of familiar scents reached his nose. It took him a moment to place them, but when he finally did, they had him flipping over so fast, he almost spilled Zarina onto the floor.

"The camp is under attack," he said. He jumped off the bed, scrambling for his jeans and boots as he strained his ears for the sound of gunfire. Spencer and Peter were out on the perimeter somewhere. If he was smelling the assholes, they should have, too.

As Zarina hurriedly put on her clothes, Tanner had to clamp down on the impulse to tell her to hide under the bed until the fighting was over. But he couldn't do that, no matter how loudly his instincts demanded he do so.

Not wanting to take the time to bother with looking for his shirt, he snatched up the AR-15 he'd leaned
against the wall last night. "I'm picking up the scents of
at least two of the men who hit the camp up north. I have
no idea why Spencer and Peter haven't raised the alarm
yet, and that scares the hell out of me."

Zarina stepped in front of him as he started for the
door. She already had her shirt, jeans, and boots on. The
sight of the revolver on her belt stopped him cold. It was
terrifying to think Zarina might have to shoot someone,
mostly because he wasn't sure she had it in her. But he
had to respect her right to protect herself and others.

"Be careful out there," she said, going up on tiptoe
to kiss him. "And don't get so wrapped up in worrying
about other people that you don't watch out for yourself."

He kissed her back, closing his eyes for a second as
worry almost overwhelmed him. Then he nodded and
reached past her to grab the doorknob. "The same goes
for you. Focus on protecting people, not going after the
men attacking the camp."

Then he was out the door and running for the north
side of the camp, letting the scents of the men attacking
the camp lead him. There were at least half a dozen men
moving in from the north, and they were already well
within the perimeter of the camp. That meant there was a
good chance they'd already taken out Spencer and Peter.

He pointed his weapon skyward and popped off three
rounds. "The camp is under attack!" he shouted at the
top of his lungs. "Inbound from the north!"

Wishing he could do more to get the camp's residents
moving but knowing he'd already done as much as he
could, Tanner turned his attention to the men intent on

taking them by surprise, using his nose to pin down their location. They must have regrouped long enough to get reinforcements so they could hit Chad's camp right before dawn, when the people who lived there would be caught unaware.

Around him, the camp came to life. Tanner prayed it wasn't too late.

His first instinct was to go after the four men circling around the camp from the west. But then he picked up Spencer's and Peter's scents the other way, along with those of two men. He veered that way, remembering how he'd seen the men trying to kidnap the tranquilized preppers up north. He had to make sure they weren't doing that to the hybrids.

Tanner's body shifted as he ran. No shock there. He always lost a little bit of control when the battle adrenaline started flowing. However, he was surprised that this time, even though he was worried as hell about Spencer and Peter, not to mention Zarina, he was able to keep the hybrid in control. Was it because of the acceptance he'd found in Zarina's arms? Maybe. Regardless, he was able to limit the changes to his muscles and his senses, things that would help him in the coming fight while still letting his human mind take the reins.

Tanner found Spencer and Peter three-quarters of a mile outside the camp, just as two men in tactical gear were loading them in the back of one of the same SUVs he'd seen earlier. He could make out their heartbeats, so he knew the hybrids were alive, but they'd clearly been tranquilized. He had no idea how these men had been able to dart the hybrids with enough of the drug to knock them out before Spencer or Peter could sound the alarm. Ultimately, he didn't care. He wasn't letting them kidnap his friends.

Tanner could have stopped and taken a shot at the men, but he didn't want to risk hitting Spencer or Peter. So instead, he growled and let his body shift further, putting all his effort into closing the distance between him and them as fast as he could.

The men must have heard him, because they both turned at the same time. The NVGs they wore hid their expressions, but they both brought their weapons up quickly, as if they weren't shocked at all to see a man running at them through the dimly lit forests at thirty miles an hour.

Tanner dodged to the right to avoid the incoming submachine gunfire, sure they'd missed him. But then something smacked into the center of his chest, and for a second, he'd thought he'd been hit. Then he realized the sting didn't feel like a 9mm. He glanced down to see a metal dart tube sticking out of his chest mere inches from his heart.

Shit.

He slapped it away but knew it wouldn't help. The damage was done.

His mind raced. He might only have seconds before he ended up in the same condition as Spencer and Peter. He growled, letting the beast inside out all the way, praying it would help him fight off the drug for a time. It might not have helped the other hybrids, but maybe being partially shifted before getting hit would make a difference.

He avoided more darts, letting his claws and fangs extend completely as he lunged at the men. They tried to line up for another shot with their tranquilizer guns, but Tanner was on them too fast to let that happen.

Both men scrambled backward, suddenly desperate to get away, but the SUVs blocked their way, and they had no choice but to deal with him. Tanner didn't even consider pulling the trigger on the weapon he was carrying. That wasn't the way his inner beast chose to fight. It was the one disadvantage of letting his hybrid half take the lead.

He roared loud enough to shake the trees around him, hitting the first guy between the eyes with the butt of his AR-15, delighting in the crunch of cracking bones as the man dropped like a sack of potatoes. Then he spun and threw himself at the second one.

That's when he found out just how much the drugs dumped into his system had already affected him. The leap that normally would have taken him ten feet barely covered five. He came up far short of his prey, giving the man time to get his dart gun up again.

Tanner moved a little to the side, hoping to make the man miss. It worked. A little. Instead of getting Tanner in the chest again, the dart clipped his right arm. But Tanner still felt some of the drugs pour into his bloodstream before he plucked the dart out.

He snarled, and the man with the dart gun stumbled back a little in fear. But while the guy might be scared, he wasn't giving up. Grabbing the automatic pistol holstered at his hip, he pulled it out with the practice of a man who handled weapons for a living. Tanner didn't think. He took two strides and slashed out with his claws, raking them across the man's throat.

Tanner stopped and looked around, wondering what

he should do next. His thoughts were getting fuzzy as hell, and it was all he could do to keep from dropping to the ground right on the spot.

A sound filtered through his muddled head, and after a few seconds, he realized he was hearing gunshots from the camp. He forced his mind to clear, remembering the four scents he'd smelled from the west. *Shit*. Those men had reached the camp.

He glanced at Spencer and Peter. He couldn't leave them out here like this. He'd grab them and hide them in the woods. That plan proved much more difficult than he'd imagined. The tranquilizer had made him so weak, he could barely drag Peter out of the back of the SUV, much less carry him. By the time he finally got the big hybrid shoved under the low-hanging branches of a fir tree, he was gasping for breath. Cursing, he walked over to get Spencer.

He'd only gone a few feet when a woman's scream echoed in the air. That was Zarina. He knew it in his soul. She was in trouble.

Leaving Spencer where he was and hoping the brush would hide him, Tanner started toward the camp. His head spun as he ran. He was so dizzy now, he wasn't sure he'd be able to help once he got there. He brutally shoved the doubts from his mind. Zarina was in trouble. He'd do anything he had to do to save her.

He stumbled into the camp, his arms and legs feeling like they weighed a ton. But he was still moving, honing in on Zarina's scent, and that was all that mattered. She was somewhere near the main building.

But as he rounded the corner of one of the cabins and headed that way, another scent smacked him in the face hard enough to stun him. Not because it was so strong, but simply because it belonged to someone he knew. That couldn't be right. The tranquilizer drug had to be playing tricks on him.

Tanner was still trying to convince himself of that when a pair of black-garbed mercenaries stepped out from the next cabin ahead of him, dragging an unconscious woman between them. Tanner smelled the blood before he even saw the red streak running down her face.

Growling, he lunged at the men in full-on shifter mode. It felt like he was moving through molasses as he crashed into them, only realizing as they all went flying that the girl was Lillie, not Zarina. A part of him felt horrible for being relieved it wasn't Zarina, but he pushed that guilt aside as he fought to save the younger girl.

One of the men came up with a .40-caliber pistol in his hand. Tanner knocked it aside and slashed the man across the face as hard as he could. The guy shouted in pain, and Tanner's inner beast roared in approval.

He spun for the second man, scrambling over Lillie's unconscious form in the process. But as he closed one clawed hand around the man's weapon and the other around the guy's throat, something thumped into his back. It wasn't hard enough to knock him forward, but it stung like a son of a bitch.

The man twisted away from his grip and punched him in the face as he fell against him, but Tanner couldn't feel a thing. Then his whole body went limp, and he was on the ground, doing everything in his power to get back to his feet despite the tranquilizer dart. When that didn't work, he tried to sit up, but that wasn't possible either.

His whole body was one solid chunk of lead now, and none of his parts would do what he told them. Breathing was even getting to be a chore.

A man suddenly leaned over him, his face a blur. But Tanner didn't need to see the man to know who it was.

"Ryan?" he rasped.

Tanner tried to force his numb mind to focus, to come up with some rational reason for his old friend to be here. But no matter how hard he tried, he couldn't make sense of what he was seeing.

"Damn," Ryan said. "I'd always thought you were a little screwed up, but I guess I underestimated just how fucked up you are. You really are a freak, aren't you?"

Tanner tried to tell the other man to go to hell, but he didn't have the energy to even speak now.

Ryan turned and looked at Lillie. "Get her up and back to the vehicles. I don't know what we can do with her, but I'm sure I'll come up with something."

Tanner's eyes locked on the .40-caliber he'd knocked out of the man's hand earlier, lying on the ground nearby. Gritting his teeth, he strained to reach over and pick it up. It took all his strength to get the weapon pointed toward the blond man scooping Lillie off the ground, but the guy merely slapped the weapon aside and threw the girl over his shoulder like she was a sack of Christmas presents.

"What about Everett?" the man asked, motioning with his chin at the guy Tanner had slashed. He was still rolling around with blood pouring between the hands he had clapped over the shredded remains of his face.

Ryan looked over casually, as if just noticing the man. "Don't worry about it, Anton. I'll take care of him."

The blond man hesitated but then shrugged and headed toward the woods.

"Once you get her tucked away, come back and help me drag this big bastard through the woods," Ryan called after him. "He's going to weigh a metric ton."

Anton grunted and disappeared, leaving Tanner lying there paralyzed and nearly unconscious with Ryan and the injured man.

Ryan gazed down at Tanner for a long moment, then shook his head. "That tranquilizer has been in you for at least five minutes and you're still conscious? What the hell are you?"

Tanner couldn't tell the asshole who used to be his friend that he'd been hit three times, but he enjoyed the displeasure his continued consciousness brought the man. There was still shooting going on all around the camp. Maybe if Tanner was able to stay awake a while longer, Malcolm or one of the preppers would stumble over them.

Ryan must have heard the shooting, too, and thought the same thing Tanner had. "Guess I'll need to start dragging your ass to the truck myself."

The man on the ground—Everett—groaned again, maybe trying to remind his boss that he was still there. Ryan frowned at the man in annoyance, then pulled out a .45 and put three rounds point-blank into the man's chest without blinking an eye.

He looked at Tanner. "Don't worry. You're too valuable to shoot."

Smirking, Ryan lifted a heavy, booted foot and kicked Tanner in the face, leaving nothing but stars followed by darkness.

Chapter 13

TATE LET CHASE DEAL WITH THE DOCTOR WHILE HE FOCUSED on leading them into the woods and away from the people after them. His gut instinct had been to head for their vehicle parked north of the house a mile down Highway 11, but he'd immediately dropped the idea. The bad guys had followed them here and would certainly know exactly where they'd parked. They were smart enough to make sure the Oxford County cruiser wouldn't be of any use to them on the off chance he and Chase got past them and back to the vehicle.

Unless they wanted to try and swim their way to freedom, that left them with no other choice but to skirt the edge of the lake and head due south through the woods until they reached Highway 114. If they were lucky, they'd be able to flag down a vehicle and get the hell out of there before the people hunting them even realized they'd left the house.

Their chances weren't as horrible as it seemed. The bad guys had been on the far side of the lake house the last time Tate had seen them on the security cameras. That meant they'd need a few more minutes to get to the house, then another minute or two to search the place. With that much of a head start, he and Chase might be able to beat them to the main road.

Then reality—in the form of Mahsood, who was currently gasping for breath as he tried to keep up—made an appearance, and Tate knew his plan had the potential to go to crap really fast. He glanced over his shoulder to see Chase practically dragging the man through the woods by one arm and not making very good time even then. They'd fallen a good fifteen feet behind him already.

"Can't you just carry him?" Tate suggested, pausing for a moment to check behind them.

Chase snorted. "If you're so hyped up about someone carrying the evil doctor, why don't you do it?"

Tate chuckled. "While I'd like to get Mahsood back to the DCO alive, I don't want it badly enough to carry him. Besides, you're younger than I am by a few years and obviously need the workout."

Chase scowled.

"I can't help but think I would be better off on my own out here," Mahsood panted as Chase picked up the pace. "If you let me go and simply create a diversion, I can escape, then meet up with you somewhere later. Once I'm out of the area, they'll ignore the two of you, since it's obvious you have no value to anyone."

Chase pinned Tate with a look as they caught up to him. "Can we just leave him here? Maybe tie him to a tree with a bow around it?"

Tate cursed and grabbed Mahsood's free arm. "Unfortunately, no. So let's get going."

He and Chase took off running again, making pretty good time. Almost good enough to convince Tate they were going to reach the highway before anyone caught up with them. He only hoped someone driving by would stop and pick them up.

Behind him, Tate heard the sound of running feet. He barely drew his weapon, when two blurs slammed into him and Chase at the same time. Mahsood let out something that sounded like a screech, but Tate didn't do more than grunt as he flew ten feet through the air like he'd been hit by a train.

He lost his weapon when he hit the ground, pain exploding through his body from the force of the impact. The moment he bounced to a stop, the feline shifter was on him, straddling his body, one clawed hand cocked back and ready to rip out his throat. Tate immediately lifted an arm to protect himself, but before he could counterattack, the man's curved claws sliced through his forearm. Ignoring the pain, Tate brought the heel of his right hand up and slammed it into the shifter's nose. The crunching sound it made was rewarding as hell.

The man threw back his head and roared, and while it didn't incapacitate him, it definitely distracted him. Tate used that to his advantage, knocking the shifter off his chest. Tate jumped up, searching wildly for his weapon. Unfortunately, it was nowhere in sight. Neither was Mahsood. However, Chase was tussling with the female wolf shifter and having nearly as much trouble as he was. His arms were bloody from claw marks, and the way he was favoring his left side indicated he might be dealing with some cracked ribs. Getting blindsided by a shifter running at full speed could do that sometimes.

The wolf shifter's claws and fangs were fully extended, and she looked ready to kill. But as much as Tate would have liked to run over to help, he needed his damn weapon first. He spun in a slow circle, wishing for the first time in his life that he'd gotten a weapon in some color other than black.

He caught sight of it half buried in the leaves and dirt just as the feline shifter pulled his hand away from his smashed nose. He looked at Tate with pure murder in his eyes.

Tate lunged for the weapon at the same time as the shifter launched at him. Tate hit the ground, his fingers closing around the familiar grip of his pistol just as the man landed on him. Tate barely had a chance to tighten his hand on the weapon before the shifter yanked him over onto his back. He tried to bring the weapon up and point it in the right direction, but the shifter grabbed his wrist and slammed it to the ground.

Tate twisted, reaching for the claws digging into his wrist. That was when he realized his pistol was now pointing straight at Chase. Or more precisely, the wolf shifter pinning his partner against a tree as she prepared to tear him apart.

Tate didn't hesitate, even though he knew it was likely to end up with him getting his own throat ripped out. He simply squeezed off four rounds in the general direction of the wolf shifter.

The sounds of the gunshots shattered the morning calm, making everyone jump, and while three of the rounds completely missed their marks, the last one hit, going through the woman's right thigh. She screamed in pain and tumbled to the side, hitting the ground hard, then spinning back up to throw Tate a look that suggested she couldn't wait to shred the flesh off his bones.

But instead of coming at him, she lifted her head and sniffed the air. Giving her feline partner a hard look, she turned and darted into the forest.

Over by the tree, Chase was just dragging himself to his feet. Tate knew the man wasn't going to be able to help him. Out of the corner of his eye, he saw the feline shifter lift his clawed hand for another killing slash and knew his forearm wasn't going to stop it this time.

Suddenly, a blur flashed past him, and all he could do was lay there stunned as Ashley appeared out of nowhere and landed on the feline shifter's back. The guy's eyes widened, but there was absolutely nothing he could do to stop the smaller, faster coyote shifter from sinking her fangs into the back of his neck.

The man howled in pain and threw himself to the side. He hit the ground rolling as he tried to shake her off. He finally managed it, but not before she'd dealt a lot of damage. When they both came up snarling at each other like rabid animals, the feline shifter took one look at Ashley and apparently decided he had business elsewhere. He turned and hauled ass like his wolf partner had done earlier.

Tate glanced at Ashley, and she snarled at him. He could see why the feline shifter had bailed. Ashley took batshit crazy to a whole new level.

She stared at him for another second, then ran off into the woods, where she stopped and dug down into a thick section of brambles, dragging Mahsood out kicking and screaming. She cuffed him once in the head, then tossed him over her shoulder and disappeared into the trees.

Tate blinked in shock, mostly at the fact that he and Chase were alive, but also at the realization that Ashley had stolen their prisoner.

He climbed to his feet and ran over to check on Chase. The cop waved him away. "I'm fine. We need to go after her. She can't run as fast while carrying Mahsood."

Tate nodded and started after the shifter and her prey. Chase kept up with him, cracked ribs be damned.

Tate couldn't believe they were risking their lives to save a man who'd experimented on dozens of people. Maybe he should just let Ashley have him.

"Would now be a bad time to point out that Ashley didn't seem to have an issue with carrying Mahsood?" Tate asked as they ran.

"That's because she's part animal and I'm not," Chase said, his breath coming a little labored. "Apparently, she has much more motivation to carry the man than I had. I'm pretty sure she's planning to drag him off and kill him for all the crap he did to her over the past decade."

Tate couldn't argue with that logic. The need for revenge could drive a person to some incredible lengths. He knew that for a fact.

"Your arm is bleeding a lot," Chase said. "You going to make it?"

"Yeah, I'm good. How about your ribs? You able to breathe okay?"

"I'm good," the deputy said. "You think we've seen the last of those other two shifters and their mercenary buddies?"

"That would be nice, but we need to be ready for them to catch up to us."

"Great," Chase said. "Then we can fight them and Ashley at the same time."

"Exactly. They'll be all together in one place, so that should make it easier."

Zarina screamed as the ground exploded in a hail of bullets a few feet to her left. The sound was purely involuntary, just like her instincts to spin around and throw herself over the three children she and Lillie had been leading to safety. The poor kids were so terrified, they simply froze in place, their faces shoved tight to the ground as if they thought the crazy people shooting at them wouldn't see them. She and Lillie quickly got the three kids moving, nudging them toward the corner of the nearest cabin as more bullets flew over their heads.

Zarina was surprised and relieved when they reached the safety of the cabin and darted around the side of it. Upon seeing the three heavily armed men in their path, she'd been sure it was over. Even though the morning's light was already beginning to brighten the eastern sky, somehow, the shooters had missed. So far.

The crazy thing was, she wasn't scared for herself. She was more worried about the kids. And Tanner. It would tear him apart if she got hurt—or worse.

"Get them to the main building!" Lillie shouted, leaning around the corner of the building and peppering the three men with several shots from her oversized handgun. "I'll keep these guys busy."

"I don't think splitting up is a good idea," Zarina said, holding her revolver ready in case she had to shoot someone. She prayed it wouldn't come to that, because it would take a miracle for her to hit anything.

Lillie pulled back from the corner, dropping the ammo clip from her weapon and loading another one so fast, Zarina had a hard time seeing exactly what she was doing. "We don't have a choice. Someone has to slow them down a little, and there's no way in hell I'm letting you do it. Take the kids and get them out of here. You can get some help and come back."

Before Zarina could protest anymore, Lillie slipped around the corner and disappeared. A moment later, Zarina heard the booming of the woman's weapon and knew Lillie was doing something stupid to give her time to get these little kids to safety.

Damn if Lillie wasn't just like Tanner!

Zarina turned and gathered the kid closest to her—a red-haired girl with eyes bulging in fear—and urged her forward. "All right, you heard Lillie. Let's get back to the main building. Fast!"

The trio obediently began moving as fast as their terrified feet could carry them. Zarina did her best to look in every direction at once, praying they didn't stumble over any more bad guys.

She'd run into Lillie only seconds after Tanner had taken off, and together they had immediately begun passing information to the confused preppers who'd just started sticking their heads out of their cabins, wondering what the hell Tanner had been yelling about.

Then Chad had come running, getting some of the men out to the perimeter while directing everyone else back toward the main building. He'd asked Lillie and Zarina to take care of the youngest of the camp's children so their parents could focus on defending the place. Zarina knew the older man had made the request because he thought it was the best way to keep his own daughter safe. How was he to know they'd stumble across a group of the men attacking the camp within minutes of leaving his side?

Zarina heard Lillie's big automatic go off several more times, but it sounded farther away, like she was leading the men toward the perimeter. By the time she and the kids reached the entrance of the main building, the shooting stopped. Zarina held her breath, praying she'd hear it again, but she didn't. Even as she banged on the door of the building, she knew there was something wrong.

The door swung open, and eager hands reached out to pull them inside, but Zarina resisted.

"I have to go back," she said firmly as Burt tried to tug her in.

"What's wrong?" he asked urgently.

"Lillie is out there. I think she's in trouble."

The other man didn't hesitate. "Let me get my weapon."

He disappeared from sight for a few seconds, then slipped out the door, carrying the same kind of rifle she'd seen Tanner with earlier.

"Where's the last place you saw her?" Burt asked, yanking a handle on the top of the weapon, then releasing it with a metallic clank.

Zarina turned and stepped off the porch, trying to remember exactly which direction Lillie's last shot had come from. She knew she didn't have a hybrid's tracking ability, but she was sure she could find the girl.

"Follow me," she said, hoping she sounded confident.

As they ran toward the north side of the camp, she realized she didn't hear much gunfire. She prayed that was a good thing.

As they rounded the last row of cabins before entering the tree line, she saw a man lying on the ground, bleeding from a gunshot wound, while two big men dressed in black tactical gear dragged Tanner into the woods. Lillie was nowhere in sight.

Heart in her throat, Zarina ran after them, not sure

what the hell she was going to do. She wasn't deluded enough to think she was good enough with her revolver to hit the men taking Tanner while not hitting him.

The pair must have heard her, because they both spun halfway around and fired off a burst of rounds in her direction. Burt tackled her, knocking her to the ground behind the dead man. That was fortunate, as the guy's body absorbed half a dozen bullets while they hid behind it.

She was trying to make herself as small as possible when she saw the man's face had been clawed open. Tanner's work for sure. She also saw Lillie's big automatic pistol lying on the ground beside the man.

Crap. There was no way Lillie would have given the weapon up without a fight. That meant the guys who had Tanner probably had Lillie, too. If she was lucky.

The gunfire coming their way abruptly stopped, and she looked up to see the men disappearing into the woods. She climbed to her feet, but then hesitated, her eyes darting toward the machine gun beside the dead man.

Zarina didn't think about the fact that she had no idea how to use the weapon. She only knew it was better than the small revolver she was carrying. Shoving the pistol into the holster on her belt, she grabbed the machine gun and took off running after the men who had Tanner.

Burt ran after her, but she ignored him, focused on catching up to the men she was after. Despite carrying someone as big as Tanner, the guys moved fast. It was all she could do to keep up with them, much less make up ground. Every time she did, one of them would turn around and shoot in her direction.

Zarina was gasping for air by the time she saw the

three SUVs ahead of her and Burt. Even as she watched, they tossed Tanner in the back of one of them alongside Lillie and a big man she thought was Spencer.

The blond-haired man who'd abducted Tanner turned slightly as he opened the passenger door of the SUV, and Zarina gasped when she saw it was Ryan.

She kept running, not understanding what Ryan was doing here or why he'd taken Tanner and the others. Beside her, Burt stumbled over something near the base of a fir tree, but she paid no attention. All she could focus on was Tanner and getting him back.

All three of the vehicles were pulling away by the time she caught up to them. She pointed the machine gun in the general direction of the tires. She knew if she missed, she could kill Lillie. Tanner and Spencer would survive a bullet, but the girl might not. Zarina had no choice though. She couldn't let them get away.

She did her best to aim, even though her hands were shaking like crazy, then pulled the trigger. The weapon bucked in her hands, and the passenger side windshield of the front SUV exploded into pieces.

She held the trigger down and lowered the weapon, trying again for the tires, but she missed. Undeterred, she kept shooting until the SUVs had completely disappeared from sight.

Zarina dropped to her knees, tears streaming down her face, her whole body trembling with fear. She wasn't a shifter or a hybrid or any kind of hero like that. She wasn't a fighter or a spy or even a computer hacker like everyone else at the DCO. She was simply a normal woman who wanted to help the man she loved, but she didn't have a clue how she was supposed to do it.

"Come on," Burt said, gently taking her arm. "I found Peter back there. He's still alive. We need to get him back to the main building, then let Chad know what happened. He'll know what to do."

She let Burt help her to her feet, not understanding what the man was saying about Peter until she saw the hybrid lying unconscious on the ground, two tranquilizer darts sticking out of his back. She yanked the darts out and checked his pulse, relieved Burt was right about him being alive. But at the same time, her mind was spinning over the fact that talking to Chad or any of the other preppers wasn't going to do anything to help Tanner, Lillie, or Spencer.

Then it hit her that Chad wasn't the person she should go to for help. She needed someone a lot better than Chad at dealing with dangerous men like Ryan.

<hr/>

"Who are you calling?" Chad asked suspiciously the moment Zarina took the satellite phone out of her pack. He wasn't the only one who was suspicious. While half the people in the main building were eyeing her hopefully, just as many were staring at her with open distrust.

She frowned at him, her finger hovering over the speed dial button Landon had programmed in for her. "Does it matter?"

The older man nodded. He was still being stubborn, even after finding out that his daughter had been kidnapped along with Tanner and Spencer. "We don't bring outsiders into our problems. It's not our way."

Zarina felt like punching the man, no matter how much she knew he was hurting over Lillie being gone.

"When it was just your people missing, it was your prerogative to try rescuing them on your own. But now your stubborn pride has gotten Tanner captured, so I'm done standing around wasting time. Your thick-headed belief that you don't need help from anyone is part of the reason Lillie got kidnapped. But you're too stuck in your ways to even see that."

Chad flinched a little at her words, along with everyone else in the room, but it was time they heard the harsh truth. For their own good.

"You may be willing to let your daughter die because you can't bring yourself to trust anybody, but I don't have that problem," she snapped. "I'm going to call the people Tanner and I work for, and they're going to turn this world upside down to save him and your daughter and everyone else who was kidnapped, because that's what they do."

Zarina didn't give Chad the chance to argue. Satellite phone in hand, she turned and headed for the door. She thumbed Landon's speed dial button the moment she stepped outside. She only prayed he'd answer. These days, Landon and Ivy were busy running all over the world, recruiting new operatives for the DCO or taking part in covert operations.

"Donovan."

Thank God.

"Landon, it's Zarina. Tanner's in trouble, and I need your help," she said simply, then dumped everything on the man who'd been watching out for Tanner since the day the DCO had found him. If anyone could rescue Tanner, it would be Landon.

Halfway into the conversation, he put the phone on speaker so Ivy could hear, too.

"You'll come, right?" Zarina asked when she was done. There was a long pause on the other end of the line.

"We'll be there, but it's going to take us a while," Landon said. "We're in the middle of Belarus right now, so it's going to be a few days before we can get there."

Zarina's heart dropped like a rock, tears springing to her eyes. This was hopeless.

"But that doesn't mean we can't help you right now," Ivy added quickly. "We'll get Kendra to dig up everything she can on Ryan. We're going to know more about him than he knows about himself. We'll figure out what he's up to and where he's taken Tanner and the others."

"While Kendra is doing that, we'll get as many operatives out there as we can," Landon said. "It might take a few hours, but by the time we have the info on Tanner's location, a team will be there, ready to do whatever is needed. You have our word on that."

Zarina started breathing again. "Thank you. I knew you wouldn't let me down."

"Not a chance," Ivy said. "But just in case, is there anyone out there we can count on for help?"

"Tanner has a brother," she said. "He's a cop in Seattle. I'm going to call him as soon as I hang up with you."

"Anyone else?" Landon asked.

She was about to say no, but just then, the door of the main building opened, and Chad, Burt, and Malcolm came out, determined expressions on each of their faces.

"There might be a few more," she admitted. "I'll call you back and let you know for sure."

Landon told Zarina they'd call the moment they dug up anything. "I'll send you the location of the nearest

DCO supply point south of Seattle. Head there as soon as you can. I'll have everyone meet you there."

"Okay," she said. "And Landon, thank you again."

Zarina hung up, ready to let Chad have it if he started arguing with her about bringing in outsiders again. But he surprised her.

"Burt and I have guns, and we know how to use them," Chad started. "We're not soldiers or cops, but we're willing to fight with you to save the people we care about. That includes Tanner."

She sighed, relieved. "Good. I don't know exactly how long it will take for my friends to get here, but we need to be there to meet them as soon as they arrive."

"We'll be ready," Chad assured her.

Chapter 14

TATE HAD TO HAND IT TO ASHLEY. SHE WAS ONE DETER-mined woman.

They'd chased the coyote shifter for nearly a mile through deep brush and cold, marshy ground, closing the distance between them little by little. The woman had a dozen chances to dump Mahsood and get away, but she didn't do it. Hell, there were a couple of places the shifter could have smashed the doctor's head against a tree trunk and called it a day. She didn't do that, either. Instead, she simply kept running until he and Chase caught up and tackled her.

They all tumbled to the ground in a heap, Chase gasping in pain, Mahsood screeching again, and Ashley leaping back to her feet with a snarl.

Tate pushed himself to his feet, then pulled his gun and aimed it at the center of her chest. She growled and took a step closer to him.

"I completely get why you want to kill this man, Ashley. I just met the guy today, and I already want to kill him, too," Tate said. "But unfortunately, we can't let you do that. So maybe we can all calm down and figure out a way to deal with this situation."

Ashley stared at him for a few seconds before turning her attention on Chase, who was climbing to his feet and heavily favoring his left side. Then her gaze dropped to Mahsood, and the expression of distaste that crossed her features didn't do anything to make Tate think she was ready to give up her prey. She growled and extended her claws.

Shit.

"Ashley, don't do it," he said softly. "Don't make me kill you, not over this piece of crap."

She tensed but didn't retract her claws. Out of the corner of his eye, he saw Chase drawing down on her, too. Tate really didn't want to have to kill her.

Just when he was sure Ashley was going to take a swipe at the doctor and tear his throat out, she jerked her head up and sniffed the air. In a blink, she turned and darted off to the side, disappearing into a thick stand of evergreens.

"Okay, that can't be good," Chase murmured.

Tate was thinking the same thing. He spun in a circle, trying to see which direction trouble was coming from, when he heard the first gunshot. He barely registered the sound when the bullet ripped a chunk of bark out of the tree where his head had been two seconds earlier.

Cursing, he shoved Chase and Mahsood behind the nearest group of trees, tackling them to the ground as dirt erupted around them in a hail of bullets. He didn't need to see who was shooting at them to know the people after Mahsood had finally shown up.

Chase rolled over onto his back, pulling a spare weapon magazine from his equipment belt and holding it ready for a quick change out. Tate did the same thing. *Shit*. Things were going to get really bad in a minute. To say they were outnumbered was an understatement. That wasn't even taking into account the whole machine gun versus pistol thing. That was almost unfair.

Oh yeah, and there were still the two shifters some-where around here, too.

Mahsood cowered between him and Chase. If the guy hugged the ground any tighter, he was going to start dig-ging in like a hermit crab.

"Now probably isn't a good time," Chase said casu-ally as guys with guns circled around to the left and right of them. "But are you ever going to tell me what the hell DCO stands for? Is that who you really work for?"

Tate took aim at some bushes off to his side that were starting to shake suspiciously. "What makes you think that?"

"Nothing specific," the deputy murmured, most of his attention focused on the mercenary in black who was low-crawling behind a fallen tree on their right. "But I couldn't help noticing that what we're doing now sure as hell doesn't show up as a typical Homeland mission on your website."

"I see your point," Tate said softly, waiting for the person behind the bush on his side to pop up and start shooting. "It's kind of complicated—and classified— but since we're both likely to be dead in the next few minutes, I can't see an issue with telling you."

"If not telling me will improve our chances of sur-vival, feel free to keep the secret to yourself."

Tate chuckled. If he had to be in a situation like this without Declan and the rest of his old team, he couldn't ask for a better person than Chase. Tate appreciated people who were cool in the face of impending doom.

"The DCO is the Department of Covert Operations," Tate said. "It's a classified organization buried in the guts of Homeland. Few people know it exists, and even fewer realize the government uses shifters for classified intel work."

Chase took the announcement in stride. No shock there. Nothing they'd been through had affected him yet, so why would hearing there was a secret government organization using shifters be any different?

"You don't have a shifter you usually work with?" Chase asked, poking his head around the tree to see where the bad guys were.

Tate shrugged. "I had one, but his wife had twins recently, and now he's home helping her take care of them. They're trying to find me another partner, but shifters don't grow on trees, you know?"

"Twins, huh?" Chase nodded. "That's cool."

Tate would have agreed, but that's when the mercenary guy on his side popped up and started shooting. It must have been the signal for all the others, because all hell broke loose after that.

The guy on Chase's side opened fire, too, while the two shifters—who'd quietly worked themselves all the way around until they were in front of them—jumped up and came racing at them full speed through the brush. The feline shifter had blood on his face and neck, as well as the front of his uniform. He seemed to be moving slower, too.

Tate ignored the two pissed-off shifters heading their way and instead focused on the man coming at him from the right. It was one of the guys who'd been on the stairs at Joanne's house.

Tate was still lying on his back when he remedied that problem by putting two bullets through the man's chest. The guy looked shocked for a second, then tumbled to the ground in a twisted pile of arms and legs.

Tate came up on one knee, his weapon swinging around fast to engage the feline shifter who was closing quickly on them. Even as he squeezed the trigger, he knew it was too late. The shifter was going to take him out before he got a shot off.

Then, out of nowhere, Ashley smashed into the feline shifter like a frigging truck. They hit the ground growling, yowling, and going at each other with their claws. Tate shifted his aim to the wolf shifter at the same time as Chase started shooting at her. Together, they forced the woman to veer sharply and race past them without engaging.

Tate probably would have cheered if Mahsood hadn't chosen that moment to jump up and run off into the woods, barely avoiding Ashley and the feline shifter rolling across the forest floor, tearing each other apart. The ungrateful bastard didn't make it more than thirty or forty feet before two of the bad guys rose up out of the bush and grabbed him, dragging him away.

"We're about to lose our prisoner!" Tate shouted.

Chase had gotten to his feet and was now moving toward the man behind the log on their left, shooting as he went. "I'm a little busy here," he called out without looking at Tate. "Go get him. I'll catch up."

Tate cursed and raced after Mahsood, slowing when he got close. Lifting his 9mm, he took slow, careful aim at one of the men leading the doctor deeper into the woods. He lined up his sights on the center of the man's back, steadying his hands. He was just about to squeeze the trigger when a strangled growl off to his left interrupted him. He threw a quick glance in that direction to see that the feline had Ashley pinned to the ground and was slowly choking the life out of her.

Shit.

Tate shifted his aim from the men dragging Mahsood away to the feline shifter and popped off a quick shot, clipping the shifter in the shoulder. The shot wasn't fatal, but it distracted the asshole enough for Ashley to push his hands away and rake her claws across the man's throat with a snarl, killing him. Ashley apparently didn't know that, because she shoved the shifter off her, then straddled his body, both hands swinging in a blur as she screamed in totally out-of-control fury.

Damn. Had he just shot the wrong shifter?

Ashley leapt to her feet and turned to glare at him, like she could actually hear his thoughts. She growled at him once, giving Tate a look that implied he shouldn't follow, then took off after Mahsood.

But he did, because he was stupid like that.

She was too fast for him to catch up, so he fired a few rounds in their direction, hoping to slow them down enough for him to line up the same shot he'd been about to take earlier. Instead, it earned him a burst of automatic weapon fire that had him diving for the dirt. He immediately came up and returned fire, cursing as the slide on his weapon locked back on an empty magazine.

Tate was in the middle of his reload when he sensed someone step out from behind a tree ten feet away. He looked up and saw the female wolf shifter standing there with an MP5 leveled straight and steady at his chest.

He was fucked. He couldn't reload faster than she could squeeze that trigger and obliterate him, and at this distance, any defensive move would have merely delayed the inevitable. He locked eyes with the woman, waiting.

She stared at him for a moment before dropping the

nose of the weapon down a few inches and plowing a dozen rounds into the dirt a few feet in front of him. He wasn't a fool. He didn't know what that was about, but he took the unexpected gift and got the hell out of there, finding refuge behind the nearest tree.

He finished reloading his weapon but still waited a few seconds before leaning out to take a look around. The men with Mahsood were long gone, and so was the wolf shifter. He caught sight of Ashley just before she disappeared from view into the trees, a furious expression on her face.

Tate was about to go after Mahsood and the men again when the sound of running feet from behind had him spinning around and lifting his weapon. He pulled up sharply as Chase slid to a stop in front of him.

"What happened?" Chase asked.

Tate wasn't sure himself. Mahsood had run right into the arms of the men trying to kill him while Tate had helped Ashley kill another shifter, and the wolf shifter had let him live after having him dead in her sights.

"That's a long story we can get into later," he told Chase. "Right now, we need to get moving if we hope to have any chance of catching up to them."

Tate started heading in that direction when his phone vibrated. Slowing to a fast walk, he pulled it out and thumbed the green button, then held it to his ear.

"Evers."

"It's Landon. I need you in Seattle ASAP."

"Now?" Tate frowned. "I'm in the middle of a shoot-out with Ashley Brannon and a group of hired guns who just kidnapped Mahsood. If I leave now, Mahsood is probably dead."

"That's Mahsood's problem," Landon said. "Tanner and Zarina are in deep shit out in Washington, and helping them takes priority over everything else. Get your ass to the airport. Kendra is arranging air transport right now."

"Shit." Tate stopped in midstride. Beside him, Chase did the same, a curious look on his face. "I knew I should have gone out there with Zarina. What happened?"

"An old army buddy of Tanner's kidnapped him. Kendra's trying to figure out where the asshole took him, and I want you out there to help with the rescue the second we have anything."

"I'm on the way." Tate hung up and looked at Chase. "Change of plans. Mahsood and Ashley are now my second priority."

"What's your first priority then?"

"Getting to Washington State to help out that lion hybrid I told you about. He's in trouble."

Chase frowned. "What the hell am I supposed to do, act like I never heard about any of this shit?"

Tate thought a moment. "You have any vacation days saved up?"

The question caught Chase off guard. "Yeah. Why?"

"Feel like taking a trip out to Washington State? I hear it's nice this time of the year."

"Is someone out there going to end up shooting at me?"

"Probably."

Chase seemed to consider that. After a moment, he shrugged. "When do we leave?"

Chapter 15

TANNER WAS NUMB ALL OVER WHEN HE WOKE UP, AND FOR A while, he lay there with his eyes closed. *Shit*. His head felt like it was full of cotton. *What the hell?*

It took him a minute to remember, but he slowly pieced everything together. Images of Lillie's unconscious body and Ryan kicking him in the face flashed in his head. He opened his eyes and bolted upright, terrified by the thought of what might have happened after he'd passed out. Most importantly, what had happened to Zarina?

While his mind was alert, his body hadn't quite caught up yet, and he nearly blacked out again. But he clawed and thrashed against the darkness, refusing to let it have him back. He had no idea how long he'd been unconscious, but he needed to figure out where he was and how to get out of there.

He looked around the pitch-black space, his eyes immediately shifting and allowing him to see as clearly as if someone had flipped a light switch. He was in a small, dank room with a single wooden door. Seven people lay curled up on the floor around him. They were so still that, at first, he thought they were all dead. But then he picked out seven individual heartbeats.

He sniffed the air for Zarina's scent, and even though the dark space was filled with a bewildering array of everything from sawdust to alcohol, he was relieved he couldn't pick up even a trace of her. Then he realized he couldn't smell Lillie either. Maybe she'd gotten away?

But while Zarina and Lillie might not be in here, there were other scents he recognized. One was Spencer. The other two were Bryce and Josh. He was also picking up blood. Lots of it.

Eager to help whichever captive was bleeding, he started to get to his feet only to stop when he realized there was something around his wrist keeping him from moving more than about two feet in any direction. He couldn't even stand up straight.

Frowning, he looked down and saw a heavy metal manacle around his right wrist attached to an equally stout chain running down to an eye bolt in the bare concrete floor. There was no way he was going to get loose from the thing, at least not easily.

Tanner glanced at the other captives and saw they were all wearing manacles like him. He called Spencer's name softly, then Bryce's, trying to rouse them. Spencer didn't stir, but Bryce lifted his head and pushed himself into a sitting position. He blinked at Tanner in the darkness, his eyes glowing ever so slightly. Bruises covered one side of his jaw, and there was a cut above his eye. He'd been hit hard—recently.

"I'm awake," he said quietly. "I thought you were still unconscious. I can't believe they grabbed you and Spencer, too. I was kind of counting on you guys to figure out where we were and get us the hell out."

Tanner grimaced. That had been the plan. At least the young hybrid seemed okay. "Help me wake Spencer up. We need to get our asses moving."

It took him and Bryce a few minutes before they

could wake Spencer. He sat up slowly, shaking his head as if trying to shake off the effect of the tranquilizer.

"What the hell hit me?" Spencer rasped. "I feel like my head has been used for batting practice, then recycled as the lining in a canary cage."

Yeah, that was a good way to describe it.

"They darted you and Peter while you were patrolling the perimeter of the camp," Tanner said. "They must have hit you with enough to put you guys under without giving you a chance to raise the alarm."

Spencer growled and yanked on the chain that held him prisoner. "Did they get Peter, too?"

"No. At least I don't think so," Tanner said quickly. "I was able to hide him in the trees before they got him."

All Tanner needed right now was for Spencer to completely lose it and rip his own hand off in an attempt to get free. He decided not to mention Lillie. If Spencer even got a hint she might be in trouble, there'd be no controlling him.

"Speaking of those assholes, any idea what they want with us?" Spencer asked. He'd given up on the manacle and chain. "It's got to be more than just kidnapping and murder, or they would have killed us already. And there's no way they're holding us for ransom."

"They're using us for sport," Bryce said, his lip curling. "And so far, the only people who have gotten out of here are the ones who've died."

Tanner frowned. "What do you mean, using us for sport?"

"He means they put us in a cage like the octagons you see on those pay-per-view MMA events and make us fight."

Josh sat up and slowly scooted around on his butt to face them. Tanner stared at him, stunned. The kid's nose had been broken, and his lip was busted. From the way he was slurring his words, his jaw was probably broken, too. Dried blood stained the front of his shirt, and more covered the legs of his jeans.

"They put me and two other people in the cage against five guys from the audience," Josh continued, staring into the darkness his regular human eyes couldn't pierce. "They let them have baseball bats while we had to fight with our bare hands. It was brutal. The crowd kept shouting for more even after the first person went down so hard, he couldn't get back up." He swallowed hard. "They beat a woman to death right in front of me, and people cheered."

Tanner didn't know what he'd been expecting, but getting thrown into some kind of gladiatorial fight wasn't it.

"The octagon is one level up from where we are now," Bryce added when Josh fell silent. "There's a dance club of some kind above that. At night, I can hear the music. I haven't had to fight yet. They said something about holding me back for the Saturday night crowd. Unless I've completely lost track of my days, I think today is Saturday, right?"

"Yeah," Spencer said.

Bryce nodded. "I guess I'm up next then."

Tanner couldn't believe how well Bryce was holding it together. Unfortunately, the same couldn't be said of Spencer. The hybrid's breathing was getting faster, and his heart rate was climbing. Rage was getting the best of him.

Tanner opened his mouth to say something to calm him down when a loud clank outside the room interrupted him. A moment later, the heavy wooden door opened, and a row of overhead fluorescents flickered on. The sudden brightness was almost blinding after the near-total darkness. It was even enough to shock Spencer out of his shift.

Tanner had to shield his eyes with his hand until he pushed his hybrid half firmly into the background and his gaze returned to normal. If he hadn't been so focused on the four men entering the room, he might have spent a few more seconds celebrating the fact that his control of the beast seemed to be getting stronger by the hour.

Ryan led the way into the room, looking even more arrogant and smug than he had back at the prepper camp. Two big men followed at his heels, spread out wide to either side like they were protecting a frigging dignitary. One was the blond, Scandinavian-looking guy—Anton. The other was darker skinned, South American maybe. Both had the look of professional muscle, definitely prior military. Tanner had seen their type before. They were well-trained men who lacked any form of moral compass. They evaluated threats and dealt with them as violently as necessary.

As they moved closer, Tanner caught sight of the large handguns each had tucked away in their underarm holsters beneath their suit jackets. A quick glance revealed the outline of backup weapons strapped to their right calves. He wouldn't be surprised if they were carrying other weapons, too.

There was another man with Ryan, too, a middle-aged Asian guy with shrewd, dark eyes.

Anton and his buddy scanned the room before

focusing their attention on Tanner. Maybe they thought he represented the most serious threat. That made sense, especially if they had no idea that Spencer and Bryce were hybrids, too. Tanner might be able to use that to his advantage.

"Told you he'd wake up fast, even with all those tranquilizers in him," Ryan said with a laugh. "But this is even better than I thought. You can't even see all that damage I did to his face from kicking him." He regarded Tanner admiringly. "Damn, you're one amazing freak."

Tanner would have preferred to stand toe-to-toe with Ryan, but the chain around his wrist made that impossible. So he settled for making himself comfortable on the floor. Bending his knee, he rested his forearm on his thigh. When he looked up at his old friend, he saw nothing but a piece of shit.

He swung his gaze from Ryan to the middle-aged Asian guy who had yet to say a single word or even crack an expression. He studied Tanner for a few moments with dark, flat eyes before surveying the other captives in the room.

Tanner glanced back at Ryan, who was still regarding him like a bug under a microscope. "You're the one forcing people to fight to the death in the basement of your club for money. So who's the freak here again?"

Ryan smirked. "We all do what we have to do to get by, old buddy."

Tanner shook his head as he surveyed the other captives. Like Josh, every one of them had bruises and were covered in blood. He turned back to Ryan. "No, we don't all do what we have to do. Some of us still remember what the hell we used to fight for and the things we believed in. The Ranger I used to know, the man I fought and bled with, wouldn't do shit like this."

Ryan's jaw clenched. "The man you fought and bled with was an idiot. He watched his brothers die so the rest of America could binge-watch their favorite TV shows, drink their soy lattes, and eat their avocado toast. War does strange things to us all, but it taught me an important lesson—take care of yourself, because no one else gives a shit whether you live or die. This is just me taking care of myself."

"We all had a hard time over there, Ryan. I lost friends, too. But you don't see me feeding innocent people to a bloodthirsty crowd for a few bucks."

"No, but I do see you growing fangs and claws," he answered. "War turned me into an entrepreneur who sees the profit potential in a little spilled blood. It turned you into a freak."

"Enough!" the Asian man snapped. "You said you had something to show me, Ryan. Something that would move the needle."

Ryan glanced at the man, then gave Tanner a speculative look. "So, how about it, old buddy? You going to show Mr. Nguyen what you're made of? Impress him as much as you impressed me?"

Tanner lifted a brow. "You're kidding, right?"

"I know how to get what we want." Grinning at the other guard, Anton pulled a large knife from behind his back. "The monster came out when he was in pain. I say we stick him once or twice in the leg. Something tells me that will work."

Even though he'd gained a lot more control over his inner beast lately, thanks to Zarina, Tanner felt his gums and fingertips tingle as the hybrid tried to take over and protect him against the attack it knew was coming.

Tanner did his best to keep the beast at bay, promising it that he'd make his move when the man got close enough to strike. He could take Anton hostage and pin the knife to the man's throat. If he did this right, he might be able to get everyone out of here.

But Ryan put a hand on Anton's shoulder. "Stand down. You too, Emilio. You'd only be wasting your time anyway. That's not how it works with Tanner. All that'll do is piss him off. If you really want to get a reaction out of him, you don't go after him. You go after someone else. Someone innocent."

Tanner stiffened, his fangs elongating ever so slightly. Ryan knew him too well.

"Someone like..." Ryan glanced around the room, his gaze falling on the middle-aged woman. She had a nasty bruise on her left cheek and an ugly gash starting at her right temple and disappearing into her hairline. "Her." He gave Anton a grin. "Stab her anywhere but in the leg. I want her to be able to stand in the cage."

Tanner's fangs and claws ripped their way out before he could stop them. He lunged at Anton with a roar. The man froze, and Tanner could have finished him right then and there if it wasn't for the damn manacle around his right wrist. He groaned in frustration as the chain stopped him short, his arm nearly ripping out of the shoulder joint as the claws of his left hand tore into the man's suit jacket. While he grazed the skin, he did no real damage beyond that.

Anton scrambled back, his eyes huge as he reached for his gun. Beside him, Emilio did the same. Tanner didn't care. He snarled and lunged again, straining against the chain holding him as he fought to get a piece of the men.

It was Ryan's applause that snapped him out of his rage. That and the fact that he could sense both Spencer and Bryce getting ready to lose it, too. Knowing how bad that would be was enough to get him to rein his inner animal back in. It complained but conceded much faster than Tanner would have ever thought possible given the situation.

Breathing hard, he let his fangs and claws slowly retract.

"Think that would move the needle?" Ryan asked Nguyen.

The man nodded approvingly. "It will indeed. In fact, he'll be tonight's main event. One flash of those fangs, and our offshore bets will go through the roof."

"I'm not going to fight for you," Tanner growled. "I don't care what you do. I won't hurt people for your entertainment."

Ryan glared at him. "You'll do anything I say, or I'm going to do all kinds of unspeakable things to that girl I grabbed."

Tanner went still, terrified his worse fears had come true and that Ryan had kidnapped Zarina. "If you hurt Zarina, I'll—"

"Tear me apart with your claws, I know." Ryan sneered. "Believe me, I wish I'd been able to get my hands on that beautiful Russian girlfriend of yours, but it didn't work out that way. However, I do have the dark-haired girl you tried to save, the one with the scars on her neck. A gift from you, I'm guessing?"

Ryan barely got the words out before Spencer shifted

and lunged for him, Bryce at his heels. Ryan might have been careful to stay out of Tanner's reach, but he'd put himself dangerously close to the other two hybrids. He would have died right then if it wasn't for Emilio. The man moved fast, yanking Ryan out of the way just as Bryce and Spencer got there.

Bryce pulled up, but Spencer refused to give up. Eyes glowing red, he snarled and yanked at the chain so hard, Tanner heard his arm bones crack.

Ryan laughed. He looked like a frigging kid at Christmas. "This keeps getting better and better. I had no idea there were three of you freaks. Is there something in the water out there or what?"

Tanner didn't answer, not that Ryan seemed to need one. The asshole turned to Nguyen. "I think we have some more opponents for the main event. With these three in the ring, we'll have a hard time counting all the money we're going to make."

Nguyen nodded, his mouth curving into a smile. After a moment, he turned and walked out, leaving Ryan and the other two men behind.

"If you hurt that girl—" Tanner started, but Ryan cut him off.

"That's up to you, not me. You do exactly what I tell you, and she'll live through the night. You try anything, and the pain she'll go through before she dies will make you sorry you were ever born."

The threat drove Spencer even further over the edge. He jerked at the manacle until his wrist bled, but it did no good.

Tanner bit back a growl as his old friend—or the man who used to be his friend—turned and walked out of the room, taking Anton and Emilio with him, slamming the door shut as they went.

It took almost an hour to calm Spencer down, during which he roared and howled so loudly, the human prisoners put their hands over their ears to block out the sound. Tanner could have told them it wouldn't work. He knew because he'd tried it when those doctors had injected Spencer with the hybrid serum all those months ago. Tanner hadn't been able to do anything to help the man's agony then, and there wasn't anything he could do now.

—⁓—

"How do we know that Tanner and the others are even in there?" Zarina tried to keep the terror out of her voice as she looked at pictures of Ryan's club spread out on the table, but she was sure she failed. "What if they've already killed them?"

Zarina had done all she could to keep it together, but the endless hours of doing nothing but sitting on her hands at the DCO's storage unit in Seattle had been hard as hell. She'd practically made herself sick imagining all the horrible things that might be happening to Tanner. Was he hurt—or worse?

She'd known it would take time for Landon to get help out here, but she'd never dreamed it would be close to sundown before most of the DCO operatives showed. And now that they were here, all they were doing was wasting time looking at stupid maps and satellite photos.

Why the hell weren't they already at The Cage, going in to get Tanner and the others out?

Beside her, Cam reached out and covered her hand

where it rested on the table, giving it a reassuring squeeze. It didn't help very much. Tanner's brother looked as worried as Zarina felt.

It was Danica Buchanan, FBI-agent-turned-DCO-operative and one of her best friends at the covert organization, who answered. "There aren't a lot of traffic cameras around the Wenatchee area, but we accessed enough of them to get an idea of which direction the three black SUVs you shot up this morning were heading. They made a beeline for Ryan's club, which is located about forty-five minutes outside Seattle, just west of Redmond."

Zarina gazed down at the big map with the red circle drawn on it. The corners of the map were held down with boxes of ammunition that were merely a small sample of the hoard of bullets and explosives stored in the place. In fact, there were enough weapons, night-vision goggles, computer equipment, and communication gear to start a small war. Apparently, the DCO kept places like this all over the world in case their operatives needed anything special for a mission. She was glad they did, even if the thought of them having to fight their way into Ryan's club to rescue Tanner and the others scared the hell out of her. Not enough to dissuade her from going in with everyone else, but enough to make her stomach clench even more than it already was.

"Satellite photos confirm the vehicles showed up at the club immediately after they grabbed Tanner and your friends," Clayne Buchanan, Danica's husband, wolf shifter, and DCO partner, said softly. "There's no indication they've left since."

Danica and Clayne had gotten to the storage unit

forty-five minutes ago. The two DCO operatives had immediately gotten the computer equipment running, then printed maps, photos, and intel reports. Zarina was glad the couple were there. Danica was extremely good at thinking through problems and making plans, while Clayne was equally good at skipping those and going straight to the fighting and killing. Zarina only wished they'd spend less time on Danica's part and get on with Clayne's.

"As far as them still being alive, we have to believe they are," Chase said, leaning forward to catch Zarina's eye, even though the movement made him wince in pain. "We don't know why Ryan took them, but the asshole went to a lot of effort to tranquilize them and take them to his club. He must have a purpose for them. That means they're going to be alive long enough for us to get in there and rescue them."

Tate and the sheriff's deputy from Maine had shown up twenty minutes after Danica and Clayne, somehow swinging a nonstop flight from Boston. Chase was obviously dealing with some kind of injury, but when she offered to take a look at it, he waved her off and told her he was fine.

"I can't believe the DCO doesn't have a single clue why Ryan kidnapped Tanner and all those other people," Staff Sergeant Carlos Diaz said. "I thought you people could find anything on anyone."

Zarina had been stunned when Diaz had shown up. A Special Forces soldier from Landon's old A-team, he'd fought alongside the DCO on several occasions but had only recently discovered he was a coyote shifter. She'd assumed the soldier would be deployed off to some dark corner of the globe with the other members of his A-team, but luckily, he'd been home on leave in San Diego and had decided raiding a night club to rescue a hybrid who tried to kill him two months ago sounded like fun. Zarina didn't understand why most men did the things they did, but she was glad to have him there.

Danica frowned. "I wish we knew. When Landon told us about Westbrook and his club, we spent a good portion of the flight from Mexico trying to come up with a possible connection between a club and the abductions. We considered everything. Drugs, illegal gambling, human trafficking, the black-market organ trade, even hybrid research. But nothing fits with the facts as we know them so far."

Walking over to the printer, Danica pulled off a stack of photos and spread them out on the table. Zarina thought they looked like mug shots, but she wasn't sure.

"When one of our analysts discovered a Vietnamese gang out of Tacoma with known ties to the LA drug trade paid for the renovations to The Cage, we were sure drugs were the answer," Danica said, setting down the last picture.

"But?" Chad prompted. Worry over his daughter's kidnapping was visibly wearing on him. Waiting for the DCO agents to arrive had been as difficult for him as it had been for Zarina. It didn't help that he was also concerned the people he'd left at the camp would be attacked again while he, Burt, and Malcolm were trying to save Tanner and the others. That was why he wouldn't let Peter come with them. He'd wanted there to be at least one fighter back to protect everyone.

"But the drug angle hasn't panned out," Clayne put

in. "While we know they're selling some party drugs out of the club, there isn't nearly enough stuff being moved through there to justify the number of gang members who seem to be providing security for the place. Besides, if this is simply about drugs, what the hell do they need with Tanner and the others?"

"Wait a minute," Burt said. "There are members of an Asian gang pulling security for the place in addition to the mercenary types who attacked our camp? How many guys are we talking about?"

"There's no way of knowing exactly how many we'll face when we go in there," Danica answered. "But if the pictures our analyst at the DCO has pulled off Facebook are any indication, there are probably at least a dozen at any one time. More at night when the club is open."

Everyone at the table looked a little concerned at that, Zarina included. While their group had a Special Forces soldier, two cops, three covert operatives, a hybrid, and three people willing to do anything to save the people they loved, there were still only ten of them.

"If there will be more security at night, why aren't we going in now before the club opens?" Zarina demanded.

Danica shook her head. "We can't go in there blind. If we try to go in through the front door without knowing what's waiting for us, we won't be any help to Tanner and the captives, because we'll all be dead."

Zarina almost screamed in frustration. She wasn't eager to go charging into that club carrying a weapon, but the thought of Tanner being in danger for another minute was more than she could handle.

"Okay, so it's agreed. We need a plan," Tate said, breaking the silence that had invaded the tight space of the storage unit. "What do we know about the club? Any floor plans?"

"Unfortunately, we know very little that will help," Danica admitted. "Before it was a club, it was a sawmill. While it's been renovated, we can still expect an almost industrial warehouse-like feel when we go in, most likely with limited lighting and lots of small rooms everywhere. Once the shooting starts, we could have people aiming at us from fifty feet away or less than ten, and we might not be able to see them in either situation."

Zarina didn't understand the significance of anything Danica said. But it didn't matter. They were going in that club, one way or the other.

"I might be able to help with that," Cam said, looking up from the cell phone Zarina hadn't even noticed he'd been holding. "I knew the building The Cage was in was old, so I had a friend of mine who's an amateur historian do a little digging. It turns out the mill had been set up over the remains of a gold and silver mine in the 1930s. The basement of the club is actually the sections of the mine that weren't sealed off. My friend's almost certain there are other ways for us to get into the basement without going through the main entrance. He's digging out maps of the mine right now."

Zarina silently said a quick prayer of thanks. "How long do you think it will take for him to come up with them? We need to get in there before Ryan does whatever it is he has in mind for Tanner and the others."

Cam nodded as he shoved his phone back in the pocket of his jeans. "He promised he'll have the maps within the hour."

While that still seemed like an inordinately long

amount of time to Zarina, Danica, Clayne, and Tate clearly didn't agree. They immediately began handing out weapons, ammunition, and equipment.

"I know nobody wants to talk about this, but I have to bring it up, because I've been on the wrong side of this situation before," Diaz said, taking the boxes of bullets Clayne offered.

Tate frowned. "What do you mean?"

"I mean that when we go in there, it's almost certainly going to be bad," Diaz explained. "Between those gang members and Ryan's ex-military buddies, there's going to be shooting, and probably a lot of it."

"So?" Tate asked. "It's not like we haven't dealt with people shooting at us before. Lots of people in fact."

"Yeah, well, the last time we all got into a bad situation with Tanner, he completely lost it and nearly killed me." Diaz's face was grim. "What do we do if he loses it again?"

"He might not be the only one." Clayne glanced at Malcolm. "Don't take this the wrong way, but bringing another hybrid in with us to go with the other two who are already in there is asking for trouble. The chances of one of you guys going apeshit is damn high."

Malcolm frowned, but instead of getting angry like Zarina thought he would, he merely nodded. "You're right. There's a good chance one of us will lose control."

Zarina wanted to think that what Diaz and Clayne were suggesting wouldn't happen, but she knew better. As much as Tanner's control had improved, he was still a hybrid. When the gunfire started and the blood started flowing, there was no telling what would happen. Hell, it might not even be a matter of losing control. If Tanner thought innocent people were in danger, he'd purposely let the beast inside take over, no matter the cost.

Cam paused in the middle of checking the machine gun he was holding to look at everyone in confusion. He probably wanted to ask what the hell they were talking about, the same way he almost certainly wanted to know why they couldn't call in Seattle SWAT and have them raid the club. But there hadn't been time to talk to him about anything, especially the part about his older brother being half animal.

Zarina picked up her backpack from where she'd placed it on the floor and took out the case with the antiserum. "If it comes to it, I'll use this on Tanner or any of the other hybrids."

Diaz eyed the injector solemnly. "Is that the antiserum?"

She nodded. "The whole reason I came out here was to get Tanner to take this and reset his body back to the way it had been before he was experimented on. But he didn't want to take it."

"Why not?" Clayne asked.

She sighed. "A lot of reasons."

On the other side of the table, Malcolm's gaze was locked on the plastic case. "Are there any side effects to taking something like that?"

"Yes, but that's not why Tanner didn't want to take it," Zarina said. "Because the antiserum resets the body, Tanner—or whoever else takes it—will go through nearly as many physiological and psychological changes as they did the first time around."

"What kind of changes?" Malcolm prompted.

Zarina hesitated. "There's a good chance whoever takes the antiserum might not be able to have children."

He considered that, then nodded and blew out a breath. "Anything else?"

"You might not remember most of the things that have happened since becoming a hybrid," she said quietly.

Danica blinked. "Wait a minute. Are you saying that Tanner might not remember you if you give him the antiserum?"

"It's possible, yes," Zarina admitted.

Clayne bit back a growl. "You don't have the right to use something like that on Tanner or any of them. To take away Tanner's memories of you..." He shook his head. "It's not right."

"Do you think I want to do it?" Zarina demanded. "Of course I don't. But I might not have a choice."

"There's always a choice," Clayne said. "Something tells me Tanner would rather die than lose a single memory of the time he's had with you."

Zarina pinned the wolf shifter with a look. "Well, I'm not ready to let him die, even if it's what he'd want. If it's between him forgetting me or accidentally killing someone he cares about, I'll do what I have to do."

In the silence that followed, Chad cleared his throat. "Lillie would hate me for saying this, but if it comes down to Spencer losing control, the antiserum is better than the alternative. Same goes for Bryce."

Tate frowned. "Wait a minute. You only have that single injector, right? What happens if more than one of the hybrids loses it? How do we decide who gets the antiserum and who doesn't?"

There was another long silence.

"Let's pray it doesn't come to that," Zarina finally

said. "If it does, we'll use the antiserum on the first one
we can get to and deal with the others as best we can."

Everyone nodded, then went back to what they'd
been doing. A few moments later, Danica told everyone
to get the last of the gear packed up. They'd leave for
Redmond in fifteen minutes.

Zarina was looking through a wall locker for extra
bullets for her trusty revolver, a task made more difficult
since she didn't know the caliber of the weapon, when
Cam grabbed a box marked .38 Special.

"Here," he said.

She opened the box and pulled one of the bullets out,
going the extra step of comparing it to the kind already
loaded in her revolver. They looked like an exact match
to her.

"Thanks," she said, slipping the box in the pocket of
her jacket. It was heavier than she thought it'd be.

"No problem." He gazed down at her with blue eyes
so like his brother's, it made her heart pang. "So, do
you think you can tell me what the hell is going on?
Because I didn't understand half the crap you guys were
talking about. Hybrids, people going crazy, and antiserum that takes away a person's memory? None of this
makes any sense."

Around them, everyone was hurriedly loading weapons and trying on night-vision goggles. They didn't have
a lot of time for this.

She looked at Cam. "Remember in the diner when
Tanner said those bad people he mentioned had done
some experiments on him? Well, you're going to see
the effects of those experiments tonight, and it's going
to freak you out. Tanner, as well as Malcolm and two

other men Ryan kidnapped, are part animal now. When
they lose control, the animal takes charge, and they can
be extremely dangerous."

Cam did a double take. "Damn. When he said that, I
had no idea... What kind of sicko does that to another
person?" He shook his head. "It doesn't matter. I don't
care if my brother is part animal. Tanner would never
hurt me."

"He wouldn't want to, and it would destroy him
afterward, but if he was far enough gone, he'd rip your
throat out without even realizing who you are." Zarina
swallowed hard. "If something happens, and you see
Tanner doing things that scare the hell out of you, get
away from him and find me. Okay?"

Cam regarded her thoughtfully. "So you can give him
the antiserum that might make him forget you?"

Tears burned Zarina's eyes. The possibility that
Tanner might not remember her and everything they'd
shared tore her heart out, making it suddenly hard to
breathe. "Yes."

Chapter 16

IT HAD TAKEN TANNER AND BRYCE ALMOST TWO HOURS TO get Spencer to calm down, and by then, Spencer's wrist was mangled and bloody. If he were human, losing his hand would have been a forgone conclusion, but he barely seemed to notice it. The craziest part of the whole thing was no one else in the small room had freaked out. Perhaps they had experience with shifters before. More likely, their spirits were so crushed that caring about anything was impossible.

"We're going to figure a way out of this," Tanner told Spencer. The other hybrid sat huddled on the floor beside him, his arms wrapped around his knees, his eyes staring at nothing. "I have no doubt Zarina has already called the organization we work for. They'll be here soon. In the meantime, we're going to find Lillie and get her out of here. I swear it on my life."

Maybe Spencer heard him, maybe he didn't, but Tanner kept talking, hoping to snap him out of the nearly catatonic state he was in. Tanner didn't know what the hell was going to happen next in this place, but when they had a chance to move, he needed Spencer to be ready.

"This is all my fault," Spencer whispered.

At least he was talking now. That had to be a good thing, even if his words didn't make a lot of sense. Tanner glanced at Bryce to see if he knew what Spencer was referring to, but the younger hybrid only shrugged.

"What do you mean?" Tanner asked Spencer. "None of this is your fault. There's no way you could have seen this coming."

Spencer looked at him, his eyes full of regret. "I've already hurt Lillie once. No matter how much I love her, I knew if we stayed together, it would only be a matter of time before I hurt her again. She got kidnapped because she was with me."

Shit. Tanner suddenly had a vivid sensation of what it must be like for Zarina when he took responsibility for every bad thing that happened in the world. Was it as frustrating for her as it was for him right now? Probably.

Tanner was seriously considering using one of Zarina's lines on Spencer and telling him Lillie was an adult who made her own decisions when the door opened. Ryan, Emilio, and Anton strode in, followed by three big Asian guys.

Even though he knew he had to stay calm, Tanner's heart beat faster. They were almost certainly here to take someone upstairs to fight. This might be their chance to make their move. Tanner didn't like the odds, though. Three hybrids chained to the floor against six trained men with weapons wasn't the most ideal situation. If they uncuffed more than one of them, that might improve their chances.

Ryan had clearly learned his lesson last time, because he didn't come anywhere near Tanner. He regarded Spencer for a moment before turning to Bryce. He gave the men with him a nod, then motioned to Josh and a few of the men along the far wall.

"Bring the woman, too," Ryan said. "For whatever reason, people love seeing a woman in the cage.

Hopefully sending the freak out there with them will give us a better fight than the last group gave us. The betting barely started before they all got thrashed."

The three Asian men moved in to unchain the people Ryan had selected, while Emilio and Anton focused on Bryce.

"You don't have to do this, Ryan," Tanner said, his gums tingling as the hybrid inside tried to make an appearance. "It's not too late to fix this."

Ryan's lip curled. "Damn, Tanner. Do you ever give it a rest? Stop trying to save my soul. The army burned it out a long time ago."

"Is that what you tell yourself so you can sleep through the night?" Tanner demanded. "That the army's to blame for all this?"

Ryan chuckled and stepped closer but still well out of reach. Tanner gave Bryce a quick look, then glanced at Emilio, still unlocking the manacle, hoping the hybrid got what he was trying to tell him. Bryce nodded slightly in understanding.

"You don't have to worry about me, Tanner," Ryan said, dragging his attention back to him. "I sleep just fine at night."

Bryce made his move the moment Emilio unchained him. One moment, he was sitting on the floor docilely; the next, he was sinking his fangs into the man's shoulder.

Tanner lunged for Ryan at the same time, but his old friend quickly backpedaled, and Tanner's outstretched claws missed the man's neck by inches. Tanner slammed to the floor in frustration just as a gun went off. Cursing, he jerked his head up, trying to figure out where the gunshots had come from, only to see Bryce tumble to the floor, dragging Emilio down with him. The man immediately rolled away and jumped to his feet. His shoulder was bleeding badly, but otherwise, he was uninjured. He reached under his jacket and pulled out his weapon, quickly pointing it at Bryce, but the move was unnecessary. Bryce was already down, and judging from the two dark stains spreading over his shirtfront, he wasn't getting up anytime soon. That son of a bitch Anton had shot him in the stomach.

"What the fuck did you do that for?" Ryan shouted. "He was going to earn us a million dollars in bets tonight. Mr. Nguyen is going to go ballistic."

"The asshole was going to kill Emilio," Anton said, his weapon still pointed at Bryce, curled up on the floor with his hands cradling his stomach. "He had his teeth buried in Emilio's damn shoulder!"

Ryan didn't seem to give a shit about that. He completely ignored Emilio as the man peeled back the collar of his shirt and checked the damage, muttering something about turning into one of those damn freaks. Instead, Ryan shoved a hand through his hair and cursed, his eyes darting back and forth between Bryce and Spencer, who was still sitting there staring at something only he could see.

"What the hell are we going to do now?" Ryan muttered. "The crowd up there is frothing at the mouth for the big fight we promised them."

"Drag him up there," Anton said, gesturing with the gun at Spencer.

Tanner tensed. Spencer was still out of it. If they tossed him into a fight right now, there was no telling what would happen.

Ryan frowned. "I don't know. I think Mr. Nguyen has other plans for him."

"I'll do it," Tanner said before Ryan could change his mind. Or suggest that his men drag Bryce up to the ring to fend for himself. A hybrid could take a lot of punishment, and Tanner hoped Bryce survived long enough for him to figure a way out of this, but the man was in too much pain to fight.

Ryan gave Tanner an appraising look. "Mr. Nguyen has something special planned for you, too, and as much as I'd love to see you get your ass whooped, I can't have anyone damaging our star attraction before the main event."

Tanner shifted just enough to make his eyes glow red, grinning as Ryan took a quick step back. "You seriously think anything you have waiting up in that cage is going to damage me?"

Ryan gazed at him for a moment longer, then turned to Anton. "Take off his chains. He'll go up in place of the other one."

Anton stepped forward but then hesitated.

Ryan laughed. "Emilio, stop whining about that boo-boo on your shoulder and point your weapon at the freak staring at nothing over there."

Emilio did as he was told, though he didn't look too happy about it. He was obviously in pain and getting paler by the minute.

Ryan turned his attention on Tanner, pinning him with a look. "Here's the deal. Emilio is going to stay down here with his gun pointed at the head of your freaky friend. If you try anything when Anton releases you, he'll shoot your freaky friend in the head. If you try anything when we get upstairs, like decide not to fight, he'll shoot your freaky friend in the head. And just in case you think it might help to take me out first, if I don't call him every two minutes and let him know everything is going peachy, he'll shoot your freaky friend in the head. Is there any part of that that doesn't make sense to you?"

It was then Tanner realized he was actually looking forward to killing his old friend. He told himself it was his hybrid half putting those thoughts in his head, but he wasn't sure. Maybe it was his subconscious trying to get him to accept there wasn't much chance of this working out any other way.

Anton holstered his automatic and nervously unlocked the manacle around Tanner's wrist, his eyes focused on him the entire time. When he was done, he quickly stepped back and pulled his weapon again as Tanner got to his feet.

"I know you, Tanner," Ryan said as he led the way out of the room and headed down a brightly lit corridor that had been neatly carved from the very bedrock of the club's foundation. Smaller tunnels branched off on either side of them, and Tanner could smell stale air coming from them. "You're probably already trying to come up with some daring scheme to rescue yourself and your friends. I'm telling you now you can forget it. Between the club level and the cage level, I have more than twenty heavily armed security people. Anything you try will only get you and all your friends killed."

"You have heavily armed security people?" Tanner asked as they approached a set of broad, smooth stone steps. "Or does Mr. Nguyen have them?"

Ryan glanced over his shoulder as he started up the steps, mouth twitching. "Does it really matter? You'll be dead regardless."

Tanner ignored him, focusing on the pair of heavy metal doors at the top of the stairs. He could already hear the muted cheering and applause coming from the other side. The sound by itself was enough to make his gums ache again. Behind him, Josh's heart was beating like a drum along with the other two captives. The two men and the woman were terrified.

When they reached the landing, Ryan turned to look at him. "Before we go in there, let me give you some more advice, Ranger to Ranger. Don't embarrass yourself. The moment we walk through those doors, every guard in the place is going to have eyes on you. You need to get into that ring and put on a good show for the crowd. And please, when you start getting your ass kicked, don't expect me to step in and save you."

Tanner glared at him. "Don't worry. I no longer have any expectations when it comes to you. You've already shown me exactly what kind of dirtbag you really are."

Ryan's only answer was to laugh and shove open the heavy double doors.

Loud music and shouting slapped Tanner in the face, along with the acrid scents of sweat and blood and an almost tangible wave of excitement. His fangs elongated in response, and he felt the first twisting and tearing of muscles that came before a shift.

Shit.

He'd thought after being with Zarina, he'd made a breakthrough of sorts. Yeah, the tingling gums and fingernails had still been there, and he'd shifted out of pure instinct a couple of times, but it had been nothing like this. He'd thought he'd be able to stay calmer than this. He'd obviously been wrong.

Tanner was so busy trying to hold off his hybrid half that he almost missed what Ryan was saying. Some crap about these fights being transmitted to a hundred places around the world all without anyone knowing where they were going down. He was only dimly aware of the huge open-air space around them and the crowd of people dressed in designer clothes, sipping fancy drinks, as he followed Ryan up to the big octagonal fighting cage.

As they got closer to the ring, the stone ceiling above him ended, revealing a second viewing area enclosed in lightly tinted glass. A part of him vaguely wondered what the hell a space like that was doing in what had probably been a sawmill at one time. It was like he was in a frigging football stadium. Although he guessed a gladiatorial ring would be more appropriate. Multiple tunnels exited the big room, and he instinctively picked up on which ones led toward the fresh air upstairs and which ones held nothing but dank air.

Tanner quickly lost interest in the sheer scale of the underground stadium as his inner beast continued to try and push its way out. He couldn't let that happen. Not here in front of all these people. He took a deep breath and forced himself to relax as he envisioned the same door he'd constructed a thousand times in his mind before tonight. Opening the imaginary door, he nudged his hybrid half into the room and closed the door on that part of himself, believing with everything he had that he could control the monster within. The animal let itself be locked away with hardly any fight at all. Almost as if it knew there'd be time to get free later.

Tanner slowly backed away from the hybrid edge, silently congratulating himself on getting past the worst of the inner battle. Then he looked up and saw the cage. His inner beast woke up and slammed against the door, wanting back out.

He ignored the animal and forced himself to take in every detail of the cage, knowing he might need the information later. It was positioned on a platform five feet high with heavy-gauge fencing fully enclosing the sides and the top. There were two entrances, one on either side, both guarded by beefy guys with weapons openly displayed on their hips.

Five large, muscular men stood inside the cage. Shirtless, they wore black military-style cargo pants and combat boots. Each man weighed in at two hundred and twenty pounds minimum. One looked closer to three hundred. All of them held aluminum bats that were stained with dark-red blood.

Anton nudged Tanner toward the entrance closest to them even as the crowd began to cheer louder. Off to the side, Ryan raised his hands with a grin, urging them on.

"Remember to put on a good show for me unless you want Emilio to get bored down there and start shooting people," Ryan said as one of the guards opened the gate.

Before Tanner could reply, a hand on his back shoved him into the cage. Someone else did the same to Josh, then the other two captives. A moment later, one of the stocky guards wrapped a heavy chain around the gate and the nearest fencing post, locking them in.

The cheering became deafening as Tanner turned to the five men Ryan expected him, Josh, and the others to fight. Over an intercom system, he could barely make out a voice calling out numbers he assumed were some kind of betting line. Based on the way the people in the crowd were tapping away at the screens on their phones, Tanner guessed all the betting was done online. Wasn't that convenient?

Tanner turned away from the five men to take in the view of the stadium from inside the cage. He saw at least four individual cameras and wondered if there were others he couldn't see. There were at least a hundred and fifty people on the main floor, with easily fifty or so behind the glass in the enclosed luxury seats above. In one of them, Ryan took a seat beside Nguyen and smiled at Tanner.

What an asshole.

Out of the corner of his eye, he saw the five men spread out. Two of them, including the big guy, looked like they intended to deal with him, while the other three moved to handle Josh and the others.

"What do we do?" Josh said nervously from behind him, his slurred words barely audible over the screaming crowd. The jackasses were stomping their feet now like they were at a frigging sporting event.

"Stay behind me in a tight group against the fence and protect each other," he said firmly. "I'll take care of these assholes."

The men with the baseball bats chuckled at that, but Tanner didn't care. If these men wanted a fight, he'd give them exactly what they were asking for.

Gaze locked on them, he let his body shift a little.

Bones popped and muscles tore as they took on his hybrid form. The urge to completely let go and let the beast out was overwhelming. Part of him didn't care if everyone saw what he was and thought him a monster. Because he knew while he might be the one with fangs and claws, he wasn't the real monster. They were up in the luxury seats and out there in the crowd.

But he resisted the urge. He couldn't reveal what he and the other hybrids and shifters of the world were. While he, Spencer, and Bryce might be in terrible danger at the moment, it was nothing compared to the danger their kind would be in if their secret slipped out. He'd have to do this without fangs and claws.

The smaller of the two men grinned smugly as he cocked his bat over his right shoulder and came in swinging. Tanner immediately closed the distance and caught the aluminum club in his hand just before it connected with his temple. Then he lunged forward and drove his fist into the man's face. There was a crunch, some of which probably came from the bones in his own hand breaking. But the minor pain was worth it to see blood spatter from the man's nose as he collapsed with a thud on the floor of the cage.

While he'd been occupied with the first man, the bigger guy had used the distraction as an opportunity to attack, the bat in his hand nearly forgotten as he charged in like a bull. The animal inside Tanner surged at the challenge, and he let go a little more, growling out loud as he launched himself at the man.

They came together with a crash, neither giving ground, and Tanner felt the pain as muscles and bones in his shoulders and chest popped. His hybrid half growled louder in pleasure at the opportunity to take on someone it felt worthy of its attention.

The giant dropped the bat and came up swinging. Tanner avoided the blow easily, letting the momentum of the attack spin the man around in a half circle. The guy's momentarily exposed back presented too good a target to ignore, and Tanner lashed out instinctively, punching the man in the right kidney as hard as he could. The shout of pain the big guy let out was easy to hear even over the roar of the crowd.

Before the big man could fall, Tanner grabbed him by the back of the neck and his belt, yanking him off his feet and tossing him toward one of the three men who'd been slowly working toward Josh and the others. A three-hundred-pound bag of anything hurt when it hit a person, and the unsuspecting man let out a grunt as he was crushed to the floor. He'd probably be getting up again, but not for a bit.

Tanner turned slowly, a growl rumbling from his throat as he regarded the remaining two men. They regarded him uncertainly now, clearly realizing this fight wasn't going to go the way they thought. One of them frantically motioned at the guard closest to the gate on his side of the octagon, like he wanted out. That earned the man a frown from the guard and a round of boos from the crowd.

Knowing he wasn't getting out of the ring before this was over, the man turned and looked at his remaining partner, nodding his head. The other guy seemed to agree with the wordless communication, and both men rushed Tanner at the same time.

They split wide at the last second, coming at him from

two sides at once. Tanner ducked the first bat swung at his head and kicked out, knocking that man back all the way to the cage fencing. The move left him open to the second guy coming in, and he got an arm up just in time to keep from getting his face caved in.

The thud of the aluminum club against his forearm cracked something hard enough for him to feel it, and the beast slipped out a little more as the pain overrode Tanner's control. He tried to stop it, but his fangs slid out, and he roared in the guy's face, fangs and all. To say the man was stunned was an understatement. Bastard just about shit himself. Guess Ryan never bothered to tell the men what they were up against.

The guy tried to swing at him again, but Tanner was too close for it to do much damage, and the weak blow bounced off his left shoulder. With a snarl, Tanner wrapped a hand around the man's throat and shoved him across the ring to the far section of fencing, pinning him there as the beast inside howled for blood. Tanner fought against the urge as much as he could, and that hesitation cost him. The man slammed his knee into Tanner's groin.

The pain was intense, but Tanner refused to release his grip on the man. Clenching his jaw, he brought his foot down on the guy's leg. The man's knee buckled as ligaments and tendons tore, and he screamed in pain as the will to fight anymore fled. Tanner's hybrid wasn't done yet, though. Lifting the man off his feet, he head-butted the guy, knocking him out cold.

Now his hybrid half was done with the man.

Tanner spun to face the last guy, only to get knocked backward by a three-hundred-pound giant running at full speed. The air exploded out of his lungs as the man drove him across the cage and slammed him into one of the support poles for the cage. The impact hurt like a son of a bitch and shredded his control that much more. Clasping his hands together, he brought his bunched fists down hard into the center of the big man's back with a roar, stunning the collective crowd to silence.

You could have heard a pin drop as the big man fell to the floor, and a part of Tanner agonized over the thought that he'd almost certainly paralyzed the guy. Another part of him didn't care. His hybrid half was getting closer and closer to the surface with every passing second. Much more of this, and he didn't think he'd be able to stop the animal from completely taking over.

A pitiful cry from behind made him whirl around. The last of the five guys was over by one of the gates, the woman pinned against his body like a shield, his bat pulled up tight to her throat with both hands. Josh and the other male captive were writhing on the floor in pain.

The crowd remained silent as Tanner strode across the ring.

"Stay the fuck back!" the man warned, yanking the bat against the woman's throat, making her gag. "I'll kill her if you don't!"

Tanner didn't slow. The man would likely kill her no matter what he did. The guards weren't going to open the gate until this was done, one way or the other.

The woman's eyes bulged as Tanner got closer, but the look of trust in their depths stunned him. Reaching out, he caught one of the man's hands in a crushing grip. Bones snapped as he wrenched the bat aside. The woman collapsed to her knees, gasping for breath.

Tanner jerked the guy to the side and punched him in the center of the chest as hard as he could. Air exploded out of the man's lungs in a whoosh as he hit the gate behind him. The force of the blow cracked ribs and sternum and bent the gate all to hell. Tanner thought for sure he'd killed the man, but then he heard the thumping of the guy's heart. The part of Tanner that didn't want to kill anymore was relieved even as he realized that emotion was likely to be short lived. None of them were out of this yet.

Taking a deep breath, Tanner slowly turned around to see Josh helping the woman off the floor and leading her over to the side of the octagon. He might have just saved all of them, but that didn't stop the kid from looking at him in terror. Tanner couldn't blame the kid. What he'd done probably didn't look a whole hell of a lot different than what the men did who'd beaten Josh up when he'd first been captured and forced to fight.

Around him, the crowd stamped their feet and cheered again, though Tanner wasn't sure whether it was because they'd enjoyed the fight or were hoping Tanner would finish off the last men he'd beaten.

Tanner glanced up at the luxury boxes and realized Ryan wasn't in the suite with Nguyen anymore. Was it too much to hope that he'd bet against Tanner and was even now drinking himself into a stupor over losing?

The gate on the far side of the cage opened, and Tanner turned to see Ryan standing there with a dozen guards. Eight of them kept their weapons pointed at Tanner while the rest led Josh and the other two captives out of the cage and herded them toward the door that led down to the cell. The moment they were out of the cage, four guards came in to haul out the injured and unconscious men Tanner had bested, unconcerned by their grunts of pain or the blood they left behind on the floor.

Tanner assumed they'd take him out next, but the remaining guards kept their weapons trained on him.

"You didn't really think I'd let you leave already, did you, old buddy?" Ryan sneered. "Your night is just getting started, and something tells me this next matchup is going to be a bit more of a challenge for you."

Smiling smugly, Ryan glanced over his shoulder at something behind him. Tanner's gut clenched at the sight of Anton forcing Spencer down the aisle, the barrel of his weapon pressed against the hybrid's back. If the crowd was concerned about the fact that a man was actually going to be forced to fight at gunpoint, they didn't show it. If anything, they cheered louder.

At first, Tanner was relieved Spencer seemed to finally be fully aware of his surroundings, but then he noticed the hybrid's eyes were glowing red, and the tips of two upper fangs were already visible as he breathed deep in an opened-mouth pant.

Shit.

Ryan must have seen the look on Tanner's face, because he grinned. "Yeah, I think this fight is going to be so much better than the first one." Gaze still on Tanner, he stepped aside to let Spencer enter the octagon. "Don't you agree, Tanner?"

"You're never going to be able to make us fight. You know that, right?" Tanner asked, praying he was right as Anton led Spencer into the center of the cage and removed the manacles from his wrists.

Ryan laughed. "Of course I will. If you don't fight, I'm going to have Emilio put a bullet in the heads of those three people you just worked so hard to protect."

Still smiling, Ryan took Spencer's arm and turned him around until he was facing toward the luxury box where Ryan had been sitting earlier. Tanner cursed at the sight of a terrified Lillie standing there beside Nguyen, his gun pressed to her temple. Even from here, Tanner could see the tears in her eyes.

"And if your friend here doesn't fight," Ryan continued, "Mr. Nguyen will shoot that sweet girl in the head, and you can both watch her brains spatter all over the glass."

Before Tanner could say anything, Ryan turned and walked out of the cage. On the other side of the octagon, Spencer growled long and low at Tanner, his fangs and claws fully extended.

Oh shit. This was going to be bad.

Chapter 17

"I'M PICKING UP TRACE SCENTS FROM THAT DIRECTION," Diaz said softly, gesturing at a slightly narrower section of tunnel to his left.

Tate shined his flashlight down the dark opening, eyeing the rubble-strewn floor that looked like it hadn't been disturbed in a hundred years, wondering if the shifter's nose was playing tricks on him. Frowning, he played the light over the map in his hand, courtesy of Cam's historian friend. As he traced the squiggles on the map with his finger, he decided maybe Diaz was onto something. It certainly looked like they should be getting close to their objective.

If Cam's friend was right, somewhere just ahead of them should be a clear section of tunnel with half a dozen small rooms along it. Those rooms, which were two levels directly below the club, were where Tanner and the other kidnapping victims were most likely being held. Unless they were all in the club's walk-in fridge, which, while scary sounding as hell, was highly unlikely.

Tate glanced over his shoulder to make sure the other members of his team were still sticking close. Chase, Chad, Burt, and Malcolm returned his look with expressions that suggested they were as ready to get the hell out of the dark, claustrophobic tunnels as Tate was. Like him and Diaz, all four of the men carried M4 carbines they'd gotten from the DCO storage unit. That worried Tate a little bit. He trusted Chase with an automatic rifle, but the other three, not so much. Hopefully, they wouldn't get in a situation where the men had to use the weapons.

Behind Malcolm, who was bringing up the rear, Tate saw the glow of the green high-intensity ChemLights the team had left in their wake as they moved through the tunnels. While they were taking their time on the way in, there was a good chance they'd be hauling ass on the way out. They didn't want to have to guess about which way to go if they were being chased.

He nodded at Diaz, motioning him forward, then followed as Burt popped another ChemLight and left it at the intersection of the two tunnels. Tate breathed deeply as he felt fresh air hit his face. They must be getting close. That was good.

Even so, Tate couldn't help but worry about what was happening with the other team. They'd all entered the tunnels together about a mile back but had split up soon after, with Zarina, Cam, Clayne, and Danica heading through tunnels one level above. The map said there was a large open space between the rooms on this level and the club, so Danica's plan called for her team to set up there and provide security for Tate's team as he and the others rescued the kidnapping victims. If anyone tried to stop them during the rescue, Danica and her team would be positioned to take them down.

It was a good plan, giving Tate extra help in case they had to carry some of the prisoners, while also hopefully keeping Chad, Burt, and Malcolm out of the worst of the shooting, if it came to that. Tate would have preferred if Zarina were down here with him, too. Hell, he would have really liked it if she'd stayed outside. But that wasn't an option. Danica, Clayne, and Cam had needed help, too, and Zarina was the only one available. Not that she ever would have agreed to stay outside anyway. She was bound and determined to help save Tanner.

With any luck, they'd find Tanner and the others down on this level, and it would be a simple matter of evacuating them back out through the tunnels. Then they'd call the cops and be done with it.

The part of the plan that had him worried the most was communications. They'd known their radio headsets probably wouldn't work in the deeper parts of the mine, but everyone hoped the reception would improve once the teams got closer to each other. If it didn't, Danica's team wouldn't know when to fall back. Worse, Tate wouldn't know if Danica's team got into trouble. Maybe they'd get lucky and the damn radios would work the way they were supposed to.

Tate was still thinking about what they'd do if the radios didn't work when he realized Diaz had come to a standstill up ahead of him. Tate noticed the tunnel wasn't as dark as it had been only minutes ago. He flicked off his light, and the rest of the team behind him did the same, dumping him into pitch-black for about thirty seconds until his eyes adjusted.

He moved closer to Diaz, who was testing the air with his nose, his eyes glowing yellow-green in the darkness. "What do you got?"

"I smell Tanner," the coyote shifter said. "But I smell blood and smokeless powder, too. Someone has been shot down here recently."

Tate's heart thudded. "Tanner?"

Diaz shook his head as he started moving slowly

along the tunnel again, keeping close to the wall. "No way to tell yet. The air currents are doing strange things to the scents down here. But we're close. That much I'm sure of."

A minute later, Diaz led them out of the narrow tunnel they'd been moving through into a much broader and cleaner corridor lit with a series of bright fluorescent bulbs hanging every few feet.

Tate glanced at the stairs at the end of the corridor that led up. He didn't have a shifter's ears, but even he could hear the near constant throb of sound coming from that direction. It sounded like he was in the basement of a football stadium during a game. Maybe he was hearing people partying in the club two levels up. Would have been nice to have sent someone to the club to give them a heads up about what was going on up there, but they didn't have enough people in their rescue party for that.

He opened his mouth to ask Diaz if he was right about the noise, but the Special Forces soldier was already heading down the corridor to the right and the door down there.

Tate and the others quickly spread out around Diaz. Tate was glad to see that Burt and Chad seemed to know what the hell they were doing with their weapons. At least they had them pointed in a safe direction.

Malcolm, on the other hand, had him a little worried. The guy's eyes were starting to pulse with that familiar red hybrid glow, and the tips of his frigging fangs were showing.

"Bryce is in there," Malcolm said, as if feeling Tate's eyes on him. "It's his blood we're smelling."

Tate glanced at Diaz. The coyote shifter nodded.

"Definitely hybrid blood. There are other people in there, too. Maybe half a dozen. Tanner was there at some point, but I don't think he is now."

Shit.

Tate tried to get Danica on the radio to let them know what the hell was happening down there, but all he got was static. He cursed again. They didn't have time for this. One of the captives was hurt, maybe more than one. They had to move. Now.

He motioned Diaz in through the door first and to the right, then gestured for Chase to go in next and to the left. Tate would take the middle of the room while the others stayed out in the corridor. He simply didn't trust Chad and his people in a close-quarter combat situation, especially with hostages in there.

Everyone nodded, though Malcolm still worried Tate. The hybrid was getting visibly agitated by the second. The scent of blood must be getting to him.

Tate counted down from three with his fingers then motioned Diaz to go. The shifter reared back and kicked the heavy door off its hinges like it was made of paper, then disappeared inside. Chase followed.

Tate charged in next to see a scene out of some kind of horror movie. Six people huddled together on the floor, all of them showing signs of abuse. One of the men was curled into a ball, clutching his stomach as blood seeped from between his fingers.

A big man stood in the center of the room, his weapon pointed at the captives, but he spun at their entrance, the gun in his hand turning their way.

Diaz, Chase, and Tate fired at the same time, hitting the man before he could squeeze the trigger. The

ear-splitting noise of three automatic rifles going off
in the tight confines of the small space was deafening,
and Tate whirled around, expecting the rest of the bad
guys who had to be down there to rush in. There was no
way they'd leave one guard down here to cover all these
prisoners. But apparently, that was exactly what they'd
done, since no one showed up.

That didn't mean people wouldn't come running
down the steps at any moment. He needed to see how
badly the captives were hurt and get them out of there.
If anyone headed this way, Danica and her team would
deal with it.

"The keys for the manacles are outside the door," the
youngest of the prisoners said.

Chad ran to grab the keys, then hurried back into the
room. As he hurriedly unlocked the manacles, he asked
if anyone knew where Lillie was, but no one did.

Tate didn't need a shifter's nose to tell him the captive bleeding from a gunshot wound was Bryce. While
everyone was beaten up and bleeding from cuts and
abrasions to the face and what looked to be defensive
wounds to their hands and arms, none of the injuries
were life-threatening. But the hybrid Bryce was bleeding so much, any normal human would have been
unconscious already, if not dead.

Tate tried to get a look at the wound to see how bad
it really was, but the hybrid growled at him, revealing a
mouthful of long teeth.

"Stop it, Bryce," Malcolm murmured, firmly pulling
his friend's claw-tipped hands away. "He's trying to
help."

Bryce relaxed enough for Tate to get a look at the

two bullet holes perforating the hybrid's stomach. Unfortunately, there wasn't much Tate could do for the injury. He wasn't a frigging doctor. Hell, they didn't even have a first-aid kit. Why the hell hadn't he insisted Zarina come with him?

He glanced at Diaz and Malcolm, knowing his bed-side manners sucked. "Do either of you know how long a hybrid can handle a gut shot like this without medical treatment?"

Both men shook their heads.

"I'm fine," Bryce growled.

Tate ignored him. It was obvious he wasn't fine.

"We need to get these people out of here and get Bryce to a hospital ASAP," Tate said.

Malcolm immediately reached down to scoop up his friend, but Bryce stopped him. "We can't leave. They took Spencer and Tanner. They're upstairs."

Tate frowned. "To the club? What the hell are they doing up there?"

"Not the club," said the kid who'd told them where the keys were. "They're one level up in the octagon. They just put Spencer in there with Tanner a few min-utes ago. They're making them fight each other. The crowd tonight is huge, and they're screaming for blood."

Tate knew he looked pretty stupid kneeling there with his mouth hanging open, but he couldn't help it. He'd been ready for almost anything when they'd come in here, but finding out the big open space they'd seen on the map was being used as some kind of gladiatorial ring and Ryan was forcing two hybrids to fight each other while a crowd cheered them on wasn't something he would have expected in a million years. His team looked just as shocked.

"Why would Tanner and Spencer fight each other?" Diaz asked in confusion. "They're friends, right?"

"They have Lillie, and Spencer knows it," the kid said softly. "He's nearly insane with worry already. If they threatened to hurt Lillie, there's nothing Spencer wouldn't do to keep her safe. Even if that means fighting Tanner in front of a couple hundred people."

Tate cursed, his head spinning as he tried to count how many ways this could go horribly wrong for them. Beyond the obvious fact that Danica and her team were likely about to step into a meat grinder—if they hadn't already—there was also the serious issue of how a crowd of bloodthirsty fight fans were going to react when they finally realized the creatures up there with claws and fangs were real.

He was still imagining how that scene might turn out when a wall-shaking roar ripped through the air, paralyzing everyone in the room.

"Shit, that's Tanner," Diaz growled, his yellow-green eyes glowing brighter as he sprinted for the door.

Tate got to his feet. "Chad, you, Burt, and Malcolm get everyone out of here and away from the cave. I'm going upstairs with Chase and Diaz to find the others."

Malcolm scooped up Bryce and headed for the door while Burt herded the other prisoners in that direction. Chad didn't move.

"I'm not going anywhere," he said with an angry shake of his head. "They have my daughter up there."

"Yes, they do," Tate agreed. "That's why I'm sending you out with the others. You run up those stairs thinking like a father, and both you and Lillie will end up dead. Let my team and me handle this. It's what we do."

Chad looked like he wanted to argue, but he finally nodded. "I'm trusting you, something I've never done before. Don't make me sorry. Save my daughter."

The older man turned without waiting for a reply, getting one arm around the female prisoner who was having a hard time moving and following Burt and Malcolm out the door.

Tate took off after Diaz, Chase at his side. They caught up with the shifter halfway up the steps at the end of the hall. That was when Tate heard the screams from above. Not shouting or cheering, but bloodcurdling screams, as if a whole lot of people had just seen something they wished they hadn't. Then the shooting started.

Shit. They might be too late to save anybody.

"Spencer, you don't have to do this," Tanner said, trying to sound as calm and soothing as possible. "We can figure a way out of this and save Lillie at the same time."

His words had no visible effect on the other hybrid. Spencer merely growled louder and dropped into a crouch, circling to the left, like he was trying to work himself into a better attack angle.

"There's no way out of this," Spencer murmured, the words so slurred from the mouthful of teeth that Tanner could barely understand them. "The only way Lillie will be safe is if we fight."

Spencer threw a glance at the luxury boxes. Tanner followed his gaze. Lillie was still standing near the glass with Nguyen on one side, his gun still pressed to her head. Ryan was on the other side of her, one hand around the back of Lillie's neck, making her watch.

"You know you can't trust anything Ryan said." Tanner backpedaled and moved to the right to keep his distance from the other man. "Even if we tear each other to bloody ribbons, he's not going to let Lillie go. You have to believe me on this."

But Spencer wasn't even listening now. He was too far gone and had been from the second he'd learned Ryan had Lillie. His face twisted with rage and despair, he launched himself at Tanner with a snarl.

Tanner lunged to the side, but as fast as he was, it didn't save him completely. Spencer was still able to get his claws into him, tearing four parallel lines across his right shoulder as he flew past. The hybrid hit the floor of the cage with a thud that shook the whole ring, crashing forward in an out-of-control tumble that didn't stop until he slammed into the fencing on the far side of the octagon. Then Spencer was up and readying himself for another attack.

The beast inside Tanner howled as much in frustration as pain, and he felt his claws and fangs slip out. He might not want to willingly hurt Spencer, but he doubted his hybrid half was interested in letting his body get ripped to shreds either. Tanner was in control for the moment, but he wasn't sure how much longer that was going to last.

The crowd was going absolutely batshit, shouting and cheering for more. Tanner risked throwing a glance in that direction, shocked to see some of the people were shoving each other out of the way to get closer to the cage. Some were snapping pictures or taking videos as he and Spencer went at each other, but most only seemed to want to get closer to the bloodshed.

Tanner was still worrying about how much worse things could get if those videos ended up on the internet when his instincts warned him Spencer was coming again. He jumped to the side and hit the floor in a roll, coming up ready for anything.

That turned out to be Spencer coming at him in a full-on hybrid rage, his red eyes now devoid of even the tiniest shred of human intelligence, his mouth open wide in a growl that displayed more teeth than any human could possibly possess. Tanner wondered if this was what he looked like when he lost control. If so, he could understand why so many people were terrified of him.

Tanner blocked the claws coming at his neck, then punched the other hybrid in the face, hard. Spencer stumbled back a few feet but otherwise barely seemed to register the blow, even though Tanner was sure he'd caused some damage. Snarling louder, Spencer came at him again, his mouth opening wide as if he intended to tear Tanner's throat out with his fangs.

Tanner darted to the side, slamming his heavy boot into Spencer's gut at the same time. The move slowed the hybrid, but only for a moment. Then he lunged for Tanner's neck again. Tanner tried to sidestep him, but there was no time. Spencer was too close and too fast.

Heart pounding, Tanner tried to get his arm up to protect his vulnerable neck, but even that seemed too little, too late. The best he could do was shove his forearm up against Spencer's upper chest, shoving him aside and deflecting the hybrid's aim. Instead of his friend's fangs slamming into his vulnerable throat, they came down on the left side of his neck and shoulder, burying deep in the muscles there.

The pain was beyond intense, and Tanner's inner beast crashed through the door out of pure survival instinct. Tanner knew if he continued to try to do this on his own, he'd end up dead, so he relinquished control, letting his claws and fangs fully extend as he forcibly ripped Spencer away from his neck.

Tanner didn't want to think about how much damage he was doing to himself, which was good, since the wave of agony that tore through him made thinking impossible. So he stopped thinking and roared, the animalistic sound easily drowning out the crowd's cheering and screaming.

Spencer growled and charged again. Tanner met him midlunge, spinning him around and slinging him across the octagon as hard as his inner beast would let him. Spencer was still three feet off the ground when he slammed into one of the gates and kept going, his weight and momentum tearing the gate partially off its hinges. Spencer smashed his head hard, then hit the stone floor outside the cage just as hard. He was up in a flash, growling and enraged even as blood poured from a wound across the side of his face.

Two guards who'd been serving as crowd control outside the cage ran straight at Spencer, weapons coming out at the same time. Spencer must have smelled them, because he spun in a move so fast, it was a blur. He swiped at the first guard's neck, then the other, before he was on the move again.

The crowd had already been stunned to complete silence by Tanner's roar and the sight of Spencer getting thrown right through the fencing of the cage. Now that Spencer was free, the crowd became completely unglued. First were the shouts and screams of panic, then the struggle to get away.

It only got more insane when Tanner climbed out of the cage, shoving aside the door that still hung there by one hinge and the chain that had been used to lock it closed. People took one look at Tanner up close and began climbing over each other to get away. That just made the panic worse. People got trampled, but Tanner couldn't find it in himself to care.

A blur of movement caught Tanner's attention, and he caught sight of Spencer making his way through the crowd, heading toward the steps leading to the second level. Tanner glanced up at the luxury box where Lillie had been, but there was no sign of the girl now, or Ryan and Nguyen for that matter. But Spencer must have believed he could find them in that direction, which was enough for Tanner.

He didn't have to worry about the crowd getting in his way. Even the people taking videos of him on their phones practically killed themselves to get out of his path. He didn't bother trying to exert his control over the beast and shift back. It was already too late for that. He might as well make use of his hybrid's talents now that the secret was out.

Tanner had only taken half a dozen strides when another guard pushed his way through the crowd, knocking people aside with the butt of the assault rifle he carried. Tanner didn't want to waste the time fighting with the guy, but he had little choice. The man was standing between him and where he needed to go.

He charged forward and met the guy just as he broke through the crowd. The man tried to get his weapon down and pointed in the right direction, but Tanner never gave him the chance. Closing his left hand around the gun, he shoved it up and away. The rifle shattered in his grip, the bullets clanging and pinging as they ricocheted around the room. At least one of them went through the glass window on the luxury boxes, shattering it into a million pieces. The already panicked people on the lower level scrambled for cover as glass rained down on them.

The man didn't try to fight Tanner for control of the assault rifle. Instead, he let go and reached for his backup piece. Tanner wrapped his claw-tipped fingers around the man's neck, gave a hard squeeze, then slung him across the room. He didn't bother to see where the man landed, but from the thud he made when he finally hit the floor, Tanner knew he wouldn't be getting up again.

Tanner had just turned and headed after Spencer when he caught a scent that stopped him cold and froze his heart.

Zarina.

What the hell was she doing here?

Chapter 18

CLAYNE SKIDDED TO A SUDDEN STOP A FEW FEET AHEAD OF her and Danica just as Zarina heard an undulating sound she could feel through the soles of her boots. She frowned and glanced over her shoulder at Cam, who was bringing up the tail end of their little team since they'd entered the tunnels. He looked as confused as she felt.

"What's that noise?" she asked Clayne.

She kept her voice barely above a whisper, worried someone at the other end of this insane network of tunnels would hear them. If there was another end. Zarina wasn't so sure, since it'd been nearly thirty minutes since they'd left Tate and his team, and the tunnel they were in now looked exactly like the tunnel they'd started in. They could have gone in one big circle for all she knew.

"I think it's people shouting and cheering," Clayne said. "And if the scents I'm picking up are any indication, it's a lot of people."

"Do you think we've gotten turned around in these caves and ended up on the club level somehow?" Danica asked as she surveyed the map in her hand.

Clayne scowled at his wife. Danica might have the map, but they'd mostly trusted the wolf shifter's nose to lead them through the tunnel. "Are you asking if I got us lost?"

Danica lifted a brow. "Do you have another explanation for all the noise if it's not the club?"

Clayne looked like he was more than ready to let Danica know what he thought of that question, but before he could get the words out, a rage-filled roar pierced the stale air in the tunnel, making the hair on Zarina's arms stand on end and her heart seize up. She'd know that roar anywhere.

"Shit, that was Tanner," Clayne muttered.

With a growl, he turned and sprinted down the tunnel in the direction they'd been heading. Zarina, Danica, and Cam followed, running after the wolf shifter as fast as they could, trying to keep up.

They hadn't gone very far before Zarina heard screams of panic and fear. A few steps later, the claustrophobic darkness they'd been traveling through for half an hour brightened, then disappeared completely as they stepped out into a large, well-lit room the size of a large movie theater.

Going from the pitch-black tunnels to the bright lights of the open space was blinding, and all Zarina could do was blink through the stars as her eyes adjusted while she tried to guess what was happening based on nothing more than the screams of terror and the growls and roars of an angry hybrid. Then gunshots rang out, followed by the sound of breaking glass, and the screaming got even louder.

When her vision finally cleared, she realized the situation was even worse than her overactive imagination had come up with. The place was in total chaos. Men were running around waving guns while people in fancy clothes screamed and trampled each other as they tried to get away.

Tanner had just climbed out of what looked like

some kind of metal-enclosed fighting ring, and while the men with guns were frightening, everyone was running from him.

Zarina had no idea what the cage was about, but she knew Tanner was in trouble. There were two dead men on the floor with their throats ripped out, and even as she watched, he wrapped his hands around the throat of another man holding a rifle and tossed him fifteen feet across the room. The man bounced off the cage like a rag doll, crumpling to the floor in an unmoving pile of arms and legs.

Blood covered the side of Tanner's neck, his eyes were scarlet red, and his jaw had broadened to accommodate his teeth. The muscles of his arms and shoulders rippled as his body continued to shift, going further than she'd ever seen him go before.

"What the hell is happening to him?" Cam breathed in horror.

"He's completely lost control," she shouted.

Shoving her hand in the pocket of her jacket, she pulled out the auto-injector still safe in its plastic case. She popped the injector out then looked at Cam, who was still standing there, stunned by the intensity of Tanner's rage.

"You have to help me get to Tanner before he kills someone he shouldn't," she said.

Cam looked at the injector in her hand, then back at Tanner. "We'll lead the way. Stick close."

There was more chaos as they circled around the outside edge of the huge open space, trying to cut Tanner off. Clayne and Cam moved out in front, shoving people aside and making a path for them through the crowd.

On the far side of the cage, Zarina heard gunfire. She looked over to see Diaz, Chase, and Tate engaging with a group of armed men. She hoped that meant Chad and the others had found their friends from the prepper camp and gotten them out of there.

She was stunned to see half a dozen people filming the chaotic scene with their phones. That was going to be bad. But there wasn't anything they could do about it. All she could focus on was getting to Tanner, then doing whatever she had to do.

They tried to reach Tanner before he got to the tunnel leading out of the main area, but there were too many people in the way, and he disappeared from view down the semidark corridor.

Clayne and Cam moved to follow, but as they reached the entrance to the passageway, a handful of Ryan's mercenaries suddenly bullied their way out of the crowd, swinging their weapons in Zarina's direction. She didn't even have time to consider throwing herself to the floor before Clayne and Danica reacted, leaping in front of her and knocking the first two men backward in a move so perfectly synchronized, it was like they'd practiced it a hundred times before.

"Keep going!" Clayne shouted as he lashed out at the man in front of him then turned toward the next. Beside him, Danica did the same thing. "Find Tanner before it's too late."

Zarina didn't pause to think about the fact that she was abandoning her friends. Instead, she ran into the tunnel after Tanner, squeezing the auto-injector firmly in her hand so she wouldn't drop it. A few moments later, she heard heavy feet running behind her. She knew it was Cam but didn't slow down to let him catch up. Tanner had too much of a lead on her already.

The tunnel she was in soon split into a Y-intersection, and she instinctively went left. But then she ran into another intersection, then another. There were only a few lights in this part of the tunnel, and the darkness, combined with the absolute maze of twists and turns, quickly convinced her that she had a better chance of getting lost than finding Tanner.

Zarina slowed down, hoping she might be able to hear the sounds of Tanner's footsteps when she heard a heavy thud behind her, quickly followed by a second one. Pulse pounding, she spun around, realizing with a start that Cam wasn't behind her anymore.

"Cam?" she called softly, heading back the way she'd come. "Is that you?"

When she got to the last turn she'd made without seeing or hearing him, she started getting worried. She was sure he'd been right behind her. There was no way she could have outrun him. She wasn't that fast.

"Cam?" she shouted, starting to freak out a little. Coming back here without Clayne and Danica had been really stupid. "Where are you?"

Zarina saw Cam's boots first. She ran toward him, her heart in her throat as her mind suggested all kinds of horrible things that could have happened to Tanner's brother.

She was so focused on Cam, she didn't even realize someone was in the adjacent tunnel until Ryan slammed into her and knocked her against the wall. She grunted in pain, crying out in dismay as the auto-injector tumbled out of her grip and disappeared into the darkness.

Zarina quickly stopped worrying about the injector as

she saw another big man with pale-blond hair step out of the tunnel, carrying a large automatic pistol. He leaned over Cam and, for a moment, Zarina thought he was going to shoot Tanner's brother. But after yanking him partway into the light and seeing the blood covering the side of Cam's head, the blond guy muttered something and shoved him aside. Oh God, Cam had been hurt bad.

"Let me go!" she yelled, trying to shove Ryan away, first in an attempt to get to Cam, but then to get to the revolver on her belt.

Ryan must have seen the move, because he caught her wrist and pinned her arm to her side easily. "I don't think so, Zarina."

Grinning, he casually reached up to slam her head back against the stone wall. The blow didn't seem that hard, but stars still exploded in her vision, and she felt her knees go weak as she tried to keep her legs under her. She blinked and shook her head, refusing to let herself black out. She had no idea what Ryan had planned for her, but she was going to fight it no matter what.

"I couldn't ask for a better hostage to help get me out of here," Ryan added as he tugged her revolver out of its holster and tossed it aside. "Tanner won't risk coming within fifty feet of me if I have a gun to your head."

She could have pointed out that Tanner likely wouldn't even recognize her at the moment but decided not to bother. Instead, she jerked her wrist out of Ryan's hand and punched him as hard as she could.

Zarina hadn't ever done anything like that before, and it likely hurt her hand more than his face, but she drew back her fist, ready to try again. Ryan cursed and slammed her against the wall again. Her legs buckled as pain stabbed through her, but she refused to be cowed, instead swinging at him again, getting in another glancing blow.

Ryan's face twisted in anger, and he shoved her back, looking like he was ready to kill her this time. As his fist came up, Zarina didn't think she was going to get out of this one with a thump to the back of the head.

Then a blur passed through her peripheral vision, and Ryan disappeared as Tanner slammed into him, knocking him five feet down the dark corridor and crushing him to the floor. Without Ryan there to hold her up, Zarina's knees gave out, and she collapsed to the ground. Growls and screams echoed around her as Tanner tore into the man who used to be his best friend.

Shadows continued to threaten her vision, but Zarina ignored them when she saw the big blond man turn his weapon Tanner's way, trying to line up a shot at him. She scrambled for her lost gun, crawling over Cam as her hands flailed around, searching for it. She found the auto-injector first, scooping that up out of instinct as she kept searching for the revolver.

She felt something hard under her hand and scrambled to pick it up even as the blond man shoved the barrel of his weapon up against the back of Tanner's head. Even though she knew she was out of time, she got the weapon up, pointed at the man, and squeezed the trigger.

The gun jumped in her hand just before the blond man's did the same in his. She had no idea where her bullet landed, but his hit the wall right over her head, peppering her with stone fragments and then ricocheting back and forth down the corridor. She flinched hard but kept pulling the trigger until the weapon didn't fire anymore. She had no idea whether she'd hit anything until the blond man dropped to his knees and then fell forward onto his face with a thud.

Everything was quiet then, except for the horrible ringing in her ears. She wondered if she should reload the revolver when it occurred to her that Tanner wasn't growling or fighting with Ryan anymore.

She pushed herself into a sitting position and twisted around, fearing the worst. Tanner crouched a few feet away from her, his eyes glowing vivid red. She had to force herself not to flinch. She might love him like crazy, but in the dim light, he looked pretty damn scary.

His fangs were still extended, and his long claws scraped against the floor as he clenched and unclenched his fists. His jeans and bare chest were covered in dark stains that were impossible to mistake for anything other than blood. She searched his red eyes, hoping to see some indication the man she loved was in there somewhere, but all she saw was the beast and the rage.

She looked over his shoulder at the torn and twisted shape lying in the darkness behind him. Ryan was dead. Tanner's hybrid half had killed him. While she had no doubt the man deserved everything Tanner's inner animal had done to him and more, she knew Ryan's death was one more thing that would eat at Tanner for the rest of his life.

Swallowing hard, Zarina slowly placed the revolver as far away from her as she could reach, then carefully push herself up to her knees. Tanner would probably think the auto-injector in her hand was much more dangerous than the gun, but there was no way she could set it aside now, not when he was this far gone. Gaze never leaving his, she slowly crawled toward him, the injector cradled protectively in her palm.

"It's me…Zarina," she whispered softly when Tanner growled at her a little. "I want to help you, but you have to trust me. Okay?"

He growled again, but this time, it almost seemed like he understood what she'd said, or at least realized she wasn't going to hurt him. Zarina prayed that was the case, because she didn't want to use the antiserum on him. Not without talking to him about it first.

Stopping in front of him, Zarina sat on one hip, then very slowly reached up to gently cup his jaw. He closed his eyes at her touch, giving her hope that everything was going to be okay.

"Are you in there, Tanner?" she asked in a low murmur. "Please be in there. Because I don't want to give you this drug if I don't have to."

He leaned into her touch for a moment, but when he opened his eyes again, they were as scarlet as ever. His fangs and claws were just as terrifyingly extended as before, too. She continued to murmur soft words to him in English and Russian like she had so many times in the past, praying they would soothe the beast inside the man she loved.

But this time, her words seemed to have no effect. Normally, Tanner's more obvious hybrid attributes would have faded away by now, leaving him exhausted and heartbroken over yet another loss of control. It was like the hybrid had decided it wasn't going to relinquish control.

As if she needed an example, a loud scream from somewhere in the tunnels reached them, making

Tanner's head jerk around in that direction, a deeper growl rumbling from his throat. Zarina immediately caught his chin with a finger, tugging his face back around so he was looking at her.

"You have to come back to me now, Tanner," she told him, her voice breaking a little as tears clouded her vision. "Before it's too late and you do something you'll regret for the rest of your life."

Tanner glanced at her, but most of his attention was focused on whoever had screamed, or maybe an errant whiff of blood she'd never be able to pick up. Either way, Zarina knew he could be seconds away from bolting on her. If he ran, a lot of people could die. That was blood Tanner would never want on his hands.

Knowing what she had to do but hating it nonetheless, Zarina lifted her hand and showed him the injector. His eyes sharpened on it immediately.

"This can help you," she said, more tears coming as she realized this was where they'd been heading for a long time. Maybe even from the very beginning. "It's the only thing that can help you now, I think."

Tanner regarded her almost curiously, and she lied to herself, thinking maybe he understood what she was saying.

"I never got the chance to fully talk to you about the antiserum, but it will reset your DNA to what it was before any of the hybrid stuff ever happened to you," she continued. "You'll still have the PTSD to deal with, but at least you'll have a chance to focus on that without worrying about the claws and fangs."

Tanner's eyes tracked the injector as she placed the tip carefully against the thickest, most muscular part of his left shoulder. "There might be some side effects we didn't talk about, too."

His eyes narrowed as if he understood.

She forced a smile to her lips, wanting him to be as calm as possible before she triggered the injector. The canister of the unit had a two-inch needle, and if he jerked away too quickly, he wouldn't get the full dose of the antiserum into his system. She had no idea what a half dose would do to him.

"The worst side effect of the drug is you might not be able to remember me when you wake up from this," she whispered, tears running down her cheeks even though she still had that fake smile pasted on her face. "That's not really a problem, though. It just means we can start all over again."

Then she shook her head, knowing things were never that simple. "But just in case it doesn't work out the same way the second time, I guess I should tell you now that I love you. More than I ever dreamed possible. I have since the first day I met you. My only regret is that I never told you sooner."

She took a deep breath, starting to apply pressure to the auto-injector. She knew exactly what she was risking by doing this, but there was no other choice.

Tanner reached over and gently wrapped his fingers around hers, taking the injector away from his shoulder. Zarina stared at his nails for at least ten seconds before she realized his claws had retracted. She lifted her head to see Tanner's beautiful blue eyes gazing back at her.

"You didn't tell me," he said quietly. "But I always knew."

—•••—

"If it's okay with you, I'd prefer if we skip the antise-rum," Tanner whispered. "The idea of forgetting even one second of my time with you isn't something I'm interested in."

Zarina knelt there on the stone floor, staring at him like he was a pig wearing a Rolex for so long, he wasn't sure she heard him.

"You're back," she finally breathed. "You're really back."

He nodded.

She flung her arms around his neck and hugged him tightly. "I thought your hybrid half had taken over and wasn't ever going to let you come back."

He hugged her back just as fiercely, inhaling deeply as he buried his face in her silky hair. "It's complicated, but I think my other half and I have worked out our dif-ferences. I don't fight so hard to keep him trapped away in the dark, and he doesn't seem so interested in destroy-ing everything he sees. It's not as simple as saying I'm completely in control now, but we have an arrangement of sorts."

"Simple or not, its sounds like a good deal to me," she said against his neck, bathing him in her scent and making his hybrid half nearly delirious with pleasure.

"I think I have you to thank for this new arrange-ment," he admitted, pulling away to gaze at her. "Everything changed the moment I finally believed you truly accepted me for what I am—a veteran with PTSD as well as a hybrid." His mouth edged up. "It also doesn't hurt to know you love me, too."

"You heard that part, huh?" She smiled. "I wasn't sure."

Tanner grinned. "Yeah, I heard. I love you, too." He gently cupped her face and kissed her. "Are you okay? Did Ryan hurt you? Or Anton?"

She looked confused for a moment, then glanced over at the blond man she'd shot. "Oh, you mean him. No, he didn't hurt me. I'm fine. Because of you."

Tanner sighed in relief and hugged her again, so damn grateful he'd been lucky enough to hear Zarina calling out Cam's name in panic. If it wasn't for that, he likely would have never turned around. He'd been so focused on chasing after Spencer that he'd nearly let the woman he loved die. But he'd gotten there in time, and she was okay.

He glanced at what was left of Ryan, having a hard time finding even a small part of him that regretted what he'd done. Maybe later, after this was all over with and he'd had some time to reflect, he'd be able to remember a time when his friend hadn't been completely evil. But not right now.

Tanner still had his arms around Zarina when he heard a groan a few feet away. Zarina had obviously heard it, too, because she pulled away with a concerned look.

"Cam!" she said.

Shit.

Cursing silently, Tanner scrambled over to check on his brother, Zarina at his side. He'd heard Cam's pulse and rhythmic breathing, so he knew his brother was okay, but it freaked him out to think he'd forgotten him even for a second.

Cam was already trying to stand up by the time they got there, but Zarina pushed him back down, leaning over to examine the wound above his ear.

"Don't try to move yet," she said. "You could have a concussion."

"No kidding I have a concussion. I'm lucky I still have a head," Cam said with a snort as he pressed his hand to the gash along his temple. "But unless that blow to the noodle screwed up my hearing, I'm pretty sure all the shooting has stopped. Which means this place is likely going to be overrun with cops soon. We need to round up everyone else and get the hell out of here."

Tanner silently agreed as he carefully helped his brother stand. He'd been preoccupied at the time, but he thought the shooting stopped about the same time he'd been tackling Ryan, which meant the fighting was over.

"Before we go, there's something I need to handle first," he said. "Spencer."

Zarina bent to scoop up her revolver, then quickly came around to lend another shoulder for Cam to lean on. "We haven't seen Spencer since we got here. I'm guessing you were chasing after him when you came this way?"

Tanner nodded, leading the way toward the main room, then down another side tunnel that took them to a set of stone steps leading to the luxury boxes. He'd been halfway up when he'd heard Zarina's cry. He hated to think Spencer and Lillie's lives had been the price he'd had to pay to save Zarina and Cam, but if the total silence from upstairs was any indication, that was exactly what had happened.

"Ryan put both of us in the cage and threatened to kill the other prisoners if we didn't fight each other," he said over his shoulder. "When Spencer saw they had a gun pointed at Lillie's head, he completely lost it. The second he got out of the cage, he raced up here to help Lillie, but in his condition, I'm worried he's just as likely to hurt her as save her."

Tanner's steps slowed as he approached the top of the stairs. The stench of blood coming from the luxury boxes was nearly overwhelming. He tried his best to separate the different scents and hone in on Lillie's and Spencer's, but there was simply too much blood for his nose to wade through.

The moment he got to the top of the stairs and looked down the well-lit corridor leading to the luxury boxes, it seemed his worst fears were realized. Four men lay on the floor, their bodies clawed and ripped apart.

He wasn't sure he even wanted to keep going, but he heard a soft voice he recognized as Lillie's. Beside him, Cam lifted his weapon higher while Zarina reloaded her revolver with trembling hands. As Tanner took off running in the direction of Lillie's voice, he hoped neither of them had to use their weapons.

Tanner found Lillie sitting on the floor of one of the suites, Spencer in her arms. He was still in his hybrid form and covered in blood. It looked like he was one wrong move away from going into a rage and killing anyone he could reach, including Lillie.

"He can't shift back," Lillie whispered, her voice choking with emotion, tears running down her face. "He's had bad episodes before, but nothing like this. He's always settled down within minutes of being provoked. I've been trying to calm him down now for nearly five minutes, and it's not helping."

Out of the corner of his eye, Tanner saw Cam lower his weapon and take a small step back. Tanner didn't blame his brother. This wasn't a problem a cop could fix, not with a weapon at least.

Zarina holstered her pistol as well. "Will he let you touch his face?" she asked softly. "Gently caressing his jaw might help."

Lillie shook her head, more tears spilling onto her cheeks. "I've tried that. And running my fingers through his hair, too. Nothing works. It's like he pushed himself too hard, and now he's trapped in this form."

Tanner heard a commotion out in the corridor, and Cam darted out to deal with it, somehow knowing they sure as hell didn't need any more stress in the room. Ten seconds later, he was back and looking even more worried than before.

"Diaz says SWAT is on their way down here from the club level," Cam said. "They're being held up a little by the crowd, but Diaz thinks we'll be lucky to have another five minutes before our escape routes are cut off."

Tanner cursed softly before stopping to wonder how the hell Diaz had gotten involved in this situation. Zarina had obviously called in for reinforcements, which had been smart as hell. He wanted to ask Cam who else was here, but there wasn't time for that.

"Tell Diaz to get everyone else out of here. That includes you," he told his brother. "I'll deal with this situation as fast as I can, then track your scents to follow you out."

"I'll tell them to go, but there's no way I'm leaving." Cam's mouth tightened. "You disappeared on me once. I'm not letting you out of my sight this time."

Tanner would have argued, but there wasn't time for that, either. He nodded, then turned back to figure out how to deal with Spencer. Maybe he could knock him out? It wasn't the best plan, but he couldn't come up with anything better at the moment.

Taking a deep breath, he started toward the hybrid, but the desperate look Spencer gave him brought him up short.

"Kill me, Tanner," he begged. "I can't live like this anymore. It's like I'm going to fly apart into a million pieces. Just end it. Please."

Lillie's face filled with horror. "Spencer, no!"

Spencer lifted his gaze to hers, tears running from his blazing red eyes. "I'm sorry, Lillie. I know I promised to stay with you no matter what, but I can't. Please let me go."

She shook her head, turning pleading eyes on Tanner. "You have to help him. There has to be another way. I won't let him die. I can't."

Tanner could never kill Spencer, even if he understood why the other hybrid was asking him to do it. Hell, there'd been enough times in his recent past when he'd wished someone would have put him out of his misery because there hadn't seemed to be any other way out. Now, Spencer was dealing with the same situation, only worse.

But this time, there was another way out.

Cam poked his head through the door of the suite. "Tanner, whatever you're going to do, you need to do it now. SWAT is heading this way."

Tanner cursed and looked at Zarina to see her gazing at him as if she'd been thinking the exact same thing as him. Nodding, she reached into her coat pocket for the injector, then popped it out of the plastic case and held it out to Lillie.

"I know you'd rather there was another way, but there isn't," Zarina said gently. "If the police find us in here, it's not going to end well. For anyone."

Lillie nodded. "Shouldn't you give it to him? You're a doctor."

Zarina shook her head. "I might be a doctor, but you're the woman he trusts and loves."

Lillie reached out and carefully took the injector. "What do I do?"

Zarina talked the other woman through the process, then Lillie took a deep breath and placed the tip of the cylinder against Spencer's shoulder.

"After I give you this, you might forget a lot of what we've been through," Lillie whispered, more tears flowing. "But I want you to remember one thing. I love you, Spencer Black, and I always will."

The hybrid looked at Lillie with the most trusting eyes Tanner had ever seen as she leaned in and kissed the man's blood-spattered cheek, then pressed down hard on the injector with an audible pop. Spencer flinched, then let out a long, low growl. Tanner tensed, worried for a moment that the hybrid would attack Lillie out of pure instinct, but he didn't.

Unfortunately, the growl had been loud enough for the SWAT cops to hear. They were calling out to each other, trying to figure out where the noise had come from. *Shit*. They'd find them even faster now.

When Tanner had been injected with the original hybrid serum, the effects had been immediate, so he'd expected much the same from Zarina's antiserum. But after another, softer growl, Spencer's eyes closed, and he went limp in Lillie's arms.

"Is he okay?" she asked fearfully.

Zarina nodded as she hurried over to check the hybrid's pulse. "Yes. I designed the antiserum to put the patient into a light coma as it reset the body's DNA. It will work much slower than the original hybrid serum, making incremental changes over a period of days instead of minutes. He'll likely be unconscious the entire time."

Zarina looked over her shoulder and nodded at Tanner. He quickly scooped Spencer up out of Lillie's arms and headed for the door. Zarina might think the changes would come slowly, but the hybrid's fangs had already retracted.

Cam took point while Zarina and Lillie followed behind as they moved quickly down the stairs, barely avoiding the SWAT cops as they slipped into the warren of tunnels that would lead them to safety.

Chapter 19

ZARINA PRESSED HER HANDS FIRMLY AGAINST TANNER'S muscular chest as she rode slowly up and down on him. Little electric shocks rippled through her every time she came down on his thighs, making her moan. Tanner lay on his back on the big hotel bed, blankets and pillows shoved aside to make room for their latest lovemaking marathon. His eyes glowed a soft shade of red, a sure sign he was getting close to orgasm even though he tried to act like he was fully in control of himself. But after being locked up in this room for three days making love, she was getting extremely good at reading his body language. And right now, he was on the edge.

Zarina moved her hands from his chest and rested them on the bed on either side of his shoulders, then leaned forward and pressed her breasts against his chest. She trailed teasing kisses along his jaw, moving her hips a little faster. Tanner grabbed her hips, trying to slow her movements even as his eyes blazed brighter.

"You keep wiggling like that, and I won't be responsible for the noise I end up making," he warned.

She laughed softly. "We can't have you making any noise, can we? Not if we want to keep a low profile. Fortunately, I have a way to help you stay quiet."

Before he could say anything, she kissed him hard, reveling in the sensation of his sharp fangs scraping against her tongue.

Tanner growled against her mouth, his whole chest vibrating. He must have decided he'd held out long enough, because he squeezed her bottom tighter and yanked her down harder on his cock.

She willingly let him control her hips, sighing as those electric shocks joined together to become one continuous tingle. It didn't take long after that for her climax to start, building up fast and cresting in a wave of ecstasy.

Tanner thought he'd be noisy, but it turned out she was the one who screamed as her orgasm hit. He kept his hands firmly on her hips, pushing her pleasure higher and higher before coming himself. She dragged her mouth away from his and buried her face in his neck, muffling her cries against his warm skin.

Her breathing had barely returned to normal when Tanner scooped her up and carried her off to the shower, where he washed all those hard to reach places for her. That led to more kissing, which led to other, more intense pleasures. Fortunately, they didn't have to pay the hot water bill for this place, because they were in there well over an hour.

She stayed in the shower a bit after Tanner stepped out, luxuriating in the feel of the warm water running down her skin. She only wished they could stay here in this little sanctuary forever and forget the outside world.

Zarina heard the TV the moment she stepped out of the shower. Sighing, she dried off quickly, then pulled on jeans and a sweater. She'd planned to run out and get something for them to eat, but she wasn't sure it was a good idea leaving Tanner alone with the television. She hated running out even for a few minutes, but they couldn't take the chance of using room service too often. Tanner ate as much as four men, and she didn't want the hotel getting suspicious, since she'd said there were only the two of them when she'd checked in. One thing they definitely couldn't do right now was draw unwanted attention. While she might have gotten out of the club without getting her face plastered all over the TV and internet, the same couldn't be said of Tanner. Now that the media had figured out who he was, his name was getting more clicks on the internet than the Kardashian clan.

She walked out of the bathroom to see Tanner sitting on the couch, flipping through the channels. His hair was still damp from the shower, and he was dressed in jeans and a flannel shirt.

"Why do you keep watching that stuff?" she asked. "You know it's only going to make you mad."

"I'm hoping to hear something about Cam."

He continued flipping through channels, ignoring the ones that were talking about him, Spencer, Diaz, or Clayne. There'd been more than enough news coverage on them, and Zarina could understand why Tanner didn't want to hear any more of it. Most of the media outlets were making him and the others out to be monsters, even after the details of what Ryan and the Asian gang had done with their fighting cage had come out. Few seemed to care that Ryan had been the real monster. They only wanted to talk about the guys with the claws and fangs.

That was why they were hiding out in this hotel an hour north of Seattle. Right after the raid, they'd talked about crossing the border into Canada, but they'd decided to stay where they were for the time being so she could be close to help Bryce and Spencer, and Tanner could keep up with what was going on with Cam. Both of them had been hoping all this would blow over, but it looked like things were getting worse.

Zarina sat down on the couch beside Tanner, praying they wouldn't see anything about Cam but knowing they almost certainly would. Cam's part in the raid, as well as Tate's and Chase's, had already come out. They hadn't received the same attention as Tanner and the others, but the press kept poking around and found out that Cam was Tanner's brother. Then the digging had really started.

She tensed as Tanner stopped on a local channel showing a photo of his brother in his Seattle PD uniform. A moment later, they showed a video clip from earlier that morning of Cam walking out of the police station as cameras flashed in his face, reporters shoving and jostling to get a word from him.

"Damn," Tanner muttered, sinking back on the couch, his shoulders slouching like the weight of the world was on them. "I knew it was going to be bad, but I'd hoped he could somehow avoid being suspended."

She rested her arm on the back of the couch and ran her fingers through his thick hair. "Cam knew what he was getting into when he decided to help us. I can guarantee he doesn't regret his decision for a second."

Tanner looked at her doubtfully. "Maybe. But what about Chase? It's one thing for my brother to destroy his career for me, but a cop from Maine who I'd never even met before? You don't think he regrets his decision to come out here to Washington and get involved in this crap?"

Zarina sighed. Tanner had blamed himself for every-thing that had happened at The Cage since they'd gotten to the hotel, which was stupid. None of it was his fault.

"Give Chase some credit, Tanner. He came to help because Tate asked him to. Once a person learns about shifters and hybrids and how the world really works, it's difficult for them to go back to their old lives. When he and Tate left a few days ago, he didn't seem the least bit upset. In fact, I get the feeling he'd been looking for a change anyway. I have no doubt we'll be seeing him working at the DCO soon."

"Okay, maybe so. How about Diaz then? Do you think the DCO is going to be able to hide him now that the army knows he's a shifter?"

Zarina winced. That one was going to be tougher. While Spencer and the preppers had slipped back into their mountain camp, and Clayne, Danica, Tate, and Chase had all disappeared to some safe house in the middle of nowhere, Diaz had gone back to Fort Campbell to accept whatever the army was going to throw at him. She liked to think the DCO would be able to cover it up, but she didn't know for sure. The knowledge that there were shifters like Diaz in the world was already bringing out a lot of ugliness in people. Zarina had no idea where it was going to end.

"Somehow, Diaz is going to be okay," she told Tanner. "Landon and Ivy aren't going to abandon him, even if they have to go break the guy out of a military prison. And if Landon decides he needs our help to do it, that's what we'll do. Because that's what they did for us."

Tanner wrapped an arm around her and pulled her

close, pressing a kiss to her hair. "You're amazing, you know that?"

She laughed. "No, but feel free to keep telling me. I'm sure it will sink in at some point."

He grinned, but his amusement quickly faded. "Okay, let's assume you're right and that Cam and everyone else will make it out of this okay. What about us? I know you want to stay close to Wenatchee in case Bryce or Spencer have a setback, but we can't stay here forever."

He was right. The longer they stayed at the hotel, the greater the odds were that someone would figure out Tanner was here. Bryce and Spencer were both doing fine, so there was really no need to stay. Bryce was currently in a nearby hospital under a fake name, recovering from the gunshot wounds he'd sustained, while Spencer had awakened this morning. Zarina wouldn't be sure until she got a sample of his DNA into a lab, but from everything Lillie told her when she'd called, the antiserum had done exactly what it was designed to do. Spencer was no longer a hybrid. Even better, the side effects weren't nearly as severe as Zarina had feared. There were some memory gaps to be sure, but most importantly, Spencer remembered Lillie and that he loved her.

"You're right," Zarina said. "Bryce and Spencer are out of danger now, so there's no reason we can't leave. But where do we go?"

Tanner tipped her face up and kissed her. "What about Russia? We could see your family. If the place you grew up in is still as rural as you said, I doubt anyone would recognize me. What do you think?"

She smiled. He was the amazing one in this relationship. "Haven't you figured it out yet? I don't care where

we go as long as we're together. If you want, I'll happily
go live in the Wenatchee Mountains with you again. I'm
sure Chad wouldn't mind us staying with them."

He chuckled. "I appreciate the offer, but I've seen
how much you enjoy hot water. I'm not taking you anywhere without indoor plumbing."

She was about to insist that wasn't necessary—even
though it really was—but just then, he jerked his head
around to look at the door. He sniffed the air, a sure sign
that someone unexpected was approaching their room.
A moment later, there was a knock at the door.

Zarina tensed as Tanner stood and walked over to the
door. She followed, her stomach clenched into a knot.
What if it was a reporter? Or the cops?

Tanner opened the door without looking through the
peephole. Cam stood there, a petite girl with a color-
ful pixie hairstyle beside him. An older couple stood
behind them, as well as a blond woman about Tanner's
age. Between the stunned look on Tanner's face and the
obvious family resemblance, it was easy figuring out
who their visitors were.

No one said anything, not even Cam. Everyone
simply stood there staring at each other. Clearly, Zarina
was going to have to make the first move. Reaching
out, she took Tanner's hand in hers as she motioned his
family forward.

"Come in," she said, giving them a smile.

When they hesitated, Cam stepped back and herded
them into the room. He peeked down the hallway, like
he was worried someone might have followed them,
then closed the door.

"We're clear," he said, as if reading her mind. "I still

have a few friends on the force, and they made sure we weren't followed."

Zarina thought after they had come inside that someone would say something, but no one made a peep. She was just about to speak when Tanner's youngest sister closed the distance between them and enveloped Tanner in a big hug, burying her face against his chest with a sob. Tanner wrapped his arms around her, his eyes filling with tears.

"Hey there, Jelly Bean," he said softly. "I see you're still coloring your hair to match your socks."

The girl laughed, and just like that, the tension in the room disappeared. Eyes misting with tears, each family member hugged Tanner one by one.

"These are my sisters, Kellie and Raquel," Tanner said to Zarina when they were done. "And this is my mother, Madeline, and my father, Cedric."

Madeline seemed to be one of those women who never showed her age. While she had to be in her fifties, her hair was still dark blond and her face had few lines. Cedric was a big man and still carried a lot of muscle on his broad frame even though he was probably at least sixty. His hair was mostly gray, but there were still stray strands of blond showing up here and there.

"Everyone," Tanner continued, "this is Zarina Sokolov, the woman I love and the reason I'm alive today."

Madeline's smile broadened as she gave Zarina a warm hug. "Cam has told us a lot about you. I have to admit, at first it sounded like he was describing Wonder Woman, but after he told us what you've done for Tanner, I'm starting to think he's right."

Blushing, Zarina motioned everyone to the couch and chairs around the TV. "I was about to go out and get something to eat, but since you're here now, why don't I order takeout instead? That way, we can sit around, and you can ask all the questions I'm sure you have."

"Takeout would be fine," Cedric said before offering Tanner a small smile. "And while we do have a lot of questions, we don't want to push. If you're not ready to talk about it, Son, we're okay with that. The only thing that matters to us is that you're safe."

Tanner glanced at Zarina, then gave his father a nod. "I'm ready to talk, but I'm warning you in advance, it's a long story."

"Long stories are the very best kind," his mother said, taking a seat in one of the chairs across from the couch. "Take all the time you need. We're not going anywhere."

Tanner caught Zarina's hand and squeezed it, then moved over to sit on the couch while she grabbed the menu from the pizza place they'd ordered from a couple of times already.

"You probably think the story started in that compound in the Kunduz Province of Afghanistan during my last tour in the Rangers, but the real beginning was in a ski lodge in the Wenatchee Mountains," Tanner said. "That's where I met Zarina and where everything changed."

His gaze drifted to hers, his mouth curving into a smile that made her heart sing, then he turned back to his family and started from the beginning.

Epilogue

"HOW THE HELL DID THIS HAPPEN?" REBECCA BRANNON demanded, flipping through the contents in the folder in front of her on the table.

"They pitted two hybrids against each other in a cage in front of a room full of cell phones," William Hamilton said. "The results were inevitable."

His gaze was locked on the CNN news feed playing on the projection screen at the front of the conference room. The volume was turned down, but she didn't need to hear the sound to know what the panel of so-called experts were saying. It was the same crap they'd been rehashing for days.

"I wasn't talking about the fiasco out in Washington State," she said with a sigh. Why the hell had she appointed him director of the DCO? Then she remembered. Because he was easy to control and relatively loyal. Valid reasons, she supposed, but possibly short-sighted. "I was referring to what happened in Maine. How is it possible that Tate Evers just happened to be in the same part of the country as Mahsood and our daughter, and you didn't know about it?"

William dragged his gaze away from the news to lift a brow at her. "You don't believe it was coincidence he was on vacation and merely thought he'd stumbled onto a hybrid experiment gone wrong?"

Rebecca didn't believe for a moment that William

bought that ridiculous story. "That would be easier to believe if he and that local deputy hadn't made such a mess of your team of *highly trained* mercenaries. The ones you insisted were the best money could buy."

William shrugged. "They are. They ultimately succeeded in the task we hired them to do. They took care of Mahsood. That's what we sent them there to do, wasn't it?"

"Yes, but they missed the opportunity to deal with our daughter," she pointed out. "Leaving her free to cause problems later."

William ran his hand through his salt-and-pepper hair, his brow furrowing. "They'll find her. Now that they know she's back in the States, it shouldn't be difficult for them to track her down again. They said she's little more than a wild animal."

Rebecca wasn't so sure of that last part. The mercenaries he had hired obviously wrote their report to make their minimal accomplishments out to be more than they were, while implying that Ashley had simply gotten lucky. Reading between the lines suggested their daughter had been completely in control of herself and in the process of tracking Mahsood down, almost certainly to gain information. What information, Rebecca wasn't sure. She didn't doubt it was somehow connected to a mother-daughter reunion in the very near future.

She shuddered at the thought.

"So, beyond your disappointment with the situation in Maine, do you have any idea how we're going to deal with this crap out in Washington State?" William asked.

Rebecca glanced at the image of Tanner on the screen, his red eyes and three-inch long fangs on full and obvious display. Damn, he was terrifying when he looked like that.

"I was hoping the media would have moved on to something else by now," she admitted. "That some terrorist attack in Europe or an embarrassing tabloid article involving some idiot politician would distract them. Unfortunately, that hasn't happened. I'm considering planting a few false sightings of these 'monsters' around the U.S., then making sure they turn out to be fake. By the time the dust clears from that, no one will remember the events that started all this, much less think shifters and hybrids are real."

William opened his mouth to say something, but whether it was to agree or not, Rebecca didn't know, because Landon Donovan and Ivy Halliwell walked into the conference room.

"I think it may be too late for that," Ivy said.

Rebecca cursed silently. She'd forgotten that shifters could pick up a quiet conversation from half a building away. What else had the woman heard? Did it really matter? Landon and Ivy already knew more than they should. In fact, they were the ones who'd almost certainly sent Evers up to Maine. She'd have to deal with those two as soon as this current crisis was taken care of.

"What do you mean by that?" she asked, hating having to drag it out of them.

Landon might be the deputy director, but Rebecca didn't like the idea of the man knowing something she didn't.

He reached over and grabbed the TV remote from the table, flipping through several channels until he reached some footage of a reporter standing in front of some

kind of security gate with a microphone in her hand and
the bright lights of a camera in her face. The sound was
still turned down, but the big banner across the top reading "Breaking News" was impossible to miss.

"What am I looking at?" Rebecca demanded.

Ivy folded her arms. "Recognize the gate behind
her?"

It took Rebecca a few moments, but then it hit her.
She frowned. "Isn't that the main gate here at the training complex? What the hell are they saying?"

Landon turned up the volume, and she and William
sat there stunned as the reporter described how she was
standing in front of the entrance to a secret federal organization known as the Department of Covert Operations,
also known as the DCO.

"How the hell...?" William started.

Landon's jaw tightened. "It gets worse."

Rebecca couldn't imagine how that could be possible, but then the eager reporter began talking about
how the DCO paired animal-like shifters and hybrids
with military and law enforcement agents to conduct
dangerous, even illegal, missions all over the world,
including places like Washington State. As the woman
spoke, a collage of personnel records of various field
agents, human and shifter alike, appeared on the screen.
Tanner's was first in line, followed by Landon's and
Ivy's and at least a dozen other operatives who were
currently in the middle of classified operations.

Those photos disappeared to be replaced with ones of
William Hamilton and the members of the Committee.
Rebecca gasped as the reporter named her as the lead-
ing force behind the DCO and its effort to siphon off

millions in taxpayer's dollars for at least a decade to run the unsanctioned government organization.

"Oh God," she whispered. All the work she'd done over the past twenty years to get here was falling apart in front of her eyes. "How could they have uncovered all this information so fast?"

"The intel section is still trying to figure that out," Landon said. "They think the information was leaked by someone in human resources."

William cursed. "How much more info do they have?"

Rebecca noticed he was looking a little pale. She couldn't blame him. She'd pulled him into this to be little more than a figurehead, and now it looked like accepting the position was going to cost him more than he'd ever imagined.

"We don't know, but I think we can expect it to get worse," Ivy admitted, looking a little worried herself.

Rebecca took a deep breath. "What do we do to get in front of this? How do we contain it?"

The grim expression on Landon's face told her everything she needed to know before he said a single word.

"Over the past few days, we've watched the country lose its collective mind over the existence of shifters and hybrids and the fact that the world they thought they knew is a lie," the former Special Forces soldier announced. "Tonight, they've learned a covert government organization not only knew about shifters and hybrids but has been using them to conduct missions in secret around the globe." He snorted. "There's no getting in front of this, Rebecca, and there's no containing it. Every secret this organization has fought to keep hidden has been exposed. The only thing that matters now is what happens next. And we're going to have to deal with the fact that it won't be us deciding how this plays out. It's going to be those people out there."

On the screen, a crowd of angry people had already started gathering at the gates of the DCO.

Rebecca stared at the TV. How were any of them going to survive everything coming their way after this?

Acknowledgments

I hope you enjoyed *X-Ops Exposed*! Tanner and Zarina's story was a long time coming, and they had to go through some crazy stuff before they got their happily ever after.

Even though this story is fiction, soldiers experiencing PTSD from things they've seen in combat is all too real. Sadly, a veteran commits suicide every twenty-two minutes. If you or someone you know is dealing with PTSD, always know that there are people out there to help.

As for X-Ops, now that the world knows about shifters and hybrids, nothing is ever going to be the same for the Department of Covert Operations.

This whole series would not be possible without some very incredible people. In addition to a big thank-you to my hubby for all his help with the action scenes and military and tactical jargon; my agent, Bob Mecoy, for believing in me and encouraging me and being there when I need to talk; my editor and go-to-person at Sourcebooks, Cat Clyne (who loves this series as much as I do and is always a phone call, text, or email away whenever I need something); and all the other amazing people at Sourcebooks, including my fantastic publicist, Stephany, and their crazy-talented art department. The covers they make for me are seriously drool-worthy!

Because I could never leave out my readers, a huge thank-you to everyone who has read my books and Snoopy-danced right along with me with every new release. That includes the fantastic people on my amazing Street Team, as well my assistant, Janet. You rock!

I also want to give a big thank-you to the men, women, and working dogs serving in our military, as well as their families.

And a very special shout-out to our favorite restaurant, P.F. Chang's, where hubby and I bat storylines back and forth and come up with all of our best ideas, as well as a thank-you to our fantastic waiter, Andrew, who takes our order into the kitchen the moment we walk in the door!

Hope you enjoy my next book, coming soon from Sourcebooks, and look forward to reading the rest of the stories as much as I look forward to sharing them with you.

If you love a man in uniform as much as I do, make sure you check out my other action-packed paranormal/romantic-suspense series from Sourcebooks called Special Wolf Alpha Team (a.k.a. SWAT)!

Happy Reading!

About the Author

Paige Tyler is a *New York Times* and *USA Today* best-selling author of sexy, romantic suspense and paranormal romance. She and her very own military hero (also known as her husband) live on the beautiful Florida coast with their adorable fur baby (also known as their dog). Paige graduated with a degree in education but decided to pursue her passion and write books about hunky alpha males and the kick-butt heroines who fall in love with them.

Visit Paige at paigetylertheauthor.com. She's also on Facebook, Twitter, Tumblr, Instagram, tsu, Wattpad, Google+, and Pinterest.

Also by Paige Tyler

X-Ops

SWAT: Special Wolf Alpha Team